'I love you Derek.' She stood at the end of the platform, waving. The train was pulling away fast and he had gone, but his face was still visible, a pale blur as the train receded, and she could see his hand waving back. And although she knew that he could not possibly hear her now, she called to him one last time, her throat aching with the pain and the tears and the effort of trying to make him understand.

'*I love you . . .*'

In the train, Derek caught the whisper of her love, not through his ears but through some deeper part of him, a part where only Olive dwelt and only Olive could reach him. And tears ran unchecked down his cheeks as he stood at the window and watched the familiar streets of Portsmouth pass him by.

Soldiers didn't cry. But Derek Harker was crying, and he wasn't going to apologise to any man for that.

Lilian Harry's grandfather hailed from Devon and Lilian always longed to return to her roots, so moving from Hampshire to a small Dartmoor town in her early twenties was a dream come true. She quickly absorbed herself in local life, learning the fascinating folklore and history of the moors, joining the church bellringers and a country dance club, and meeting people who are still her friends today. Although she later moved north, living first in Herefordshire and then in the Lake District, she returned in the 1990s and now lives on the edge of the moor with her two ginger cats. She is still an active bellringer and member of the local drama group, and loves to walk on the moors. She has one son and one daughter. Her latest novel in hardback, *A Stranger in Burracombe*, is also available from Orion. Visit her website at www.lilianharry.co.uk.

By Lilian Harry

Bells of Burracombe
Three Little Ships
A Farthing Will Do
Dance Little Lady
Under the Apple Tree
A Promise to Keep
A Girl Called Thursday
Tuppence to Spend
PS I Love You
Kiss the Girls Goodbye
Corner House Girls
Keep Smiling Through
Wives & Sweethearts
Love & Laughter
Moonlight & Lovesongs
The Girls They Left Behind
Goodbye Sweetheart

The Girls They Left Behind

LILIAN HARRY

An Orion paperback

First published in Great Britain in 1995
by Orion
This paperback edition published in 1996
by Orion Books Ltd,
Orion House, 5 Upper St Martin's Lane,
London WC2H 9EA

Reissued 2007

7 9 10 8 6

A CIP catalogue record for this book is available
from the British Library.

Printed and bound in Germany by
GGP Media GmbH, Poessneck

The Orion Publishing Group's policy is to use papers that
are natural, renewable and recyclable products and
made from wood grown in sustainable forests. The logging
and manufacturing processes are expected to conform to
the environmental regulations of the country of origin.

www.orionbooks.co.uk

For my sister Christine
with love

CHAPTER ONE

Olive and Derek Harker arrived for the latest possible train on that Sunday evening, but Portsmouth Town Station was as crowded as if it were morning. The carriages were filling with soldiers and airmen going back off leave, and the platform was crowded with the women and children who were bidding them goodbye. Some were smiling bravely, but most were already in tears and few would be dry-eyed as the train steamed out of the station.

'I can't bear it,' Olive wept as Derek held her in his arms. 'You don't seem to have been here five minutes. It's so cruel, taking you away like this. We've only just got married.'

'I know.' He stroked her hair. He was having difficulty with his own feelings. Men didn't cry – especially men who were soldiers, going off to war – but he felt disturbingly as if he might. His throat ached in a way he couldn't remember since he was twelve years old. He swallowed the ache and buried his face in Olive's hair, and she turned her head so that their lips met. She clung to him, her body shaking with sobs, and he wondered how he was ever going to bring himself to break away.

'Livvy, I've got to go,' he whispered despairingly. 'If I miss the train –'

'I know. It'll be jankers.' She tried to smile and it nearly broke his heart. 'It's all right, Derek, I'm not going to make a fuss.' The engine was pouring out steam and it billowed around them, enveloping them in a humid cloud. She stared at his face, her eyes dark and hungry, as if she were trying to memorise each tiny iota. She had made love with the same hunger last night, he remembered, and he had been caught up in her desperation, turning to her again and again as if every moment must be used for loving.

Suppose I didn't go? he thought suddenly. Suppose I just walked away from the train, from the station, from the war itself and said to hell with it, it's not my war, I've got a life to live with my wife and my family – if there is one. And what chance do we have to start one?

Suppose I just refused to go . . .

But he knew what would happen. He was a soldier. He couldn't even plead the excuse of conscience. He'd be posted as a deserter. He'd be caught, court-martialled and imprisoned. Perhaps even shot.

He hadn't been through Dunkirk to end up like that.

The guard blew his whistle. The engine blew its own shrill note. Doors began to slam and one by one the men broke away from their girls, from their sweethearts and wives, and climbed aboard. The women stood, their handkerchiefs at faces that streamed with tears, and watched helplessly. Some of them held children in their arms, children who looked bewildered and lost.

'Derek . . .'

'Livvy, I love you.' He caught her hard against him and kissed her fiercely, then tore himself away and scrambled up into the train. The door slammed and he twisted to stare down at her. 'I love you . . .'

'Derek – Derek.' She could not say the words she knew he longed to hear. She had said them in the night, over and over again, but now her throat closed against them and her lips could only form his name. She gazed up at him, her misery tightening about her like a straitjacket, and heard the slow thump of the pistons as the train began to move. He was going from her, slipping away, leaving, and she could say nothing, only stand mute, shaking her head and feeling the tears like rain upon her face.

'Livvy . . .'

'Derek – Derek –' Suddenly her tongue was freed and she ran beside the train as it moved slowly along the platform. 'I love you, Derek. I love you.' He had heard, she knew he had heard. He was smiling, an odd, distorted smile, and there was rain on his cheeks too, but it wasn't raining and she knew it must be his own tears. *Derek*, in tears? Her eyes flooded again, blurring her vision, but there was no stopping her now and she ran along the platform, blundering into other women, young girls, mothers with babies, giving them hardly a thought for all her thoughts were with the man who was going back to war and leaving her behind.

'I love you, Derek.' She stood at the end of the platform, waving. The train was pulling away fast and he had gone, but his face was still visible, a pale blur as the train receded, and she could see his hand waving back. And although she knew that he could not possibly hear her now, she called to him one last time, her throat aching with the pain and the tears and the effort of trying to make him understand.

'*I love you . . .*'

In the train, Derek caught the whisper of her love, not through his ears but through some deeper part of him, a part where only Olive dwelt and only Olive could reach him. And the tears ran unchecked down his cheeks as he stood at the window and watched the familiar streets of Portsmouth pass him by.

Soldiers didn't cry. But Derek Harker was crying, and he wasn't going to apologise to any man for that.

Olive went back to work the next morning just as if she hadn't got married on Saturday morning and had a thirty-six hour honeymoon. There didn't seem to be much point in doing anything else, despite her father's disapproval.

Ted Chapman had been stubbornly opposed to his daughter continuing to work at all, even though she was employed by Derek's father in the office of his builder's yard.

'Your mother's never gone out to work and I don't like the idea of my girls doing it, once they're wed,' he said for the dozenth time as Olive came down to breakfast. 'Married women ought to stop at home and look after their men.'

'Chance'd be a fine thing,' Olive retorted, feeling the tears dangerously close again. 'How can I look after Derek when he's living in a Nissen hut down in Devon? And we haven't even *got* a home. What am I supposed to do all day if I haven't got a job?'

'You could give your mum a hand.' But Ted knew his argument was unconvincing. Annie had the housework well under control, and both Olive and Betty did their share. And Annie herself had something to say about that.

'More and more women are having to work these days, what with all the young men being called up for the Forces. If she wasn't doing that, she'd be doing something else. At least Harker's is only a few streets away.' She refilled the big teacup the girls had given him for Christmas a few years ago. 'Anyway, you can't tell her what to do now, she's a married woman.'

It was hard enough to believe that, all the same, and Annie had to keep reminding herself by thinking of Olive and Derek's wedding day only the day before yesterday, with Olive in the white dress she'd borrowed from a friend and her chestnut hair glowing in the sun.

'She's still living under our roof,' Ted muttered, and Annie clicked her tongue in exasperation.

'Honestly, Ted! Anyone would think our Olive was out on the razzle every night and bringing back sailors, like Nancy Baxter. All she's doing is getting married, and it's not her fault she can't start with her own home and her man coming home at nights like a couple should. She's a good girl and you know it, and Derek's a decent chap. You were keen enough for them to get married when you came back from Dunkirk.'

'I never said anything against them getting married. It's her working I don't like. But I suppose you're right. Nothing's the same any more, and you can't tell young people what to do.'

He finished his tea and got up, going out into the back porch to find his bicycle clips. Olive and Betty made a face at each other and Annie sighed.

'I don't know about your dad, I'm sure. He's all on edge these days. He's never properly settled down since he came back from Dunkirk. It upset him a lot, that did.'

'It upset a lot of people,' Olive said, thinking of the things Derek had told her. Young soldiers, no more than kids really, shivering and crying all the way home from Dover in the

4

trains, their uniforms still soaked from having to stand in the water, many of them wounded by the bombing and strafing they'd suffered on the beaches. Her dad had been brave, she knew, taking his ferryboat over to help get them away, but he hadn't had to suffer like they had. And he didn't have to go back. She thought of Derek again, going off on the train with all those others, knowing what they might be going back to.

It was queer to think she was a married woman now. It didn't seem right that her life hadn't changed. Apart from that one day and night with Derek, everything was the same. She got up each morning, helped her mum get breakfast ready, went off to the office and spent the day typing out letters and invoices. A lot of building had stopped because of the war, and business was slack, but John Harker wasn't worried about that. 'It'll pick up soon enough, once the bombing starts,' he said grimly. 'There'll be plenty needs doing then.'

On Thursday evenings Olive usually finished a few minutes early and went to the pictures with Betty. There didn't seem to be any point in changing that, just because she was now a married woman. The men had already gone home and she was shuffling together her papers when her father-in-law came in.

'That's right,' he said. 'You go off and enjoy yourself. A couple of hours at the Odeon'll do you good.'

Olive smiled at him. It already seemed an eternity since Derek had gone away and she missed him more each day. Funny to think that this time last week they hadn't even been married . . .

The air was split by the sudden wail of a siren. Its sound rose and fell like the howl of a banshee. For a full minute it maintained its unearthly shrieking, and then it died slowly away. In the silence left behind, it was as if the whole world held its breath.

Olive stopped what she was doing, a bundle of papers slipping from fingers that had suddenly frozen, and stared at John Harker. For a brief moment, the man and girl stood riveted, their eyes locked. Then John reached out and grabbed Olive's arm.

'The shelter! Quick – leave that.'

'But the invoices –'

'Leave them! This is it, Olive. I can hear the planes already.'

'Maybe it's another false alarm –'

'There've been German planes around all day. They've been all along the coast. They've tried twice already – I heard it on the news. But this lot's got through. Drop the papers, Livvy, and get over to the shelter quick. I'll fetch Florrie.'

He pulled her through the door and they ran across the yard. The Anderson was in the garden, through a tall gate set in the wall that separated the Harkers' home from the business. John Harker put his hand between Olive's shoulder blades and gave her a shove that sent her staggering through the gate and halfway down the garden path. Then he turned and ran into the house.

He and Florrie Harker scrambled down into the dim, musty shelter only seconds before the first explosion.

Olive's cousins, Tim and Keith Budd, were involved in a game of cowboys and Indians. Each armed with a toy pistol, they had scurried out as soon as tea was over to join the children who were, for one reason or another, still at home in Portsmouth, and not evacuated to the country. Some had been evacuated and returned after a few weeks, homesick or even badly treated, some had come to the conclusion that there was, after all, no danger from bombing or gas, and some had never left Portsmouth at all, despite the entreaties of the authorities.

Micky Baxter was one of these. Always the wild boy of April Grove, he had exulted in the sudden freedom of no school and formed a small gang of boys who had nothing to do and all day to do it in. Together, they had roamed the streets, looking for mischief and having no trouble in finding it. Their exploits had come to a head when they had held up an assistant in a jewellery shop with a pistol left over from the 1914–18 war. Micky was still on probation for that, but it didn't seem to make much difference.

Jess Budd didn't like her boys playing with Micky Baxter, but although they were half afraid of his scapegrace nature,

6

they were also fascinated by it. And although a lot of children had come back, their own special friends were still out at Bridge End, where they'd been evacuated.

They gathered at the end of April Grove, near the Budds' house. Tim and Keith were both cowboys, like Micky, and the Indians were Martin Baker, who had come back from evacuation with appendicitis, Jimmy Cross and Cyril Nash, who had a pale, angelic face with large brown eyes and spent most of his time trying to undo the impression that his name and appearance invariably created.

Only those who possessed pistols were allowed to be cowboys, and Micky was undisputed leader because his was reputed to be real. Tim and Keith, who had heard the story of the jeweller's shop, glanced at it with respect, and kept their distance, thankful that they weren't Indians. Suppose it was still loaded? But Jimmy Cross scoffed at them.

'Course it ain't that one. They took it off him, didn't they? Anyway, me and Cyril's got real catapults, better'n any old toy guns, they are.'

He displayed the weapons, made of forked sticks and a wide strip of rubber. Tim watched enviously as he bent, picked up a stone from the road, and sent it zinging down the street. Mrs Seddon, who kept the corner shop, came out of her side gate just as the stone whistled past her and she looked up sharply. The boys skittered hastily into a nearby alley.

I hope she doesn't tell Mum, Tim thought anxiously, but the game was starting now and the three Indians were fleeing up the alley looking for places to hide.

The cowboys turned their backs, as the rules of the game demanded, and scuffed their toes in the dust.

'I s'pose you'll be goin' back to the country soon,' Micky observed. 'Runnin' away from the bombs.'

'We're not running away.' Tim protested, uncomfortably aware that they were. 'We only came back to see our Olive get married. Anyway, it's good in the country. There's all sorts of things to do.'

'Oh yeah?' Micky sneered. 'Pickin' flowers? Countin' sheep? That's girls' stuff.'

'There's plenty of things besides that. Good trees to climb.

7

Birds' nests. And we help on the farm, too. We can milk cows.'

'Milk cows? I'd sooner get it out of a bottle. Catch me goin' to the country. I'd rather stay here – no school or nothing, do what you like. It's good.'

'There are schools,' Keith said. 'Our school's open, I heard Mum say so when she and Dad were talking about us stopping here. But Dad says there's going to be bad bombing soon and he wants us out of it.'

'I 'ope there is,' Micky said. 'I *want* the bombs to come. I ain't scared of 'em. Smash! Crash! Just like Saturday morning pictures, it'll be.'

'But suppose *Germans* come?' Keith asked, speaking the name in a whisper. 'S'pose they invade? That means they'll come and live in our houses, they'll take away everything. What'll you do then?'

'I'll fight 'em, that's what I'll do.' Micky lifted his arm and bent it, clenching his fist to make the biceps stand out. 'Tell you what, they're goin' to come in parachutes. I'll catch one of them, tie him up in his own parachute and take him down the police station.' He frowned, thinking of his last visit to that establishment. 'No, I won't, I'll take him up Hilsea Barracks, let the soldiers have him. They won't get *our* house.'

'You're daft,' Tim said. 'There's going to be hundreds of them – thousands. They'll have guns and bayonets and everything. You'll have to hide and keep out of their way. And I tell you what, it'll be better out in the country then. The people out there, they've taken all the signposts down – the Germans won't be able to find their way anywhere, they'll be lost. *We'll* know where we are, but they won't.'

'They won't want to go out there anyway.' Micky glanced over his shoulder. The alleyway was deserted, the Indians long vanished from sight. 'I reckon they've had long enough to find hideouts now. Anyway, I bet I know where they've gone. They'll be round Carlisle Crescent. Just because Jimmy Cross lives near there, he thinks it's the only place to hide.'

The three boys cocked their pistols and ran up the alley, keeping an eye open as they passed open gateways in case the

8

Indians were skulking in someone's garden. There was no sign of them as they passed along the back of September Street and came to the railway line and level crossing. Carlisle Crescent was on the other side of the track, and Tim and Keith hesitated.

The railway line formed a natural boundary to their normal territory. Although they were allowed to go out to play in the streets, they were not supposed to go beyond certain limits without first letting their mother know. April Grove, March and October Streets, with their maze of alleyways created a small, tight neighbourhood where all the children and adults were known to each other. Cars seldom appeared there, especially in the evenings, and only tradesmen's carts and wagons made regular appearances during the day. Ball games, skipping, hopscotch and marbles could be played unhindered, and although some of the less tolerant residents might object to the constant thud of a ball against the wall of their house, and even forbid the chalking of cricket stumps or goal posts on the bricks, they did little more than make occasional testy appearances, chasing away the offending children. Usually, the children returned after a few days, chalked up their goal posts again and resumed their games.

Children from other streets were less welcome. They were looked upon with suspicion and told to 'Go and play in your own street'. And by the same unwritten rule, if you went to someone else's street you were likely to be sent off with a flea in your ear.

But Jimmy Cross lived in Carlisle Crescent, or near enough, Tim reasoned. So it ought to be all right to go there. And as for letting Mum know, she couldn't expect him to break off from a game of cowboys and Indians to run home and tell her they might be going over the railway. Specially after what Micky Baxter had been saying about them running away from the bombs.

Anyway, they'd be back long before she came out to call them in for bed, so she'd never know. And as long as they didn't run into Dad, walking home from work, they'd be safe.

The crossing gates were closed and a train approached along the track. The boys scampered up the steps of the

9

bridge and the engine chugged beneath, its roar filling their ears. Steam and smoke billowed around them and they capered about in the cloud, delighted, flapping their hands in front of their faces and grinning at each other through the swirling mist before scuttering down the steps on the other side and into Carlisle Crescent.

The houses here were posher than in April Grove. They weren't in a terrace but were separate, some in twos and some on their own. They were all slightly different and some were bungalows. They had front gardens, big enough for a bit of lawn, and in a few there were bushes and even a tree or two. A couple had greenhouses with tomato plants growing in them. It was almost as good as the country, Tim thought, wishing he could live in such a house. Fancy having grass in your garden, just like a real field!

The three cowboys entered the crescent cautiously, their pistols still held at the ready as they searched for signs of Indians. One of the gardens had a low wall running along beside it and they ran across to it, half-crouching, and peered cautiously over the top, as cowboys did at the cinema.

Tim's hero was Roy Rogers, who had a marvellous horse called Trigger. He modelled himself on Roy Rogers now, imagining himself in cowboy gear, with chaps on his trousers and a holster slung at his waist. He noticed that Keith was limping slightly. Keith's favourite was Hopalong Cassidy.

Zing! A stone whistled past their ears and bounced off the wall beside them. The cowboys jumped, startled, and Tim remembered the catapults. He waved his pistol, regretting the lack of caps. At least he could have made a noise. As it was, he felt helpless.

Another stone whizzed past, almost grazing his cheek, and he was suddenly angry. His mum and dad had always laid down very strict rules about throwing stones. You only threw them into the sea, and even then only when there were no swimmers about. And you never, never threw them at people.

'They're cheating,' he hissed. 'Stones are dangerous. They could hit us in the eye.'

Micky too was feeling disgruntled. The catapults had put the Indians at an advantage, and that was against the rules.

The cowboys were supposed to win. He debated introducing a new rule, that only cowboys could have catapults, but knew that the Indians would claim that they were nearer to bows and arrows and should therefore be theirs. Perhaps it would be better if catapults weren't allowed at all. But that would mean he couldn't have one either, and he'd already made up his mind to get himself the best in the street.

If only he hadn't had to give up the old Army pistol. It hadn't actually been his, but he'd been the only one with the nerve to carry it. If he still had that – and could get some ammunition for it – well, there wouldn't be any dispute then. He'd win every time.

He thought of the German parachutist he meant to catch. He'd be armed. Perhaps Micky could get his pistol off him – and some bullets as well. He wouldn't even have to worry about swearing the man to secrecy, since he wouldn't be able to talk English.

Feeling suddenly cheerful, he brought his mind back to the game in hand and nodded.

'You're right,' he said. 'Stones aren't allowed.' He stood up, braving the hail of stones now flying at them from the alleyway across the street, and shouted, 'The game's over. You're cheating, so we've won. Come out or we'll come over and take you prisoner.'

For answer, the biggest stone of all came flying towards him. He ducked, and two things happened very quickly.

From immediately behind him came the sound of splintering glass as the stone smashed into a greenhouse. And from above, from all around, vibrating in the very ground beneath their feet, came the howl of the air-raid siren.

It swelled through the air, filling the sky, spreading over their heads, shrieking its way through the streets, between the houses, along the alleyways and into every narrow passage. It forced its way into houses and woke babies in their cots; it startled old men and women dozing in chairs. It transfixed lovers in quiet corners, and froze women standing at stoves as they cooked their families' suppers. It shrieked at people on the way home from work, leaving them stunned as the unearthly wail rose and fell about them. And as the droning sound died away at last, everyone turned their eyes to the sky to see the approaching aircraft.

There was a moment's silence and then the street erupted into action. Families poured from houses into their gardens, making for the shelters. Firewatchers hurried out, dragging heavy stirrup-pumps and still fastening on tin helmets. An air-raid warden cycled past, intent on reaching his post, never noticing the children. There was a tumult of shouting, of panic, of orders yelled and frightened screams. And then, again, silence as the shelters were reached and closed.

The boys huddled together by the wall. They could hear the faint throb of the planes as they neared the coast. They looked at each other, their faces pale, eyes wide.

'What shall we do?' Tim muttered. 'We ought to be in shelters too.' They all knew what they should be doing. They had rehearsed it often enough. But their rehearsals had always been on the assumption that they would be close to a shelter – either their own, at home, or in their own street or at school. Here, they were on alien territory, in a street where they were not supposed to be playing, and they would as soon have thought of going into someone else's shelter as they would have thought of walking uninvited into the house.

He noticed that somehow the Indians had come across the road and joined them. The catapults dangled from their hands. It didn't seem to matter now that they'd been cheating. Martin Baker was looking white and scared but Cyril Nash's eyes were bright. And Jimmy, although within a hundred yards of his own home, was making no effort to run for shelter.

'They're coming,' he breathed, his voice wobbly with excitement. 'I can hear 'em now. Listen. *Look*!'

The boys craned their necks. Away to the south, where Southsea Common met the sea, they could see a black cloud of aircraft, like starlings gathering for their evening roost. They approached steadily, their engines snarling, and as they came over the city itself, Tim saw the first of the bombs begin to fall.

They dropped like black eggs from the belly of the aircraft and tumbled slowly towards the earth. He stared at them, fascinated. His eyes watched as they descended, falling through the network of balloons that floated above the city, falling towards the ships in the harbour, falling towards the Dockyard where his father worked, falling, falling, falling . . .

The explosion shook the ground under his feet and thundered through the air in great waves of brutal sound that battered against his ears and tore at his body. Almost before it hit him, he flung himself to the ground, and the six boys huddled together on the pavement while the first air-raid of the war stormed over Portsmouth.

Jess Budd stood at the front door of number 14, April Grove, holding her baby daughter Maureen in her arms, and watched her sons scamper along the street. She looked up at the blue sky and shivered. For a moment, she was almost inclined to call them back, but before she could raise her voice Peggy Shaw opened her front door and came out to stand beside her.

'Making the most of the fine evenings,' she remarked. 'What're you going to do about your kids, Jess? Are they going back to the country?'

'Oh, yes. We only had them home for the wedding. Rose wanted to be bridesmaid, and we had to give our Olive a day to remember – she's got precious little else. But Frank says there's going to be bad raids soon and the children have got to be out of it.'

'And are you going too?'

Jess shook her head firmly. 'I'm stopping here. I had enough of being away all through the winter. And Frank needs his wife to look after him.' She looked down at Maureen, who was wriggling in an effort to get down, and set her down to toddle on the pavement. 'I know it means keeping the baby at home too, but there's nothing we can do about that.'

'Well, I won't say I shan't be glad to have you back next door,' Peggy commented. 'It felt really queer all those months, without you about. And the street's like a morgue without Tim and Keith and the other kids playing out there. I'll be sorry to see them go. Mind, I wouldn't moan if it was

Micky Baxter. The mischief that boy gets up to, you wouldn't believe.'

'Maybe when the raids start Nancy'll change her mind and send him off after all.' Jess looked up again at the evening sky. It was still blue, with only a faint flush of apricot to show that the sun was beginning to go down. It was good that the weather had been fine these past few weeks, so that Frank could get over to the allotment and work in the fresh air. It blew all the dust of the Dockyard boiler-shop out of his lungs and he always looked a bit happier when he came home with a basket full of gooseberries or blackcurrants or vegetables that he'd grown himself. 'You just can't believe there's people out there killing each other,' she said. 'Bits of boys like your Bob and our Colin, climbing into aeroplanes and coming over to drop bombs on people they've never ever seen. And our lads –'

Her words were drowned by the shriek of the siren. Maureen began to scream in panic and Jess bent and scooped her up in her arms, holding her close. She looked at Peggy Shaw, her face white.

'Is it another false alarm?'

'I don't know.' Peggy stared at her. 'We ought to go down the shelter, just in case . . .'

'But the boys – Tim and Keith. They're out playing somewhere. And Rose – she went up to the Brunners –'

'She'll go in their shelter then.'

Jess bit her lip in a torment of indecision. 'I'll have to go out and find the boys. Can you take the baby for me, Peg?'

People were coming out into the street, looking fearfully at the sky, asking each other if it was real. They heard the throb of aeroplanes.

'That's not our lads!' They had grown used to the sound of British aircraft, but this was different. There was a snarl in the sound, a menace as if a vicious dog was growling deep in its throat. Jess caught her breath.

'That's it! They're here. Oh, *Peg* –'

'Down the air-raid shelter, quick,' Peggy said. 'There's no time to waste. I can hear the guns. Quick, Jess.'

'But the boys – Rose – Frank . . . they're out there

somewhere – I can't just –'

'You can't go looking for 'em, either.' Peggy's hand was on her arm, pulling her back through the door. 'Jess, you can't go out in the streets, you'll just have to hope they've got the sense to make for shelter. They know what to do, we've all practised it enough, goodness knows. But you've got Maureen to think of.' She hustled Jess to the back door and they stared at the sky again. It was still clear, still cloudless, but now the blue had taken on a hard, sinister sheen and they could hear the snarl of approaching aircraft. Suddenly, the barrage balloons seemed a weak and flimsy defence against the advancing wave of destruction.

'*Quick*, Jess,' Peggy urged again, but Jess shook her head and broke away.

'You go. Take the baby. But I've got to find the boys. I can't leave them out there . . .'

She hurried back through the house, her breath coming in quick, frightened gasps, and out into the street. The aircraft were visible now, like a cloud of black starlings high above the balloons. Her body ached with terror. She ran across to the corner by Mrs Seddon's shop, staring up October Street.

Peggy was behind her again, Maureen still crying in her arms.

'They're coming,' she panted. 'Jess, you've got to come down the shelter. The boys must have gone in with someone else. They're not here – you can see that. Someone'll be looking after them. Jess, for God's sake, come back . . .'

Jess took one more frantic look up the deserted street. The throb of the planes was closer. In a few seconds they would be overhead. The bombs would begin to fall.

'They must be up the alley.' She dashed to the end of April Grove, where the boys had scampered on their hunt for the Indians, but it was empty. Everyone had run for cover.

Despairing and guilty, she turned and Peggy hustled her through the little house, leaving the doors open as she went. The two women pelted down the garden path and dived into the Anderson shelter. Panting, half sobbing, they squatted on the low benches that Frank had fitted against the walls, and stared at each other. The baby wailed in Peggy's arms, and

Jess took her back and cradled her against her breast.

'Oh, Peg –' she began, but the rest of her words were lost in the explosion of the first bombs.

In Portchester Road, Kathy Simmons had just finished giving her children their supper when the siren went.

Stella and Muriel pulled faces. 'Do we *have* to go down the shelter, Mum? It'll only be another false alarm.'

'Yes, we do,' Kathy said sharply, although she would have liked to ignore it herself. 'One of these days it's going to be real, and then what would we do? Anyway, we've got to keep practising, you don't know how quick the planes can –'

She stopped, suddenly aware of a throaty grumble from the sky. Hardly believing her ears, she went to the back door. The sound was closer. She felt a wave of fear, and the baby inside her seemed to jerk as if he felt it too.

'Quick!' she snapped, snatching up the box that contained all the family birth certificates and other papers too important to be lost. 'Come on, Stella – leave that – get down there as fast as you can.'

'But my dolly – I've left her upstairs.' Muriel's voice began to rise in a wail but Kathy grabbed her arm.

'There isn't time for that – she'll be all right – come *on* when I tell you!' The garden path had never seemed so long. She hurried the girls down it and into the Anderson shelter Mike had dug out before he went away. The drone was coming closer, it sounded almost overhead although with her last frightened glance before she ducked through the low doorway, she could see only a cloud of black freckles in the sky, like swarming ants. Oh God, she thought, they're really coming, we're going to be bombed, and Mike not here and our baby boy not even born . . . She folded her arms across her stomach and bowed her head, shutting her eyes tightly as if by doing so she could shut out the terrifying reality.

But reality would not be shut out. She heard the first bomb fall, and was forced to open her eyes and pull her two little girls into her arms, to try to give them the comfort she so desperately needed herself. And as if that first bomb were a signal, others began to fall, sometimes singly, sometimes in clusters, so that the explosions seemed to merge together in one massive blast. As the shock waves ran through the earth, shuddering beneath Kathy's feet, the corrugated iron of the Anderson shelter rattled in her ears. The girls screamed and she clutched them to her convulsively, feeling the unborn baby tremble again in her womb. Be still, she begged it silently, be quiet. You're too small to kick like that, you've only just quickened. But the fluttering movements continued, as if her own fear communicated itself to the tiny, developing life, and would not let it rest.

The detonations continued, deafening her. Surely the planes must be directly overhead. How safe was an Anderson? She'd heard that no shelter could survive a direct hit. The thunder of the bombs threatened to burst her eardrums, shatter her skull. Nobody had ever told her an air-raid would be like this.

In the worst moment of all, it was as if the air inside the dimly-lit Anderson turned into vapour, as if she could see it shimmer all around. The iron of the walls wrinkled, almost as if they cringed in pain. The earth floor split into a thousand tiny cracks. And the noise was no longer noise. It had become something greater, something that took her whole body and shook it without mercy, as a tiger might take and shake its prey until it was senseless.

Dimly, Kathy was aware that she was screaming, although she could hear no sound of her voice. She could feel the vibrations in the children's bodies and knew that they too were crying with terror. She wanted to comfort them, but had no power over her own fear. It swamped her, leaving her no strength for anything else.

For a long time, after the sound of the last plane had faded, the three of them lay still on the splintered floor. The turmoil of the raid still sounded in their ears and it was only gradually that the silence crept back. At last they heard the tentative note of the Raiders Passed signal, and Kathy lifted her head.

'They've gone,' she whispered, and crawled to the steps that led up into the open air.

What she saw then was no surprise. She had known, from that first terrifying explosion, that the bombs were falling

17

dangerously close. She had known that she and the two little girls would have no home to go back to.

But she was still not prepared for the sight of the house she and Mike had loved so much, shattered and gaping like a smashed tooth. Still shaking, she dragged herself out of the shelter and gripped the distorted iron to pull herself upright, staring in misery and despair.

The house was a mess of torn brickwork and splintered wood. There was nothing at all left of the roof, and the upstairs rooms were totally demolished. Downstairs, all she could see was ruin – smashed furniture, ornaments and knick-knacks scattered and broken, a curtain still half hanging from a crooked rail, filthy with dust.

The two girls scrambled out and stood beside her, still sobbing.

'My dolly,' Muriel whispered. 'My dolly . . .'

CHAPTER TWO

Frank Budd had just left the Dockyard when the siren sounded.

Carrying his leather-bound lunchbox, he walked through Unicorn Gate and turned to go along Flathouse Road towards the Royal Hospital. From there, he would make his way through the maze of narrow side streets towards Kingston and Copnor.

Sometimes he took the bus, but it was too hot this evening to be cooped up on a crowded bus, and it was ten hours since he'd tasted any air other than the steamy heat of the boiler-shop. With no overtime tonight, for the first time in weeks, he could afford to walk. Jess wouldn't be expecting him till seven and there would still be time to spend a few hours over on his allotment in the fresh air and evening sunshine. There was plenty to be done – hoeing and weeding, and perhaps some soft fruit to pick, if Jess hadn't had time to get over there herself during the afternoon.

The allotment was thriving this year. After the bitter winter and cold spring, he'd been afraid everything would be late, but instead they'd had this glorious summer and the vegetables and fruit had flourished. He'd never seen the beans so high at this time of year before, and the goose-berries and currants were fat and glowing. The row or two of strawberries had done well too, and they'd had them for tea once or twice as well as providing a good bowlful for Olive's wedding last Saturday. Strawberries were, in Frank's opinion, a luxury and he only grew them because Jess liked them so much. They did make a good jam, with a few gooseberries to help them set.

The road was full of men leaving the Dockyard, some on foot like Frank, others cycling. There were buses too, taking them all over the city and down to the Hard, where the ferryboats waited to take those who lived in Gosport on the five-minute trip across the harbour. It was a vast exodus, and other folk kept clear when the Dockyard was coming out.

It was at that moment that the siren sounded.

The wail filled the air. Frank stopped as its shriek hit him, and felt the jolt of shock, followed by a tingling shudder that ran over his whole body. He glanced quickly up and down the street. In that moment, everyone must have done exactly the same – stopped as if frozen. Then there was sudden movement everywhere as people began to run and shout. An old lady who had been creeping slowly along with her hand on the low garden walls to steady herself, stood with confused, frightened eyes, her lips trembling as she clutched her shopping bag close against her.

For a few seconds, Frank stood as uncertain as the rest. Then he remembered that there was a public shelter two streets away. He set off towards it, then turned back and approached the old woman.

'They're coming,' she whispered. 'They're coming to get us.'

'They're not going to, though, are they?' He spoke cheerfully, although already he could hear the snarl of the bombers approaching. Had the warning come too late?

It had certainly come too late for a lot of people to find proper shelter. Especially people like this poor old dear, who was now sobbing helplessly and wetting herself into the bargain. He saw the puddle forming round her feet and tugged her arm gently.

'Come on, missus, let's get you home. You don't want to be out on the street in this.' The planes were very close now and he felt the first shock of explosion as bombs fell in the harbour and the Dockyard. The old woman whimpered and clutched him and he forgot to be gentle and dragged her along the street, ignoring the shopping bag that she had dropped.

'Me rations! Me rations!' she wept as she stumbled along,

but Frank was concerned only with getting her indoors. I hope to God she didn't lock the front door, he thought as they reached it, and breathed a sigh of relief as it swung open at his touch. He pushed her inside.

'Have you got a shelter?'

'No. We're a sixer, see, we couldn't have no Anderson, I dunno why. Something to do with the water-pipes in the gardens, they come through every sixth house. My daughter's hubby says we'll have to make do under the stairs, they say that's the safest place, don't they . . .' Her voice faltered as Frank pushed her along the narrow passage. The space beneath the stairs had been boxed in as a big cupboard, with an old mattress shoved inside to sit on. He bent and thrust the old lady inside, then scrambled in beside her as another explosion shook the house.

'Here, that was close.' She seemed to be recovering a little now that she was home. Together, they crouched on the floor in the dimness, listening to the roar of planes overhead and the thunder of the exploding bombs.

'It's bad, innit,' the old woman whispered. 'They're going to bomb us out of our own homes. They're going to keep on bombing till there's none of us left and then they're going to take our homes away and live in 'em and do what they like.' She began to cry again. 'It's not fair. It's not *fair*. Not after what we went through before. I lost my husband in the last lot, killed in action he was, to make England a land fit for heroes to live in, and what good did it do? Tell me that, eh?'

'Ssh.' Frank found her hand and patted it. 'Don't think about it now. It's happening and we've just got to live through it and not let it get us down.' But he spoke absently, for his thoughts were with Jess and the children. For God's sake, he thought, don't let those boys be out roaming the streets in this lot. And he made up his mind that they would be sent back to the safety of the countryside as soon as possible.

The explosions rocked around them. What's happening out there? he wondered. I ought to get out there and help.

He began to crawl out of the cupboard. 'I've got to go now, love. You stay here till they sound the Raiders Passed signal and your daughter gets back, then you have a nice cup of tea.

21

You'll be all right here.' He hoped it was true.

She clutched him with feeble fingers, entreating him to stay, but he gently disentangled her hands. 'You stay here. You're safe here,' he repeated, and stood up, ducking again immediately as an explosion thundered almost overhead and he heard the sound of breaking glass and falling masonry. For a moment, he hesitated. He could have his head blown off the minute he stepped through the front door.

But someone was going to get killed anyway, in this lot. Probably hundreds, maybe thousands of people. And others would be hurt, and buried under collapsed buildings, needing help.

The next explosion was closer still. It sounded as if it were almost next door. The window of the room he was in shattered, glass flying everywhere, and if he hadn't ducked he would have been peppered with it, slashed to pieces perhaps. But this time the thought of scrambling back into the safety of the home-made shelter didn't enter his head. Without another word to the old woman, who was now whimpering with terror, he wrenched open the door and ran along the passage to the street.

Whatever was happening out there, he had to be part of it. He couldn't stay here while his own family and home were in danger, somewhere across the city, and he couldn't take shelter when he had a duty to do.

The front door was still ajar. He pulled it open and stood for a moment looking up and down the street. God knows what I expected, he thought. Complete devastation? Houses knocked down, on fire, bits of bodies lying about all over the place? In fact, his mind had shown him no pictures of what a bombed city might be like. Until now, although he had known the facts, he had been unable to imagine the consequences.

But to his surprise, there was little sign of destruction. At first glance, everything seemed normal. And then he noticed that almost every window in the street was shattered. A few chimneys had fallen or stood askew, ready to topple. And a boy of about twelve – not all that much bigger than his Tim – came by, crying and holding his head. There was blood dripping down through his fingers.

Frank ran out and grabbed his arm. The planes seemed to have passed over now, but more might come at any moment and he could still hear explosions. Smoke rose in black clouds above the rooftops. The danger was by no means over.

'What are you doing out here? You ought to be in a shelter.' His voice was rough with fear and concern, but sounded merely cross and the boy flinched and tried to pull away.

'I wasn't doing nothing wrong, mister. I tried to get 'ome, but the bombs come. I couldn't find nowhere to shelter. And then summat hit me, it hit me head, look. I'm *bleedin'*.'

He began to sob again and Frank felt a flash of rage. He knew now what Jess had meant when she'd railed against the war, saying it wasn't fair that ordinary people who just wanted to live their lives should have to get caught up in such things. Old women like the one he'd left behind in the house, alone and crying with terror, nippers like this one with a wound that could have killed him. And this was just the start.

'Come on,' he said more gently. 'Let's get you to a First Aid post.' He prised the boy's fingers away from his scalp and examined the cut. It was more of a graze, but it had taken off a fair lump of skin and blood was oozing through the matted brown hair. It needed proper attention, from someone who knew what they were doing.

He thought of going back to the Royal Hospital but they'd be too busy with real casualties. There must have been any amount of people killed and hurt in the raid. He could hear the streets coming back to life now as people ventured out, and there were shouts and yells as folk discovered what had happened. There'd be plenty needing help. He felt a stab of fear as he wondered again how Jess and the kids had fared.

But he couldn't just leave the boy. Best get him to a First Aid post, where he could be properly looked after.

Drayton Road Infants' School. It had been taken over by the ARP, they'd have people there who could help. It wasn't too far away. He hoped to God they could get there. There didn't seem to be any bombs falling at the moment, but the sky was filled with black smoke now, split with streaks of orange flame, and he could smell the acrid tang of burning. It looked as if there was a bad fire somewhere, and from the direction he thought it could be the gasholder at Rudmore. If that was on fire, there could be another explosion at any minute, worse than a bomb.

He gripped the boy's arm and began to run. The lad made no more effort to escape and ran along with Frank, still half sobbing. He kept his other hand pressed to his head, the blood still oozing between his fingers. Frank hoped he wouldn't pass out before they got to the First Aid post.

An ARP warden cycled down the road, his wheels wobbling as he avoided glass and broken tiles.

'Get back under shelter!' he shouted. 'There's not bin no Raiders Passed signal yet. There could be another lot coming over any minute. Get inside, all of you.'

Frank took no notice. He had only one thought in his mind, to get this boy to a place where his head could be attended to, and then to get home. His own family might be buried and calling for help, needing him.

He stopped the warden.

'I'm a firewatcher – got to get on duty. But I want this youngster seen to first. Can I get through to Drayton Road?'

The man stared at him. His face was already grimy with dust and smoke. He looked as scared as the rest, and why not? He'd never been bombed either, it was the first time for him same as everyone else.

'Drayton Road?' he said, as if the name were new to him. 'I dunno, mate. There's bin bombs up there, I know that.' He glanced up at the sky, so blue only half an hour ago, now filled with the menacing cloud of fiery black smoke which darkened the streets. 'Summat's burning down near the Yard.'

'I thought it might be Rudmore,' Frank said, and the warden nodded.

'Yeah, it might. And if that goes up we'll cop another packet. This your boy? His head don't look too good.'

Frank shook his head. 'I just want to get him somewhere he can be seen to. Then I'm off up Copnor.'

He set off again. The warden was already turning away to shout at some children who were throwing stones at one of the few unbroken windows left. At the corner of the street a man passed him, his face grey with shock, eyes staring. He looked at Frank and put out a hand.

'The Anchor – you should see what they done to the Anchor.'

'The Anchor?' Frank said. 'The pub, you mean?'

'You should see what they done,' the man repeated. He seemed to be on the verge of tears. 'The bastards. The bastards.' He shook his head blindly and stumbled on, purposelessly, as if he had nowhere to go, nothing in mind but the agony of what he had seen.

'Come on,' Frank said, taking the boy's arm again. 'I can't help it if there are more planes coming, I've got to get back up Copnor.'

They were in Kingston Road now, one of the busiest thoroughfares in the city, leading from the London Road across Portsbridge, and eventually to the beach at Southsea. It was all one long road really, with several different names as it passed through different districts – easy to see from the air, Frank thought, looking up again to see if there were planes. But the sky was still black with smoke. At least that might stop the enemy spotting their targets, he thought grimly.

And it seemed that the danger was, for the moment, over. As he hurried across the main road, aware that a little further along people were shouting and crowding towards Kingston Cross, as if something had happened there, the siren began to wail again. But this time, instead of the fearsome, swelling lament that warned of enemy approach, it was like a long-drawn sigh of relief – the signal that the raid was over.

Kingston Cross. That was where the Blue Anchor Hotel stood. Frank had never been inside, for he was a teetotaller and avoided public houses, but he knew them all by name and used them as landmarks. The family often teased him about his knowledge of local public houses, revealed whenever he gave directions. 'That's just opposite the Coach and Horses.' Or, 'Turn left by the Star and Garter and then keep straight on till you get to the Black Lion.' How did anyone who never touched a drop know so much about pubs, his brother-in-law Ted would ask. But Frank would point out that it was just a matter of knowing the city you'd been born in, knowing it like the back of your hand.

He could see Kingston Cross now, from where he stood at the corner of Powerscourt Road, and it was obvious that something up there had been badly damaged. Already fire engines were appearing, dashing along the roads with bells ringing, but they'd heading for the fire over at Rudmore. He hesitated, wanting to go straight up to the Anchor, but the boy beside him was sobbing again, clearly frightened and in some pain. He'd have to get him seen to first. And he was desperately anxious about Jess and the children.

He turned and made for Drayton Road. Only a few yards now, and he could hand over his burden and go and give whatever help he could.

And then, on the corner of Wymering Road, he stopped dead.

The main part of the school, where the older children went, was still standing, its wide brick façade and narrow tower untouched. But the infant school had received a direct hit. The buildings where five-year-old children had learned to read and write and add two and two together, were little more than a heap of rubble, smashed beyond recognition, and a dense cloud of dust hung over the ruins, swirling in its own breeze, and settling like a miasma of despair over the wreckage.

Frank stared at it, his mouth moving in silent expostulation.

Some of the walls were still partially standing, the rooms inside chaotically exposed, children's drawings and maps of Europe still pinned to the walls along with posters giving instructions about the war and diagrams of bandages and slings. Tables, desks and chairs were tossed and jumbled amongst the wreckage of collapsed ceilings and partitions. First-aid boxes and equipment, stacked ready for the first emergency, were broken and torn, smothered with dust, half buried under wooden laths and plaster. Sandbags, piled outside as an extra protection, had been torn and split open, their contents blown in all directions to add to the gritty cloud of filth.

And amongst it all, bewildered and dazed, staggered the survivors and less badly injured of the people who had manned the post and been there when the sound of the siren first ruptured the air.

'My God,' Frank said in a whisper. And then, more loudly, 'My God. Oh, my *God* . . . '

'It's bad, innit, mister,' the boy beside him said in a frightened voice.

'It is. It's bad.' Frank glanced down at him. The seeping of blood seemed to have stopped and where it had run down his face and neck it was now darkening against the grimy skin. 'Look, you'd better get off home. It don't look as if there'll be any bandages for you here. D'you reckon you can make it by yourself? I'll have to stop here now.'

The boy shook his head a little and flinched as if it still hurt. But his eyes were on the devastation before them. 'I can stop and help too, mister. I ain't hurt that bad.'

Frank hesitated. It didn't seem right, a nipper like this seeing the sights he felt sure they would see. But if there were people buried under that rubble, they'd need all the help they could get. And the kid was looking better, though the shock of seeing the bombed school had turned him a shade or two paler under all the dirt.

'All right, then,' he said. 'But you get off home the minute you want to, see? Your mum'll be half out of her mind worrying about you.' Half an hour ago, he would have given that priority, just as he'd been first anxious to see the old lady into safety and then determined to get home to Jess. But now it was different. There were people here who needed help this minute, if they were to be saved, and they had to be put first. Old ladies who were frightened and mothers worrying about kids – even Jess, his own wife, came second.

He ran across the road towards the school. Other people were flocking round too, appalled, staring at the ruin of the buildings they knew so well. The playground, where children had run and shouted and laughed, was a mass of rubble, the little row of lavatories knocked almost flat. And from the wreckage came a sound that chilled the hearts of all those who heard it – the first, wailing cry for help.

It rose from the broken earth where the bomb had struck. And it seemed to Frank Budd that it was the cry, not of one

27

person, not of one man or woman or child, but a cry that expressed the anguish of all those who were to be a part of the war that was now storming its way over the world.

The war that had begun for Portsmouth on this warm and sunny evening in July 1940.

Jess did not wait for the Raiders Passed signal. As soon as the thunder of the explosions and the roar of the aircraft began to fade, she was at the door of the shelter, gazing out at the sky. She stared in dismay at the dark smoke billowing overhead, and turned to her neighbour.

'God knows what they've done, Peg! The whole place is alight. I've got to find the boys!'

Peggy came to crouch beside her. Together, they watched as the smoke was slashed by orange flame. She twisted her head to look at the row of terraced houses, dreading what she might see.

'Well, they haven't hit April Grove,' she said with relief. 'That's something to be thankful for. We've still got homes to go to.'

'The children . . .' Jess said again. 'I've got to go and look for them.' She turned her eyes up to the blackened sky. 'I can't hear any planes now. They've gone.'

'We're supposed to wait,' Peggy began doubtfully, but she knew that Jess would not be able to rest until she had her family safe at home again. 'Well, I daresay it's all right to go out now. I'll keep Maureen with me.'

'Thanks, Peg.' Jess scrambled out of the shelter and ran up the path. The house stood just as she had left it, all the doors wide open, and she went straight through to the front and out into April Grove. As she came out on to the pavement, the siren sounded again and she gasped, then realised that it meant safety. The raiders really had passed.

Granny Kinch and her daughter Nancy emerged from number 10, Granny Kinch swathed as usual in a grubby flowered pinafore with her grey hair tightly bound in metal curlers. They looked up at the smoke-filled sky.

'Somewhere's caught it, look. I bet that's Rudmore. It'll go up like a torch any minute, see if it doesn't.'

Jess paused. 'Have you seen my boys? They're not with you, are they?'

Nancy Baxter shook her head. 'No, love, they're not here. Nor's our Micky, come to that. Didn't they go off up the street somewhere?'

'I don't know where they are.' Jess stared at the two women. 'You mean your Micky's out somewhere too?'

Nancy shrugged. 'Went out straight after tea. I saw him with that Nash boy and little Martin Baker. Playing cowboys'n'Indians, they were.'

'But they must have been scared to death!'

'Our Micky?' Nancy laughed. 'He'll be all right, he'll have found somewhere to hide, and your two with him. Takes a lot to frighten our Micky.'

'They could have been killed,' Jess said. 'I've been half out of my mind –' She gazed desperately up October Street. People were beginning to come out now, looking up at the sky and turning to each other, needing the reassurance of contact.

Jess's sister Annie appeared, hurrying down from the house at the top of April Grove. She too had an apron on, though it was a good deal cleaner than Granny Kinch's, and her face was anxious.

'Jess! Are you all right? I had to leave the supper half-cooked, ruined it is, and where we're supposed to get more when everything's on ration, I don't –'

'I've lost the boys!' Jess burst out, and saw Annie's face whiten. 'They went out to play and never came back. I don't know where they are.'

'Oh, my goodness.' Annie leaned against the wall, her hand over her heart. 'I thought for a minute . . . You mean they were out in all that lot?'

Jess nodded miserably. 'I've got to find them, Annie. If anything's happened to them – and Frank's not home yet either –'

'I'll come with you.' The two sisters set off up October Street, asking everyone they met if they had seen Tim and Keith. But nobody had, and everybody wanted to talk about the raid. Fred and Ada Brown stopped them as they hurried past. They were both trembling with agitation.

29

'I thought the bombs were coming right through our ceiling,' Fred Brown said, his old voice quavering. 'Me and our Ada, we got under the stairs, and the whole house was shaking round us.'

'I bet there's hundreds dead. Thousands.' Ada Brown shuddered and stared at Jess. 'You mean your two were out in it? That's terrible.'

'Someone must have seen them,' Jess said. 'There was five or six of them, playing cowboys and Indians. They must be somewhere.'

Her voice was ragged and jerky. Annie gave her a quick look and took her arm. 'Come on. We'll try September Street.'

'They're not supposed to go on the main road.'

'What boys are supposed to do and what they do are two different things,' Annie said. 'What about Rose? Is she all right?'

'She went up to see Joy Brunner.' Jess's steps quickened. 'Peg said she'd have gone in their shelter.'

'Well, that's what she did, then. Maybe the boys are there too.' They turned the corner of September Street. There were one or two cars and vans parked near the shops, and a bus was coming over the level crossing. You'd hardly know there'd been a raid on, except for the acrid smoke overhead and the people standing about in knots talking.

'Oh, my God, look at that.' Mr Hines, the butcher was out in front of his shop. 'Looks like they were trying for the Dockyard.'

'And looks like they missed,' old Mr Clogg said sourly. He ran a tiny hardware shop over the road. He had no shelter and had shuffled over to the Hines's when the warning sounded, still wearing the old carpet slippers he always wore in the shop. 'That fire's not in the Yard.'

'It's not just one fire. I reckon half the city's going up in flames.'

'I thought we were going to as well,' Mrs Hines said. 'Those bombs sounded right overhead. I didn't think we'd see a thing left standing . . .' She shook her head. Her lips trembling, her face white.

'I don't suppose they're all that interested in Copnor,' Mrs Marsh from the dairy said. 'There's nothing here they'd want to bomb.' But no one looked convinced.

Mr Hines was first to make a move. He shrugged his shoulders, glanced at his wife and said, 'Well, we'd better carry on, I suppose. I was halfway through chopping up some ox-liver. I hope you turned the gas off, Freda.'

'So do I,' Mrs Hines said, with an attempt at a smile. 'Else we'll have burnt potatoes for supper.' She looked at the sky again, at the smoke and the flames, and her mouth quivered. 'It's horrible,' she whispered, and Jess saw the tears in her eyes. 'Horrible . . .' She turned and almost ran into the house.

Mr Hines looked embarrassed and gave Jess and Annie a twisted half-grin. 'Freda gets upset,' he said unnecessarily. 'She was in London during the last lot, y'see.' He shrugged helplessly and followed his wife into the shop, and Mr Clogg shuffled back across the road.

Jess heard a sound on the other side and turned to see Alice Brunner and her daughter Joy emerging from their shelter. Rose was close behind them. She saw her mother and ran to her, burying her face against Jess's breast.

'Thank goodness you're all right,' Jess said, her voice choked. She held Rose close against her. 'I've been worried stiff. D'you know where the boys are?'

Rose shook her head. 'Oh, Mum, it was awful . . .'

'I know, love, I know.' Jess stroked the dark hair but her eyes were searching the street. 'But it's over now. It's the boys I'm worried about.' She looked at Alice Brunner. 'Did you see them before it started? Were they up this way?'

Alice was white-faced and Joy's eyes huge with fear. Like everyone else, they looked around them and then stared at the smoke. Alice began to cry.

'They'll be all right,' Mrs Marsh said. 'It doesn't seem to have hit anything round here.'

'And you think that's all right?' Alice's voice was high and shrill. Ever since the war began, she had been living on her nerves. The arrest of her German-born husband Heinrich had brought her close to breaking-point, and since news had

31

come last week of the torpedoing of the *Arandora Star* she had been trembling on the brink of collapse. 'People are being killed, and you think it's *all right?*'

'No, of course I don't.' Jess saw Mrs Marsh bite her lip. 'None of it's all right, Alice. But we've got to carry on, haven't we? We can't just go to pieces. That's the only way we'll win this war – by carrying on, by not *letting* them beat us.' She turned to go indoors. 'I was just going to clean out my big fridge when it started, and that's what I'm going to do now, Germans or no Germans. If Hitler *is* going to invade, I'm not having him say I keep a dirty dairy! And if I were you, Alice Brunner, I'd do the same. Keep your shop tidy and everything as it should be. Your husband would have wanted you to do that, wouldn't he?'

Alice nodded. Her mousy hair was hanging loose about her pale face. 'There wasn't a neater man in Pompey than my Heinrich.'

'Well, then. What'd he say if he walked in and found it in a mess, and you looking like that?'

Joy took her mother's arm. 'Come on in, Mum. I'll make you a cup of tea.'

Jess was still holding Rose. In her imagination, she saw Tim and Keith lying dead in some alleyway, their toy pistols still clutched in their hands.

'I'll never forgive myself if anything's happened to those two,' she said, beginning to run again. 'Frank *said* they should never have come back, he said there'd be bad raids, but I would have them home and now – oh, those Germans, those wicked, *wicked* Germans!'

'They'll be all right.' Annie and Rose kept pace with her, Rose still hiccuping. 'Mrs Marsh was right, you can see there's been no bombing round here. They've just taken shelter somewhere, that's all, and – look!' She quickened her steps further. 'That's them now! Just coming over the railway.'

Jess felt as if her legs were stuck in treacle. They wouldn't move fast enough. She saw Tim and Keith hurtling towards her, their faces wreathed in grins, and she felt the sobs rise in her throat.

The smiles were of embarrassment, appeasement and a half awareness of relief at having survived the bombing. But to Jess they were an affront. Her fear turned to anger, and her relief, so enormous that it demanded instant expression, merged with her anger. A moment ago, her fury had been directed against the Germans; now it was focused for a few moments upon her sons.

'You naughty, naughty boys!' she exclaimed, catching them roughly by the shoulders. 'Whatever do you think you've been doing, staying out in the streets in that lot? Where have you been? I looked for you everywhere when the sirens sounded. Don't you realise you could have been killed? D'you think it's something to laugh at, worrying me like that?'

Tim and Keith stared at her, shocked by her outburst. Jess rarely shouted at them. She could tell them off, and frequently did, and they were well aware of the limits they had better not cross, but she hardly ever shook them like this, with rough hands, and raised her voice. And she was *crying*. Their grins faded and they glanced sideways at each other and ducked their heads.

'We only went over to Carlisle Crescent,' Tim said, trying to sound aggrieved. 'We were playing cowboys and Indians –'

'Carlisle Crescent? That's over the railway. You know you're not supposed to go down there.' Jess shook them both again. 'If you don't stop in your own street, you won't be allowed out to play at all.' Frank was right, they were better off in the country. You couldn't keep track of boys like this, and you couldn't keep them indoors all the time either, they needed to be out playing, letting off steam.

She saw that Keith had begun to cry, large tears creeping down his cheeks, and even Tim's lips were wobbling, and she felt suddenly guilty at the way she had yelled at them. Her hands more gentle now, she pulled them close and hugged them tightly.

'There, it's all right,' she muttered. 'I was just so worried, not knowing where you were and hearing the bombs falling. You mustn't go so far away again. You must always be close enough to get home, see? Come on now, let's go back indoors before they come back.'

Subdued now, the three children walked back down the street beside her. Peggy Shaw was still in number 14, making cocoa. She had fed Maureen and put her to bed, and now she went back next door to her own family.

'And now you two can go to bed as well,' Jess told the boys. 'I don't care if it is before your usual bedtime. Drink your cocoa and scrub that dirt of your faces and then get upstairs.'

Rose, still white-faced and shaking, crept into Frank's armchair and curled up there. She looked at her mother.

'I don't have to go yet, do I? Can't I stop up till Dad comes home?'

Jess's heart gave a lurch. Until now, she'd been too worried about the children to give way to her fears about her husband. Now terror flooded back into her heart and she felt sick all over again.

But there was nothing she could do. She couldn't even go out to look for him.

'Yes,' she said, not wanting to wait on her own. 'You can stop up for a bit. But not too long mind. Your dad might be a bit late tonight.'

The boys went to bed without a word. But Jess and Rose sat together, watching the smoke drift slowly across the sky and worrying about Frank.

It was almost ten o'clock when Frank finally arrived home. For three hours he worked in Drayton Road, helping to pull away the rubble that had buried so many of the ARP wardens and helpers who had been preparing to give aid to others. With his bare hands, he dragged at bricks and laths and plaster, tugging frantically because under all this, somewhere, he could hear a woman's cries or a man shouting for help. Or perhaps there was someone who couldn't cry or shout, who was unconscious but still alive, choking in the dust, crushed by a beam of timber or a pile of broken bricks.

Frank was a big man, powerfully built. He took charge of a little group of men who could lift heavy weights, and they moved from place to place over the ruins, shifting what other people couldn't budge. They needed to take special care because sometimes it was clear that a beam which must be

34

shifted could bring down a whole wall, or a portion of roof that was still hanging as if by a thread above their heads. And sometimes, although they knew that the person who lay buried beneath could only be saved if the beam was moved, they dared not touch it, for fear of its killing others.

As well as moving rubble, there were bodies to be shifted. The bodies of first-aid workers, men and women who had attended classes since the war was declared, determined to be of use, but had had their lives slashed away before they could attend so much as a cut finger. And they were not neatly laid-out, covered with white sheets, as if they had died in hospital or been tidied up by others more accustomed to such things. Instead, they lay like broken dolls amongst the wreckage, their bodies crushed, their limbs smashed, their eyes open and staring from the mess of raw flesh and blackened blood and bone that had been their faces.

Some of them were not even whole. Their legs had been torn from their bodies, their arms lay draped across upturned tables or tangled with chairs, there was even a head that had been wrenched from its neck and rolled by itself to lie perched on a tottering pile of bloodstained bandages. When Frank first caught sight of it, it seemed to be watching him and he turned away and vomited. And I've been in a war before, he thought. How is this going to affect these other people, who never dreamed of such things? How about the boy with the grazed head, that I brought here?

All these fragments must be collected and put together, like some gruesome jigsaw puzzle, and you couldn't turn your back and say it wasn't your job. It was everyone's job.

At last the terrible work was over. Firemen had come and gone, ambulances had taken the injured away to the hospital. The rubble still filled the playground where small children had played hopscotch and fivestones, and would have to be left until there was time to deal with it. But as far as anyone could tell, there was no one left under the chaos of smashed masonry and torn beams. No one alive, anyway.

Eleven dead. Eleven people who had been fit and healthy but for one reason or another not expected to fight – men too old or too young, women who had been glad to offer their time. Eleven people who had left their homes that afternoon expecting to be home in time for supper and would never go home again.

'One of them was the Superintendent,' Frank told Jess when he finally came in through the front door to find her sitting doing nothing, with Rose now asleep in his chair. 'And there was others hurt, some of 'em aren't going to live, you could tell that.' He shuddered a little, thinking of the injuries, things that ought never to happen to human bodies. 'And all the time I was thinking about you and the kids and wondering what was going on up here. I couldn't tell where all the explosions were coming from, and no one seemed to know anything. It seemed as if the whole city had been smashed to bits. And the sky was so full of smoke and flames, I thought they'd set light to whatever was left anyway.'

'I know.' Jess held him tightly, not caring that his clothes were filthy, that his hair was full of dust and plaster. 'We could see it from here. Whatever was it? Someone said it was one of the ships in the Yard on fire.'

Frank shook his head. 'There might've been some ships hit, I dunno. But the fire came from the gasholder at Rudmore. A bomb fell right inside. It wasn't full, one of the firemen who came to Drayton told me that. It could've been nasty, all the same, if they hadn't got it under control so quick.' He sat down wearily at the table and leant his head on his hands. 'Thank God you're all right, Jess. All the way home, I was thinking what it'd be like to turn the corner and see number 14 just a mass of rubble. There's a whole row in Portchester Road, with hardly a slate left and all their windows out. And houses in Farlington Road they'll never be able to patch up, almost nothing left of them, bricks and stuff all over the place. And the Blue Anchor's gone, and half a dozen houses and a garage in Gamble Road. And that's just around this part of Pompey. God knows what the rest of the city's like.'

Henry, the big tabby cat, got up from the rag rug and came over to lay a paw on Frank's knee. Frank reached down and pulled the cat on to his lap and Henry purred and rubbed his head against the dirty shirt. He had spent the raid crouched against the wall of the coalshed and had hardly left Jess's side since she had come back to the house.

'Poor old chap,' Frank said, scratching the hard, furry head. 'You can't understand it at all, can you.'

Jess went out to the scullery to make some more cocoa. As she came back into the room, she saw Rose stir and open her eyes. She saw her father and scrambled out of the chair to run to him and bury her face against his chest.

'Rose!' Jess remonstrated. 'Your father's all dirty still.'

But Frank held his daughter's head and his big hands stroked her straight black hair. He looked down at her trembling body and Jess felt her own heart soften at the expression on his face.

Frank wasn't a man who was demonstrative towards his children. He hadn't had enough of that kind of loving in his own childhood to be able to pass it on. But she knew his heart was tender and that he longed to be able to cuddle them, or even to give them a casual pat, without feeling awkward. And, just occasionally, there were moments when his emotions overcame his reticence and he was able to express them freely and without embarrassment.

This was one of those moments, and Jess felt her eyes fill with tears as she watched her husband and eldest child hold each other closely. And she felt a sharp poignancy and a deep sadness that it took a war, sometimes, to bring people as close as they ought to be to one another. That eleven people had to die before Frank's eyes before he could hold his daughter in his arms and stroke her hair.

CHAPTER THREE

'Mind you don't go too far away, now. I don't want to have to go looking for you again if there's another raid.'

Jess looked at her sons with some misgivings. After last night, she was half afraid to let them out, but it was impossible to keep them indoors on such a fine morning.

'We'll be all right, Mum.'

Tim and Keith hopped from foot to foot. They had been awake early, gazing out of their bedroom window over the allotments, talking about the raid. It was nothing but a game to them. They hadn't seen what Frank had seen, nor did Jess want them to see such things.

'I want them back out in the country,' she'd said to Frank last night, after Rose had gone to bed. 'Back out at Bridge End, where they'll be safe.'

'We'll take them on Saturday,' he agreed. 'And you can stay there too, at Mrs Greenberry's.' But Jess had shaken her head. She'd liked Mrs Greenberry well enough, and loved being in the country, but she'd hated the months away from Frank when she'd gone with the first evacuation. A wife's place was with her man, and she didn't intend to leave him again.

Tim and Keith raced up the street, as excited as puppies let off the leash. They stopped near the end of April Grove, where the road widened and there was space for a game of cricket. Someone had chalked stumps on the blank wall of the end house of March Street.

'Shall I go back for the bat?' Keith suggested, but Tim shrugged.

'Don't feel like cricket. I want to go exploring.'

Keith looked around. They were near their Auntie Annie's house here and knew every inch of the three streets. He looked through the fence at the allotments. There were footpaths across them, but the boys weren't supposed to go there unless they were going to Frank's allotment, to take him a jug of tea or tell him dinner was ready.

'There's Micky,' he said. 'And Jimmy Cross and Cyril.'

The three boys came through a hole in the fence and joined them. Micky was grinning.

'What happened to you last night? Mummy make you go to bed early?'

Tim flushed. 'We wanted to listen to the wireless.' They hadn't been allowed to, but Micky didn't have to know that. 'D'you want a game of cricket? We could get our bat.'

'Cricket!' Micky said scornfully. 'We've got better things to do than play cricket. We're going down to look at the bombs.'

'Bombs? You mean there's still bombs? Ones that haven't gone off? Bet there's not.'

'Bet there are, then. Bet we'll find some.' Micky strutted cockily. 'We'll get 'em for souvenirs. My mum says she'll put 'em on the mantelpiece if we find any.'

'Not *unexploded* bombs. That'd be dangerous.'

'Well, ones that have gone off, anyway. And shells and bullets and that. There'll be all sorts down Drayton Road way. The school got bombed and hundreds of people were killed. We might find bodies.'

Tim wasn't sure he wanted to find bodies, but the idea of shells and bomb cases was alluring. He hesitated and looked at Keith.

'We're not allowed to go right down Drayton Road.'

'Mummy's boys,' Micky sneered. 'Well, we're going, ain't we?' Cyril and Jimmy nodded. 'Don't suppose we'll have to go that far anyway. There was bombing nearer than that. Bet we'll find all sorts of stuff.'

He turned away, and the other two boys followed him. Tim and Keith stared after them enviously.

'I wouldn't mind finding a few bombs,' Tim said. 'That'd be something to take back to Bridge End. Give that Brian

Collins something to think about!'

'But we're not supposed to go out of the street,' Keith said wistfully.

Tim thought for a moment. 'We only promised not to go over the railway. Drayton Road's not over the railway – it's in the opposite direction. And we don't have to go all the way. We can always come back if we get fed up.'

Keith hesitated. He glanced back down the street towards number 14. Their mother had gone back indoors and the only person in sight was Mrs Glaister next door, scrubbing her step. She wouldn't take any notice of them, she never did.

'Come on,' Tim said, setting off up March Street. 'The Germans won't come this early in the morning. And if we go back to Bridge End tomorrow we'll never get another chance to find a bomb of our own.'

Filled with fresh excitement, the two boys scurried up the street and caught up with Micky and his henchmen as they turned the corner into September Street. There were plenty of people about now, opening up their shops or walking to work. A few stood at bus stops, but there weren't many buses about. Perhaps they couldn't get through the bombed streets.

'There's whole rows of houses smashed to bits,' Micky said with relish. 'I bet some of 'em are still burning. We could help put 'em out. We might find a parachute. That's how they're going to invade, by parachute. They'll all come down from the sky, with guns and hand grenades.'

'They won't,' Tim said. 'They'll come in ships.'

They crossed over Copnor Road. The two Budds had never been so far away from April Grove without permission. At first they'd been nervous, half expecting to be called back or spotted by someone who knew them and might tell Mum or Dad. But now there was less chance of that and they relaxed and look round eagerly for signs of bomb damage.

By the time they reached Chichester Road, Keith's short legs were tiring and he was finding it difficult to keep up with the others. But at the first sight of broken windows and debris littering the streets, he forgot his weariness.

'Coo-er! Look at that . . .'

They gazed at the windows, already being boarded up.

There were people up on roofs too, putting back slates. A woman with a scarf wound over her head like a turban swept broken glass out of her front door.

'Come on,' Micky urged as they slowed down, 'there's better'n this to see. I want to see some real smashed houses.'

But when they reached Portchester Road, even Micky stopped in awe. They stared at the ruined street, at the piles of debris that still blocked the road, at the shattered roofs and torn walls. Some of the houses had been completely destroyed. Others had whole rooms exposed, with pictures still hanging on the walls and teacups still on the tables.

'There's someone's lav, stuck out in the middle of nowhere.' Micky pointed to a bathroom that had been partially demolished. He sniggered. 'Wonder if they were sittin' on it . . .'

'I could do with a pee,' Cyril said, and ran over to the lavatory bowl which hung at a drunken angle at the top of a splintered staircase. The other boys giggled and someone shouted at them. Cyril came back grinning and they went on down the street, kicking at loose bricks and clambering over piles of rubble.

'There's all sorts of stuff just bin left,' Micky said. 'Look. Tins of peas, beans, all bent and twisted. And kids' toys. I bet some of it's still all right.' He bent and scrabbled through a pile of objects that had been heaped in the gutter. 'There's a Dinky car here, nothing wrong with it at all.'

The other boys began to do the same, turning over broken dolls and mangled train sets. Most of it was beyond repair, but there were a few bits and pieces that could be slipped into pockets. They moved slowly along the pavement, pushing the muddled heaps with their toes, keeping out of the way of the people who were clearing up.

'You can get right into these houses,' Jimmy Cross said. 'I wonder what it's like.'

The nearest house was partly destroyed, with the upper walls torn away to expose its upstairs rooms, while downstairs remained closed and mysterious. Through the broken window, they could see tumbled furniture and doors hanging at crazy angles.

'I wonder if anyone got killed in there,' Tim said in a hushed voice.

Micky's eyes lit up. 'Let's go and see.'

Keith hung back a little. 'Will there be blood? I don't like blood much, it makes me feel funny.'

'Stop out here then.' The bigger boys were already pushing open the front door. It swung back, revealing a mess of broken laths and torn wallpaper. The stairs were covered with broken plaster, with bits of blue carpet showing here and there. Micky glanced up and down the street. 'Quick – no one's watching.'

Tim looked at his brother. He was uneasily aware that they ought not to be here, that this was something that would definitely be forbidden. If Dad ever got to hear about it . . . but the temptation was too strong to be resisted. Yet he couldn't leave Keith out here all by himself.

'Come on,' he said. 'There won't be any blood. They've taken away all the people who got hurt.' He turned to go after the others. Keith, his lips trembling a little, followed him unhappily.

Micky was in the front room, rummaging through a cupboard that had once had a glass front. Most of its contents were broken, but there were a couple of glasses that were only slightly chipped, and he took them out and stood them on the windowsill.

'They'll do for our mum. She likes a glass of port and lemon. So does my gran.' He looked round the filthy room and his eyes gleamed. 'Here, this'd make a smashing den.'

Jimmy Cross was sifting through another heap of rubble. 'It's all girls' stuff,' he said in disgust. 'Look at this – a china doll with its face all smashed. And a teddy-bear with all its stuffing coming out. We're not going to find anything worth having here.'

'This is all right.' Tim had found something else. He wiped the dust off with his sleeve and held it up. 'It's a donkey.'

The other boys crowded round to look. The donkey was made of twisted and woven cane. It carried panniers on its sides and wore a straw sombrero with its ears poking through.

'It's just a kid's toy,' Micky said, but Tim shook his head.

'It's not, it's from Gibraltar. Our Auntie Annie's got one just like it. Her Colin brought it home once – he's a sailor. He helped sink the *Graf Spee*.' He looked at the donkey again. 'I'll take it home for Mum.'

'Oy! What you doing in there?' They jumped as an ARP warden pushed his way into the room and grabbed their shoulders. 'Don'tcher think things is bad enough without looters and sightseers? Clear off, before I calls a copper.'

Micky turned indignantly. 'We're not looting! My auntie lives here. Least, she did till yesterday.' He looked around him at the ruined house. 'We just come over to get a few things for her.'

The warden stared at him. His face was tired and grey, and he looked as if he had neither slept nor shaved for the past two days. The harsh lines softened and he laid his hand on the boy's arm.

'I'm sorry, son,' he said more quietly. 'I wouldn't have bawled at you, only we had a lot of nosy parkers round here today, snooping round to see what they could see – and take away, too, some of 'em. I dunno what they want to come gawping for, they'll see plenty more of it before they're much older. But you didn't ought to be poking round inside, all the same, it ain't safe. The whole lot could come crashing down any minute.'

He led them back on to the littered pavement, and they stood looking up at the ruins of the house. Tim looked at Micky.

'We'd better go home,' he muttered. 'Our mum'll be looking for us again.'

'I was just goin' anyway,' Micky said loudly. 'There's nothin' else worth takin'. Our auntie'll be ever so upset.' He turned and swaggered away up the street.

The rest of the boys trailed after him. Tim felt uncomfortable. He wasn't above telling the odd fib himself, but he felt that there was something wrong about Micky's lie about an auntie living in that house. Only yesterday, someone *had* lived there – someone real, who didn't have a home any more, who might even have been killed. It didn't seem right to take things out of their house and then tell lies about them.

43

He was still carrying the donkey. He wondered what to do with it. He could drop it in the road, but somehow he didn't like to do that. He wiped some of the dust from its head. Perhaps Maureen would like it.

But by the time he arrived home, he knew that he would never be able to produce it without a lot of explanations about where he had found it. He went up the back garden path, relieved to find that his mother was out shopping, and hid it in the coalshed.

Kathy Simmons woke that morning to find herself sharing a large school hall with a crowd of other people who had been bombed out of their homes or evacuated because of the danger of explosion. She lay for a moment on the hastily made-up camp bed, staring miserably at the sunshine filtering dustily through the tall windows.

For a few moments, before opening her eyes, she had tried to convince herself that the raid had been no more than a nightmare, that she was still at home and had never spent the evening and half the night being pushed from pillar to post, sent first to this rescue centre, then to that, until at last she and the girls had finished up here. But it was no use. Already she could hear the voices of the helpers as they prepared breakfast, the weeping of other people around her and the sobs of her own little girls.

Dragging herself back to reality, she sat up and brushed back her hair with fingers that still trembled. She didn't seem able to stop shaking, even though she'd slept, on and off, for the past three or four hours. Last night it had been worse – great shudders that seemed to tear her body apart. She'd felt so guilty, being unable to control them when Stella and Muriel needed all the comfort she could give them, but someone had given her a cup of tea with a lot of sugar in it and that had helped. For a bit.

Muriel was crying again now in her little nest of blankets. There hadn't been enough beds for everyone, and she and Stella had been put to bed on a heap of old cushions. Kathy hadn't been at all happy about those cushions, they were stained and tattered and she wouldn't have given them house

44

room, but there was nothing else and she'd been too worn out to argue. She bent over and touched Muriel's shoulder, drawing her into her arms.

'Don't cry, pet. It's all over now, we're quite safe. Come into my bed for a minute.'

The child allowed herself to be pulled into bed and lay there in Kathy's arms, sobbing bitterly. Kathy felt her heart wrench. It wasn't fair, bombing little children out of their homes. It wasn't Christian. She stroked the fair hair, wondering if Muriel would ever get over it. She was only six and didn't understand. Stella was nine and had a bit more idea, but she'd never expected the sort of horror that had happened last night. Kathy hadn't expected it herself.

Muriel was trying to say something now, the words choked by sobs. Kathy held her tightly, crooning and smoothing her hair. 'Don't try to talk. It's all over now. Everything's all right now.' She wished she could believe it.

Stella was awake too, sitting up and watching them. Her face was white but she wasn't crying. She looked as if she'd buttoned up everything tightly inside her.

'She wants her dolly,' she said. 'She wants Princess Marcia.'

Kathy's heart sank. They had found the doll last night, during that first unbelieving survey of the bombed house. Almost everything had been smashed. The doll's china face had been broken beyond repair, its arms and legs crushed. Kathy had wept herself at the sight of it. She remembered the day Mike had brought it home, when he'd come back from one of his Mediterranean trips. He'd brought her a little basketwork donkey at the same time . . . She'd turned away, too sick at heart to look for anything else. There wasn't any point.

'I'm sorry about Princess Marcia,' she said, rocking Muriel in her arms. 'We'll get you another dolly.' But she knew it wouldn't be the same.

After that, there wasn't time for crying. The helpers had poured out cups of tea on a trestle table at the end of the hall and everyone was crowding round trying to grab the sugar. There was bread and marge too, but nothing else. Some of the children picked at theirs and left it, others stuffed it into their mouths as though they hadn't seen food for a month. Kathy put the pieces Stella and Muriel couldn't eat into her pocket. There was no knowing where the next meal might come from.

'What are we supposed to do now?' she asked one of the helpers, a woman with grey hair and a tired face. She'd probably been up most of the night, trying to sort out the endless stream of people who'd been bombed out. 'Where can we go?'

The woman shook her head. 'Don't ask me, love. I'm just here to pour out tea and make sandwiches. There'll be someone come in from the council later on to sort all that out for you.'

Kathy went back to the corner where she and the girls had spent the night. It was the only home they had now, that rickety little camp bed and the pile of old cushions. She wondered how long they would have to live here, and what they would do for clothes and food. They had nothing but what they had been wearing when the siren had sounded.

The morning wore on. Nobody seemed to know quite what to do with themselves. People sat on their beds or gathered in small groups to talk about how awful the raid had been. A couple of women started an argument. Most of them were still feeling shaken, and one girl kept being sick.

Helpers came and went, and two or three women carrying briefcases came in and set up a sort of office on the trestle tables. One of them called for attention and asked all those whose names began with A to form a queue to be interviewed.

'That's us at the back as usual,' Kathy commented ruefully. Muriel had stopped her bitter crying now and was sitting miserably on the camp bed. Stella, still white-faced and subdued, had asked if she could go outside to play, but Kathy had shaken her head.'I'd rather you stopped here, under my eye. We might have to go somewhere else and I don't want to have to go looking for you.'

There were quite a few children, who had either not been evacuated or had been brought back when it seemed as if there was going to be no bombing. A few had toys they'd managed to salvage, but most of them were growing bored and restless. The smaller ones clung to their mothers, whining and grizzling, and some of the bigger boys started to chase round the hall, jumping on and off beds and shouting.

'I 'opes to Gawd we don't 'ave to stop 'ere long,' said a woman near Kathy. 'You'd think they'd 'ave summat better than this ready. I mean, what're they going to do if there's another lot like last night? We'll be crowded out.'

'I suppose they're trying to get something organised now.' The queue of people had now reached those whose names began with D. The As, Bs and Cs had already returned to their little spaces and gathered up what belongings they still possessed. 'What does your name start with?'

'W,' the woman said gloomily. 'Wilson. It'll be the middle of next week before they gets round to me.'

'Well, I don't see why we got to wait,' someone else chipped in. She had frizzled ginger hair and the end of a cigarette drooping from her lip. 'I'll be going to stop with my sister at Farlington. I don't see as that's their business. They never took no interest in us before.'

'Yes, but they'll give you money, won't they,' Mrs Wilson said. 'To buy new clothes and furniture and stuff. And they wants to know just who's bin bombed out, for their records.'

The ginger woman looked as if she didn't give tuppence for the records, but the possibility of being given money didn't seem to have struck her before. She sat down again and lit another cigarette.

At midday the tables were cleared again and urns of soup and tea brought in. There was more bread and marge, and this time most people ate it. There was milk for the children, but it was obvious that supplies were scarce. Presumably the bombing had made it difficult to get fresh food through, though there seemed to be a good store of tins and packets in the school.

At last the queue reached S, and Kathy found herself sitting in front of the trestle table with the girls one on each side of her. The woman behind the table was wearing a floral dress and looked hot and sticky. She was rather fat, with wavy grey hair that looked as if it had been polished.

47

'Name?' She had a scratchy pen and an inkpot. 'Address? And how many in your family?'

'Just the two girls,' Kathy said, and the woman looked at her sharply.

'Husband away?'

'He's in the Merchant Navy.'

'I see.' The woman wrote down all the details. 'You've managed to save your documents, that's a good thing. Some people have got nothing, just nothing. What else is salvage-able?'

Kathy stared at her.

'What else did you bring with you? Can you get much out of the house? Furniture, clothes, utensils?'

Kathy shook her head numbly. 'Nothing.' She felt the ache in her throat, the hot threat of tears in her eyes. All day she'd been trying to keep them back for the sake of the children, but now her control was slipping.

'Nothing at all?'

'We couldn't even get Princess Marcia,' Muriel said suddenly. 'And Stella's donkey that Daddy brought home.'

The woman looked at the children, then back at Kathy. All day she had been interviewing people who had been bombed out of their houses and now had nothing at all, and she had begun to harden herself towards the tragedy of it all. It was the only way to get through. But the sight of Muriel's face, mourning her lost doll, touched her heart and brought her own tears perilously close.

'Well, there'll be other dolls,' she said briskly, forcing them back. 'The main thing now is to find you somewhere to live and give you some money. Now, you can be housed for a short while in a reception centre about half a mile away – a church hall. This one is being kept for immediate emergencies. You'll be allowed enough money for your immediate needs such as soap and a change of clothes, and when a house is found for you, you'll be given money for furniture.' She opened a tin box and gave Kathy a pound note and a ten-shilling one, entering the figure in a column beside Kathy's name. She signed the sheet of paper, then tore it off and handed it over. 'Keep that safe. It tells us what you've had.

You're allowed a total of five pounds but it's not to be frittered away, mind. And if you're evacuated the sum will be different, of course, since you won't be requiring furniture.'

'I shan't be evacuated,' Kathy said. 'I want to be in Portsmouth for when my husband gets home.'

The woman pursed her lips. 'You'll be sending the children away, though.'

Kathy shook her head. 'I'd rather we stayed together.'

'They'd be a lot safer out in the country.'

'We'd rather be together.' She tried a shaky smile. 'Anyway, they say lightning never strikes twice in the same place.'

The woman sighed and shrugged. 'Well, it's up to you.' She looked past Kathy at the queue behind her. 'Next.'

Kathy folded the blankets they'd used and piled them neatly at the end of the bed, wondering if they would be used that night by some other bomb victim. With the two little girls, she walked through the streets to the church hall, where she found another camp bed, another pile of blankets, and another pile of battered cushions. Here she was told that she was on high priority for a house and could go to look at one at once.

She sat down on the bed and cuddled Stella and Muriel against her. She had done nothing all day, yet she was exhausted. Tomorrow they'd have to go out and find some cheap clothes, maybe in a second-hand shop. The grey-haired woman was right. Five pounds – even one pound ten – seemed a lot of money. But it would have to be spent carefully to buy all the things they would need.

'Will I be able to have a new dolly?' Muriel asked, and Kathy cuddled her closer, feeling the hard ache once again in her throat.

'Yes,' she said, 'we'll find you a dolly.'

Betty Chapman spent the morning cleaning the windows of the dairy where she worked. Even though they were criss-crossed with brown paper strips, Mrs Marsh insisted that they must be kept clean. A dairy had to be hygienic.

'She'll have me dusting and polishing the sandbags next,'

49

Betty grumbled to her sister Olive as they ate the sausages and chips their mother had prepared for their midday meal. 'I'm sick of frittering my time away in the dairy. Any old woman could do that job. There's better things for people like me.'

Olive sniffed and Betty felt exasperated. Although she had been married for less than a week, she seemed to think she'd gone up in the world, somehow. As if being a 'married woman' as she now liked to call herself, made her better than her younger sister. As if she knew more.

Well, maybe she does, but I bet it's not all that much, Betty thought. I reckon I know as much about the facts of life as she does – except that she knows what it *feels* like. She gazed at Olive's face, trying to see whether there was any difference. Her sister was certainly apt to go off in a dream these days, staring into space with her fork halfway to her mouth. Was she thinking about it then? Was she remembering her wedding night, she and Derek in bed together, thinking about what they'd done?

'I don't think you've heard a word I said,' she exclaimed crossly. 'If you're not going to be a bit more chatty than this, I might as well read *Tit-Bits* while I have my dinner.'

'You'll do no such thing,' Annie said sharply. 'I'll have no reading at table in this house. And it's lunch, not dinner.'

Betty made a face. All her friends called the midday meal 'dinner' and thought her stuck-up when she called it 'lunch'. But Mum had picked up these ideas when she'd been in service in a big house, and you couldn't argue with her.

'Well, it's like a morgue,' she grumbled. 'Our Olive sitting there with a face as long as a wet weekend and nothing cheerful on the wireless. And there's been nothing but the air-raid in the shop this morning. Everyone was either in it or knows someone else who was in it. They can't talk about anything else.'

'And can you blame them? There's been people killed here, in Portsmouth, only half a mile away from this house. It could be us next time, don't you realise that?'

Annie's voice trembled a little. The raid had frightened her badly. All the time she'd been worrying about Olive and Ted. Olive was at Harker's and would almost certainly get into their shelter, but Ted was on evening shift, taking the *Ferry King* across the harbour to Gosport, and she knew how much he hated it, especially since Dunkirk.

'And how d'you think I feel?' Olive demanded suddenly. 'I was married last Saturday, remember? Two days married life I had, and now my Derek's miles away down in Devon, and God knows when I'll see him again.' She glowered at her sister and Betty shrugged.

'That's not my fault is it? I didn't tell you to get married.' She bit her lip. She and Olive had always been good friends, never squabbled much, yet these days it seemed they were always bickering. She said more quietly, 'I'm sorry, Livvy. I know you miss him. Same as I missed Graham when he was away. And he'll be off again soon, once they get the ship sorted out, and I don't know what might happen to him, do I. But that's just what I'm saying. They're both doing something and we're just *stuck* here. I want to be doing something too. Something really important. Don't you?'

'I reckon it's important to keep on going same as always,' Olive said. 'The men have got to have homes to come back to and it's up to us women to make sure they do. Look at that raid last night. Dozens of houses smashed. People have been coming into the office all morning trying to get Mr Harker to do their repairs. How d'you think he'd manage without someone to run his office?'

'Oh, I daresay he needs someone to do all his paperwork for him,' Betty agreed. 'But it doesn't have to be you, does it? Mrs Harker could do that. Anyway –' as she saw her sister's face darken again '– I wasn't talking about you, I was talking about me. I want to do something more than count bags of eggs and make up pats of butter. Not that there's much butter to pat these days, nor eggs to count neither.' She laid her knife and fork together on her plate as Annie had always taught her, and sighed, 'I wish they'd call me up into the Land Army. It's ages since I put my name down.'

'I don't reckon they're going to,' Olive said. 'They've got too many girls registering. I tell you what's happened, with people not using their cars any more, and farmers going back to horses, all the blokes who worked as village garage mechanics have gone on the land. That's why they don't want the girls after all. And there's plenty of old men, farm labourers who know what they're doing and pleased enough to earn themselves a bit of money. I shouldn't think you'll ever get called up.'

'Well, I'll go into one of the other Services then. The Wrens. Or the WAAFs.' She got up and looked into the mirror that hung over the fireplace, pulling with her fingers at the golden-brown curls clustering over her head. 'Which uniform d'you think would suit me best?'

Annie clucked with irritation. 'Honestly, our Betty, you make me so cross at times. You don't go into the Services just because of a pretty uniform. Anyway, I don't expect your Dad would let you go. He's never said yes to you joining the Land Army, you know that.'

Betty pouted. 'He's an old stick-in-the-mud. Why shouldn't I join the Land Army? Or anything else? It's for my country, isn't it? To help win the war? What's wrong with that?'

'Yes, why shouldn't Bet do what she wants?' Olive joined in. She was well aware that her father had been against her marrying Derek before she was twenty-one, until Derek had come back from Dunkirk and made it clear he wasn't waiting any longer. Now she was a married woman and therefore outside her father's jurisdiction, even though she was still living at home with her parents, and she could afford to stick up for her sister. 'If she wants to go and milk cows and dig potatoes, why not?'

Annie sighed and fetched the pudding. It was stewed apple tart with some custard made more with water than milk. The custard was thin, and a year ago she'd have felt like throwing it away, but things had changed since then. You couldn't get the ingredients to make decent puddings and you couldn't afford to waste what there was. You had to make do – she'd already tried making 'banana pudding' with parsnips and a bit of flavouring, and some of the other economy wartime recipes they'd started putting in newspapers and giving out on the wireless, and she had to admit that some of them weren't bad at all.

She set the tart down on the table and cut it into portions, leaving one for Ted when he came home.

'I don't know, I'm sure,' she said. 'Everything's so different these days, I can't keep up with it all. I thought we had our lives all nice and settled, with our Colin in the Navy and you girls growing up and getting nice jobs for a few years before you got married. Now there's you with your man miles away, and our Bet talking about uniforms, and Colin goodness knows where . . .' She shook her head. 'It's like you can't be sure of anything. And then the air-raids –' Her voice broke and she sank into her chair and put her hand up to her quivering mouth. A moment later the tears were pouring down her cheeks, and Olive and Betty stared at her and simultaneously reached out to lay their hands on her arms.

'Mum, don't.' Olive got up and went to her mother, drawing the greying head against her breast. 'Don't cry. It's over now, the air-raid, and we're all safe.'

'Over? It's not over. It's only just started.' Annie looked up at her. 'It's going to be like that all the time now – sirens going off when you don't expect them, bombs exploding in the next street, perhaps on our own house. Never knowing where you all are when it happens, never knowing if you'll walk out of here one morning and not come back. And if our Betty goes off, how'll I know she's safe then, eh? She might be ill or hurt and it'd be days before we heard anything, *days* . . .'

'But that's no different from being evacuated,' Betty said. 'And I'd be safer out in the country –'

'Shut up,' Olive snapped. 'Can't you see she's upset? It's the shock, that's what it is, it's enough to upset anyone. It's all right, Mum,' she murmured, bending her head down to her mother's. 'It's all right. None of us got hurt in the raid, and we won't neither, as long as we make sure and get in the shelter every time. And I don't reckon they'll get through so easy again. Our lads'll be on the watch for 'em now, you see. They won't let those dratted German planes in again.'

Maybe they wouldn't, Betty thought, but she remembered seeing the planes high in the sky, flying steadily, as if determined that nothing would stop them. She looked up and saw the fear in her sister's eyes.

The war had been brought right to their doorstep.

CHAPTER FOUR

'Come on,' Jess said as soon as dinner was finished and the washing-up done.'We're going down North End to see Grandma and Grandpa.'

She'd half expected an objection from the boys, but none came. They'd been unusually quiet ever since she'd arrived home from the shops to find them already back, and Tim was wearing his guilty look. She wondered what they'd been up to.

Perhaps they'd let it out on the way to North End. Annie had already been last night, to make sure that they were all right after the raid, but Jess was anxious to see them herself.

Rose pushed Maureen's pram. Since coming back from Bridge End she had almost taken over the baby, playing with her, feeding her, washing her – though she still refused to have anything to do with nappies – and taking her for walks. Sometimes Joy Brunner came with her, but Joy was more often busy in the shop, helping her own mother.

The boys wandered alongside, still rather quiet. No, they hadn't been playing cricket, Tim had said when Jess asked him. No, nor cowboys and Indians.

'So what were you doing all morning?' she inquired, as they walked through the streets. 'Hide and seek?'

'Yes,' Tim began, but Keith, speaking at the same moment, said a little more brightly, 'No. We've been exploring.'

'Exploring?' Jess repeated, noticing Tim's scowl. 'Where were you exploring? You haven't been too far away, I hope.'

Keith too had seen his brother's frown and dropped his eyes, saying nothing. His ears had turned red. Jess kept her gaze fixed on Tim's face and he glanced up and reddened as well.

'Where were you exploring?' she asked again.

'Nowhere much,' Tim said, with a shrug, and she was convinced that they had been doing something they shouldn't.

'Where?'

Tim looked at her. He knew that if he told her the truth he and Keith would be in serious trouble. Worse still, they'd be in trouble with Dad. It was bad enough having Mum cross with them, but if it was something she thought Dad should know about, it meant real punishment. A lot of shouting. Probably the cane.

'Africa,' he said, wiith sudden inspiration. 'And Australia. That's where we explored, wasn't it, Keith?'

Jess looked at them. She knew perfectly well that Tim was evading the truth, and she knew why. She considered insisting, then decided against it. The boys were going away again tomorrow – she didn't want their last day to be a miserable one.

All the same, she had to try to satisfy her need to know.

'You haven't been going down any of the bombed streets, I hope,' she said. 'You know what your father would say if you did. It's dangerous.'

Tim met her eyes so guilelessly that she knew at once that this was just what they had done.

'The bombed streets?' he said. 'But they're miles away. We're not allowed right down there.'

Jess looked into the hazel eyes and sighed. She knew, and Tim knew she knew, that he was lying. I suppose he went down there with that Micky Baxter, she thought, and was glad all over again that her boys would be out in the country again tomorrow, safe from Hitler's bombs, and away from the influence of the bad boy of April Grove.

Arthur and Mary were just finishing their dinner. They got up, glad to see Jess and the children, and Mary went out to the scullery to put the kettle on.

'I'll do that, Mum,' Jess said. 'You sit down and have a rest. You must have had a nasty shock last night.'

Her mother fetched a tin of broken biscuits and handed it to the children. Tim and Keith ran out into the back garden, where Arthur had fixed up a swing from the old apple tree, and Rose went and sat on the step, rocking the pram with one hand.

'We were a bit shook up', Mary confessed. 'But we got ourselves in the shelter and stopped there till it was safe to come out. We were glad to get our gas masks off, I can tell you!'

Jess couldn't help smiling at the thought of the two old people, sitting there in their gas masks, but her amusement was only fleeting. She hadn't even thought of putting on her and Maureen's gas masks, and the boys had gone out to play without theirs.

'They 'ad gas in the first lot,' Arthur said in his thin reedy voice. 'Mustard gas, it was. Cruel stuff. I seen men with their lungs burnt right through their chests with it.'

'Don't, Dad,' Jess begged him, glancing towards the open door. She could hear Tim and Keith calling to each other, and Rose singing softly to the baby. But she knew that he would not be stopped. He seemed to need to go over it all, over and over again, as if by doing so he could make some sense of what was happening now.

But there wasn't any sense to be made, not when you were almost eighty and had already lived through two or three wars, including one that was supposed to end all wars and had failed dismally.

'So what are you going to do about the children?' Mary asked. 'You can't keep them under your eye the whole time.'

'Oh, they're going back straightaway,' Jess said firmly. 'Me and Frank have settled that. Tomorrow, we're taking them. Mr and Mrs Corner wrote saying they're looking forward to having the boys back and I know that nice Mrs Greenberry'll take care of Rose. We're going on the train. I asked Ethel Glaister if she'd like us to take her Shirley along too but no, Bridge End isn't good enough for her. She's decided to send Shirley off to America, or Canada.' Jess sniffed. 'It's one extreme or the other with that one. Wouldn't let her go off with the others last year, thinking nothing was going to happen, then gets scared silly.'

'Ethel Glaister was silly already,' Mary said caustically. She had known Ethel ever since she and Jess had been neighbours. 'Still, I'm glad she's letting Shirley go. It's daft, keeping kiddies at home these days. There was nowhere for the child to go to school, nobody much to play with. But there, I suppose that's how Ethel liked it, she always did think she was a cut above the rest of us.'

Tim came racing in.

'Grandpa, show us your bullets. The ones you got in the last lot.'

Jess flinched. She hated hearing the children use such terms. It seemed so casual, as if the Great War hadn't mattered. And she didn't much like her father showing them souvenirs he'd brought back, either –the cartridge cases and empty shells that he'd polished lovingly and set up on the mantelpiece. It was like keeping bones.

'Come on,' she said abruptly, getting up. 'It's time we went back. I've got a lot to do at home. They're asking us to do half as many sailors' collars again, and I don't know where I'm going to find the time, I'm sure I don't.'

Back in September Street, she let the two boys run on ahead while she and Rose did their own shopping. She went into Atkinson's, the greengrocer, where Molly Atkinson was weighing out potatoes.

People were still talking about the raid. Some of them were frightened, doing their shopping hastily in order to get home as quickly as possible in case there was another. Some were angry, cursing Hitler and using language that caused Molly to speak sharply, telling them to leave her shop if they couldn't keep their mouths clean. One or two were in real distress, for they had lost friends or relatives in the raid and were finding it hard to take in.

'That Mrs Jenkins that used to clean at Drayton Road School, she's gone,' old Mrs Stokes was saying over and over again as Molly made up her order. 'I saw her only Tuesday afternoon. Bright as a button, she was, laughing and joking, doing a bit of a dance because her chap had come home unexpected. And now she's gone. It don't seem possible.'

'My Jack always called in at the Anchor for a pint on his way home,' Carrie Barnes, from Carlisle Crescent, chipped in evidently forgetting this had been a habit she had strongly disapproved. 'He'll never be able to go there again now. Flat as a pancake, and all the beer running away like drainwater.'

'There's one or two would say that's all it was anyway,' someone else remarked caustically, and the other customers laughed, though there was a nervous edge to their laughter. They went out, leaving Molly and Jess alone.

Molly went on sorting the few boxes of potatoes into a display, with her five-year-old son Alan and his sister Wendy helping her. She gave Jess a rueful smile. She looked tired and thin, and no wonder, Jess thought, seeing what she'd been through already in this war.

'Not too good last night, was it, love?' she said. 'Still, I expect you got the children into the shelter, didn't you?'

'We were down there even before the siren had stopped. I know some people didn't bother, thought it was another false alarm, but I wouldn't take the risk.' She laid her hand briefly on Alan's head. 'I've been through enough worry over these two already.'

'I know,' Jess hesitated. 'You won't think of sending them away again, then?'

Molly Atkinson shook her head firmly. 'I'll never let 'em out of my sight again. I know some kids have found good places in the country, but I'd rather have 'em home with me. If we go, we go together, but I couldn't go through all that again, not knowing what's happening to them.'

Jess could understand that, for she knew that Alan and Wendy's experience of evacuation had not been a happy one, but she still felt anxious for these two little ones, kept at home to face bombing such as Portsmouth had known last night. Still, it was Molly's decision and she couldn't blame the young mother. And she'd heard that Alan still hadn't got over it, he was as clinging as a baby, terrified of the dark and screamed in the night as if he were having the most dreadful nightmares.

She went into the newsagent's shop and found young Joy, Rose's friend, serving. Alice Brunner came out from the back, her face pale and her eyes red-rimmed. It was only ten days since news had come of the sinking of the *Arandora Star*, on her way to Canada with fifteen hundred internees, and Alice's German-born husband Heinrich had been amongst them. Reports were still slowly filtering through about survivors, but when Jess asked Alice if there had been any news, the woman shook her head.

'He shouldn't never have been on the ship in the first place,' she said with weary indignation. 'Calling him an alien! He'd lived here over twenty years, we went to Deniston Road church together every Sunday. He was a better Christian than a lot of people I could mention around here, saving present company, of course. He wanted to join the LDV, didn't he? He wanted to help, and instead of that, they take him off in handcuffs and put him in prison like a common criminal, and then send him off to be torpedoed.' She pushed a straggle of hair back from her forehead. 'It's not fair.'

It wasn't fair, but then war never is, Jess thought as she tried to give Alice some comfort. But what could you say? Heinrich might be amongst the survivors but he might have gone down with the ship. And until poor Alice knew for sure, she was going to be tortured by her imaginings, seeing him struggle in the oily water, perhaps badly injured, crying for help, crying for her . . .

It didn't bear thinking about. But you had to think about it. You couldn't just walk away and forget. And there was going to be more of it, more every day until the whole terrible business was over.

'Well, at least you've got Joy,' Jess said lamely, wondering uneasily if this was the right thing to say. 'Maybe it'd be better if . . . ' Her voice trailed away but Alice picked up the words sharply.

'Better if what? Better if I let her go off to the country, where she'd be safe?' Her face twisted and crumpled, as if she were trying not to cry. 'I suppose you think I'm selfish, keeping her here. But I can't let her go off too. I'd have nobody then.'

And Alice wasn't a person who could manage with nobody, Jess thought, gazing at the misery in her friend's face. She'd always had someone to depend on – her own mother, when she'd been a child, and then Heinrich. Now it was Joy.

'Anyway, she wouldn't go,' Alice went on, looking at the two girls who were now marking up the *Evening News*. 'She didn't want to go last September, when all the other children went, she just wanted to stay home with us. It was almost like she knew something like this was going to happen.'

Jess collected her newspaper and walked down October Street, her heart heavy. So many lives being disrupted . . . As she came nearer to Mrs Seddon's corner shop, she noticed a young woman with two little girls on the other side of the road, standing outside number 16. At the same moment, Tim came running up to her.

'There's someone who's been bombed out. She's going to live in that house.'

'Ssh,' Jess said sharply. 'People don't want their business shouted up and down the street for all to hear. How do you know, anyway?'

'She told Granny Kinch,' Tim said in an injured tone, and Jess thought that in that case the young woman might just as well let the town crier know her news. Granny Kinch was a grapevine all on her own. She looked across the road again, and saw that the woman was pregnant.

She hesitated, then went across. The young woman was fitting a key into the lock.

'D'you need any help? I don't want to seem nosy, but my boy's just told me you were bombed out last night. If there's anything I can do . . .'

The woman turned. Why, she's not much more than a girl, Jess thought, for all she's got a couple of kiddies of eight or nine. And expecting another one, too!

She was reminded of herself a few years ago, coming down this same street with two children and another on the way. Only in her case there hadn't been a war on, and she and Frank had been coming from rooms to their own house.

'Thanks,' the girl said. 'I don't really know what I've got to do. It's been a bit of a shock.'

'I should think it has. Where d'you live?'

The girl's face twisted. 'We *did* live down Portchester

61

Road, but there's not much left of it now. We got a proper bashing, I can tell you.'

'Portchester Road!' That was where Frank had been yesterday evening. 'D'you mean your house was –'

'Smashed to bits,' the girl said bitterly. 'Had it looking like a little palace too, we did, and then along comes Hitler and smashes it to pieces. Everything we've scrimped and saved for. They say they'll get it rebuilt, or pay compensation or something, but they never will.' She shrugged. 'How can they, the amount that's being bombed? Anyway, if the Germans come and take away the whole lot, *they* won't be paying out no compensation. So now we've got to start again.' She turned and looked at the front of the little house, its windows smeared with dust and grime. 'We're lucky, really, they've put us up the list on account of the children.' Her hand touched her stomach lightly. 'And the one coming. There's some people'll be in those emergency centres for weeks.'

'You poor soul.' Jess gazed at her, wondering what she could say next. 'So what have you got to do?'

'Look at this house, say if we want it or not.' The girl laughed shortly. 'If we want it! What choice have we got? We're lucky to get anywhere.'

'Would you like me to come in with you?' Jess offered diffidently. 'I mean, there might be quite a lot needs to be done. I wouldn't mind giving you a hand.'

The girl's eyes warmed a little. 'Would you really? But you must have a lot to do – those two boys are yours, aren't they? And you've got a baby, too.'

'The boys'll be away tomorrow. We're sending them back to the country.' Jess looked at the two little girls, wondering why they hadn't been evacuated too. Of course, a lot of children had come back, thinking there weren't going to be any bombs. 'And Maureen's no trouble.'

'Well, if you'd just come in with me.' The girl laughed again, a little nervously. 'It's silly, but I've got a sort of funny feeling about going in. Almost like it might be haunted. Daft!'

'It's not. It's reaction.' Jess parked the pram in the tiny scrap of yard in front of the house. 'My name's Jess Budd, by the way. I live just over the corner, in April Grove – number 14.'

'I'm Kathy Simmons.' Kathy turned the key and pushed open the door. 'Well, let's see what they've given us, shall we?' She went into the dark, narrow little passage and sniffed. 'Phew! What a pong. Who lived here before?'

'An old woman. She'd been on her own for years, except for her cats. She had quite a few – just let them breed.' Jess surveyed the discoloured walls. 'You can see nothing's been done to the place since she died. Her family came and took away what bits of furniture were any use and Mr Carter – he's the landlord, owns four or five houses in this street – he cleared out the rest and got a shilling or two for it from the rag-and-bone man.'

Kathy opened the door into the front room and looked in at the bare floorboards and grubby walls. 'Ugh! How could anyone live like this?' Her mouth twisted. 'Well, it looks as if I'm going to find out, doesn't it, me and the girls.'

Jess gazed at her in dismay. Kathy had said that her house was smashed to bits. She must have almost no furniture, clothes or anything. How was she going to manage?

'Do they give you anything to help out?' she asked, wondering if she sounded nosy. 'I mean, surely they give you a bed or something.'

'Five pounds. That's all. Five pounds, for everything you possess. After that, you're left to yourself.' Kathy shut the door and walked through to the tiny back room and scullery. There was nothing in the scullery but an old earthenware sink with a cold tap. The smell of cats was everywhere.

Five pounds to buy furniture seemed like a fortune to Jess, but when you thought about having to get enough beds for a family of four, with another one on the way, and buy all the things you needed for your kitchen, and chairs to sit on and clothes for everyone, well, you could see that it wouldn't go far at all.

'We've got nothing of our own,' Kathy said. 'Just the clothes we were stood up in. And they weren't nothing special, not on a Thursday afternoon.' She grinned suddenly. 'You'd think he could at least bomb us on a Sunday, when we'd got our best clothes on, wouldn't you!'

'If you need any help –' Jess began awkwardly. She couldn't imagine what help she could give – there was no spare money in the Budd household, let alone spare clothes or furniture – but it seemed wrong not to offer. 'I mean, I'll help you scrub out a bit if you like. And when the baby comes, I'd be glad to come over and give you a hand. I've got a few of Maureen's baby things too, you're welcome to them if you'd like them.'

'Oh, I *would*. That's really nice of you.' Kathy smiled at her and Jess thought how brave she was. Fancy being able to make jokes about being bombed out of your own house!

They stood for a moment in silence, surveying the dirty room. Kathy went across to the back door and opened it, letting the afternoon sunlight straggle in. It made the dirt look even worse. She took a deep breath and managed a watery grin.

'Well, I suppose there's no use just looking at it. I'll have to start getting straight. I'll go round the second-hand shops for a few bits and pieces of furniture and some clothes to get us started.' She looked around at the house she must turn into a home for her family. 'You don't realise how much you've got till you lose it. And you've got to get the blackout done before you can even think of anything else.'

'I know,' Jess said. She followed Kathy to the front door and they went out into the fresh air with some relief. Kathy's two little girls were standing by Maureen's pram, holding up a woolly rabbit that Frank's sister-in-law had knitted for her. The street was quiet. 'Do you think the Germans are really going to invade?'

'Do you?' Kathy asked.

It was the question on everyone's lips. Some people didn't want to think about it, they shrugged it away. Others brooded about it the whole time. All through the previous year, when so little had seemed to be happening, although the news had been unremittingly bad about what was going on in other countries, no one had really been able to believe that Hitler would forget Great Britain.

Jess shook her head.

'I don't reckon the Germans are going to come,' she said

stoutly. 'Our boys are fighting them off. Look at the way they've gone up after the raiders, day after day. The bombing would have been a lot worse without the RAF to look after us.'

'And it'll get worse yet,' Kathy said darkly. 'Aren't we one of the biggest powers in the world? Stands to reason he wants to take us over! Same as he's taken everyone else over.' She laid her hand over her abdomen and looked at the two girls. 'It's the little ones I worry about. Them, and him in here.'

'I know,' Jess said quietly. 'And maybe if we'd thought there was going to be a war, we'd never have had this little one.' She bent forward and prodded Maureen in the stomach. The baby squealed and chortled. 'But we wouldn't be without you now, would we? Specially with the other three evacuated.' She looked at Kathy. 'Didn't you want to be evacuated? Is your husband in the Forces?'

'In the Merchant Navy. He doesn't believe in evacuation. Nor do I, really. I think everyone ought to stay where they are.' Kathy's face flushed a little. 'Anyway, I never know when he's going to get home for a night or two and I'd rather be here.'

Jess nodded. She knew how Kathy felt, for she hated the idea of leaving Frank. But if he weren't here ... Still, everyone had to make up their own mind.

'D'you want another girl?' she asked, changing the subject. 'Or would you rather have a boy this time?'

'Oh, a boy,' Kathy said, with a passion that startled her. 'I only want a boy. I only *ever* wanted boys. Well, I don't mean I don't love Muriel and Stella now they're here – and I wouldn't change them, not for the world – but I really do want a boy this time.' She looked at Jess. 'You've got a nice family, haven't you. Three others, is it?'

'Two boys and a girl. They're a bit older than Maureen – she was our afterthought!' She laughed self-consciously. 'Rose is thirteen now and the boys are nine and eleven.'

'Oh, you'll miss them,' Kathy said. 'I don't think I could bear to let my kids go away without me.'

'I will miss them,' Jess said. 'But it's war, isn't it. You just have to do the best you can. And I don't want to go through

65

another experience like last night, not knowing where the boys were and then finding they'd been out in the street the whole time. It still makes me feel sick to think of that.' She shook her head. 'You can't keep them in all the time. Specially boys. They're better off in the country, where they can roam about and play. And we go out to see them whenever we can. My husband goes out on his bike if we haven't got enough for the fare.'

'Well, if I get a boy this time I'm never going to let him out of my sight,' Kathy said. She shut the front door. 'Well, it looks as if we're going to be neighbours. It's a poky little place but it's better than a corner of the church hall.' She looked at Jess and gave her a wavery smile; it was clear she wasn't far from tears. 'Thanks ever so much for coming in with me. I think if I'd been on my own . . .'

'That's all right.' Jess felt her own eyes sting. 'And don't forget, as soon as you want a bit of help you come over and say. I'll be glad to give you a hand – take my mind off other things.' She knew she was going to miss the boys and Rose dreadfully. But at least she had Maureen to think of, and Frank at home. She felt sorry for Kathy Simmons. Being bombed out of her home with a baby due in a couple of months and no husband at home, she needed a friend or two. And the two little girls seemed nice enough. They seemed to enjoy playing with Maureen.

She pushed the pram across the road and round the corner to number 14. Kathy was the first real casualty of the war that she had met, but there would be plenty more. She might even be one herself, before long.

The boys were playing leapfrog on the pavement outside the house. She went indoors to get their tea. This time tomorrow, they'd be back out in the country and Maureen the only child she had at home.

The quiet of the afternoon was split by the sudden wail of the siren. It rose and fell, filling Jess's ears with its shriek, filling her heart with fear. She ran to the door but the boys came tumbling in before she could reach it, and she gathered up the baby and pushed them before her down the garden path.

*

Back at Bridge End the following week, the Budds found themselves centres of attention as their friends gathered round them to ask what it had been like to be in an air-raid.

'It was smashing,' Tim declared, swaggering along the country lane. 'Planes flying over the top of us, dropping bombs all over the place. Terrific explosions. And a huge great fire, the sky was all full of flames. We thought the whole of Pompey was going to catch fire.'

'Go on,' Brian Collins sneered. 'It couldn't've been that bad. There wasn't that many houses burnt down.'

'It was the gasholder. It could've gone up like a bomb itself. They had every fire engine in Pompey there trying to put it out.'

'Weren't you scared?' a little girl asked, awed, and Brian Collins sniggered again.

'Course he was. That's why he's come back, ain't it? Scared out of his wits, not that he had many to start with.'

Tim scowled. He and Brian Collins had always been enemies. 'I wasn't scared,' he said hotly. 'It was my Dad said we had to come back. Anyway, I like being in the country. After the war we're all going to come and live here, Mum and Dad and our baby, all of us.'

'You're welcome to it,' Brian said. 'I'm fed up with the country. Old man Callaway treats me like a slave. I'd sooner be back in Pompey, going mudlarking.'

'You're not allowed to do that now,' Tim said. 'The harbour's full of unexploded bombs. You'd get blown up.'

Brian made a face at him and Tim turned away. His Dad had told him often enough not to let Brian Collins goad him into a fight. 'You should always stand up for yourself,' he said, 'but you shouldn't start it. Anyway, it's not worth bothering with people like that. Just take no notice.'

Tim tried to follow his father's advice, but it wasn't easy when he saw the sneer on Brian's face. He wanted to wipe it off with a good hard punch. But that would mean he'd hit out first and put himself into the wrong, which Dad had told him was just what Brian wanted.

Rose was less eager to recount her air-raid experiences. She told her foster-mother Mrs Greenberry about it, and the countrywoman's face grew pale.

'You mean you weren't even at home with your Mum? And the boys were out in the streets? That poor soul, she must have been worried sick.'

'Dad wasn't home either,' Rose said. 'He was on his way home from work. He had to stop and help. There was people killed, bodies everywhere.' Frank hadn't told her that, but her own imagination told her it must have been so. She had lain awake, wondering what it had been like. It would have been better if he had told her, she thought, then she wouldn't have to keep imagining it, but she hadn't dared ask him. Even Mum had been cross when she'd mentioned it.

'Little girls don't have to worry about things like that,' she'd told her. 'That's why you're going back to Bridge End. You just help Mrs Greenberry like you help me, and forget about the war.'

Rose hadn't wanted to come back to Bridge End. She liked the Greenberrys and she'd been frightened during the raid, but she'd still rather be at home with Mum. Especially when they knew that Southampton was being bombed and heard on the news that there'd been more raids over Portsmouth.

Suppose something happened to number 14. Suppose Mum and Dad were hurt – killed even – and Rose wasn't there to help. Suppose someone forgot to let her know.

'Of course they won't forget,' Mrs Greenberry said. 'Anyway, nothing's going to happen to your mum and dad. Now, you stop thinking about it and go down the garden and pick us a few peas. Mr Greenberry's brought home a nice rabbit for our supper, and you know you like rabbit.'

But rabbit wasn't enough to stop Rose worrying. And she picked at her dinner that evening, and went to bed with her stomach filled with the leaden lump of fear instead of Mr Greenberry's homegrown vegetables and the rabbit he'd brought from the farm.

Reg and Edna Corner had their worries too. They waited until Tim and Keith were in bed before discussing them.

'I just don't see how we're to manage,' Edna said. 'You're bound to get called up soon, and with a baby coming as well . . .'

'I'm sure Mr Callaway will let you stop on in the cottage,' Reg said. 'I mean, he's not going to get another worker, is he? He'll get one or two of the older men – Simon Barrow, he's still pretty spry, he'll be glad to earn himself a bob or two. Or maybe he'll get a Land Girl.'

'And where's she going to live?' Edna demanded. 'He's already got young Brian billeted on him at the farmhouse. He'll want this cottage, that's what, and he'll probably put up two or three more as well. No, the minute you're called up he'll have me out. I'll have to go and stop with Mum.'

Reg gazed at her. It wasn't what he wanted, starting a family this way, with him away in the Forces and Edna having to go back to her mother's cramped little cottage. He looked round the little room. They'd got it so nice. Even though it wasn't theirs, it was still their home for as long as he worked on the farm, and he'd expected that to be for a good few years, if not for life. What reason was there to move, if you were happy? And he and Edna had been happy, there was no doubt at all about that.

'So what are we going to do about Tim and Keith?' he asked.

Edna shrugged. 'What can we do? You know how I feel about them, they're smashing boys, I feel like they're almost our own. But we can't keep them here once the baby's born. I don't think I could manage it all, specially if you're going to be away. And anyway –'

'Mr Callaway won't let you stop on,' Reg finished for her. 'Well, I daresay you're right. I suppose we'd better let the billeting officer know.'

Edna looked miserable. 'Not too soon, Reg. I don't want to lose them yet.'

'But it's not fair on them, letting them settle in again and then get pushed on somewhere else. We ought to tell their mum and dad at least.' He looked at her. He knew how fond of the two boys she had become. 'Tell you what we'll do, Edna. We'll look out for somewhere for them ourselves. Somewhere we know they'll be happy. And then we'll tell Mrs Budd and the billeting officer.' He put his arm round her and drew her close. 'And now you've got to start thinking about yourself and our own little one. I'm fond of the boys too, but you're more important to me. You and our own baby. That's what you've got to be thinking about.'

Edna smiled. But her heart was sore. Like Reg, she felt bitterly disappointed that things had turned out this way – that their first baby should be coming into such a world, with its father about to be sent off to war and their home taken from them.

It wasn't fair. But the past year had taught everyone that you could no longer expect fairness.

Micky Baxter did not go to Bridge End. He had no wish to leave Portsmouth, and his mother Nancy didn't bother to insist. She hardly looked on Micky as a child anyway; from an early age he had been allowed to fend for himself, running the streets, living by his fists, pinching the odd apple or orange from greengrocers' displays, pocketing all sorts of oddments that it was best not to enquire about.

'It was just left lyin' about,' he would explain. 'There wasn't no sense in just leavin' it, was there?'

'Funny,' Nancy said, 'last time I saw something like that it was lying on a counter in Woolies. You'd better watch yourself, Micky.'

'Oh, leave the boy alone,' Granny Kinch said. 'All boys gets up to a bit o' mischief. There ain't no real harm in him.'

But even she had been shaken when Micky was taken to court for the jeweller's shop incident. At first, she'd refused to believe it had been Micky at all, and then she had tried to blame the boy who had given him the gun. Now she looked on it as a prank that had gone too far. 'He's learnt his lesson,' she said. 'He won't do nothing like that again.'

Micky had no intention of doing anything like that again. He had learned that it was best not to let yourself be seen. Then no one could identify you. Instead of marching into small shops where twelve-year-old boys stood out like sore thumbs, he and the others skulked around Woolworths and British Home Stores. They filched things from barrows in Charlotte Street and slid purses off the top of careless women's shopping baskets. There was never much in the purses but a few coppers soon mounted up.

Not that there was much to spend money on, not when you could pinch most of what you wanted. Even fags could be nicked when the tobacconist was looking for something you'd asked for and he hadn't got. And you could get into the pictures, three for the price of one, by sending one in on a ticket and then waiting by the fire exit.

'We oughter have somewhere to keep the cash,' Micky said. He knew that if he kept it at home his mother or grandmother was likely to find it, and that would be the last he saw of it. And he wasn't prepared to let either of the other boys be treasurer. 'We needs a den.'

'We got a den,' Cyril said. 'Our garden shed. Nobody ever goes in it now Dad's away.'

Micky shook his head. 'Nah. There's better'n that. You come with me.'

Jimmy had a tin money-box with a key that nearly always worked. They put their loot into it – three and sevenpence three-farthings – and set off through the streets.

'Are we going down the bomb sites?' Cyril asked. 'There'd be some good places there.'

Micky nodded but said nothing. He had been exploring the bombed houses several times since the raid and looked on them as his territory. There'd been other boys about too, but he was fairly confident that the place he had discovered was safe.

'Here,' he said, as they turned into the derelict street, 'this is the place.'

The boys looked around them, still awed by the extent of the damage. Only a few houses were left standing, down at the other end, and most of those were damaged. Piles of bricks and rubble still filled gardens, and shattered rooms stood open to the weather.

'These places'll make smashing dens,' Cyril said.

'You wait.' Micky led them into the third house of the row. The front walls were still standing, though badly damaged, and the front door hung crookedly on its hinges. He pushed it open and a sour smell of food gone bad, excreta and cats, hit their faces. Cyril wrinkled his nose.

'Eugh! Something's died in here.'

'Nah. It's just cats' muck.' Micky scrambled over the fallen bricks and plaster. There was a cupboard under the stairs, its door propped shut with a brick. He moved the brick and the door fell open.

'Coo!'

'It's a cellar,' Micky said unnecessarily. 'It's just right for a den. Nobody else knows about it, I bin testing.'

Jimmy and Cyril gazed down into the black abyss. The steps were black and slimy, and the walls green with mould. The air was dank.

'It's smashing,' Cyril said. 'It's the best place we ever found.'

Micky nodded. He produced a box of matches and a stub of candle and led the way down the grimy steps. By the flickering light, they could see that this had been a coal-cellar. There was no coal here now, except for a few lumps piled in one corner, but someone had brought down a rickety table and a couple of broken chairs. Micky touched them proudly.

'See, we even got furniture. I fetched these down. And I left this, just to see if anyone else was nosin' round.' He picked up a battered Dinky car from the table. 'They'd've took this, so that means no one's bin here. It's safe as houses.'

'S'pose it gets bombed again?' Jimmy suggested, glancing at the crumbling walls.

Micky shook his head derisively. 'Nah. They never hits the same place twice.' He sat down in one of the chairs and put his feet on the table. 'Better'n an old garden shed, eh?'

Jimmy put his tin money-box on the table. 'Where we going to hide it?'

'Over here.' Micky swung his feet down and went over to the wall. The guttering candle threw deep shadows but he felt along until one of the bricks came out in his hand. 'See, there's a space here. We can put the tin there. No one'll ever find it and we can come down here whenever we like and get some money, have a fag, whatever we want.'

'We could bring some grub,' Cyril said, his imagination taking flight. 'We could light a fire – cook meals.'

'We can do better'n that.' Micky paused while the other

two gazed expectantly at him, then said slowly and dramatically, 'We can keep a parachutist here.'

Jimmy and Cyril drew in their breath. They looked about them at the dark, clammy walls. 'A parachutist? You mean a *German*?'

'Well, we wouldn't keep a British one down here, would we?' Micky said impatiently. 'But we could keep a Jerry for as long as we liked. Pile up stuff against the door so he couldn't get out. Nobody'd hear him shout. He'd be our prisoner.'

Jimmy had a practical question. 'Isn't there a hatch, where they used to deliver coal? He could get out through that.'

'Nah. It's all blocked up with bricks and stuff. I've looked.'

The candle was almost burnt out. Micky put the tin box into the hole and replaced the brick. He picked up the Dinky toy, hesitated, then put it back on the table.

'I'll leave that, just so we always know if anyone's bin pokin' about. And mind you don't come down here without me.'

Jimmy and Cyril shook their heads. They went back up the steps, replaced the door and heaped rubbish against it. Then they went back outside and looked up at the sky.

They were almost disappointed not to see it filled with the billowing umbrellas of German parachutes.

CHAPTER FIVE

Betty Chapman was beginning to think that her application to join the Land Army had been lost for ever, when she found herself opening a brown envelope one morning to find that she had been ordered 'over the hill' to Bishop's Waltham, to work on a farm.

'Bishop's Waltham!' she said in some disappointment. 'Why, that's no distance at all. I thought I'd be sent miles out into the country.'

'There's as good countryside at Bishop's Waltham as you'd find anywhere in England,' her mother said with some asperity. 'Were you looking forward to getting away from us, then?'

'No, of course not.' Betty bit her lip. Nobody in the family had been keen on this idea of her going to work on the land and her father had been downright suspicious about it. Just as if she'd suggested doing something immoral, she thought indignantly. 'I just thought I might get the chance to see a bit more of England, that's all.'

'I've told you before,' Ted Chapman told her curtly, 'this war ain't no holiday camp. If you go and work on a farm you'll have to *work*. It won't be doing the odd bit of weeding and picking a few blackberries for a pie. It'll be getting up at five in the morning, summer and winter, to milk cows, spending all day slaving at some other job and then milking half the evening as well. If you ask me, they're mad to take you on, a bit of a thing like you, and that doctor who gave you your certificate wants his head looking at.'

'Well, it's either that or the Services. They're going to want all us girls, Dad. I might as well start now as wait to be called up and find myself somewhere I don't want to be.'

Ted grunted and didn't answer. He felt increasingly bewildered these days, as if his head was full of cotton-wool, and he no longer felt in control of his own life, let alone those of his family. He was dismayed by the way his daughters had so suddenly grown up. There was Olive, married before she was twenty-one, which was something he'd always declared he wouldn't allow. And now Betty leaving home to go and live out in the wilds. Well, Bishop's Waltham wasn't exactly the *wilds*, but it was country, wasn't it, and there was nobody there he knew. In Pompey he knew hundreds of people, people he'd grown up with, people he'd known since they were nippers. And country folk could be funny, there was no saying they couldn't. Look at some of the tales you heard about the way evacuees got treated.

But parents were the last people to be consulted about their children these days. Girls could do whatever they pleased now and treated their mums and dads as if they were something out of the Ark, as if they knew nothing. And the Government was aiding and abetting them.

'She ought to have gone and got a job at Airspeed,' he said to Annie. 'She'd have been in a reserved occupation then and earned good money too. They're making planes hand over fist up there, and can't get 'em out fast enough.'

'And no wonder, the way they're being shot out of the sky,' Annie observed. 'And she wouldn't be any safer there, would she? Airspeed got hit themselves the other day, and if it hadn't been after working hours any amount of people would've been killed.' But she didn't argue back too much. She knew how Ted's nights were filled with bad dreams, how the things he had seen at Dunkirk still haunted his mind.

There were still plenty of air-raid warnings, though no more bombs had fallen on Portsmouth in the weeks that followed the July attack. And the city was fighting back – two days later, the *Evening News* had launched a 'Buy a Spitfire' appeal, and they had collected the six thousand pounds needed in only a fortnight.

And they certainly needed planes. Every day now, aircraft

could be seen in the sky, dodging and swooping crazily as they fired at each other. You could stand and watch the 'dogfights' as they were called, almost as if they were some kind of aerial circus, a spectacle laid on for entertainment.

But the entertainment was a deadly one. The newspapers were full now of reports of the battle which was being waged in the skies. *Twenty-Eight Raiders Shot Down*, the headlines announced on 26 July and, a few days later, *Fighters' Fine Work Over Portsmouth* with a detailed report of the Spitfires which had met a hundred and fifty enemy bombers coming in from the south. Aided by Hurricanes and Defiants, they drove off the German Heinkels and Messerschmitts, shooting down several which fell either into the sea or in open countryside.

One was reported as having dived nose-first down a disused well on the Isle of Wight, only its tail sticking up above the ground with the swastika to prove its nationality. Another crashed into a field, its pilot and navigator captured by a local milkman. A third, flying over in the early hours of the morning, managed to penetrate the barrage and dropped three bombs on a farm, with a total casualty rate of fifty chickens and a rabbit.

'And you reckon our Betty'll be safer, out at Bishop's Waltham!' Ted commented sarcastically, but Annie just shook her head at him. She was beginning to come round to the idea of Betty's going away. Always more down-to-earth than her husband, she accepted the fact that the war had changed everything and you couldn't expect anything to turn out the way you'd thought it would. The best you could hope for was that everyone would get through it alive, however long it lasted – and how long would that be? A year? Two years? – and that the German invasion would be kept at bay. The thought of enemy soldiers marching down September Street made her shudder.

She looked at the photographs in *Picture Post*. Millions of French people, fleeing from Paris and other big cities, carrying whatever possessions they had been able to snatch up in their panic as their Government capitulated. Old men and women, small children and babies in prams, trudging bewildered along endless roads, with no idea of where they

76

were going. Derek Harker had seen them as he came through Dunkirk, and spoke of an old woman who had told him this was the second time she had had to leave her home. The first time was twenty-five years ago in the Great War, and when she had returned it was to find her home razed to the ground. 'I thought I had suffered enough,' she said, picking up the pathetic bundle, wrapped in a tattered blanket, that was all she could carry. 'But it seems one has never suffered too much in this world.'

Annie and Jess had agreed that the only way to carry on was to keep busy. Constant activity would keep your mind off it. And heaven knew there was always plenty to do.

The arrival of Betty's uniform a day or two later helped. Together she, Betty and Olive unpacked the parcel and turned over the garments inside, holding them up for inspection. Olive gave a snort of laughter.

'Look at these gum-boots! Imagine them, all caked in mud. You'll never be able to lift up your feet. And what about this overcoat, it must weigh a ton. They've sent you a soldier's uniform by mistake.'

'And this hat,' Annie said. 'It looks like Roy Roger's, caught in a rainstorm. Mind, these long socks look all right. They'll keep your feet warm.'

'Well, they'll help fill up the boots, anyway. And how about these?' Olive pulled out a pair of fawn trousers. 'You're never going to wear these, our Bet! They look like riding-breeches.'

'You don't expect me to wear my best skirt for milking cows, do you?' Betty retorted. 'Anyway, I think they're rather smart.' She held her head to one side and examined the corduroy breeches. 'And they go well with the green jumper.'

'Go on, you'll look just like a patch of muddy field,' Olive jeered. 'Here, try 'em on, I want to see what they look like.'

Betty slipped off her skirt and blouse. There were three short-sleeved shirts in the parcel as well and she pulled one over her head.

'Well, that's not bad.' Annie said. 'Quite nice, for summer.'

'It's aertex. See all these tiny holes, they help keep you warm or cool, like a string vest.' Betty struggled into the breeches and fastened them up. 'Not a bad fit. I was expecting to have to tie them up with string.' She climbed on to a chair to see herself in the mirror. 'What d'you think of that, then?'

'I don't know what your dad'll say, seeing you in trousers. You know he don't like it for women.'

'Well, he can't tell me not to, can he,' Betty said, exasperated. 'I mean, I've got to wear 'em. I suppose he'd rather have me climbing up on a haycart in a skirt and all the blokes looking up my knickers.'

'Betty! There's no call for talk like that. That's just the sort of thing that worries me, hearing you get so coarse. If that's the kind of thing you'll say at home, what's it going to be like when you're on a farm?' Annie shook her head. 'I think you're dad's right, you ought to have stopped at home. You could easy have got a job round here. You're too young to be going away.'

'I'm nineteen,' Betty said. 'In two years I'll be able to do what I like anyway. If you can't trust me now –'

'It isn't a matter of trusting you –' Annie began, but she was interrupted by the shrill peal of the doorbell. Sighing, she went off to answer it, while Betty looked into the mirror again and twisted herself this way and that.

'I want a nice belt to go round my waist,' she said to Olive. 'That brown leather one of yours would do, you never wear it. Don't you think these breeches make me look slim?'

'Skinny, I'd say,' Olive said, but there was no malice in her voice. She looked at her sister, pivoting on the chair. 'Aren't you going to try on the jumper? And look, here's a tie, you ought to put that on too. And the hat.'

Betty took the tie and tied it rapidly round her neck. She put her hands on her waist and posed again. The two girls looked in the mirror and giggled.

'Ride him cowboy!' Olive said, plonking the hat on her sister's head. 'Well, if the farmer sends you home you can always get a job in films. Here comes Mum, give her a surprise.'

Betty struck another pose but the chair overbalanced and she shrieked and grabbed Olive's shoulders. The two girls staggered and collapsed on the floor in a tumbled heap. Olive's skirt rucked up around her waist and Betty's breeches half unbuttoned. They lay giggling and Annie, coming back into the room, stopped abruptly.

'Whatever are you two doing? Get up at once, and make yourselves decent, for goodness' sake. Here's Graham to see you Betty, he doesn't want to find you making a fool of yourself, and as for you Olive, you're a married woman now, you ought to know better. Whatever would Derek think if he could see you?'

Hastily, Olive smoothed down her skirt and scrambled to her feet. She turned away, scowling slightly. There were times when being a 'married woman' could be a disadvantage. Did it mean you couldn't have fun any more, even with your own sister? And it wasn't fair of Mum, reminding her that Derek was miles away. Anyway, she knew very well what he'd think if he could see her lying on the floor with her skirt up round her waist. Her lips quivered a little at the thought.

Betty fastened her breeches quickly, hoping that Graham didn't notice what she was doing. She definitely needed that belt. She pushed back her curls and grinned at him.

'Hullo, Gray. What d'you think of my new uniform, then?'

There was a hint of defiance in her tone. Graham had never liked the idea of her joining the Land Army. He seemed to think she ought to stay at home, ready to be there whenever his ship happened to come in. But Betty wasn't prepared to stay at home darning socks just because her boy was away at sea. It was her life too, wasn't it? And if she wanted to spend her time digging potatoes, why shouldn't she?

All the same, she was disappointed when he gave her new clothes no more than a brief glance and then said tersely, 'I've got something to tell you, Bet. We're sailing tomorrow.'

'Tomorrow?'

She looked at him in dismay. Of course, she'd known he'd be going soon. They'd only stayed in harbour so long because the repairs had taken longer than expected, and there'd been so many other damaged ships coming into the Dockyard. And the battle – the Battle of Britain, they were calling it, as Winston Churchill had foretold – was getting fiercer every day. Only yesterday, there had been the biggest fight yet, with four hundred German aircraft seen off the Island, and sixty shot down, which made four hundred in less than four weeks. And although the battle was taking place in the air, the RAF still needed the support of the Navy.

Betty had known that Graham couldn't be in Portsmouth for long. But she had hoped they'd have this last week together, before she went off to Bishop's Waltham.

Still, maybe it was just as well. Graham wouldn't have taken kindly to her going away first, even if it was only just over the hill.

'You two'd better go in the front room and have a talk,' Annie said. 'Olive, you can help me get supper ready. Your Dad'll be in soon and he'll want it on the table.'

Betty and Graham went into the front room and sat down on the settee. Graham sat upright, saying nothing. His ginger hair was tousled, his bright blue eyes staring straight ahead. Betty glanced sideways at him and took his hand.

'Aren't you going to give me a kiss, then?'

'Didn't know you wanted me to,' he said stiffly. 'You seemed to be having a pretty good time without me. Nobody'd think, to hear you and Olive laughing and joking, that me and Derek Harker might be going to get killed any day. You don't seem a bit worried about me going away.'

'Graham! That's an awful thing to say.' She put her arms round his neck and kissed him. 'Of course I don't want you to go away,' she whispered. 'But we both knew it was going to happen, didn't we? And we've had a lovely time while you've been here.'

'Maybe you have,' he said sullenly. 'It hasn't been much fun for me, I can tell you. Bloody welding going on night and day, the bulkheads half torn off, dockyard workers crawling all over the ship like ants . . . '

'I know,' she said. 'But when you've been ashore, when we've been together, that's been nice, hasn't it?'

'It could've been nicer,' Graham muttered, not looking at her.

There was a moment's silence. Then Betty said, 'I've told you, Graham, I won't give way. I don't want to be left with a baby on my hands. And I don't think you ought to keep on about it.'

'Why not? We're supposed to be engaged, aren't we? I've given you a ring.'

'That's not official, you know it isn't. I only wear it like an engagement ring when there's no one else around.'

'It still means we're engaged. You said it still meant that.'

'It doesn't mean we're married, though, does it? And that's the sort of ring I want on my finger before we go any further.' She gazed at him, wishing that he would leave the subject alone. 'Graham, you know what could happen.'

'It wouldn't. I'd make sure it wouldn't. Look, what's the point of talking about getting married, you've told me time and time again your dad'll never agree –'

'I'm *not* talking about getting married!' she exclaimed, and bit her lip.

Graham stared at her. 'What d'you mean? Are you telling me you want to break it off? You're giving me back my ring, the day before I go away? Well, I think that's –'

'Graham, no!' She wrapped her arms around him again, holding him tightly. 'I didn't say that, I didn't. I just said – oh, I don't know what I did say now. I just don't want to think about getting married yet, that's all. I don't see the point, not with things as they are. Look at our Olive, been married a month and she hasn't seen Derek since. And if she wasn't working for his dad, she'd just as likely lose her job. You know what people are like about married women working. Where's the point? I don't want to be stuck at home with nothing to do.'

'It wasn't me brought up the subject,' he said. 'All I want –'

'I know what you want,' Betty broke in, 'and the answer's no.'

'Betty. It's my last night.' He pulled her close and slipped his hand up under the green jersey. He fumbled with the buttons on the shirt and put his hand over her breast. 'Bet, you don't know what it'd mean to me . . .'

'I know what it might mean to me,' she said, a little breathlessly. Graham had always had more effect on her than she allowed him to see. If he just knew what her body was doing when he kissed her like that, when he squeezed her breasts . . . I shouldn't ever have let him go this far, she thought. One of these days I'm just not going to be able to say no . . .

'I told you, I'll look after you.' His hand was on her knee now, sliding up her thigh. He stroked the crotch of her breeches and she gasped and squirmed. Even through the thick corduroy, there was no doubt as to her response. He slipped his hand up over her stomach and started to fumble with her waistband.

'Graham, don't! Mum and Olive are in the next room and Dad'll be home any minute, he could easy put his head in the door. Graham, please –'

'I love you, Betty.' His lips were covering hers, moving over her face, nibbling at her ears. 'You're the first real girl I've ever had. I just want to love you properly, just once, before I go away.' He managed to undo the top button of her breeches. 'Betty, I'm going to sea tomorrow, we don't know when we'll see each other gain, I might get killed . . . You can't say no. You've got to let me, you've *got* to . . . ' He pulled her suddenly so that she was half-lying on the settee. He leaned over her, then laid his body on hers and pushed himself hard against her. 'You've got to,' he panted.

Betty's thoughts were in panic. When Graham kissed her, when he stroked her breast or let his hands stray down over her bottom, she found it exciting. She enjoyed his touch and wanted him to go on doing it, and sometimes she knew she'd like him to go further. But she never wanted him to go 'all the way'. All her upbringing was against it, and always in her mind was the thought of her parents' disapproval, a disapproval that would amount to disgust and anger if she ever brought 'trouble' to the house.

Until now, she had always managed to keep the situation under control. But since Graham had come home a month ago and they'd had this unexpected time together, it had been much more difficult. He was restless, demanding, less ready to accept the lines she drew. And she had known that if she wasn't careful, this moment would come, when he would demand too much. The question in her mind had been, would she be able to resist him?

Not if he'd approached her more gradually, perhaps, in

some dark, secluded spot where no one was likely to interrupt them. Not if he'd started with some of those lingering kisses that left her weak and melting, if he'd stroked her body gently, not hurrying, just slowly increasing the intimacy with every caress. If he'd taken his time, whispering to her all the time about how he loved her, what a beautiful body she had. If he'd pressed himself more gently against her, letting her feel the firmness of his body and holding her close, even tightly, but without crushing the breath out of her in this sudden almost frantic assault.

She knew that she might have had difficulty in stopping him then, difficulty in stopping herself. But this was worse. She sensed in Graham a desperation he had never shown before, a desperation that would not take 'no' for an answer. And she was suddenly, frighteningly, aware of his strength. She looked up at his face, trying to see his eyes, but they were half-closed, glazed, and she knew he did not see her. She wriggled her arms up and grasped his shoulders, trying to push him away, but he was like a rock.

'These bloody breeches!' he muttered, struggling with the buttons. 'Why did you have to put these on?'

'I didn't know you were coming . . . Graham, please don't—'

Should she call out, shout for Mum? That would stop him, but the thought of her mother coming into the room and finding them like this, struggling on the settee half undressed, was too awful. She'd tell Dad and they'd both blame her, say she'd led Graham on, probably insist they get married. And if they couldn't get married because he was going away, they'd be watching her for the first sign of a baby and it would be the end of the Land Army for her, they'd never let her go. And they'd never trust her again.

'Can't you pull 'em down, Bet?' he muttered, and groaned. 'I don't think I can wait much longer.'

She gave him an agonised look. Wouldn't it be better just to do as he wanted, and get it over with? It seemed as if that was the only way of stopping him now. Let him do it and do it quick, before Mum thumped on the door or Dad came in.

But Mum would know, she thought, the minute she looked at them she'd know. And suppose there was a baby?

83

Olive had told her it didn't always happen the first time. But Betty knew one or two girls who'd got caught, and they'd sworn it had only happened once.

She gave Graham's shoulders a hard push.

'*No*. Stop it, Graham. I don't want to – and you're hurting my leg. Get off me.'

He stared at her. He had been fumbling with his own trousers and she saw the paleness of his flesh against the dark blue serge. His face was flushed and he was breathing hard.

His ginger brows came together in a frown. 'Take 'em off, Bet. This is my last night –'

'Graham, I *can't*. You know I can't.' To her relief, she heard footsteps on the pavement outside and the click of the front gate. 'There's Dad! He'll be in any minute.' Panic lent her strength and she wriggled clear of Graham's arms and started frantically to do up her clothes. 'Make yourself decent, Graham, for goodness' sake!'

'He doesn't come in this way, does he? He goes round the side, to the back door.'

'I know, but sometimes he comes in the front.' In fact, he hardly ever did, but Betty wasn't going to tell Graham that. 'Anyway, if he's home supper'll be on the table and Mum'll be knocking on the door for us to go back.' She sat up and straightened her jersey, then looked at him. 'I'm sorry, Gray. But I can't do it, not like that. And I'm scared of what might happen.'

'I told you, I wouldn't let anything happen.' He finished tidying himself and looked away from her, still breathing quickly. 'You ought to trust me, Bet. You would, if you really loved me.'

'I do love you.'

'Well, prove it, then,' he challenged her. 'Show me you love me. After supper – we'll come in here again. No one'll disturb us, they know it's my last night. And you can take those daft breeches off and put on a skirt.'

Betty said nothing. She felt miserable and heavy inside. Graham was going away tomorrow, she didn't know when she would see him again, and she felt that he was right, that if she really loved him she'd let him have what he wanted, she wouldn't deny him. So *did* she love him? She thought she did – and she wanted it too, she couldn't deny that. But not like this, she cried out inside, not struggling on a settee in her mother's front room, trying not to be heard and then having to pretend afterwards. And spending the next two or three weeks waiting in terror, and maybe the next nine months in despair.

'Please, Graham,' she said in a low voice, 'don't keep on.'

He gave her a steady look. His blue eyes were hard, the skin taut around them, and his lips were tight. The flush had died from his face, leaving the freckles standing out against the pale skin.

He said, 'All right, Bet. It's all off, then. You can give me back my ring and I'll go. Say goodbye to your mum and dad for me, and tell'em I'm sorry I won't be seeing them again.' He stood up.

Betty caught at his white summer shirt. The cotton was cool under her fingers. She remembered the day when he had first come here in the matelot's uniform, how proud she had been.

'No, Graham, don't go! Not like that. I do love you, I do, it's just that –' The tears came to her eyes and her voice broke ' – I'm scared, that's all. I've never – it's my first time, I – I don't know what it's like – I'm *scared*.' She looked up at him appealingly. 'Graham?' And then she took a deep breath and said shakily, 'All right. I'll do it. After supper.' And felt almost as if she'd signed her life away.

Graham's face cleared and broke into a huge grin. 'You will? You'll let me love you properly? Oh, Bet –' He pulled her up against him and held her tightly. 'Bet, I promise I'll look after you. I won't let anything happen.' He kissed her and squeezed her breast, and she stiffened, terrified that his passion would overtake him again. But at that moment there was a thump on the door and they heard Annie's voice calling that supper was ready. Reluctantly, Graham let Betty go, and she stepped away, conscious of a huge wave of relief.

'Later,' he whispered in her ear. 'I'll be looking forward to it, all through supper.'

Betty gave him a wavering smile. But the feeling of

heaviness still persisted inside her, and she knew that she would be unable to eat a thing.

Graham sat at the Chapmans' supper table, conscious of a simmering excitement. He was slightly ashamed of the way he'd behaved in the front room earlier. He hadn't meant to be rough with Betty, but his feelings had overwhelmed him. And he'd been upset by the sight of her in those cowboy breeches and hat. They seemed to take her away, as if she was going to have a new life that he couldn't share.

Graham didn't want Betty going away or having a life he didn't know about. He wanted her at home, where he could picture her when he was away at sea. He wanted to be able to wake up in the morning knowing exactly what she was doing – having her breakfast, walking up March Street to work in the dairy, going down town to do a bit of shopping or helping her mum around the house on Saturday afternoon. Going to church and maybe for a walk with her sister on Sunday. He'd been pleased when Olive got married, that meant there'd be no more chaps coming to the house, less chance of Betty getting off with someone else. And he was glad Bob Shaw was away in Devon, with Derek. He knew Bob was sweet on Betty and he had an idea she'd got a soft spot for him too.

But if Betty went off to the country, to some farm, there was no knowing who she might meet. Not all these country chaps would get called up. And some of them were big, beefy blokes, the sort who might easily sweep a girl off her feet and make her forget she'd got a boy in the Navy.

Still, he'd got her to promise to give herself to him tonight, and that would keep her true, he was sure of that. What's more, and perhaps even more important, he'd find out at last just what this sex business was all about.

At twenty, Graham had never experienced sex with a girl. He'd been thinking about it since he was seventeen or eighteen – before that, really – but although he'd had two or three girlfriends before Betty, he'd never got much further than kissing and the occasional more daring fumble, with his hands quickly slapped away. There had been one girl who'd let him feel her body more intimately, and who had done her own exploring too, through a hole in his trouser pocket, but he'd only been fifteen or sixteen then and a bit scared of the peculiar excitement it had caused. Usually, it had ended with tickling and giggles and, now he came to think of it, they hadn't even kissed very much.

But for the last year or so he'd been feeling increasingly restless. He wanted to know what it was all about. He wanted to know what this feeling was that other blokes talked about, usually with sniggers and dirty jokes, but still as if it was somehow the whole purpose of living, of being a man. And since he'd joined the Navy, it had been worse. You weren't a man until you'd 'done it', yet who were you to 'do it' with?

'You've got a girl, haven't you?' one of his shipmates asked him. 'Well, what's she for?'

But girls like Betty didn't 'do it'. They'd been brought up to save themselves for marriage, and they were pretty sharp when a boy tried to go too far. And the other option, the tarts who stood at the Dockyard gate and walked up and down Queen Street, carried their own risks. During his training on Whale Island, in Portsmouth Harbour, Graham had been subjected to several lectures on venereal disease, with horrific pictures to accompany them, and already on the ship he'd seen a couple of men who were getting regular, and not very sympathetic, treatment from the ship's doctor, and whose eating utensils were marked with red paint and kept separate from everyone else's.

So how was a bloke to find out? And now that he knew that the ship would be sailing, to stay at sea perhaps for weeks or months, and almost sure to be involved in action, perhaps even sunk, he was desperate to experience it, if only once. I can't die without knowing, he thought. I can't. It's not fair.

Betty had to let him. She had to. She was his girl, she'd got him to give her a ring which she wore on her left hand whenever they were out on their own, she'd said she loved him. All he was asking was to do it once, just once, just so that he knew what it was like. It was all right for her, it didn't mean so much to girls, she wouldn't sit at home wondering about it, wishing she could get the chance. And if she did, she could find a bloke easily enough – though she'd better not. But for him, away at sea, there would be no more chances. Perhaps never.

Just now, in the front room, he'd been overwhelmed by the desperation of his need. He looked at Ted Chapman, sitting at the head of the table, and silently cursed him. If he hadn't come in when he did . . . But maybe it'd be better later anyway. Betty had changed those horrible breeches for a skirt and she'd promised she wouldn't stop him, and her mum always let them go in the front room to say goodnight. And this being his last night, she'd be sure to let them have a bit longer, she wouldn't come bursting in. They'd be as safe there as if they were out in the country, with the stars overhead and nobody else around for miles.

'I had a few words with the new people in October Street, where the old lady lived with all the cats,' Annie was saying. 'A mother and two girls about eight or nine. Expecting too – it put me in mind of our Jess, moving into number 14 with Rose and Tim just little ones and Keith on the way.'

'Rose and Tim were only two or three,' Ted objected. 'You said these two were eight or nine.'

'Well, I know. I didn't say they were identical, just that they put me in mind.' Annie spoke with some impatience. Ted always had to be so literal. And couldn't he see she was just talking for something to say? Couldn't he see what was going on right in front of his eyes?

Annie had no illusions about young Graham Philpotts. She had a pretty good idea what was in his mind now, as he sat beside Betty at the supper table. He couldn't keep his eyes off her and was having a job keeping his hands off her too, if she was any judge. She'd given them both a sharp look when they came in from the front room, and seen Betty's over-bright eyes and flushed face, and Graham's smirk. She didn't think they'd actually done anything they shouldn't – well, not too much, and not yet – but Graham looked too much like the cat who'd got the cream for her peace of mind, and there was only one reason for a chap to look like that, the night before he went away to war.

If he hadn't already had the cream, he was expecting to get it.

Well, it was up to her to see that he didn't. It wasn't that she didn't trust Betty, but any girl could get carried away at times like this. That was why Ted was so against her leaving home. But Annie knew that a girl didn't have to leave home to get into trouble. It could happen in her own front room. And even a good girl could be forced into it, if the boy was persistent.

Graham had that persistent look tonight. And Betty was looking upset, as if she was half excited, half scared. She's ripe to fall, Annie thought, and she needs help to see she doesn't.

'Simmons, their name is, the people who are in number 16,' she went on. 'Jess told me she stopped and had a word. The husband's in the Merchant Navy and hasn't been home since March.'

'Where do they come from?' Olive asked. She seemed to have heard all this before, and wasn't particularly interested anyway, but there was something up with Mum, she looked anxious, and Betty and Graham had looked almost as if they'd had a row when they came in. She caught her sister's eye and was startled by the expression, almost of appeal, in her face.

'They were bombed out in that air-raid last month, down in Portchester Road. Their house is wrecked, so they've come to October Street.'

'Where've they been living till now?' Betty was trying desperately to control her juddering feelings, but her voice came out shrilly, as if she'd been crying. She could feel Graham beside her. Why did I promise? she thought. What am I going to do?

'Oh, she's been moved in a couple of weeks – took her a while to get the place fit to live in.' Annie sniffed. Jess had told her about the state the place was in. She wondered what it was like now. Annie cleaned her kitchen – and indeed her whole house – thoroughly each morning. Just as if the King and Queen were coming to visit, Ted sometimes remarked. And suppose they did? Annie would retort. Wouldn't you be thankful that someone cared enough about the place to keep it fit for visitors? And when he observed, as he had been increasingly wont to do just lately, that it was more likely to be Hitler who came walking in the door, she spoke even more sharply.

'I'll not have any German making remarks about *my* front step, nor how clean my net curtains are. And take those dirty boots off before you come in here, Ted Chapman. War or no war, I've still got my floors to keep clean, and I didn't spend half the winter making those rag rugs for you to leave muddy footprints all over them.'

She felt sorry for young Mrs Simmons, being bombed out of a home that was like a little palace and having to start again in something that was no better than a slum.

It had been a good enough start to the conversation, after all. Ted started to talk about other people who had been bombed out in that raid. He knew a couple from the ferry, men who'd gone over to Gosport to work. You got to know the regulars, they always went to the same places on the boat, some favouring the warmth of the funnel, some standing up in the bow with the piles of bikes. There were a couple of others who had never appeared again after that raid, he thought.

'Didn't one of your friends come from Portchester Road?' Betty asked Graham, grateful to be able to ask him something more ordinary. Not that air-raids were ordinary, though her dad and Uncle Frank both reckoned they were going to be. But there hadn't been another one since 11 July after all, though there'd been plenty of fighter planes coming over, and having dogfights with the RAF up there in the sky.

Graham nodded. 'Knocker White. He didn't actually come from there – his auntie lived there. But his mum always went round on a Thursday and we came up that way the next day and found the house bombed flat.'

The family had already heard the story. Graham had told them on the evening he had arrived. Later on, he'd told them that Knocker and his oppo Arnie had gone on to his mother's house and found the two women there, safe enough but a bit battered by the explosion. They had sheltered under the stairs when the raid started, too frightened to make the dash down the garden for the shelter, and had been found half buried in plaster and rubble, scratched and bruised but otherwise unhurt. The auntie had moved in with her sister now and was sleeping in Knocker's room.

Supper was over at last. The two girls washed up while Annie made Ted's sandwiches for next day and wrapped them in greaseproof paper. Ted and Graham read the newspaper and discussed the war, and then they all sat down together again. There was a moment's silence and Graham glanced at Betty. Perhaps now they'd be able to go back to the front room for the rest of the evening.

Annie caught the look and saw the blush on Betty's cheek. She sat up and said brightly, 'How about a game of cards?'

'Cards?' Ted said. 'On a Friday?' The family often played cards, but it was usually on a Sunday evening, and more often in winter than in summer. He looked out of the window. 'I was thinking of walking over to the allotment for an hour.'

'What, on Graham's last evening?' Annie saw his look of astonishment and almost laughed at herself. Why ever should Ted want to stay at home, just because it was Graham's last evening here? He didn't even like the boy all that much. And that's as good a reason as any, she thought grimly. If he doesn't want Graham Philpotts as part of the family, he'd better play his part. 'I'm sure there's nothing wants doing over there that can't wait till tomorrow.'

'It's all right, Mrs Chapman,' Graham said. 'I'm not all that keen on cards myself. I'd just as soon sit and talk for a bit.' In the front room with Betty, preferably, he thought, by ourselves and not doing all that much talking either.

'Oh, I'd like a game,' Betty said quickly. 'It'll be something to remember when you're away, Gray. A nice family evening together.' She avoided his eye. She could feel his disappointment and felt sorry about it, but she knew now that she would do almost anything to avoid being alone with him. Oh, Graham, she thought, I do love you – I'm *sure* I love you – but I'm just not ready . . .

Annie was already getting out the cards and in a few minutes the family found themselves sitting back at the table, sorting out their hands. They'd play Rummy, Annie declared, that was a nice game for five people since you couldn't play whist or solo. And after that they played Sevens, and then a game that Olive knew but couldn't remember the name of and then some silly game that involved putting a handful of farthings in the middle of the table and grabbing them. It made them laugh a lot, especially Betty and Annie, but the laughter was forced somehow and when the game was over they were all quiet, as if there was nothing left to say.

'Look at the time!' Annie said. 'I suppose you'll have to be getting back to the ship, Graham. Lucky it's not dark yet, or you might get lost!'

'I expect I'll find my way all right,' Graham said. His voice was flat. He knew, they all knew, that he'd have to leave in half an hour, not because he had to get back to his ship – he didn't have to be on board until six in the morning, an hour before sailing time – but because at ten o'clock the family would be starting to go to bed and the Chapmans would insist he was out of the house before then. And that didn't leave enough time for anything bar a few kisses. By now, he wasn't even sure that he wanted to kiss Betty anyway.

He refused Annie's offer of a cup of cocoa and she finally allowed them to go into the front room for their last goodnights. He shook hands with her and Ted, gave Olive an awkward peck on the cheek, and then followed Betty through the door. They stood in the front room, as ill at ease as if they had only just met, and then Betty looked up at his face and said, 'I'm sorry, Gray.'

'Yeah, I reckon you are.' He couldn't help his voice sounding bitter. 'I didn't notice you saying no to a game of cards.'

'I couldn't, could I? Mum knew what was up, she was set on us not being in here too long together. She'd have found some other way. We ought to have gone out for a walk.'

'And taken the whole family with us,' he sneered. 'Be honest, Bet, you were glad. You never did want us to do it, did you? You said as much. I just wish you'd said before, that's all –'

'I did, Graham! You know I did.'

'You been leading me on,' he continued as if she had not spoken. 'You wanted to get engaged, not me, you wanted a ring. What does all that mean, eh? What was it all about?'

'It was because I loved you,' she said, her voice quivering. The tears welled up in her eyes and trembled on her lashes. 'I do love you, Graham. It's just –'

'So why don't you prove it? Why don't you *show* me you love me?'

'But I do! Didn't I knit you a Fair Isle pullover? Didn't I make you a chocolate cake? Didn't I –'

'Cake!' he exlaimed. 'A *pullover*! Bet, I'm not talking about cakes and pullovers, I'm talking about –'

'I know what you're talking about,' she said, casting an anxious glance towards the wall that separated the front room from the room where the rest of the family were sitting. 'Please, Gray, don't shout, you'll have our Dad in here wanting to know what's going on. I've told you, I can't. I'm not ready for it. And I'm scared.'

'You don't trust me,' he muttered. 'And you don't love me. I've got to go away to sea tomorrow and I might be killed, never knowing what it's like. D'you realise that, Bet? I might never, never know what it's like.'

'Oh, Graham,' she said, and the tears poured down her cheeks. 'Oh, Graham, I'm sorry. I'm really, really sorry.'

She moved closer and put her arms around his body. She could feel his warmth through the white cotton shirt. She pressed her face against his chest and felt his heart beating under her cheek.

'If only there was time,' she said miserably. 'I'd do it now. I really would, Gray.'

But there was no more time. Already they could hear Olive's footsteps on the stairs and the movements in the next room as Annie and her husband prepared to go to bed. In a few minutes one of them would knock on the wall, and Betty would have to go back.

'I love you, Gray,' she whispered, and lifted her face. 'I really love you.'

He bent and kissed her lips. 'You'll write to me, won't you, Bet?'

'Every day.'

'And you won't get off with some farmer's boy?'

'I hate farmers' boys!' she declared, and they both laughed shakily.

Annie's knock sounded on the wall and they held each

other tightly, with sudden passion. Graham groaned and kissed her hard. He felt his frustration well up inside him and clenched his teeth with the despair of it. Betty burst into fresh sobs and dug her fingers into his shoulders.

'Oh, Graham, I don't want you to go. I don't want you to go.'

'I know. I know.' He almost tore himself from her arms. Annie's knock sounded again, a little louder. 'But if I don't go, your Dad'll be in here with a horsewhip.' He held her away from him, gave her a crooked grin and then one last fierce kiss. He wrenched open the door and blundered out into the street.

Betty followed him to the front door. It was still light and she watched through her tears as he strode away up March Street. At the top, he turned and waved, and she lifted her own hand and blew him a kiss. And then he was gone.

She stood for a moment, feeling the emptiness around her where only a few moments before Graham had been. She looked at her hands, still able to feel the warmth and shape of his body on their skin. She wrapped her arms about her own body, trying to imagine that she was holding him still.

He'd been here, close to her, alive and warm and real. And now he was gone, and she didn't know when she'd see him again, when she would be able to touch him.

If she ran to the top of March Street she would still be able to see him, walking along September, tall and proud in his matelot uniform. But it would only be a few more seconds before he was once again lost to sight. It was as if she would never be able to catch up with him again.

The door behind her opened and Annie came out on to the step. She slipped her arm around Betty's waist.

'Don't stand out here fretting, love,' she said gently. 'He's gone. And you did the right thing.'

Betty didn't have to ask her what she meant. And she knew that without her mother's help, or interference, depending on how you looked at it, she might very easily have done the wrong thing.

I suppose I'll be glad about it after a while, she thought drearily as she followed Annie back into the house. But just at that moment I wish I'd been doing the wrong thing all this past month, and given Graham something better than a game of cards to remember when he's at sea.

Graham walked swiftly until he had turned the corner into September Street, and then his footsteps slowed.

Bugger Betty's mum! If it hadn't been for her, he and Betty could have spent a couple of hours in the front room, snug as you like behind the net curtains, and she'd have given him everything he wanted. He knew she would. She'd promised, and Betty wasn't one to go back on a promise. But Mrs Chapman was too sharp, she never had trusted him, and she'd made sure they had no chance. And now he might never know . . .

'Hullo, it's young Ginger Philpotts, isn't it? What's the matter with you, lost a shilling and found sixpence?'

Graham looked up, startled, and recognised Tommy Vickers. He was a smallish man with wavy fair hair and a cheeky grin, who lived at the top of April Grove, by the allotments not far from the Chapmans' house, and always had something to say about whatever was going on. Graham knew him from the days when the Philpotts family had lived in September Street, before they went to live 'over the water' in Gosport. Tommy Vickers had been a popular figure with the children, always ready with a pocketful of toffees to scatter amongst them or a joke to tell.

'Hullo, Mr Vickers,' he said. 'I'm all right, just said goodbye to Betty, that's all. We're sailing in the morning.'

'Oh, so that's it. And you're feeling a bit chocker.' Tommy had been in the Navy – the 'Andrew', he always called it – in the last war. 'Well, if you're not in a hurry, why not come and have a drink?'

'A drink?' Graham said stupidly, and Tommy grinned.

'You're a sailor, aren't you? Don't tell me you don't know what pubs are for. Come on.' It was a Brickwoods house, and he pulled Graham through the door. The smell of beer came to meet them. There was sawdust on the floor and raucous laughter in the air. Graham started to feel better.

'What'll it be? Can't offer you pusser's rum.' Tommy

chuckled and Graham grinned back. Naval rum was stronger than any other kind and he had his tot every day in the mess.

'Best thing about the Andrew, the daily tot of rum,' Tommy said, 'but you can't get it outside. Well, you can –' he laid his finger against his nose and winked '– but you got to know the right people. So what is it? Pint of bitter?'

Graham nodded. Beer was another thing he might not get for a long time. The Navy gave you rum, but any other booze was absolutely forbidden, at least for the lower deck. Officers just about swam in pink gin, so he'd heard, but none of it ever filtered down to Jolly Jack.

Tommy brought the glasses over to a small table and they sat down. There was a short silence while they downed the first half. Graham had been half afraid that Tommy would suggest 'oncers' and expect him to drain the whole lot in a go, but he said nothing. Not that Graham couldn't have done it, but it would have meant he'd have to buy the next round and he was painfully conscious that he had very little money in his pocket. He set down his glass and wondered what to say.

Tommy Vickers was never at a loss for words. He cocked a bright blue eye at Graham and said, 'So you're off to sea tomorrow. How d'you like the idea? This is your first ship, isn't it?'

'That's right. I'm a writer.' When he told people that, they thought it meant he wrote books but he didn't have to explain to Tommy that all it meant was a clerk. Even ships had offices and paperwork, even when they went to war, perhaps more so, he thought.

Tommy nodded. 'I was a cook. A good one too. Nobody went hungry on my ship. Fed 'em like fighting cocks, I did. Been to sea yet?'

'Yes.' Graham told him about their attempt to thwart the air-raid a month ago, and how they'd been damaged and had to limp back to Portsmouth. 'We only got just past the Needles. They didn't warn us in time, that's what it was.'

'They didn't warn anyone in time,' Tommy said. 'There'd been two attacks already that day, down Portland, and they got there too late for those too. Caught with their pants right down. And they reckon they spotted our lot coming over the

French coast, plenty of time to get everyone into shelters.'

'That's right,' Graham said. 'We saw 'em at a quarter to six. Heinkels, they were, with ME110s holding their hands. Our lads were in Hurricanes but while they were attacking the MEs, the Heinkels just went on and bombed Pompey.' His face was angry, but he gave a sudden reminiscent grin. 'Mind you, we saw two of 'em off – a couple of Hurricanes got round the Heinkels and started driving 'em just like sheep. Two of 'em collided in mid-air and fell straight into the drink. But they couldn't do nothing about the rest.'

'It was a bad do,' Tommy said, and they fell silent. He drank the rest of his beer. 'Well, we won't be caught napping again. I reckon they must've learnt their lesson, up at Bomber Command. Drink up, son. There's time for another one before they close.'

Graham flushed scarlet and felt in his pocket. 'I – I haven't got much dosh,' he stammered, but Tommy waved a hand at him.

'Did I ask you to pay? I was in the last lot, y'know. I came through it all right, but there were a lot of blokes, good mates of mine, who didn't. This one's on me. Call it one for them if you like.'

He went back to the bar and Graham glanced around the room. It was filled with smoke and there were a couple of other sailors there and a few women, but no one he knew. Unless that face was familiar? He stared hard and then realised who it was.

Nancy Baxter from April Grove. She was sitting with a couple of other women, drinking port and lemon by the look of it. She looked much the same as he'd always known her, thin and scraggy, her dark hair cut in a short, ragged bob. She had on a summer frock, the sort women wore when it was hot and sunny, with straps instead of sleeves, and her shoulders looked brown. The front was cut low and he could see the tops of her breasts. They didn't look all that much, but he couldn't help staring all the same.

Nancy Baxter was a tart, the whole street knew that. She was supposed to work nights in a hotel somewhere, but nobody had ever managed to find out which one and it was anyone's guess what kind of hotel it was. The two women with her were probably tarts too, dressed flashily and showing more leg than his Betty ever would. One of them caught his eye and gave him an enquiring smile. She crossed her legs and swung the foot towards him and he heard her laugh as he flushed and turned away.

He was still feeling hot when Tommy came back with the drinks, and his body was behaving in an embarrassing way. He picked up the glass and gulped down some beer.

'Ta. That's good.'

Tommy nodded and gave Graham a shrewd glance. 'Still feeling fed-up?'

'Yeah.' Graham hesitated, then said, 'What did you do when you went to sea, Mr Vickers? About – you know –' he blushed again '– girls, that sort of thing.'

'So that's it, is it?' The older man gave a short laugh. He was about fifty, Graham thought, and must be past it long ago. What was he doing, asking an old man's advice?

'Oh, forget I asked,' he said quickly, picking up his drink again to cover his embarrassment. 'It doesn't matter.'

'Doesn't matter? Of course it matters. It matters a helluva lot. And drop this Mr Vickers nonsense, my name's Tommy as well you know.' He leaned forwards. 'Look, I'll tell you this, sex *never* stops mattering. Well, not till you're a lot older than I am, anyway!' He grinned. 'And there's all the time in the world to find out about it – or ought to be.' He looked more sober. 'That's what's biting you, isn't it? You're off to sea tomorrow and you're scared you're never going to know what it's all about.'

Graham looked down at the table. Some of the beer had slopped over when Tommy set down the glasses, and he made patterns in it with one finger.

'Well . . .'

'Course you are. You're a healthy young man, it'd be a funny thing if you didn't have women on your mind. Been there for a few years too, I should think, eh?' He paused. 'You've been calling round Betty Chapman's place quite a bit lately.'

'Betty and me haven't done anything,' Graham said

98

quickly. 'She's a decent girl. We –' He broke off. He wanted to tell Tommy that he and Betty were secretly engaged, but Tommy Vickers knew the Chapmans well, he lived only a stone's throw away from them and what's more he was the same generation, he'd be just as likely to pass it on. 'We're just friends,' he said lamely.

Tommy laughed. 'Tell that to the marines! Well, I can tell she hasn't given you any goodbye presents, anyway. And you might think yourself lucky, at that. You might've left her with one neither of you wanted.' He drank some of his beer. 'Are you telling me you've never done it at all?'

Graham shook his head miserably.

'What would you do, Mr Vickers? I know there's girls – women –' he couldn't help his eyes straying in the direction of Nancy Baxter and her two friends ' – I mean, I know you can get it, but –'

'But you've heard all the horror stories.' Tommy too glanced across the room. 'Well, if I were you, I'd listen to 'em. There's more than one kind of present you can get from girls, and some are worse than others. I've always steered clear, myself. Once you're at sea, you're safe, that's always been my motto, and don't drink too much on shore runs.' He gave Graham a shrewd but kindly glance with his blue eyes. 'I know it seems hard, as the bishop said to the actress, but you're better off wondering than collecting a packet of what those sluts could hand you. But you're a big boy, as the actress said to the bishop, and you've got to make up your own mind.'

Nancy Baxter had got up and was moving in their direction. She leaned over them and said, 'That's right, Tommy. He's got to decide for himself.' She winked at Graham. 'Bet I know what you're talking about!'

Graham felt his skin colour yet again and Tommy said warningly, 'You leave the kid alone, Nance. He don't need your attentions.'

'Oh, don't worry,' she said, 'this is my night off.' She picked up the glass she had set down on the table. 'Just out for a bit of fun with me pals, what's wrong with that?' She winked at Graham again and moved away, swaying her thin hips.

Tommy snorted. 'Beats me how she gets the business.

She's nothing to look at. Well, it's coming up to drinking up time and my missus'll be wondering where I've got to. Very handy with the rolling pin, is my missus!'

He winked at Graham and finished his beer. The landlord had rung the bell and more people were beginning to leave. The three tarts were on their way to the door.

'Okay, Mr Vickers – I mean, Tommy,' Graham said, still feeling awkward at using the first name of a man he'd known when he was little. 'I'll remember. And thanks for the drink.'

They walked outside. The twilight of midsummer was deepening to a shadowed blue. The sky was cloudless, with just a few stars prickling its indigo dome. Tommy stood still, looking upwards as everyone did these days. He turned to Graham and stuck out his hand.

'Good luck, Ginger. You're going to need it, I reckon, but someone always gets through, and there's no reason why it shouldn't be you. I did, after all, always reckoned I was lucky, so I'll pass my luck on to you. You remind me of myself a bit, when I was your age.' He grinned. 'Look us up next time you're in Pompey, eh?'

'Thanks. I will.' Graham shook the hand, feeling a sudden urge to hold on to it. 'Cheerio, then.'

He turned and walked away along September Street. The encounter hadn't eased his frustration, but he did feel a bit better for it. At least he'd been able to tell someone how he felt, someone who understood. Maybe Tommy Vickers wasn't past it after all. Or perhaps it was just that his memory was good!

He grinned at the thought, and then jumped as a voice spoke in his ear.

'Ginger? It is little Ginger, ain't it?'

Graham looked round, startled. Nancy Baxter was beside him, her bare shoulder almost touching his. She gave him a smile.

'Didn't you used to live in September Street? I knew your ma, Elsie. And Charlie, your dad. Course, I was only a kiddy then, but I remember 'em well.'

Some kiddy, thought Graham. Nancy Baxter had a boy of around eleven, she must have been at least twenty when he was born. Nobody knew who his father was, supposed to be a soldier, or was it a sailor, someone high-up anyway. So what were Nancy and her mum and Micky doing, living in a two-up, two-down terraced house in a backstreet in Pompey? And didn't she have another kid now? Still, it wasn't worth arguing about, and maybe she really had known his parents when she was young.

'Do they still call you Ginger?' she asked. 'I bet they do, with those carrots! So what're you doing now, then? Off back to your ship? I'd have thought you'd be stopping with Betty Chapman tonight.'

Graham stared at her. 'Stopping with Betty? Why?'

'Well, it's your last night, innit?' She laughed. 'Shouldn't know that, should I! But you'd be surprised what I get to know in my line of business.' She winked and lowered her voice a bit. 'F'r instance, I always know when a bloke's gasping for it. And when it's a nice-looking chap like yourself . . .'

Graham remembered Tommy's warning. 'No thanks. I've got to get back.'

'Why? You ain't sailing till morning.'

'You know more than you ought to,' Graham said. 'And you shouldn't be blabbing it round the streets, either. You know what they say.'

'Oh, I know! Walls have ears, be like Dad and keep Mum, there's a fifth columnist under every bed.' She sniggered again. She's had too much to drink, he thought. 'You don't have to worry about me, Ginger. And if there's anything you want, to help speed you on your way, well, you've only got to ask.'

Graham looked at her and turned away quickly, thankful that the twilight hid his blush. 'No thanks.'

'Sure?' She took his arm, turning him back towards her, and searched his face. 'You didn't look too cheerful, back there in the pub with Tommy Vickers. Just said goodbye to young Betty, had you?'

Blimey, Graham thought, everyone knows your bloody business round here. He twisted away again.

'Look, sorry. I've got to get back to the ship . . .'

'What's the hurry?' Nancy held on to his arm. She moved

closer and he caught another glimpse of her breasts, where the sundress gaped from her body. 'Look, Ginger, I'm not after business. I've seen too many young chaps going off to sea lately. I know the look – the look you all get. Specially you young 'uns. Never had it and scared you're never going to get it. That's right, innit? Don't try to flannel me, you won't have got much joy out of young Betty, I know, not with a dad like hers hovering outside the door. So what's the hurry? Why not come home with me and go back to your ship in the morning.' She grinned. 'I'll make sure you don't oversleep!'

Graham felt the heat flood over his body, from his neck upwards, from his waist down. He shook his head and stammered.

'I'm not – I don't – I can't – look, I've got to get back. I've got to!'

'Not till morning.' Nancy said calmly. 'And you are, you do and you can. What's more, you want to. Why not come and have a bit of fun while you've got the chance? Where's the harm in it?' She held her head on one side, her eyes like black buttons in the darkness, and reached down to stroke his thigh. 'No one's going to know,' she whispered cajolingly. 'Betty thinks you've gone back ages ago, and Tommy Vickers is home in bed with his own missus by now. And I know how to keep my mouth shut.'

She was thin and a bit scraggy, with bony shoulders. But she was offering him something no other woman had offered, something he badly wanted. He'd wanted it to be Betty, but it couldn't be, wouldn't, for years. And he couldn't wait for years. Nobody had the right to make him wait years.

'I can't,' he stuttered miserably. 'I haven't got any money. I'm skint.'

'Who's talking about money?' she retorted. 'Look, I told Tommy Vickers this was my night off. But that don't mean I can't accommodate a friend, does it? Specially when I knew his mum and dad years ago when I was a nipper. Call it in memory of old times, if you like!' She laughed and hooked his arm into hers. 'Come on, stop looking so worried, we'll go down the back way. And you can be out first thing in the morning, before anyone else is about. Your Betty'll never know, and what she don't know can't hurt her, can it?'

Almost without realising it, Graham had turned and was walking back along September Street, arm in arm in the darkness with Nancy Baxter. His head reeled and his heart thumped. He thought briefly of Betty, then pushed her from his mind.

This was nothing to do with Betty, nor Tommy Vickers, nor his mum and dad. This was between him and Nancy Baxter. In fact, he wasn't even sure it had much to do with Nancy. It was all to do with himself, with the body he had grown into. It was to do with his manhood, with the desperate need he had to know what it felt like to *be* a man, to know what it was all about.

He had a right to it, didn't he? He had a *right*.

Betty heard their footsteps go by as she lay in bed, her pillow wet with tears. She was alone in the bedroom – after her marriage, Olive had moved into Colin's room in the little turret. It didn't seem right, sleeping with her sister now she was a married woman, she'd said, and Betty had been glad enough to have the room to herself, though she missed their whispered conversations and felt less close to her sister now.

She was glad now to have no witness to her tears, although she would have liked the comfort Olive might have given her. And it would have proved to her that Betty did love Graham, just as much as she loved her Derek. Sometimes Olive behaved as if they were the only two who had ever been in love, or missed each other.

At least they're married, Betty thought. They can do what they like. Not like me and Graham. She thought again of his lips on hers, of his searching hands. She'd wanted to give him what he wanted, she'd wanted it herself, but she just couldn't. And she'd hated sending him off like that, miserable.

Maybe next time he comes home, she thought. I'll ask Olive about it, how to make sure nothing goes wrong. Graham's right, it's not fair, not when he has to go off to sea not knowing whether he'll ever come back.

She knew that he was afraid he would lose her to some other boy. She knew that he wanted to know she belonged to him, that he was the first man ever to make love to her. And I want to be his first girl, she thought.

And I will – next time he comes home. I'll write and tell him. It'll be a promise.

The footsteps had faded now. She turned over and fell asleep.

CHAPTER SIX

It was midday on the Monday after Graham's departure, and Betty Chapman had just handed Mrs Marsh her notice, when the sirens sounded their long-drawn, eerie lament.

'Oh no,' Mrs Marsh said with a cluck of exasperation. 'There it goes again. I suppose we'll have to shut the shop and go down the shelter. You never know but what it might be real.'

Outside, the sun was at its height, glittering on the balloons. The raiders were not yet in sight, but as she went to lock the shop door the low mutter of their approach could be heard over the dying wail of the siren. Suddenly fearful, the two went quickly to the back door and as they came out into the yard the mutter developed into a snarl, and then a low, ominous roar.

Mrs Marsh gave a gasp of fright and ran for the shelter. She had hung her washing on the line earlier and she snatched at it as she ran, pulling it with her. One of the white sheets trailed on the ground and almost tripped her up. She cried out with fear and annoyance, and gathered it up in a bundle, dragging it through the little doorway.

Next door, Alice and Joy Brunner were sorting through a bundle of women's magazines. The siren caught and froze them. Alice's pale face grew even whiter and she began to shake.

Joy dropped the magazines and grabbed her mother's arm. 'Come on, Mum. Down the shelter, quick.'

'It's a false alarm,' Alice said, shuddering. 'It's bound to be. They aren't really coming.'

'They might be.' There had been false alarms day after day, but you could never be sure it wasn't real until the other siren sounded, the one that meant it was safe again. 'We ought to go down the shelter just in case.' Joy let go of her mother's arm and locked the shop door. They'd left it unlocked once and come back to find half the sweets gone from the boxes behind the counter. She had a good idea who it was had taken them too. 'Come on, quick. Where's your gas mask?'

'It's no use, Joy. Even if it is them, it's no use. If we're meant to be killed, we'll be killed, just like your poor father.'

'*Mum*!' The snarl of planes approaching could be heard quite clearly now. Joy pulled again at her mother's arm, dragging her through the shop and out of the back of the house. She glanced up and caught her first sight of an enemy formation, like a cloud of black flies coming directly out of the sun. For a few seconds she stood frozen. Only her head and eyes moved, following the path of the aircraft as they came slowly onwards, flying in a straight, remorseless line over the city.

'Oh-h-h,' Alice moaned, covering her face with her hands. 'Oh, Joy . . . Heinrich . . . Heinrich, where are you . . .?' She broke away from Joy's hand and scuttled like a crab towards the Anderson shelter.

Joy saw the bombs, falling like a bundle of firewood from the belly of the first plane, scattering in the air, falling on Portsmouth . . .

'Joy! *Joy*!'

Alice was screaming at her, her head poking out of the Anderson. With a startled jump, Joy came to her senses and hurled herself down the garden.

'They're right on top of us!' She flung herself in behind her mother. 'They're *diving* on us!' The first explosion shook the ground and was followed by another, another and another. She crouched on the floor and Alice clutched her, gabbling with fear.

'They're not giving us a *chance*. There's people still out in the streets.' The harsh rattle of guns drowned her voice. 'Oh, Joy, what's that?'

'It's anti-aircraft fire,' Joy said. Her voice was trembling and she made a huge effort to control it. 'We're shooting at them. They won't get away as easy as that.'

'What difference does it make whether it's a bomb or an aeroplane that drops on you? You're just as dead.' Alice crouched on the floor, her hands over her ears. 'Oh, it's so *loud*. They must be right overhead. They'll kill us all.'

The planes were roaring overhead. It sounded as if they were simply circling over the city, quite undisturbed by the anti-aircraft guns. Every minute was punctuated by a fresh explosion. Alice and Joy huddled together on the damp earth floor, their arms covering their heads, their bodies jarred by the vibrations that tore through them through both earth and air.

'There'll be nothing left,' Alice whimpered. 'Nothing left . . .'

It seemed as if half a lifetime had passed, yet it was barely twelve-thirty when the Raiders Passed signal sounded. Cautiously, only half believing it, Joy and Alice looked at each other.

The sky was silent again. There was no snarl of approaching Heinkels, no 'crump' of a falling bomb. The last explosion had been several minutes ago.

'D'you think it's really safe?' Alice whispered.

'They've got ways of telling,' Joy said uneasily. 'People looking with telescopes, and that sort of thing. And it's broad daylight. They must be able to see they've gone.'

They scrambled to their feet, stretched their cramped and stiffened limbs and crawled slowly out of the shelter, blinking in the bright sunlight and almost afraid to look about them. It seemed uncannily quiet after the pandemonium of the previous half-hour, but as the thunder died from their ears they became aware of voices from nearby gardens, and then of a shadow passing beneath the sun as black smoke billowed into the sky, with flames of cruel orange and red showing like glimpses of silk lining in a torn black cloak. The Devil's cloak, Joy thought, flung over the city of Portsmouth to stifle it to death . . .

She saw Mrs Marsh and Betty Chapman looking over the

fence. Alice was crying again, staring at the black and orange smoke and shaking her head like a doll that had been wound up and couldn't stop.

'It isn't that Mum wants to give in,' she said defensively. 'But she misses Dad so much. And not even knowing what's happened to him.' Her eyes filled with tears. 'We don't even know why they had to take him away. He never did anything wrong.' Her arms were round her mother's thin body, comforting her as if she were the mother and Alice her child.

Mrs Marsh nodded. 'I know, love. It's all too much for her. You take her in and make her a cup of tea, and I'll come round and see if there's anything I can do. It's hard on us all, but we've just got to help each other as best we can.' She looked down at the washing still clutched in her arms. 'I don't know why I took this down with me, I'm sure.'

She went back into the dairy and Betty Chapman followed her. The excitement of being called up into the Land Army had faded. There wasn't much glamour after all in a war that took innocent men away from their homes as if they were criminals, and left women like Alice Brunner frightened and alone.

Ted Chapman was bringing the *Ferry King* alongside the Portsmouth pontoon when the sirens sounded.

He felt the now familiar chill of fear run down his spine. It didn't matter how many false alarms there were, you never lost that little cold shudder or the sickness in your stomach. He looked at Ben, who had just jumped ashore to wind the mooring rope to the stanchion. The other member of the crew, old Sam Hardy, was unfastening the chain to let the passengers off.

'Get up to the shelters, quick!'

Sam shook his head. 'I'll stay aboard.'

Ted drew a ragged breath of exasperation. They had this argument every bloody time. Whichever side of the harbour they were on, the men were supposed to make for the shelters at the top of the Hard. And they never would. The two of them, Sam and young Ben, always insisted on staying with the *King*.

'When you go up to the shelter, so will I,' Sam said flatly, and Ben nodded. But Ted could not bring himself to leave his boat. The *King* had been his life, his pride and joy, for years. He'd crossed the harbour thousands of times, in all weathers, tossing in winter gales, creeping almost blindfold in thick fog. And he'd taken her across to Dunkirk, where she'd worked under heavy shelling and gunfire.

The *King* had stood by him then, and he had a superstitious dread of leaving her.

'For crying out loud!' he shouted, his voice cracking with fear. 'The Jerries are coming – can't you see them?' They were coming in over the Isle of Wight, black as a flock of starlings. 'Get into shelter, for God's sake!'

The passengers were running hell for leather up the sloping pontoon. Above them on the railway station, they could see people leaping off the trains, scuttling along the platforms in a frantic search for safety. Ted looked at the sky. The flock of black planes held a horrible fascination.

Terror ran through his body like a flame at white heat. He screamed again at his crew.

'*The shelters*! *For God's sake – the shelters*!'

'You come too.' Sam ran up the few steps to the bridge and grabbed his arm. 'Ted, don't be daft – you get bombed here an' you won't know whether to burn or drown. Look at 'em! They're making straight for the Yard. They'll blow the whole bloody lot to smithereens, and us with 'em. What good'll that do anyone?' He dragged Ted down to the deck and thrust him on to the pontoon. 'Look, any more trouble from you and I'll knock you out and *carry* you to the shelter!'

Ted felt his legs begin to run. He was still gibbering a protest, but Sam and Ben were on either side of him, yanking him up the wooden slope. By the time they reached the top and began to run along the bridge, the air was filled with the drone of the aeroplanes. Panic tore at his body. It was Dunkirk all over again, and this time they wouldn't survive.

The first bombs fell as they pushed their way through the shelter door.

Tommy Vickers was working in Old Portsmouth, near

Whitewoods, the furniture depository. His job as general handyman with the Council took him all over the city. That was how he liked it. He enjoyed knowing Pompey like the back of his hand, hearing all the gossip, being a familiar figure around the place. Mending pipes, painting street signs, sweeping gutters, he didn't care what he did, so long as he was out and always had time for a cheery word or a joke.

When the siren sounded, he made for the nearest shelter and settled himself on one of the benches. Some kids had been in and pinched the paraffin lamps, but someone had a torch and flashed it around in the darkness. Most of the people were resigned to another false alarm, but the sound of the aeroplanes changed the atmosphere to one of dismay.

'Oh God, not again. It was bad enough last time.'

'What'll they hit this time? Our Fred's house had all its windows blowed out. He's only just got 'em patched up.'

A woman beside Tommy began to cry. He patted her arm.

'It's all right, love, we're safe enough in here. Look, let's have a bit of a singsong. It'll cheer us up.'

'What's there to feel cheerful about?' someone asked out of the darkness, and Tommy shrugged.

'Well, it'll help pass the time. And if we sing loud enough we won't hear the planes. Come on, I'll start and you all join in.'

He cast about in his mind for a song. *Little Brown Jug* had been popular lately. Glenn Miller had been playing it on the wireless.

> *'My wife and I lived all alone,*
> *In a little log hut we called our own,*
> *She loved whisky, I loved rum,*
> *I tell you what, we'd lots of fun.'*

He paused. One or two voices joined in, rather feebly.

> *'Ha-ha-ha,*
> *He-he-he,*
> *Little brown jug, don't I love thee . . .'*

A bomb crashed down outside. It drowned their voices, shook the earth beneath their feet, sent a wave of vibration through their bones. The woman near Tommy screamed and began to cry more loudly.

Tommy put his arm around her shoulders and gripped her tightly against him. He started again.

> *'Dear old pals, jolly old pals,*
> *Clinging together in all sorts of weather,*
> *Dear old pals, jolly old pals,*
> *Give me the friendship of dear old pals.'*

Now others were joining in. As Tommy finished his song, another one started in a far corner. More people were singing, their voices wavery and self-conscious at first, rising to a shout of defiance as the noise increased outside.

'Daisy, Daisy, give me your answer do,' someone sang, and the response came from a dozen throats.

> *'I'm half crazy, all for the love of you.'*

Another explosion rocked the shelter. The noise of aircraft, ack-ack guns and the screaming whistle of the falling bombs created a pounding cacophony that threatened to burst the eardrums of the people huddled in the shelter, but they kept singing. In every momentary lull, the voices could be heard, straggling on.

> *'It won't be a stylish marriage,*
> *I can't afford a carriage . . .'*

'Bloody hell,' a man near the door said, 'that was a close one. Something's copped it.'

> *'But you'll look sweet*
> *Upon the seat*
> *Of a bicycle made for two.'*

'We 'ad a tandem once,' the woman in Tommy's arms snuffled, and he held her closer. 'But it ain't safe to go out no more.'

'Them days'll come back again, you'll see.'

The raid continued. The same dread was in every heart – what would they see when it was over and they went out into the street? But the songs went on, defiance tempered with desperation and a need to do something together, a communication and reassurance. By the time it was over, those who had dashed into the shelter as strangers were held by a bond of both fear and comfort.

At last the noise diminished. The Raiders Passed signal sounded and those nearest the door peered cautiously out.

'Blimey.'

'What is it? What've the bastards done?'

'Only just about flattened us, that's all.'

Tommy let go of the woman and emerged into the sunlight. It was misted over now, almost obscured by the smoke of flaming buildings. The pungent smell of burning was in the air.

'That's Whitewoods bin hit. Goin' up like a torch.'

'There's a big fire down by the ferry, too. And more in the Yard.'

'It's all over the shop. I don't reckon there's a building left standing.'

Tommy left them and ran down the street. The furniture warehouse was well alight, flames leaping from the roof. The whole façade was a mass of orange fire and as he watched a great section of wall toppled slowly outwards into the road. People were screaming and running about, futilely directing stirrup pumps at the blaze, yelling orders to each other. Others wandered in a daze or slumped against walls.

Tommy did what he could, helping those who were hurt or just plain terrified out of their wits. A fire engine arrived and one of the ARP men who had been rushing about giving orders began to berate the chief.

'One bloody engine ain't enough! You can see what it's like. The whole bloody building's afire. We needs every engine in Pompey to fight this lot.'

The fire chief shook his hand off angrily. 'You go on up round Bonfire Corner and tell 'em that. It's proper livin' up to its name, that is. And Queen Street's nothing but rubble, they've got half the engines trying to put that out. And Brickwoods is smashed – that's next week's beer down the drain.'

'Well, what're we supposed to do 'ere, then?' the ARP man

demanded pugnaciously. 'That fire's goin' ter spread if it ain't checked.'

The fire chief turned on him. 'We do whatever we bloody can, don't we? It ain't our fault we ain't got the appliances.' He rubbed a blackened hand over his face. His eyes were desperate. 'The Harbour Station's going up in flames too. We 'aven't got the men, the streets are blocked, and when we do get there, the bloody mains are burst and we can't get no water. Oh, what a bleedin' mess . . .'

'The station?' Tommy stared at him. Portsmouth Harbour Station was a landmark. Everyone who ever went near the ferry knew it. It was built out over the water, so that you could look down from the platforms and see the sea lapping beneath. People came down from London on the train and walked down the platform and straight on to a boat for the Isle of Wight.

'Incendiary,' the fireman said, and turned away again. The warehouse was past saving but sparks and flames were settling on the roofs of other buildings. He ran over to the men who were struggling with the hoses.

Down by the harbour, Ted Chapman also was emerging from the blackness of an air-raid shelter. He stared at the salty blue flames and black smoke billowing from the Harbour Station, and broke into a run.

'Bloody hell, look at that! The whole station's going up. The *King* –'

'They'll never let us near.' Sam and Ben stood behind him, staring. Already people were running about like ants at the top of the pontoon, by the station entrance. A couple of makeshift fire engines converted from dustcarts were pulling up and blue-uniformed men leaping off them and unreeling long hoses.

'It would be low tide,' Sam said in disgust. There was nothing but mud below the slipway. The pontoon, which floated almost level with the road at high tide, was at the bottom of a steep wooden slope.

Which was probably what had saved the *Ferry King*. Moored to the pontoon, she was well below the station and out of the reach of the flames which had spread so quickly along the structure, turning the trains into a heap of twisted, melting metal.

She was not out of danger. Shards of burning fabric were falling on her and Ted watched in agony, certain that she would burst into flames at any moment. But the water which was being sprayed now over the burning structure of the station was turned upon the ferry-boat too, and the flames sizzled and went out.

The *Ferry King* had survived to cross the harbour another day.

Gosport had been hit as well. Frank's brother Howard lived in Gosport and he cycled the twelve miles round the top of the harbour that evening to tell them he and his family were all right. Jess opened the door to him in relief.

'Thank goodness you weren't bombed, Howard. Frank wanted to come over to you but the ferry's not running and I wouldn't let him go out again without his tea. Was there any damage round you?'

Howard nodded. 'Chap called Herbert Gadsby, killed. He lived down Oval Gardens. I used to pass the time of day with him.'

Jess gazed at him solemnly. It was the first time any of them had actually known someone who had been killed.

Howard worked at Supermarine, near Southampton. They built Spitfires there and his work was secret, he wouldn't even talk to Frank about it. But there was still a lot he didn't know, and the war was as bewildering to him as to anyone else.

'We don't know where we are with Stokes Bay these days,' he said. 'One day we can go down there, the next they're putting up barbed wire, old bedsteads, anything to keep it fenced off. And last week they told us we can go there again! They don't seem to know what's what at all. The Admiralty even requisitioned Lee swimming pool a few weeks ago. What are they going to do with that, teach sailors to sail model yachts?'

It took some time for the details of the raid to reach the people of Portsmouth, and the next day's issue of the *Evening News* was snapped up the moment it appeared on the streets.

Frank came home from work to find Jess reading it with tears in her eyes. He took it from her and spread it on the table, and they read it together.

'We've done well,' he said. 'Look at those headlines. *Too Hot for Raiders*. It was one of the German pilots said that. And here's another one. *English Too Good*. They're almost begging to be taken prisoner, look, this one even brought his hair-oil and shaving tackle with him!'

'And one of them was a boy of fifteen,' Jess said. 'Fifteen! That's not much older than our Rose. How can they send children like that to war?'

'Maybe he pretended to be older. Plenty of lads have done that.' Frank looked at the paper again. 'We shot down sixty-one planes. Sixty-one. They've lost over five hundred now. It can't go on much longer, Jess.'

'Why not? Last air-raid we had, you said it was only the beginning.' Jess shook her head. 'Look what they're doing to us. Have you heard about the Eye and Ear Hospital? Look, it says here, well, it doesn't say it was the Eye and Ear, they don't print the names, but everyone knows that's where it was, it says they were just starting a mastoid operation and they went on, right through the raid, even though it was hit. The nurses had to get the patients out to places of safety. Fancy having to drag people out of their hospital beds to go to a shelter! I mean, suppose someone was in traction.'

'They don't put you in traction for eyes and ears,' Frank pointed out, but Jess snapped at him uncharacteristically.

'It doesn't have to be the Eye and Ear gets bombed, does it! It could as easy be the Royal or St Mary's next time. All I'm saying is Hitler's got the whole of Europe now to build his planes in, he's not going to run out in the first five minutes.' She looked at Frank. 'He wants to invade us, doesn't he? He wants us under his heel along with the rest.'

Frank was silent for a moment. He wanted to offer some comfort, but could think of none. Jess was right – Portsmouth had taken a bad knock.

'Oh, Frank,' Jess said, and now the tears were on her cheeks. 'Look at this. That man, the one without any legs, you know, he used to be outside Woolworths selling matches, till it burned down in May. He's been killed. Sitting in the park in his wheelchair, he was, and got killed by flying fragments.' She laid down the paper. 'He lost his legs in the first war. I suppose he couldn't get into a shelter, not in a wheelchair.'

She stood by the gas stove, waiting for the kettle to boil, thinking of the man with no legs. What sort of a life had he had? Blown up in the first war, probably gassed as well for all she knew, scratching a living by sitting on a little wooden cart on the pavement outside Woolworths, selling matches. He hadn't been all that old, probably in his fifties. Just a young man when he lost his legs.

It wasn't only his legs he'd lost, either, she thought. Bert Shaw next door had told her he always bought matches from him and he'd spoken to him quite a few times. The man had told him he'd been engaged to be married when the Great War had broken out, but his sweetheart hadn't been able to face marrying a man with no legs. He'd had to find somewhere to live, a place in Charlotte Street, not much more than a storage room. It had a low washbasin and a lavatory and someone had fixed him up with an old stove to do his bit of cooking, and the other traders had given him some bits of old carpet to put on the stone floor and a few sticks of furniture, and that was about it. That was how he'd lived for the past twenty years or so.

'I can't stop thinking about that poor man,' Jess said, taking Frank's tea through to him. 'His legs, his dreams, his whole life, all just smashed to pieces. And what for? Just so he could crawl about like a beetle all those years and wait to be killed after all.'

'We've been through all this, Jess,' Frank said. 'We had to go in and help Poland. You know we did. Just like you had to go and help those evacuee kiddies, remember? You knew it wasn't right, what was happening to them, and we knew it wasn't right what Hitler was doing. We didn't have any choice.'

Maureen, who had been fast asleep in her pram in the front room, began to cry. Jess went in and picked her up. She brought her into the back room and sat at the table, holding her on her knee. Frank looked at her and frowned.

'It still don't seem right, you and her being in Portsmouth with all this bombing. I wish you'd go back out to Bridge End.'

'We've been through that, too. I won't leave you, Frank, and that's flat. Anyway, I'm not letting Ethel Glaister get her nose through the door again. I know what'd happen, I'd hardly be up the top of the street before she'd be in here with her perm and her smarmy ways and a bit of fruit cake for you to eat. She never has a word to say to me, but I've seen her when you're out in the garden, leaning on the fence and fluttering her eyelashes.'

'I don't give her any encouragement,' Frank protested, and Jess laughed.

'I know that! But that sort doesn't need encouragement. Thinks she's God's gift to mankind, that one does, and she's got worse since George went. I wonder if he knows how she carries on when he's away.'

'She doesn't carry on. Not really. I mean, I've never seen her *with* anyone, and nobody comes to the house.'

'Well, no, I don't mean she carries on in that sense – thinks too much of herself. But she'd like to think all the men are after her.' Jess sniffed. 'And the way she dresses up, you'd never think she had a husband in the Territorials.'

Frank smiled. He knew just what Jess meant, but it sounded funny all the same. He looked at the baby, who was chewing a crust Jess had given her, and reached out awkwardly to touch her cheek. It felt like a peach under his rough finger.

Frank was never entirely at ease with babies, not even his own. He liked the children better when they got old enough to talk to sensibly and to do things with. He liked showing the boys how to make things with wood or mend broken cups and such. But his life revolved around his family, all the same, and he would have died fighting if anyone had tried to harm them.

That's what we're doing, he thought. Fighting for our families. And if Hitler does invade us, I'll fight to the death for this little scrap, yes, and for the boys and Rose as well. And Jess. Especially for Jess.

They had been married for seventeen years and she had brought into his life the first real love he had ever known. It was not something he would give up easily.

CHAPTER SEVEN

Ethel Glaister put down her book and glanced restlessly about the room. She was fed up with being on her own. She wanted someone to talk to.

Ethel's older children, Joe and Carol, were out at work all day, and her husband George was away in the Army. And although Ethel was houseproud and liked to keep her home 'nice', her real pleasure lay in showing off her home to envious neighbours. Otherwise, she occupied herself with reading romantic novels or going to the cinema.

But it was nicer to have someone to go to the pictures with, so that you could talk about the film on the way home.

Ethel had no friends in the streets nearby. But she had noticed Kathy Simmons and her two little girls going up and down October Street and heard how they'd been bombed out. Kathy had come from Portchester Road, where the houses were a bit bigger than those in October Street and had bay windows, so she was obviously used to something better, and the girls might make nice friends for her Shirley.

She went out into the scullery, took off her blouse and had a wash at the sink. Upstairs, she put on her second-best blouse, the one with the frilly collar. Her best blouse had frills all the way down the front, but that was too much for an afternoon call. Her powder-blue jacket would be nice, though, and her grey skirt. A lot smarter than that old herringbone jacket and brown skirt Jess Budd always wore to the shops, and it would show Mrs Simmons that although April Grove might be a backstreet it was no slum.

Carefully, she polished her black high-heeled shoes, and minced across to the corner and over to number 16.

Kathy Simmons had been trying once again to rid the Anderson shelter of the smell of cats.

It had been hard work moving in. Nobody had thought to give the house a clean and Kathy, arriving from a home in which nothing had ever been out of place until Hitler got his hands on it, had found herself spending the first part of her five pounds on brooms and scrubbing brushes, just to get it fit to live in. The old lady didn't seem to have decorated for years, and the rooms were dark and dingy. There was no electricity, and only the two downstairs rooms and lean-to scullery were lit with gas. Upstairs, you had to use candles, and you had to take a candle with you to the outside lavatory. How romantic, she thought. That'd get Mike in the mood when he came home!

She had spent the morning scrubbing the scullery, and felt proud of her efforts. The walls were still brown, but at least it was a lighter shade of brown, and the old linoleum on the floor had turned out to be yellow. There were still a few stains she couldn't shift, but on the whole it looked much better. Almost cheerful, in fact. And although she'd felt tired from her efforts and knew she ought to rest in the afternoon, she'd been unable to forget the smell in the shelter, and determined to have another go at it. If they were going to have to keep on going down there, it might as well be as homely as it could be, and she didn't want to have to take her baby down there with it smelling the way it did.

Besides, she had found that it was only by keeping busy that she could keep the memories at bay. The siren wailing just as she was giving the girls their supper. The planes roaring overhead, the whistling of the bombs as they fell and the explosions all around. And then coming out of the shelter to find her home destroyed, with only a few fragments left whole. And Muriel's doll like a baby amongst the rubble, its face smashed, its body torn and broken. A baby, abandoned to the fury of the enemy . . .

Only constant work, a determined effort to put the

memories behind her and a smile on her face, could keep such horrors out of her mind.

She gave the shelter another thorough scrub and had come back into the house for more hot water when she heard the doorbell ring.

Drat! She stood for a moment, hesitating, the kettle in her hand. Could she ignore it? No, better not. The girls had gone out to have some lessons in a house up in Deniston Street, and it might be something to do with them. She'd never forgive herself if anything had happened to them and she'd refused to answer the door.

She set the kettle back on the stove. It was still whistling gently as she answered the door and found Ethel Glaister standing on the step.

For a moment or two, she thought that it must be to do with the girls. Or perhaps with the house in Portchester Street. The woman standing on her step was too smart to be anything but an official of some sort. Maybe she was from the Assistance Board, come to see what Kathy had spent the five pounds on. Or perhaps – her mind flicked to Mike. Had anything happened to his ship? The baby inside her gave a sudden kick and she covered it with her hand as if to protect it from shock.

Ethel Glaister stared at Kathy, her eyes moving from the dirty working skirt to the old blouse which was covered by what looked like a man's shirt. She looked doubtfully along the dingy passage. Mrs Simmons had seemed a clean, respectable sort of woman in the street, but this looked no better than a slum after all!

'I'm sorry,' she said, backing away. 'Perhaps you're too busy, I'll come back another day.'

Kathy smiled. Now that the first surprise had passed, she was beginning to recognise her visitor. She lived nearby, somewhere in April Grove. Kathy had seen her walking up and down the street, always smartly dressed, her yellow hair waved and her face made up. Perhaps she'd come to collect for something, war savings, perhaps, or another Spitfire fund. In any case, it would be nice to have someone to talk to for a bit.

'It's all right,' she said. 'I'd nearly finished. To tell the truth, I shouldn't have been doing it anyway. I'm supposed to put my feet up in the afternoons, but I couldn't put up with the stink any longer . . . Did you want something?'

Ethel cast a nervous glance along the passage and then up and down the street, as if afraid to be seen. 'No – oh no,' she said hastily. 'I just called, you know, out of friendliness. You being new here, as it were. I thought you might be pleased to meet one of your neighbours.'

'That's nice of you,' Kathy said cheerfully. 'Come in and have a cup of tea.'

She brushed a hand down her front and grimaced. 'Sorry I'm in such a state. I've been scrubbing out the Anderson. You wouldn't believe the state it was in, I reckon every cat in the street's had a pee in there. Cost me a fortune in Dettol, it has.'

Ethel opened her mouth to protest but Kathy was already disappearing into the back room. Distastefully, she followed, trying not to let her powder-blue jacket brush against the walls. It looked as if they could do with a scrub too, she thought, but it was clear that young Mrs Simmons had been doing her best with the back room and scullery, which both smelt strongly of yellow soap.

All the same, she was swiftly revising her ideas about making a friend of the new neighbour. And as for letting her Shirley come over here to play . . .

'Sit down.' Kathy waved at the sagging armchair. 'Not much of a place, is it, but I'm thankful for anything, I can tell you. Goodness knows where the furniture came from – I stand it out in the back yard when the sun's shining and give it a good beating, you'd be surprised what comes out! Still, it's better than nothing.' She went out into the scullery and Ethel could hear her putting tea into the pot and pouring in boiling water.

'Did you lose everything?' Ethel asked. She moved away from the armchair and perched on the edge of an old kitchen chair, hoping that Mrs Simmons had at least wiped off the grime.

'The lot. Everything we owned. Well, except for a few bits

and bobs that we managed to salvage next day. The place just collapsed, you see, got a direct hit.' Kathy rattled cups and saucers together. 'Sorry I can't offer you sugar, I keep it for the kids. They need it, poor little mites.' She came into the room with two cups of tea and handed one to Ethel. 'People don't realise that kids lose everything too, in air-raids. All their clothes, their toys and books, all their little bits and pieces. You don't get any money to replace them. My Muriel had a baby doll, thought the world of it she did, and she'd just put it in its little cradle when the siren went. I wouldn't let her go back for it and it got smashed to smithereens.' Her eyes filled with tears. 'I'll never really forgive myself for that. We found it, you see, its face all broken. Muriel cries for it every night.'

'Better a doll than her, though,' Ethel said. 'Dolls don't matter. What about your hubby, then? Someone told me he's at sea.'

'That's right, in the Merchant Navy.' Deliberately, Kathy forced her mind away from Muriel's broken doll. It haunted her dreams too. It had looked so much like a baby . . . 'He doesn't get home much now. I was hoping he'd be around when the baby's born.' Unconsciously, she caressed her rounded stomach. 'I don't suppose he will, though.'

'There's not many men round here now,' Ethel remarked. 'Only Frank Budd and Tommy Vickers and people like that who're too old to be called up. My George is in the Army, of course. He went straightaway, he was in the Territorials, you see, and they had to report for duty the minute war was declared.' She touched her hair. 'Well, we were on holiday in Devonshire when it was actually declared but naturally we came home at once. We knew our duty.'

Kathy wasn't quite sure what to say. She picked up her cup and said, 'It seems quite nice round here. Quiet.'

'Well, it isn't bad, I suppose,' Ethel said grudgingly. 'Of course, if it hadn't been for the war, we'd have moved. I want a three-bedroomed house with a proper bathroom. Semi-detached, you know. And with George doing so well at his job, we'd have been able to afford it. But now that all this has started –' She shrugged, looking irritated. 'I told him, there wasn't any need for him to go dashing off, but he would go and now we're on Army pay, and *that's* not much, I can tell you!'

Her voice had taken on a querulous note. She sipped her tea, holding her little finger out daintily. Kathy looked at her, at the powder-blue jacket and the frilly blouse and the carefully waved golden hair. What was she doing here? Why had she come?

'You've got two little girls, haven't you?' Ethel said. 'I see you've not sent them away, then.'

'No, I'd rather we were all together. And I want to be in Pompey in case Mike comes home unexpectedly.' Kathy spoke with a touch of defiance in her tone. People treated you like a bad mother, not sending your children to the country. But from some of the stories she'd heard about evacuees, it sounded as if they had a worse time out there than if they'd stayed in the city. She hated to think of Stella and Muriel, far from home, with strangers who didn't understand or care about them. Better here. And hadn't she already proved that if you got into a shelter in time, you were safe?

'I'm thinking of sending my Shirley to Canada,' Ethel said. 'You don't know who they're mixing with out in these villages, do you? They're taking a whole shipload of kiddies to Canada on a liner. I think it'll be a good experience for her.'

Kathy stared at her. Canada! It was on the other side of the world. And they might be gone for years. Why, they'd be strangers when they came back.

'Of course, you'll be used to something better than this,' Ethel remarked, glancing disparagingly round the bare little room. 'I mean, the houses in Portchester Street are quite a bit bigger, aren't they? You must miss it, coming to a place like this.'

'It's no good thinking like that. I'm just glad to have a house. And I can soon get it looking nice, once I get hold of a pot of paint and a bit of wallpaper. And then I can ask people in without apologising for the state of it!' She laughed.

'Oh, I'd be careful who you asked in,' Ethel said quickly. 'I mean, some of the people round here are very nice – in their way – but there are a few I wouldn't want across *my* doorstep, I can tell you.'

'Well, I daresay I'll soon find out who suits me,' Kathy said. 'Jess Budd's nice.'

'Oh, Jess is all right, if you like that type of person,' Ethel said dismissively. 'Rather a mousy little woman, I've never been able to see what her husband sees in her, myself. Now *there's* a fine figure of a man, Frank Budd, you'll have seen him walking home from work, I daresay. A big, tall man. He works in the Dockyard. And there's the Shaws, in number 13, on the other side of the Budds, I don't have much to do with them. Peggy Shaw and Jess Budd are very thick. And Vi Redding, next door to Mrs Shaw, well, the less said about *her* the better. Have you seen the state of her front step? But the person you really want to be careful of is Mrs Kinch – Granny Kinch, they call her. She sits on a chair at her front door all day, keeping an eye on everything that goes on. Used to stand there for hours, till her varicose veins got the better of her.'

'I've seen her. She gave the girls some toffees one day.'

'Oh yes, she does that, always likes to get the kiddies round her. A real nosy old so-and-so, she is. I wouldn't let mine get round her door. And you know what they say about Nancy, of course.'

Kathy shook her head. 'Nancy?'

'Nancy Baxter, so-called. Her daughter. Supposed to be married to some high-up, only sometimes they say he's a soldier, sometimes he's in the Navy, they don't seem to be too sure themselves, and you know what *that* means. Anyway, whatever he is – if he exists at all, which I take leave to doubt – you never see him down April Grove, though you might see plenty of other men.'

Kathy gazed at her. There was a peculiar, avid excitement in Ethel's eyes and now and then she licked her thin lips. I don't want to hear this, she thought. This is what she came for, to pass on her own spiteful gossip. I wish she'd go.

But Ethel was now into her stride. She leaned forward and spoke in an exaggeratedly low whisper, mouthing the words as if they might be overheard. Kathy drew back a little, feeling the same distaste as Ethel had felt as she walked along the dingy passage. She had the same senstion of not wanting her clothes to brush against the other woman, of not wanting to be contaminated.

'. . . a *tart*,' Ethel mouthed. 'Ever since they came here . . . bringing sailors back from the pub . . . supposed to be working in a hotel at nights. Hotel! We all know what *that* means . . . disgusting, it is . . . got a baby now, and not a clue who its father is, I'll be bound. . . And that Micky, just left to run wild . . . ought to be a law . . . '

Her whisper slunk about the room like a dank miasma, feeling its way into corners, hanging in the air. It was like a web, Kathy thought, a dirty cobweb that clung to her face and that she wanted to brush away.

'I'm sorry,' she said, getting up. 'I'll have to go soon. The girls are having lessons up Deniston Street and I'll have to go and fetch them.'

'I'll go with you,' Ethel offered. 'I'd like a nice walk. And we can arrange for you to come over to me one afternoon. Or the pictures. We could go to the pictures together. Henry Fonda's on at the Odeon this week, in *The Grapes of Wrath*, we could go and see that. Or there's Bing Crosby at the Rex. What d'you fancy?'

'I don't think I'll be able to go to the pictures,' Kathy said shortly. 'I don't have time. And it's uncomfortable sitting in the seats, the way I am.'

'Oh, well, yes, I suppose it is. Well, shopping, then. We could go shopping down North End. Or Commercial Road. C&A are advertising some lovely new coats for autumn, all in the newest colours. There's a nice alpaca for four and a half guineas. I'm looking for a new coat, before they put clothes on ration – they're talking about it, you know. You could help me choose.'

'No, thanks,' Kathy said. 'And I'll have to get ready to go now. I can't go up to fetch the kids looking like this. She ushered Ethel to the door. 'It was nice of you to come. I daresay I'll see you in the street, to say hello.'

'Oh,' Ethel began as she was pushed gently out on to the step again. 'But we haven't arranged –' There was a decisive click and she turned in astonishment to find the door closed firmly behind her. 'But – but –' She stared at it for a moment, as if expecting it to open again and Kathy appear, all smiles, in her best clothes, but there was silence from within. And when she rattled at the letter-box and pushed it open to peer inside, there was no sign that there was anyone at home at all.

'*Well!*' Ethel exclaimed. 'Well, did you ever see anything so *rude*! And after I'd been so *nice* to her, too. Telling her things, inviting her to tea, suggesting she might like to come to the pictures with me or do some shopping!' She turned and saw Granny Kinch sitting in her doorway, watching her with beady black eyes. Oh, it was just too much!

With a toss of her head, she marched away up October Street. Where she was going, she had no idea, but she wasn't going to walk past Granny Kinch and give her the satisfaction of knowing she'd been as good as turned out of number 16.

And she certainly wouldn't be calling on Kathy Simmons again. Say hello in the street? she thought furiously. Why, I wouldn't say hello to her in my *grave*!

For boys like Micky Baxter, Jimmy Cross and Cyril Nash, the raids were a huge adventure. Out in the streets from early morning until dark, they seldom went into a shelter when the siren sounded. Instead, they crouched beside a wall, gazing up at the sky, watching the planes zoom low over the city and cheering whenever one was shot down.

'Dirty Jerry bastards,' Micky said with relish as they watched a Heinkel spinning out of control into Langstone Harbour. It seemed to screw itself a hole in the water with its nose and a great spray of flame and water rose like a volcanic eruption into the air. 'Serves 'im right. I 'ope 'e was burnt alive.'

'Well, he's dead anyway.' They flinched and shut their eyes as a bomb fell a few streets away. The crash ricocheted around them. 'Coo, look at that smoke. Once they're gone we'll go an' look for souvenirs again, shall we?'

'Souvenirs!' Micky sneered. 'We can get better'n that. Let's go round the shops. You know people don't lock up proper when the siren goes. We can get some good stuff.'

Jimmy and Cyril looked at each other. Micky was already on probation for walking into a jeweller's shop brandishing a gun left over from the last war. Jimmy's dad said he'd been lucky not to get sent to Borstal.

'Come on,' Micky urged. 'Who's going to see us? They're all down the shelters like rabbits in a burrow. I bet that wireless shop along Copnor Road's open. He's got some good torches in there.' He set off, keeping close to the wall as the bombs rained down on the city.

One of Cyril's dreams was to own a really good torch. A black rubber one. They could go out at night then – it was all right as long as you kept out of the air-raid warden's way. And explore some more of the cellars they'd found in bombed houses.

They came to the wireless shop. To their disgust, the door was locked. Cyril gazed through the window and saw that there were indeed two rubber torches on display.

'I bet if you broke the window nobody'd hear us,' he said. 'Not with all this noise going on.' The bombs were exploding further down in the city, but the noise reverberated around the streets. 'Anyway, they'd just think it was blast.'

Jimmy hesitated, but Micky nodded eagerly.

'You're right. We don't have to worry about locks. Come on.' He picked up a stone, glanced quickly up and down the street, and smashed it against the glass. The dusty display inside was showered with fragments, and Cyril reached through and grabbed one of the torches.

'It's a smasher.' He moved the switch. 'Shit! There's no batteries.'

Micky had his hand on the other torch, but as he closed his fingers around it they heard a yell from the street and turned sharply. Micky, jerking his hand out of the broken window, gave a yelp of pain.

'Oy! You boys! What you up to?' An air-raid warden was advancing on them, waving threateningly. 'You oughter be in the shelter.'

'Run,' Micky muttered, but the other two were already away. Micky raced after them and they dodged round a corner and into the maze of alleyways that ran between the side streets. Half scared, half giggling, they came to a halt against a garden wall, crouching as a bomb exploded closer at hand.

'Fat old fool,' Micky jeered. 'He'll never catch us.'

'He might know us, though,' Jimmy said a little anxiously.

'Nah. He's not from round our street. So long as we don't go down that way for a bit. Anyway, they got more to think about than a broken window.' He gazed up at the sky, at the aircraft still swooping overhead, some German, some British. He could see gunfire spattering against the sides of the planes, the flare as shells burst in the air. Flames and smoke were rising from several places in Portsmouth, and the sound of explosions and the rattle of guns were deafening.

'Smashing,' he breathed, thinking scornfully of all the people who were cowering in their shelters and missing the glory of it all. 'Smashing . . .'

The Germans had named Tuesday, 13 August, *Adlertag*. It meant Eagle Day and was to have been the day when the Luftwaffe would blow the RAF from the skies and the invasion begin. But the British had other ideas.

For the rest of the week, the sirens sounded daily, sometimes more than once, as wave after wave of German bombers flew across the sky. Bad weather gave some respite on Wednesday, but there were still thirty-one German planes reported destroyed in Saturday's *Evening News*, and the resumption of heavy bombing on Thursday brought the Germans a hundred and eighty losses. The total for the week was estimated at four hundred and ninety-two, bringing the total for the war so far at almost a thousand.

A thousand planes, and each with two or three young men inside, either killed or captured. Several came down in fields north of Portsdown Hill, and there were photographs in the paper showing pub landlords or farmers who had been first on the scene, grinning over their prize.

The following week the newspapers carried a report of Mr Churchill's speech in the House of Commons. Standing with his head slightly lowered, looking as always like a bull about to charge, he had praised the RAF for its heroism.

'*The gratitude of every home in our island . . . goes out to the British airmen who are turning the tide of the war,*' he declared, his mellifluous tones rolling around the chamber. '*Never in the field of human conflict was so much owed by so many to so few. All hearts go out to the fighter pilots whose brilliant actions we see with our own eyes, day after day . . . . Our people are united and resolved as they have never been before. Death and ruin have become small things, compared with shame and defeat.'*

Four days later, the raiders came again. It was a Saturday afternoon and Betty Chapman and her sister Olive had decided to go to the pictures with the two Shaw sisters. Robert Preston and Dorothy Lamour were in *Typhoon* at the Odeon and Diane Shaw, who was just sixteen, declared herself to be in love with Robert Preston.

'I've seen it twice already,' she said as the four girls walked down Stubbington Avenue together. 'He's gorgeous! I wish I could meet him.'

'He'd never even look at you,' Gladys told her with sisterly bluntness. 'I like Dorothy Lamour, I think she's really glamorous. I reckon I could look a bit like her, if I did my hair the same way.'

'Go on,' Diane said, getting her own back, 'you've been trying to look like Norma Shearer for the past twelve months. I haven't noticed it's got you any more boyfriends.'

'Who says I want boyfriends?' Gladys tossed her head. 'I can get plenty, if I want them. I just haven't fancied anyone lately. Too much bother.'

'I bet she wouldn't say that if your brother was home on leave,' Diane said to Betty, and Gladys blushed.

'Shut up, Di. Colin and me are just friends.'

'Is that why you write to him practically every day?'

'I don't! Not every day. But a boy wants a bit of news from home when he's away at sea. It doesn't mean anything.'

Betty gave Gladys's arm a squeeze. She knew that Gladys had been carrying a torch for Colin for the past couple of years. But just writing to a boy didn't have to mean you were his girlfriend. Didn't she write regularly to Gladys's brother Bob, even though she was secretly engaged to Graham?

'Are you looking forward to being a Land Girl?' Gladys asked her now.

Betty nodded. 'I think it'll be smashing. Specially in this

weather. Just imagine being out in the fields, hay-making, while all the rest of you are slaving away in offices and shops.'

'And just imagine it in freezing rain, when all the rest of us are cosy and warm indoors,' Olive said. 'Rather you than me!'

'Well, at least you'll be away from the bombs,' Diane observed. 'I'm getting fed up with these raids. Down the shelter half the time – boring.'

'Boring! I'm too scared to be bored,' Olive said. 'It makes me shudder every time I hear that awful siren, the noise seems to go right down my back. And listening to the planes coming over, and the bombs, ugh, it's horrible.'

'Well, let's forget the war for this afternoon.' They were almost at the cinema now, and Gladys began to fish in her bag for money. 'Which seats shall we go in?'

'Upstairs,' Betty suggested, but Diane shook her head.

'I haven't got enough money. It's the ninepennies for me.'

They bought their tickets and went in. The lights had not yet been lowered and they stood for a moment by the first few rows of seats, debating which to go into. The audience was small – there would be more at the evening show – and there was plenty of room.

'Go on, our Di,' Gladys urged. 'Make up your mind, they'll be starting any minute.'

Diane led the way into the fourth row and immediately passed round a bag of toffees. Chewing comfortably, the four girls looked up at the screen and sighed in happy anticipation as the heavy curtains changed colour under the dimming lights and then slowly drew apart.

The advertisements came first, then the News. They watched as a clipped voice described the scenes that were being shown – news of the war, with pictures of soldiers setting up camp, grinning and waving at the camera, smiling and busy women setting up canteens, evacuated children playing in fields. There were also a few shots of soldiers who had come back from Dunkirk in June, looking tired but cheerful. It was extolled as a victorious rescue.

'Victorious!' Olive muttered. 'We were chased off the beaches, that's what. I wish they wouldn't show this. I came here to forget about the war for a couple of hours.'

The News was over at last and the big film began. Diane passed her toffees along again and they settled down to enjoy the story. Once or twice Gladys touched her hair, imagining it done the way Dorothy Lamour did hers, and Diane dreamed that she was in Robert Preston's arms. Olive wondered if Derek might get some leave soon, the 698 had been moved to Wiltshire, to stand by when repairs were needed to the runways at Boscombe Down, and Betty thought about Graham and wondered yet again if she should have let him make love to her that last night. If Mum hadn't insisted on playing cards all evening, she might easily have done so. But then if she had, she might have been sitting here now worrying about a baby, and that was something she could do without.

There was Bob Shaw too. Olive told her she was wrong to write to another boy when she was going steady with Graham, but she and Bob had known each other all their lives, they'd played in the street together and learned to swim in Langstone Harbour. It didn't do any harm to write to him, surely, but did it mean she wasn't really in love with Graham after all?

The film continued. Dorothy Lamour swayed seductively on screen and was adored by every man in the audience. The women sighed over Robert Preston and for a little while the war was, indeed, forgotten.

And then, at just twenty minutes past four, the siren began to sound.

There was a general groan. People began to get up, hesitated, half sat down again. A few scrambled along to the ends of the rows of seats and hurried up the aisle. On screen, Dorothy Lamour and Robert Preston drifted into each other's arms and the four girls looked at each other.

'I suppose we ought to go,' Olive said reluctantly.

'Oh, bother it!' Diane had dropped her toffees. She bent and felt about on the floor. 'Well, *I'm* not going. We're just getting to the best bit.'

'But the bombs –'

'They won't be coming up here. It's the Dockyard they're aiming at. Look, they haven't stopped showing the film, have they? So they can't think it's anything much.'

The film stopped suddenly and the lights came on. They looked at each other again and Olive started to get to her feet.

'Wait a minute.' Betty grabbed her arm. 'Someone's coming on the stage.'

Fascinated and half afraid, they watched. Perhaps the Germans had actually invaded. Perhaps this *was* a German, come to tell them what to do. Doubtfully, Betty wondered if an invading German would be likely to be dressed in a dark suit, and then realised that it was the cinema manager. She stifled a nervous giggle.

'I'm very sorry, ladies and gentlemen. Hitler's signature tune is on the air again.' There was a ripple of laughter from the audience. 'You are of course free to leave if you wish to, but the show is going on and you're welcome to stay with us.' He paused, then added, 'Good luck, and thank you for coming this afternoon.'

There was a buzz of chatter. Everyone was asking each other the same question – shall we go or shall we stay? The wail of the siren had died away again and nothing could be heard outside. Perhaps Diane was right, Betty thought, and it was going to be just another false alarm.

'I'm staying too,' she said suddenly. 'This is my last chance to come to the pictures here. I'm not letting Hitler spoil it for me.'

The two older girls hesitated. Gladys shrugged. 'Might as well. If we went outside now we'd never get into a shelter anyway. There was hundreds of people shopping. I reckon we're as safe here as anywhere else.'

'That's right,' Olive agreed. 'And if they're going to keep the film going, I think we *ought* to stay. That'll show Hitler we're not afraid of him. *I'm* not going to run down a hole like a rabbit diving down its burrow just because he starts playing his music.'

The others laughed. The film had started again and Dorothy Lamour and Robert Preston were now involved in the typhoon of the title. The wind howled and shrieked from the screen, and the building suddenly shook with the crash of thunder.

'That was guns!' Olive gasped, and grabbed at Betty's hand.

They could hear the throb of the planes now, and their roar as they passed above. There was an explosion somewhere close by and a splintering sound from overhead. The audience looked up at the darkened roof and saw gaps of daylight appear. As one person, they scrambled towards the sides of the cinema and crouched down as the gaps widened and shrapnel rained down on to the seats they had just vacated.

'Oh, my God,' Gladys gasped. 'They're bombing us, Olive – Betty – they're bombing *us*!'

Another explosion sounded from the car park outside, and the screen trembled and shook. Their laughter forgotten, the girls huddled together, staring with terrified eyes at the film, as if by watching the tumult on the screen they could somehow reduce the reality of what was happening.

'We ought to have gone,' Olive whispered. 'We ought to have got into a shelter.'

'We'd never have made it.' Betty remembered the sight of the enemy flying like a black cloud overhead, as she had stood on Mrs Marsh's garden path. 'We'd have been caught out in the street.'

'And if this place gets hit we'll be buried alive. I'd rather take my chance out in the open.'

But the other girls shook their heads. They knew there was no escape now. Outside, they would be in even more danger than in here. They just had to sit it out and hope that the cinema would make a good shelter.

'Well, at least we can see the end of the film,' Diane observed as Preston and Lamour melted into an embrace. 'I wanted to see him kiss her.'

A bubble of hysterical giggles rose into Betty's throat and she heard Gladys snort. The cinema rocked again, and the music was drowned by a shattering thud. The audience was now pressed into a tight crowd at each side of the auditorium, but the film kept running and all eyes were fixed on the screen.

'I wish we'd never come,' Olive moaned, covering her head

with her arms. Betty squeezed her shoulders.

'It doesn't matter where you are. You know what they say – if a bomb's got your name on it, it'll find you. Look – the picture's finished. At least we saw it all!'

Olive smiled weakly. The explosions seemed to have stopped now and she lifted her head and watched the last few shots. The music swelled and throbbed through the cinema and the last scene faded. There was a moment of silence.

The aircraft noise had died away. It was only five minutes since the first thunderous crash. The girls looked at each other uncertainly. They looked at the holes in the roof, at the fragments of shrapnel and the torn seats. Was it safe anywhere?

'Maybe it wasn't so bad after all,' Betty said hopefully. 'Well, we might as well see the programme to the end.'

'Yes, we might,' Gladys said. 'D'you know what the little film's called?'

They shook their heads. And then the title came up on the screen and everyone in the cinema laughed.

'*Though Shalt Not Kill . . .*'

It seemed funny when they were inside the cinema, with the manager declaring that the show must go on and a spirit of defiant bravado holding them together. It was less funny when they came out to bright sunshine and saw a crater in the car park, less funny when they realised that the houses behind the cinema had been demolished, not funny at all when they heard that the Princes Theatre in Lake Road had received a direct hit and eight people been killed. The thousand-pound bomb had crashed through the roof and exploded high above the auditorium, completely wrecking the interior and blowing seats out through the roof into the street.

'That could have been you,' Annie scolded her daughters when they arrived home. 'It's all very well saying Hitler's not going to stop you enjoying yourselves – he *can* stop you. He can stop you living. Next time, get yourselves into a shelter.'

'But I don't suppose we could have done,' Betty argued. 'The shops were full of people – it was really busy down North End. The shelters would have been full before we got anywhere near them. Anyway, the bombs started almost as soon as the siren had gone off, we wouldn't have had time.'

Annie sighed. She knew this was true – she'd barely got into her own shelter when the planes had come overhead. And the whole thing had been over in five minutes.

Gladys Shaw had refused to hurry home with the other girls. Instead, she stopped to give a hand in the street behind the cinema. People had been killed and injured there and, like Frank Budd, she had been shocked and sickened by sights she hadn't dreamed of.

She saw an old man sitting on the kerb, his arms folded over his head as he rocked to and fro. He was crying, his mouth loose and slobbery, his scant grey hair matted with blood. Gladys crouched down beside him, taking out her handkerchief to wipe gently at his head. He must have a very nasty cut.

'No,' he said, 'it ain't me what got hurt. That's my Edie's blood, that is.' He looked at Gladys, his faded eyes as bewildered as a child's. 'We was just having a cup of tea when the siren went, and now she's dead. She's still in there, all crumpled up in her chair.' Gladys followed his gaze to a small house. People were moving about inside, shifting debris, trying to ease something out from under a fallen beam. 'It ain't no good,' he said with the flatness of despair. 'She went straightaway, they might as well leave her at rest.' He told Gladys this through hiccuping sobs, and then he told her again, and a third time when a stout woman in a tweed jacket brought him a mug of tea. He was still repeating it when they led him gently away.

There had been a children's tea-party in the house next door. It had been to celebrate little Doreen's seventh birthday, from the card Gladys found lying in the middle of the littered road outside. She helped one of the First Aid workers gather the survivors together and put her arms round them while they had cuts and bruises washed and bandaged. Some of them were taken to hospital in an ambulance. She didn't ask how many had been killed, nor whether one of them was Doreen herself.

She watched the ambulances drive away and turned back

to see what else she could do. A woman was sobbing in a shattered doorway across the street. Gladys stepped off the pavement to go to her and felt something soft against her foot. She looked down, and felt the gorge rise in her throat.

It was a baby, no more than three or four weeks old. The tiny body had been split like a paper bag. It lay soaking in its own blood, its contents spilling out like those of a carelessly wrapped parcel.

Gladys stared at it. It shifted suddenly, horrifyingly, then blurred before her eyes. Her ears roared and she shook her head and turned away, her hands over her mouth. As she swayed, arms caught and held her, and the First Aider she had been helping spoke in her ear.

'Come and have a cuppa,' she said. 'You're not used to it, are you?'

'Who is?' Gladys asked, sitting down on a broken bit of wall. 'Have *you* ever seen things like that before?'

The woman shrugged. 'I was a nurse. I worked in Casualty. There's plenty happens in street accidents and such . . . But it's never easy to take, specially not with kiddies.' She handed Gladys a mug of tea. 'Sip that, it's good and sweet, it'll make you feel better.' The ambulances were beginning to return, and people were searching under the rubble for more survivors. 'Get off home if you like. I'll have to stay and help.'

'I'll stay too.' Gladys gulped down the hot liquid. 'But I don't know that I'm much help. I don't know any First Aid or anything.'

It didn't seem to matter. There was still plenty to do, helping shift debris and giving what comfort she could to the people they did manage to dig out, some of them miraculously unhurt. But it was clear to Gladys that she could have been a lot more help, and by the time she reached home at last, she had made up her mind what to do.

'I'm coming to Red Cross classes with you,' she told her mother as she sank into a chair with a cup of tea. 'I ought to have done it before. And I'm going to learn to drive.'

'Drive?' Peggy echoed. 'What, drive a car, you mean?'

'Well, I'm not going to drive a train,' Gladys said with a weary attempt at humour.

'But what will you drive? I mean, you're not thinking of going on the buses, are you? Your dad'll never –'

'I don't know what I'll do. Nobody knows what they'll have to do in this war.' Glady set down the empty cup and dragged herself out of the chair. She felt dirty and dog-tired and would have liked nothing better than to sink into a hot bath. But that meant getting in the tin bath from the yard and turning on the geyser to fill it up, and then dragging it out again, and she didn't have the energy. Besides, the family had had their weekly bathing session last night. 'I just think driving'll be a useful thing to be able to do. Oh, I'm so *tired*.' It seemed a lifetime since she and the others had been sitting in the cinema watching Robert Preston.

'You have a good wash, love.' Peggy had been out during the raid too, and was almost as weary as her daughter, but she recognised the signs of shock and knew that Gladys needed comfort and warmth. 'I'll heat you up some of that pea soup that was left over from dinner. And then I reckon you'd be best off to get to bed early.'

Early? To Gladys, it felt as if the day had lasted for ever. She went out into the scullery, took off her top clothes and ran some hot water into the enamel bowl. She stared at it and then, very slowly, washed herself.

The pictures of the typhoon that had seemed so dramatic on screen had faded from her mind. Instead, all she could see were an old man sitting on the pavement, a child's birthday card fluttering in a shattered street and a baby's body lying in the gutter.

I've got to do something about it, she thought. I've got to do my bit.

CHAPTER EIGHT

As soon as the Chapmans had finished their Sunday lunch of roast lamb – a smaller joint than they were used to, but Annie refused to lower her standards and have sausages instead – Betty set out to visit Graham's parents in Gosport.

Charlie and Elsie Philpotts lived about a mile from the harbour. Betty caught a bus and got off by the Gipsy Queen, then walked up Carnarvon Road. There were several short cul-de-sacs running off the road on both sides, and the Philpotts' lived in one of these. Charlie was pruning roses in his front garden when Betty arrived. He looked up at the sound of her voice and straightened his thin body, rubbing the small of his back with one hand.

'Every picture tells a story . . . Come over to see the missus, have you? She's somewhere indoors, or else out the back.' He called out in his dry, sandpapery voice, 'Elsie! We've got a visitor.'

Elsie Philpotts appeared, big and blowsy, her mauve satin blouse already parting company with her tight green skirt. Her ginger hair had recently been permed, and clustered round her head in curls so tight they seemed afraid to leave go of each other. She had no stockings on, but had painted her legs with something brown and streaky. On her feet, she wore pink slippers.

'Betty! Well, this is nice.' She enveloped Betty in a hug. It was like being assaulted by two feather pillows. 'Come over to see us on your last day, have you? I call that really nice, don't you, Charlie?'

Her husband blinked at her. His blue eyes always looked

half dreamy, as if he was living in another world. 'What d'you mean, her last day? She's not being took off to prison, is she?'

Elsie Philpotts let out a shriek of laughter.

'Took off to prison! What an idea! As if our Betty would do anything to be sent to prison for. *You* know what she's doing, Charlie. I told you. Going for a Land Girl, she is, milking cows and feeding chickens and all that.' She regarded Betty fondly. 'Just think, this time next week you'll be a farmer's girl. Think you're going to like it?'

'I hope so,' Betty said, and Elsie dug her in the ribs with a surprisingly sharp elbow and gave another chortle.

'You'll have to watch out for the farmer, mind! I know what these country bumpkins are like when they get behind a haystack. Eh, Charlie?'

'You'd know more about that than me,' he responded dryly. 'I never went out in the country as much as you did.'

'Well, I had an auntie out at Titchfield, didn't I. I used to go over on me bike,' she told Betty. 'My cousin Jean and me, we used to go all over the place. Oh, we had a few games, I'll tell you. But not with Charlie listening, eh?' She squawked and dug Betty in the ribs again. 'Still, *you* won't be getting up to no hanky-panky, not with Graham to think about.'

'No.' Not much chance of that, Betty thought, with all the young men being called up anyway. There would be nothing but old men left, same as in the towns. But Mrs Philpotts was right, she wouldn't let Graham down any more than he'd be unfaithful to her.

All the same, it didn't mean she couldn't have other friends. Same as she kept on writing to Bob, just as a friend. You couldn't shut yourself away from everything, just because you had a boyfriend in the Navy.

'Here, come and talk to me while I put the kettle on,' Elsie said. 'We'll take a cup of tea out in the back garden and you can tell me all about the Land Army. Have you got your uniform yet? It's trousers, innit? What do your mum and dad think of that, then?'

They went into the house, along the passage with its dark red anaglypta walls and Charlie's bike, and through to the kitchen. It was smallish and distempered in cream, with green woodwork and a green oilcloth on the table. An Ascot water heater was fixed to the wall with a long tap over the sink. Washing-up was piled on the wooden drainer, and there was a smell of cabbage.

'Sunday dinner,' Elsie said cheerfully, opening the back door to put a plate of scraps into the meatsafe just outside. 'We used to have enough meat left over to have it cold on Monday and a nice shepherd's pie on Tuesday. Now we're lucky if we got enough to give the cat a few scraps. Still, Charlie says it won't do me no harm to starve off a bit of me fat!' She laughed and her bosom shook. 'I tell him I'll need it in the winter, the way things are going I won't be able to get a new winter coat. They're talking about rationing clothes, did you know that? Clothes! They'll be rationing fresh air next.'

She filled the kettle and set it on the gas stove. Betty described her uniform and Elsie listened, raising her eyebrows, nodding and pursing her lips at all the right moments.

'I'm doing war work too,' she said. 'I've joined the WVS. Women's Voluntary Service, that is. I'm helping with canteens for people who've been bombed out of their homes.' She shook her head. 'You heard what happened over here the other day? We had fifty of the poor sods down in the Central School. Nowhere to go, no money, lost everything, they had. Well, we'd got crockery and stuff together, and food, and we were going to give 'em a hot meal. They've got good kitchens at the Central School, they used to cook the dinners for the kiddies at Leesland as well. And do you know what?' Her chins quivered with indignation. 'That old so-and-so in charge wouldn't let us cook it! There was a proper up-and-downer about it, I can tell you. I thought there was going to be a riot. Well –' she grinned suddenly '– I *hoped* there'd be a riot. Mean old skinflint, he wanted lynching.'

'What happened?' Betty asked. She knew that there had been several people made homeless by the raids on Gosport. What had it been like for them, their homes destroyed and then refused a hot dinner?

'Oh, in the end he said we could give it to the kids. Well, that was something, but what were their poor mums and dads to do, starve? So Mrs Green, she went down to the Town Hall and the Town Clerk himself came up the school and told him off proper. And he said in future we're to give them a good hot dinner whenever we want to, and never mind the high-and-mighty Public Assistance Officer.' She snorted. 'Public Assistance! Public Interference, that's what I call him.'

The kettle boiled and she made the tea, collected a bottle of milk from the safe and carried them out into the garden, leaving Betty to follow with an assortment of cups and saucers.

'We don't have a matching teaset in the house,' Elsie said, setting the tea down on a rickety table. 'It's not that we've never had one – we've had half a dozen. I just can't keep them, somehow, they break to bits in my hands. Mostly it's when I'm washing up – Charlie reckons I'm too clumsy, but I think it's the hot water.' The milk bottle tipped over and Betty caught it just before it spilled. 'But you can't get the grease off things if you don't use it really hot, can you?'

She took the milk bottle and slopped milk into the three cups. Tea followed, making little brown trails between the cups as she poured, and then she lifted her voice.

'Char-*lie*! Tea up. Sit yourself down, Betty, love, and tell me how you've got on in the raids over there. Haven't they been terrible! I heard there's been Andersons just blown apart, and trench shelters collapsed. And didn't one get a direct hit?'

'That was in the second raid,' Betty said. 'Nearly a hundred and fifty people in it, there were, but there was only one killed. A little boy.'

'Oh, that's sad,' Elsie Philpotts said, her eyes filling with tears. 'A little boy. Think of his poor ma. Mind, we've had a bit over here too – a whole team of young RAF lads looking after a balloon were killed in their shelter last week.' She looked at Betty. 'I don't know whether to be thankful that my Graham's not training to be a pilot or worried about him at sea.'

Betty didn't know what to say. It didn't seem to make any difference which Service he was in, they were all as dangerous as each other. She saw the pallor under Elsie Philpotts' makeup, the tremble of her lips, and realised that under the jollity Graham's mother was badly frightened.

She felt suddenly ashamed. She'd been thinking of Graham almost as if he was away on holiday and would soon be back. But his mother knew that he might never come back. And for her, he was the only boy in the world.

It's worse for mothers, Betty thought. They're losing their children, the only ones they've got. Girls like me, we'll go on even if our sweethearts or husbands get killed, we'll still go on living and we might find someone else. But for a mother, he's gone for ever and there's nobody else.

It didn't matter whether your child was a baby in a pram, a little boy in an air-raid shelter or a grown man fighting for his country. He was your child, and always would be, and nobody could take the place of a child.

Throughout the following week, the sirens continued to sound. Monday afternoon brought a hundred and fifty enemy planes and, amidst the fierce battle that was fought over the heads of the citizens, a direct hit was scored on the gas works at Hilsea and more than seventy properties damaged. This time warning was given sooner and the shelters reached in good time, with the result that only two civilians were hurt. The Royal Marine Barracks of Fort Cumberland, one of the Victorian 'Palmerston's Follies' that ringed Portsmouth, was less fortunate and was hit by more than fifty bombs.

By this time, Betty was out on the farm. She had left home that morning, straight after breakfast, marching self-consciously up the street in her new uniform. The whole family were standing at the gate to see her off – Annie, Ted, Olive, and even Jess with baby Maureen in her arms. Betty turned at the top of the street and waved, feeling suddenly panicky. Suppose she hated it after all! Suppose she couldn't do the work. Suppose . . .

But there was no time for 'supposing'. The bus came along and she climbed aboard, trying not to notice the stares of the passengers. She found a seat and gazed out of the window.

There was a lump in her throat as she passed the familiar

landmarks – the school where she had first learnt to read and write, the 'rec' where she'd played cricket with her brother and Bob Shaw. She'd had a letter from Bob last week, but anything interesting had been crossed out by the censor.

She'd heard from Graham too, but Graham wasn't such a good letter-writer as Bob. Nothing got crossed out in his scrawled notes! And he was still sulking a bit over her going away. He hadn't asked a single question about where she was going, and although he wished her luck at the end, it didn't seem as if he meant it.

Oh well, that was men all over, thought women ought to be there at their beck and call whenever they wanted them. This war would teach them different, she thought. Already women were doing a lot of the jobs men generally kept to themselves – why, there was a woman conductor, a conduct*ress*, Betty supposed she ought to be called, on this very bus, clipping the tickets as good as any man. And why not? It didn't exactly need big muscles.

'Off to the farm, then, love?'

Betty turned quickly. Tommy Vickers had sat down next to her and was looking at her with bright blue eyes. She smiled and nodded. She liked Mr Vickers. He had often tossed her and the boys a few toffees when they were out playing in the street, and sometimes he would even join in and bowl a few balls at the stumps chalked on the end house. Mrs Vickers had come out once and told him he'd never grow up, and Tommy had laughed and slapped her bottom and told her to be glad of it.

'I heard you were going on the land,' he continued. 'Well, you'll have a better time hoeing turnips than slaving away in some factory making munitions. And the uniform looks very fetching!'

Betty blushed. 'Dad doesn't really like me wearing trousers.'

'Well, not for pleasure, maybe, but it's different when it's work,' Tommy said. 'You can't do farm work in a posh frock. Where are you going?'

'Bishop's Waltham. There's quite a few going. We're getting a coach at the station.'

Tommy nodded. 'Well, you take care of yourself and look out for the farmer's boy.' He winked. 'I've heard a lot of tales about what they get up to behind haystacks – and if they're anything like I was when I was a lad, you'd better stay round the front. I know I wouldn't have wanted to miss a chance of kissing a pretty girl like you!'

Betty felt her blush deepen. 'Oh, I shan't be kissing anyone,' she said hurriedly. 'I've got a boy.'

'Young Ginger Philpotts. Yes.' Tommy gave her a considering look. 'Well, he's not a bad youngster, puts me in mind of myself a bit. I was in the Navy, you know, in the last lot.' He glanced out of the window. 'But it's not serious with him, is it. I mean, you'll have a good few romances before you're ready to settle down.'

'Oh, but –' Betty bit her lip. It had been on the tip of her tongue to tell Mr Vickers that she and Graham were secretly engaged. Why was she talking to him like this? 'I don't think it's fair to go out with other boys,' she said a little stiffly. 'Not when you've got someone away.'

'No, maybe not.' But he still sounded thoughtful. 'Well, I wish you both luck, Betty. I hope it all works out for you. Just don't be surprised if – well, you're both young, you can change your minds and no hard feelings. Anyway, this is my stop.' He grinned at her, suddenly cheerful again. 'Remember what I said now, take care and stand well clear of haystacks!'

He jumped off the bus and Betty looked out and saw him laughing at her from the pavement. She smiled and waved, feeling better. He always had that effect, she thought, people always walked away from Tommy with a smile on their faces.

The bus was nearly at the town station now, and the coach would be waiting. The adventure was about to begin.

The coach was filled with girls like herself or a few years older. They all looked self-conscious in their new uniforms and avoided each other's eyes as they lugged their kitbags on to the bus and found seats. A thin woman with spectacles and a clipboard counted them all on, checking their names on her list, and then checked them at least twice more before allowing the bus to move off.

Betty scrambled aboard and got a window-seat. It had taken nearly two hours to get everyone organised but it looked as if they were off at last. She stared at the crowd of girls, all dressed in their breeches and pullovers. They were from all over Portsmouth, some of them from Gosport, and mostly strangers to each other. One or two knew each other and talked in hushed whispers, as if they were in church.

'Whew! It's hot isn't it?' A tall, lanky girl with untidy brown hair had plonked herself down in the next seat. 'I hope it doesn't take too long now. I thought they'd never get us sorted out, didn't you? Where are you going?'

'Somewhere near Bishop's Waltham,' Betty said. 'What about you?'

'Same place. My Dad says it's hardly worth getting on a bus for.' She laughed, showing a row of square white teeth. 'I told him, they need someone to milk cows just as much in Bishop's Waltham as they do fifty miles away.' She brushed back a loose curl and gave Betty a friendly grin. 'P'raps we'll be seeing a bit of each other. What's your name? I'm Yvonne, Yvonne Hayter.'

The two girls talked as the coach made its way out of Portsmouth and into the countryside. It did not go directly to Bishop's Waltham, but meandered around the lanes, calling at different villages and farms. Several times the driver lost his way and Miss Andrews grew more and more exasperated.

'You'd think they'd send someone who knew the area,' she said sarcastically. 'Don't you have a map?'

'Look, lady, if you think you can do any better, I'll get out of this seat and you can drive instead,' the man retorted. 'I reckon I could do the grumbling as well as you.' He poked his finger at the map he had spread out beside him. 'They've took all the signposts down, haven't they, so Jerry won't be able to find his way about. Well, he's not the only one! And half these farms and places aren't even mentioned on this map.'

'Well, ask someone,' she said impatiently, and he groaned and rolled up his eyes.

'Who? The local cow? Can *you* see anyone to ask?' The lanes were deserted. The girls, who had found the situation funny to begin with, sighed and shifted uncomfortably. The seats were covered with oilcloth which had grown hot and sticky, and their breeches and long socks were too thick for a summer's day. The uniform included dungarees made of strong cotton, but they weren't so smart and it hadn't seemed right to wear them.

Not that many of the girls looked smart as it was, Betty thought. The clothes had been allocated as small, medium and large, and within each category there was quite a range of sizes. She had been lucky, but some of the girls looked half swamped by baggy breeches and socks that had been folded over half a dozen times at the top, and others looked as if they might burst all the seams at any minute.

Eventually, the coach driver managed to find all the places on the list, dropping girls off at each one. Miss Andrews checked and counted them all again each time – 'as if someone might have slipped through the floorboards,' Yvonne muttered in Betty's ear – and at last there were only three left, Betty, Yvonne and a slender girl with china-blue eyes and fair hair curled in ringlets. She looked more like a fairy off a Christmas tree than a land girl, even in her uniform, Betty thought, and wondered if she would be able to do the work. She caught the girl's glance and gave her a smile, but the china-blue eyes were cold and the fair head turned away. Betty felt irritated. I was only trying to be friendly, she thought.

The coach rounded a last corner and stopped in the narrow main street of Bishop's Waltham. The girls looked out with interest. There were a number of people about, all staring at the bus, and Miss Andrews poked out her head and asked for directions to the farm.

'It's another mile down that lane,' she reported. 'And we can't get the coach all the way – the last bit's too narrow. Mr Spencer's going to meet us there.'

Once more they set off, coming to a halt at a little crossroads. The coach driver stopped again.

'I'm not going any further. I'll have a job to turn round here as it is.'

'It's all right,' Miss Andrews said stiffly. 'This is as far as we have to go.' She looked out. The hedges were thick with blackberries but there was no sign of a farmer. 'Where *is* he?'

'Well, this is it,' Yvonne remarked, standing up and bumping her head on the overhead rack. 'Ouch! Why do I have to be so tall?' She glanced at the fair-haired girl. 'I bet they'll put us together. We'll get called Lofty and Titch!'

'They'd better not try,' the girl said grimly. She picked up her kitbag and pushed past them to the front of the bus where Miss Andrews was once again consulting her clipboard. 'My name's Erica Jones and I must have a bedroom to myself.'

'Coo-er,' Yvonne murmured, not too quietly. 'Someone thinks a lot of herself.' A flush touched the fair girl's neck and it was clear she had heard the penetrating whisper. She lifted her head a little higher and said coldly, 'I enquired at the recruiting office and was told it would be arranged.'

'Well, I don't know anything about that,' the woman said in a harassed voice. 'You'll have to see what Mr Spencer says about it.' She looked down the lane and tutted. 'He ought to be here now. I said we'd be here about two, and now it's gone three.'

'Maybe he thought you'd stood him up,' the driver suggested.

Erica Jones sighed impatiently and tapped her foot on the floor of the bus. Betty thought she was probably about twenty-one or two. Her golden curls shone and she wore make-up, though not so much that she looked what Betty's dad would call 'cheap'. Her uniform fitted beautifully, as if it had been made to measure, and she wore small gold earrings. Pierced ears, Betty thought enviously. Neither Annie nor Ted would have allowed her to get her ears pierced. It was obvious that she came from a home with more money than the Chapmans had.

Yvonne looked as though she had been wearing her uniform for the past three months. Her aertex shirt was crumpled and damp, her breeches as creased as if they had been rolled into a ball. Her shoes were already scuffed, her hat battered and her green pullover unravelling at one sleeve. She winked at Betty.

'Are we all going to the same place?' she asked. 'Is Mr

Spencer the farmer?'

'What? Oh – yes, that's right.' The clipboard woman had been talking to the driver. She came back looking distracted. 'You're all three down for his farm. But there seems to be some hold-up. I don't know why he isn't here.'

'Because it's milking time.'

The voice made them all jump. They peered out of the bus at the young man who stood smiling up at them. He was tall, lean without being skinny, and had a mop of brown, curly hair. He glanced at the three girls and then smiled again at Miss Andrews. 'I'm Dennis Verney. I work for Mr Spencer. He told me to come down here and meet the young ladies. I'm to take them to their billet.' His gaze travelled slowly over the three staring faces, and Betty felt a tiny shock as his eyes rested upon her face. 'Why don't you all come with me now?' he suggested, and there was a hint of laughter in his voice, as if Dennis Verney found quite a lot of things funny. 'I reckon Mrs Spencer'll have the kettle on by now and I bet you could all do with a cup of tea.'

'A cup of tea!' Yvonne exclaimed. 'Could I ever!' She jumped down from the bus and linked her arm with Dennis's. They were almost exactly the same height, Betty noticed, and she felt left out and a bit annoyed with Yvonne. Was she a flirt?

Erica too was looking annoyed. She climbed down into the lane, dragging her kitbag behind her, and made a great show of hoisting it on to her back. She looked back at Miss Andrews, who was fussing helplessly, obviously wondering if she should allow her three remaining chicks to go off with this unknown man.

'I still expect a room to myself, you know,' she said accusingly, but the woman shook her head.

'I'm sorry. We can't get the bus down the lane and I have to go back. If there's anything you're not happy about, you'll have to get in touch with the Office.' She stood back to allow Betty to dismount from the bus. 'Someone will call round in a day or two to see that everything's all right. And remember that you're here to work!'

Betty heaved her kitbag on to her shoulder and marched

away down the lane after the others. For a moment, she caught herself wishing that she was the one to be swinging along with her arm through Dennis Verney's. Then she frowned and scolded herself.

Didn't she already have a boy, away at sea? Wasn't she wearing his ring this very minute, even if it was on her right hand? And what about Tommy Vickers' warning to be careful of the farmer's boys?

Anyway, a tall, strong young chap like Dennis Verney wasn't going to be around for long. He'd be called up himself in a week or two. And then there'd be three of them – him, Graham and Bob Shaw – to worry about.

I won't get too friendly with him, she decided. It's not worth it.

Dennis Verney led the three girls down the lane. It wound away from the main road and over a little bridge with a watercress-filled stream running lazily beneath it. On either side were broad, sloping fields and the lane twisted between tall hedges to climb a steep hill.

The farm lay at the bottom of the hill, set back off the road, with a large farmyard. The girls looked about with interest.

'My, that's a big house,' Yvonne said with awe. 'It's like a mansion!'

'It's the farmhouse,' Dennis said. 'It's not as big as it looks – all that part on the end is a barn. The hay's kept there for the animals.'

The house was built of grey flints. It had several windows and to Betty looked as big as three of the little terraced houses in April Grove. She shared Yvonne's awe, but Erica sniffed.

'This yard's mucky.'

Dennis grinned.

'It's a farmyard. The cows come through here to be milked. That's the milking shed, over there. The poultry are kept in that other shed and let out during the day.'

The yard was full of hens, picking at the earth. At the far side there was a pond, half covered in green, with a few ducks paddling about at its edge. There was a patch of grass with an apple tree hanging over it and someone had left a chair and a basket in the shade. Two large horses were grazing in a small paddock.

'It's lovely,' Betty said. 'It's real country.'

'It's a farm,' Dennis said again, and smiled at her.

Betty looked at him. He had warm hazel eyes, full of laughter. She felt suddenly confused, but before she could say anything the farmhouse door opened and a woman bustled out. She was about Betty's height and rather plump, with grey hair. She was smiling but looked anxious, and her eyes moved quickly over the three girls.

'So you're our land girls.' Her voice had a soft burr to it, quite different from the sharper accents of Portsmouth. 'Well, I'm pleased to see you. You'll find things a bit different here from what you're used to, I daresay, but we'll all shake down together. Now come in and tell me your names and I'll show you where you're to sleep.'

Betty glanced sideways at Erica, expecting her to claim her own room again, but for once the fair-haired girl was silent. She had put down her kitbag as they stood in front of the house, and now she moved to pick it up.

'Here, little 'un, let me carry that for you,' Dennis said. 'Good lord, it's nearly as tall as you are. How –'

Whatever he had been going to ask was lost as Erica whirled round, fists clenched and eyes blazing, and stamped her foot at him. He backed away, an almost comical expression of amazement on his face, as she let fly.

'Don't call me that! Don't call me "little 'un" or "Titch" or "Shorty" or anything else you might think's funny – I don't like it. It's bad enough *being* short, without everybody else treating it like a joke. So just keep your funny remarks to yourself, see?' She hoisted up her kitbag and swung it on to her shoulder, then looked at Mrs Spencer. 'I'd like to see my room now, please.'

'Whew! She's a star turn and no mistake,' Yvonne muttered in Betty's ear. 'Talk about Lady Muck.'

Mrs Spencer looked taken aback. She tightened her lips and turned to Dennis. 'You'd better go and help with the milking. I can see to these girls.' She waited while he disappeared across the yard, then went back into the house, leaving the girls to follow her.

Erica went first, explaining that she had only agreed to come on condition that she was given her own room. The other two followed, more interested in the farmhouse than in the other girl's demands, and gazed about them at the big kitchen.

It was large and untidy, with a dresser taking up most of one wall and an assortment of cupboards and drawers around the others. The dresser was piled with papers, bills, invoices, numerous forms, letters and old newspapers. A rough-topped table stood in one corner, with what looked like an old church pew with a high back on each of the long sides, and chairs at the end. There was a wide range, with its fire lit in spite of the hot weather, and a door leading into a long sitting-room with two sagging sofas and a couple of armchairs. Each held a pile of washing, evidently waiting to be ironed.

It didn't look as if the Spencers had much more money than the Chapmans, Betty thought in some surprise. Her own mother would have been ashamed to let visitors come in and see the house looking as untidy as this, in fact, it never *did* look as untidy as this. And the furniture looked old-fashioned and not at all up to date.

'Fancy living in a lovely big house like this and not keeping it nice,' she whispered to Yvonne, but the lanky girl gave her a puzzled look.

'It looks all right to me. Hell of a lot better than down Rudmore Alley, that's where I live. Five of us to a bedroom and *she* wants one all to herself!' She gazed around the room, her eye wide. 'I reckon we could get our whole house in this kitchen.'

Betty said nothing. She knew where Rudmore Alley was, over near Stamshaw, where the gas-holder had got hit during the first raid. But she had never been there. It wasn't much better than a slum, her mother said, with narrow passageways of tiny houses, and too many people living too close together. They were all poor down there, working either at the timberyard or on the wharves, and a lot of the children went to school with no shoes on their feet. She wondered what her mother would say if she knew that Betty would be sharing a room with a girl from Rudmore Alley.

'But I *told* them in the office,' Erica was saying. 'I told them, I have to have my own room. I'm not *used* to sharing with other people. I won't be able to *sleep*.'

'You'll sleep all right, after you've done a good day's work.' Erica gasped and they all turned quickly and saw the doorway blocked by a large man. He stood surveying them, his hands on his hips, face shadowed. He moved forwards, his eyes narrowed. 'It's hard work on a farm, aye and mucky too. You'll be no good if you're afraid of mucking out the pigs or milking a cow. I hope you don't think you've come out here on holiday, to get away from the bombs.'

'Of course we don't,' Betty said indignantly. 'We want to help win the war. At least, I do.' She glanced at the other girls. Yvonne, thin but tall, looked ready to do her bit, but what about Erica? She didn't look as if she'd ever got her hands dirty in her life.

'So do I,' Yvonne said warmly. 'And I'm not afraid of pigs, or cows. I'll do whatever you want me to.'

The farmer looked at her, his eyes moving over her lanky body. He's looking at us just as if we were cattle in a market, Betty thought, suppressing a nervous giggle.

'Well, maybe you'll be some use when you've got a bit of flesh on you,' he remarked. 'It's soft living in the city, so they tell me. A couple of weeks harvesting'll soon build you up.'

'It's good food that'll build them up,' his wife said. 'A few eggs and a bit of butter. And proper milk, not like that thin stuff they get out of bottles.' Her voice was warm and motherly as she looked at the three girls. 'We still have to take what rations they give us, but there's always a bit extra being on a farm – a drop of milk in the pail, a cracked egg now and then. And you'll need it, with the work you'll be doing – my husband's right there.'

Erica had recovered herself. She stepped forward, tilting her head to look up at the big farmer, but before she could speak Mrs Spencer said hastily, 'I was just telling you about the sleeping arrangements. I'll take you upstairs now and then Mr Spencer can show you the farm before tea.' She turned and opened a door which Betty had thought to be a cupboard but now saw to lead to a narrow flight of stairs. Bumping their kitbags on the wall, the three girls followed her, Erica looking annoyed.

'I daresay you're hungry after your journey,' Mrs Spencer said. 'I always cook a meal at tea-time. The men need it. My husband's always had a good appetite, and Dennis eats whatever's put in front of him. Oh, you'll need to give me your ration books, I'll have to register you in the shops.' She was leading them along a narrow passage and then set off again, up a further flight of stairs. 'Here. This is your room.'

The three girls crowded into the room behind her. It was long and narrow, with sloping walls, and the windows were so low that you would have to kneel on the floor to look out of them. There were three folding camp beds, close together, and three small chests of drawers.

'Coo,' Yvonne said, 'the ceiling's a bit low. I can't stand up straight, except in the middle.'

Betty stared at the room. She felt a twinge of excitement. It was bigger than her room at home, even if she did have to share it, and the sun was slanting in through the low windows and making striped patterns on the floorboards. The curtains were old but pretty, with patterns of flowers faded to a soft blur. It was like a room out of an Enid Blyton story.

'You're expecting us to sleep *here*?' Erica said, her voice high with disbelief.

Mrs Spencer looked at her. 'What's the matter with it?'

'What's the *matter*? It's an *attic*.'

'It's the only room we've got that's big enough.'

Erica sighed impatiently. 'I've told you, I'm to have my own room. I've never shared a room. I'm afraid there's been some mistake. You'll have to do something about it.'

Mrs Spencer shook her head. 'I can't do anything about it. Nobody said anything to me about a separate room. Anyway, it'll have to do, there's nowhere else for you to go. All the rest of the rooms in the house are occupied.'

'How many people live here?' Yvonne asked curiously. 'Have you got evacuees?'

'No, but there's me and my husband, and Dennis, and old

Jonas – he's been with us for years. And we've got my sister and her two children staying with us. They've got Dick and Gerald's rooms.' She looked at them again. 'You'll have to sleep here.'

Yvonne picked up her kitbag and marched into the room. She dumped it on one of the camp beds and said cheerfully, 'Suits me. Which bed d'you want, Bet? The one by the window?'

Betty agreed eagerly. She thought of lying close to that window at night, gazing out at the stars, waking in the morning to see the apple tree outside, its leaves dancing against the sky – why, it was as good as a holiday. She dropped her bag on the bed and grinned at Yvonne, then looked at Erica.

'That leaves you the bed at the end. Come on – it won't be that bad, sharing with us. We haven't got fleas. Anyway, it's that or walk back to Pompey on your own, take your choice.' She lay back on the bed and laughed. 'I think it's a smashing room. I've never slept in an attic before.'

'We haven't even got an attic,' Yvonne remarked, and pulled open the neck of her kitbag.

Erica stared at them both. She turned to look at their hostess, but Mrs Spencer had disappeared down the stairs. She hesitated for a moment, then walked to the end of the room, her back stiff.

'It's only for tonight,' she said haughtily. 'I'll get something done about it first thing in the morning, see if I don't. I'd never have come if I'd thought I was going to be treated like this.' She dumped her kitbag on the bed and sniffed. 'Not that I'm going to be here for long anyway.'

'What d'you mean?' Yvonne was fishing out all her belongings and strewing them about her bed. It looked as if she was turning out a ragbag, Betty thought. The Land Army uniform must have been the first new clothes Yvonne had ever had. 'Where are you going?'

'Oh, I'm getting married.' Erica held up her left hand and they saw the tiny diamond glinting on her finger. 'My fiancé's in the RAF and as soon as he gets leave we'll be having a big wedding. And then I'll go with him, wherever he's stationed.'

'So why did you join the Land Army?'

'It was either that or one of the Services and I wasn't going to join *them*. In any case, we'll be having a baby straightaway so there was no point starting anything important. And then I shan't have to work at all.'

'Having a baby?' Betty said incredulously. 'But why?'

'Why d'you think? I might not get another chance. If Geoffrey gets killed . . .' she shrugged. 'At least I'd have something to remember him by. And I won't have to go into the Services.' Her red lips wrinkled in distaste.

Yvonne stared at her. 'You talk as if a baby's a – a fancy photo or something. It's a person. You can't have a baby just to get out of doing war work.'

'I can if I like,' Erica said coolly. She glanced disparagingly around the attic. 'I suppose these hooks and nails on the wall are their idea of somewhere to hang our clothes. Honestly! Not even a wardrobe. It's disgusting.'

'It's clean.' Betty didn't feel like talking to Erica any more. She opened one of the chests of drawers and began to put away her clothes. 'And Mrs Spencer seems quite nice, though I'm not so sure about the old man.'

'What about the *young* one, though?' Yvonne's eyes sparkled. 'He's a bit of all right, isn't he? Dennis, I think that's a lovely name.' She rolled her eyes. 'Who d'you suppose he is? He doesn't seem to be their son.'

'No, both their boys are away in the war.' Betty re-membered Dennis's warm hazel eyes and felt the colour rise in her cheeks. She turned her head away quickly. 'Maybe he just works here. He'll probably be called up any time. Or he might even be on leave.'

'I don't think he is.' For the first time, Erica joined in a conversation that was not centred upon herself. 'If you ask me, there's something funny about him.'

'Funny? What d'you mean?'

'I don't know,' she said slowly. She sat on her bed, unrolling a pair of thick socks, and gazed at them. 'But I don't believe he's in the Forces and I don't believe he's been working on the farm for long. He's not the kind of person who works on a farm. You can tell by his voice. And there's something about him, something I can't quite put my finger on. But I don't trust him.'

The other two girls stared at her. Betty felt a twinge of unease. Something not quite right? Something not to be trusted? She thought of the laughing eyes, the ready grin, and shook her head.

He'd seemed such a nice sort of chap. But it was funny that he was working on the farm instead of being in the Forces. And he didn't seem like the sort of chap you'd expect to find doing the milking and things like that. And his voice *was* too posh, almost as posh as one of the announcers on the wireless.

Maybe Erica was right. There were spies everywhere. And you had to be careful these days about who you trusted.

The three girls looked at each other, suddenly solemn. And somewhere in the distance, so faint that it was little more than a prickle along their spines, they heard the wail of the siren, and then the muffled thud of bombs as they began once more to fall on the city of Portsmouth.

CHAPTER NINE

The working day started early on a farm, and the three girls were up by six o'clock next morning and drinking tea at the kitchen table. And that was the last lie-in they'd get, Mr Spencer told them when they went out to the byre where the three men were already milking.

'Lie-in!' Erica exclaimed. 'I don't get up till eight o'clock at home.'

Dennis chuckled and the old farmhand, Jonas, snorted. He was sitting on a milking stool, his head pressed against the flank of a large brown cow, his hands squeezing her udder with rhythmic ease. He had already expressed his opinion of the new Land Girls when Mr Spencer had shown them the farm the evening before.

'So you're what they've sent to replace our Dick and Gerald, are you?' He hadn't even bothered to take the straw out of his mouth as he stared at them. 'Well, I suppose the three of you together might be able do the work of one of 'em, but I must say you don't look up to much. Specially you,' he said to Erica, who quivered with fury. 'Why, you're no bigger than a threepenny bit.' Yvonne stifled a giggle and he turned his rheumy eyes on her. 'And you're just a couple of yards of bloody tapwater, but at least you'll be able to reach things. As for you – he turned to Betty – you'll not be able to keep that perm, not when you're out in all weathers, so you might as well forget it.'

'My hair's not permed,' Betty said indignantly. 'It's naturally curly.'

He gave a cackle of laughter. '"Naturally curly", is it! Well, that's a load off my mind, I must say. Hear that, boss? That's one of 'em won't be bothered about setting her hair every bloody Friday night.'

And how much work could *he* do in a day? Betty had wondered as Mr Spencer led them on around the yard. He wasn't much bigger than Erica himself and was as bent as a hairpin. But he looked as tough and scrawny as an old hen, as if he was nothing but bone and sinew. And he'd been on the farm all his life, Mrs Spencer had told them, worked for Mr Spencer's father when he was alive and knew all that there was to know about the job.

Now he finished the cow he was milking and the farmer suggested that each man should show one of the girls how to milk. Betty bit her lip, trying not to giggle again as Jonas gave Erica a look of pure disgust and rose to let her take his place at the next stall.

'Here's the stool. Three-legged – it's steadier that way. You don't want it toppling over every time the beast shifts her weight.' He sat Erica down on it and guided her hands to the udder. 'I 'ope you're not too dainty to touch her teats. Put your fingers round 'em good and hard. You got to squeeze – no good bloody stroking 'em. You ain't doin' it for her delight.'

Betty and Yvonne watched as the blonde girl settled herself gingerly beside the cow. She looked even smaller beside the huge brown beast, and her fingers barely closed around the teat. She looked with some trepidation at the smooth brown flank and gave a tentative squeeze.

'That ain't no good,' Jonas said disgustedly. 'Lean into 'er. Never mind yer pretty hair. Press yerself against 'er belly and give them tits a proper squeeze. You're milkin' er, not askin' 'er to purr. She ain't a pussy-cat.'

Erica bit her lip. Betty could see the frustration on her face. She squeezed again, and nothing happened. The cow shifted as if in irritation, and Erica flinched.

'She doesn't like it. I don't believe there's any milk there.'

'So what's that in 'er bag, bloody champagne? Mebbe you'd get it out quicker if it was.' The old man elbowed her aside and set his own hands on the udder. Immediately, two streams of milk gushed into the pail. 'Looks like milk to me.'

Erica made a sound of exasperation, and Mr Spencer laughed.

'Have another go. Nobody gets it right first time, even Jonas, only he's so old he doesn't remember learning. Just keep trying, little 'un.' He didn't seem to know that Erica hated reference to be made to her smallness. 'Now you other two try. You – Yvonne – come here with me, and Betty, you go with Dennis.' He led the way into another stall and Betty and Dennis looked at each other.

'A case of the blind leading the blind, I'm afraid,' he said cheerfully. 'I've only been doing it a few weeks myself. But I reckon I've just about got the hang of it now. Come and try Buttercup, she's usually pretty generous.'

Betty sat down on the little stool. The cow looked bigger than ever. She laid her face against its side and gave a little exclamation of surprise.

'Isn't she warm!'

Dennis chuckled. 'Of course she is. And I'll tell you something, Betty, this'll be one of the best jobs on the farm in winter. Imagine it in here on a cold, frosty morning, with all the cows breathing out nice warm air and heating the place up with their bodies. The best excuse in the world to spend a couple of hours all cosy against a warm body, better than a teddy-bear any day. What d'you think?'

Betty laughed. 'I think you could be right.' Tentatively, she touched the udder. It felt smooth and firm. Remembering what Jonas had said, she took experimental hold of two opposite teats and began to squeeze.

'No, not quite like that.' Dennis squatted beside her and reached in to cover her hands with his own. 'More like this.' His fingers tightened over hers. His face was very close. She could feel his breath on her cheek. 'That's better,' he said, and there was an odd note in his voice as he drew quickly away. 'Look . . .'

Betty opened her eyes, surprised to find that she had closed them. Her heart was beating quickly and she could feel a warmth in her face that was nothing to do with the cow. She looked into the pail and saw the milk already covering the bottom.

'Am *I* doing that?' Her momentary embarrassment was forgotten as she stared in delight at the jets of milk still issuing from the teats as she squeezed. 'Hey, look, I'm really milking!'

Dennis laughed. He had moved away now and she could no longer feel the warmth of his body close to hers. She blushed again, feeling her heart skitter, then called to the other girls. 'I'm really getting milk out. How are you getting on?'

By the time milking was over each girl had managed to draw off about half a pailful from their respective cows and even Jonas admitted that it wasn't bad for beginners – 'and bloody townies, at that'. But their fingers were stiff and aching and they wondered if they would ever be able to milk the whole herd, as the men were accustomed to do.

'You'll get used to it,' Mrs Spencer assured them, serving everyone with a hearty breakfast of fried potatoes. 'Come next month and you'll be experts.'

'Experts!' Jonas said with a snort. 'Takes longer'n a few months to make experts. Takes a bloody lifetime.'

'Well, you'll have to make do without experts then,' Betty retorted. She was getting tired of Jonas. 'We can't go back to the beginning and get ourselves born on a farm just to please you.'

'Now look you here,' he began, lifting a gnarled finger to point at her. 'I don't 'ave to sit 'ere and be spoke to like that by a chit of a bloody girl –'

'You don't have to sit here at all,' the farmer's wife said sharply. 'I'll have no squabbling at this table, Jonas, and well you know it. The girls have come to help us and they've got to learn, and it's up to you to teach them and look pleasant about it, so mind your manners. *And* your language. If you don't want to share your meals with the rest of us, you can have 'em out in the barn, it's all one to me.'

The old man stared at her, his jaw dropping open so that Betty wanted to giggle again. But the look on Mrs Spencer's face warned her that it would not be welcome and she looked down at her plate instead.

Breakfast was always served after milking, and the kitchen

table was crowded, with Mrs Spencer's sister Iris Blake and her two children hurrying through their meal as well. Mrs Blake was married to an Army captain and had come to stay at the beginning of the war. It was already apparent to the girls that the two sisters didn't really see eye to eye, especially over the behaviour of the children. But these days there were plenty of people having to live together who didn't get on, and if you had the room you had to take in someone. It might as well be family as strangers. And at least the children went to school each day in Bishop's Waltham.

The meal was soon over – no time to hang about, Mr Spencer said as he led them outside again. There was a harvest to be gathered, and more things to learn. And learning made everyone slow, so the sooner they got down to it the better.

'It's all the harder because the tractor can't be used now,' Dennis told them as they left the house. 'It takes too much fuel so the horses have come back into their own. And some farmers who don't have horses use oxen, or even cows.'

The girls looked at him blankly until he explained that the farmers were using self-binders, dragged round the fields by a team of horses, which cut the crop and bound it into heavy sheaves. 'Then we come along and prop them up against each other in stooks,' he said. 'Given good weather, it'll dry out and then we can stack it up ready for the threshers.'

'What are the threshers?' Betty asked, and old Jonas raised his eyes to the heavens. 'Well, it's not our fault we don't know,' she told him indignantly. 'I daresay there's quite a few things about towns and ships that *you* don't know!'

'Don't need to, neither,' Jonas said, and spat out a piece of straw. Erica gave him a glance of disgust.

Dennis grinned. 'The threshers aren't a "what", they're a "who". They go round all the farms in turn with a machine and thresh the stacks. Nobody's allowed to have them for more than a few days, so they can only do a part of the crop each time they come. It could be March before they've finished.'

'And meantime all my money stays tied up in the stacks,' Mr Spencer said, joining them. 'And I don't want to see any of you smoking near them, understand? One of those stacks goes up in flames, and it's my livelihood gone for a burton. Now, are we going to harvest this corn or are we just going to let it stand there and rot?'

Dennis led the way over to the paddock and called to the two big horses. They ambled over and rubbed their noses against his sleeve. He fastened the head collars on and handed one to Betty to lead.

'Will he come with me?' She looked a little nervously up at the big head. She was quite accustomed to horses, for many of the tradesmen who called around the streets of Portsmouth still used them, but she had always been warned not to go too close in case they bit or kicked. This one had long yellow teeth and hooves as big as dinner-plates.

'He'll follow his mate.' Dennis turned to go out of the paddock. 'He's called Boxer, and this one's Shandy. They're quiet as lambs, the pair of them.'

He harnessed them to the binder and the work began. At first, the girls watched and then, gradually, they began to join in.

The self-binder had a sharp reciprocating knife which cut the corn as the horses dragged it round the field. It was then guided on to the canvas bed by the 'sails' which prevented it from falling loose, and transported into the box where it was bunched and tied automatically with sisal string. Finally, the sheaves were cast out into rows, the whole procedure taking place continuously as the horses plodded round and round.

Jonas led the horses. It looked the easiest job, Betty thought, but probably it wasn't – Jonas had been doing these jobs for so long that he could make anything look easy. And he was very particular about the knife, checking that it was razor-sharp. 'Makes it easier to cut the corn, and easier to work the horses,' he said, giving away the information as reluctantly as if it were a precious jewel. He hadn't forgiven them for their blundering attempts at milking, Betty realised, nor for her answering back at the breakfast table. His look as Mrs Spencer had told him to mind his manners had been murderous.

She sighed and followed the others. Dennis and Mr

Spencer were now following the binder and building the sheaves into stooks, six or eight of them, propped together like a wigwam, with a couple more laid over the top like a roof.

'That's to let the rain run off,' Mr Spencer explained. 'Come the time they're dry, we'll load 'em on to the cart and stack 'em, like Dennis told you.' He surveyed them. 'Well, I reckon I'll leave you to it now. You ought to be able to manage a simple job like that. I daresay Jonas'll tell you when it's time to knock off for half an hour.'

Half an hour! Betty thought as she laboured in the hot sun for the rest of the morning. Was that all the break they were going to get? Already, it seemed as if they had done a full day's work. She thought of the dairy in September Street and how she'd grumbled if Mrs Marsh told her to clean out the big fridge. And Mr Spencer had thought they'd look on this as a holiday!

Still, exhausted as she was when she lay on her bed at the end of that first day, she felt a warm glow of satisfaction at what she had accomplished. Building stooks hadn't been as easy as it looked, but she'd managed to get several standing unaided, although rather drunken-looking, and at afternoon milking she'd managed to draw off all the milk Buttercup had to give, and most of Daisy's as well. Not bad for a beginner, however much old Jonas might look down his battered nose. And tomorrow, she'd do better still.

But the next day the girls' muscles were stiff and sore, and their fingers painful to use. There was no respite from their work, however; cows would be in a worse case if they weren't milked, Mr Spencer told them shortly, and the country the worse off for lack of milk. And the harvest must be got in. Sun wouldn't shine for ever.

Mrs Spencer was slightly more sympathetic, but Betty could tell that she was wondering if city girls could ever be up to the demands of farm work. Perhaps old Jonas was right, she thought, and you had to be bred to it. But Dennis hadn't been, and he could tackle most jobs with a fair amount of efficiency.

'It was just as bad for me when I started,' he told them as they sat at the edge of the cornfield one day, taking what shade they could from the hedge for their midday break. 'I found muscles I didn't know I'd got and ached in places where I didn't know I had places! But it all sorted itself out after two or three weeks and I've never felt fitter than I do now.'

'Two or three weeks?' Yvonne exclaimed. 'I'll be dead by then!'

He laughed. 'No, you won't.'

'Well, I'll probably wish I was,' she retorted. 'Don't you reckon so, Betty?'

Betty smiled and shrugged. 'I think Dennis is right. I'm feeling better already. My fingers hardly ached at all when I was milking this morning.'

'That's because you did hardly any milking,' Yvonne grinned. She looked at Erica, who was sitting a little apart from them reading her latest letter from Geoffrey. 'What d'you reckon, Eric? Think we'll have snuffed it by the end of next week?'

The blonde girl glanced up. Her china-blue eyes were cold and as they moved over Dennis her lip curled slightly. Her voice was stony and bitter.

'I don't suppose so. I expect we'll all be just as alive as we are now, even those who don't deserve to be.' She glanced down at the letter still held between her fingers. 'But there'll be plenty who *will* be dead, men like my Geoffrey, who're ready to risk their lives to save other people's skins. Even the yellow ones who aren't worth saving at all.' With a sudden movement, she crumpled up the letter and stuffed it into her pocket, then scrambled to her feet. 'Come on, let's get on with the stooking. Let's show what *girls* can do to help win the war. It'll make up for some of the company we have to keep.'

She strode away towards Jonas, who was removing the horses' nosebags. Dennis gave them a rueful glance and followed her and Betty and Yvonne stared at each other.

'Well!' Betty exclaimed. 'What d'you make of that? What did she mean about yellow skins? We're not fighting to save Chinamen, are we?'

'Not that I know of,' Yvonne said quietly. 'But I don't reckon she meant that sort of yellow skin, anyway. She was talking about our Dennis. Didn't you see the look she gave him – or the way he looked at us?'

'Dennis? But why? He's not a coward. He's just doing farm work, same as we are.' Betty frowned. 'Ever since we arrived here, Erica's had it in for Dennis. And I don't understand why, do you?'

'I'm not sure,' Yvonne said slowly. She rose to her feet and dusted breadcrumbs off her dungarees. 'But I think Erica knows a bit more about Dennis Verney than we do. And tonight I'm going to ask her just what it is.'

She walked away to join the others, and Betty collected up the greaseproof paper Mrs Spencer had wrapped their sandwiches in and smoothed it out carefully to be used again next day. She thought over the past week, trying to pick out things Dennis had done which could make Erica dislike him so bitterly.

There was nothing. All she could think of were his hazel eyes, so often laughing. His ready smile. The way he was always ready to help or encourage any of them who needed it. The way he had folded his hands over hers as he showed her how to milk Buttercup . . .

I don't think there's anything suspicious about him, she thought, pulling herself to her feet. I don't think there's anything at all.

'He's a conchie.'

The word echoed around the attic bedroom and seemed to hang in the air as if waiting for someone to pick it up. Yvonne was the one.

'A conchie? What's that?'

Erica looked at her contemptuously.

'Don't you know what a conchie is? A CO. A *conscientious objector*. He won't fight.'

Yvonne's brow furrowed. 'What do you mean, won't fight? Won't fight who?'

'The *Germans*, of course. He won't go in the Forces. He probably won't even help make aeroplanes or munitions, or anything to do with the war. He'd rather leave it to someone else. People like my Geoffrey.'

By now the girls had heard a good deal about Geoffrey. He was a pilot stationed at Tangmere and would be coming to the farm soon to see her, Erica promised. But at present, like all the other airmen, he was too busy fighting.

'They have to be ready all the time. When the German planes are seen coming, they have to scramble –'

'Scramble?'

'Run for their planes. It's like a race, Geoffrey says, to see who can get into the air first. He flies a Spitfire, and they have to get right up above the Germans and shoot them down.' Erica stopped abruptly, obviously wondering if she had said too much.

'It's all right,' Betty said. 'We're not fifth columnists. We won't tell anyone what Geoffrey does.'

'It's not you. It's that Dennis. I still don't trust him.'

That was just before she had discovered what he was. Now she despised him even more.

'He's a coward. He pretends he won't fight because he's got principles against it, but it's really because he's too frightened. Principles! Does he think he's the only one with principles?'

'What sort of principles?' Betty asked. In the week that they had been at the farm, she had grown to like Dennis more and more. Her dad would have approved of him, she thought. But if he was a CO . . .

'I thought you *had* to go into the Services if you were called up,' Yvonne said before Erica could answer. 'I didn't think there was any choice.'

'There isn't, unless you can prove you've got principles. But some of these people will go to prison rather than fight for their king and country.' Erica's voice was bitter. She stared out of the window. 'I'm going to apply to be moved. There's still no sign of me having a room of my own, and I'm not stopping where there's a conchie. I don't see that anyone can force me to do that.'

Yvonne shrugged. 'Suits us. We might get someone who's not too toffee-nosed to speak to us. And I think Dennis is nice.'

'You would.' Erica turned her back and went back to the letter she was writing. She wrote long epistles to her Geoffrey and the other two wondered when he got time to read them, if he was so busy. And what could she be saying? It must be one long grumble.

Betty too was writing a letter. She wrote to Graham every day, and to Bob Shaw at least once a week. Now she had to write to her parents and Olive as well. But at least there was plenty to write about.

By the end of that first week, any romantic notions that the girls might have had about country life had been firmly dispelled. The weather was still fine, but there was little time to bask in the sunshine. Apart from the harvest there were cows to be milked twice a day, pigs to be fed and sheep to be dipped. Betty, who had been so eager on that first morning to learn to milk a cow, began to feel as if she had only to finish with one animal to turn and find a line of others awaiting her attention, and her dreams were a turmoil of milking, feeding and dipping.

'I thought I was dipping Roger last night,' she told Yvonne. Roger was the bull and lived by himself in a pen close to the farmyard. He was black and white, and the girls had been told not to go anywhere near him.

Yvonne laughed. 'I bet he put up a fight.' She looked ruefully at her hands. 'How are your blisters, Bet?'

All the girls had blisters on their hands from using unfamiliar implements, and sore muscles all over their bodies. They were scratched and bruised, and the sun had burnt their faces and arms. Betty's nose was peeling and Erica was frantic about her red face.

'Geoffrey said he'd come this weekend. I can't let him see me like this.'

'Go on, he'll see you looking a lot worse than that when you're married,' Yvonne retorted. 'How are you going to manage about your curls then?'

Erica twisted bandages into her hair every night to keep the ringlets in. Tight-lipped, she would turn her back on the other two and work in front of a small mirror which she propped on her bed. She applied a thick layer of cold cream to her face as well, and caused Yvonne to hoot with laughter the first time she saw her.

'You look like one of those pictures of Hottentots! Only they've got black spiky hair and black faces. Doesn't she, Bet?'

'She looks like a negative of one,' Betty said. 'My brother Colin develops his own photos when he's home and she looks just like the negatives.'

Erica scowled. But she continued to bandage her hair every night and to cream her face, and Betty had to admit that the fair girl's skin was standing up to the ravages of long days in the sun better than hers or Yvonne's. It was red, but it wasn't peeling.

Erica didn't answer Yvonne's jibe about her curls. She peered at herself in the mirror and rubbed in a little more cold cream. Then she took Geoffrey's photograph from the wooden box which served as a bedside table and gazed at it.

'I hope he'll be able to come over,' she said. 'It's nearly three weeks since I saw him. And they got bombed there too, you know. He could be killed any day.'

Betty felt sorry for her. She was right, Tangmere had been bombed. And Geoffrey was in danger every time he took to the air in his Spitfire. Every night the evening paper had carried reports of the battle that was going on overhead, the number of Germans shot down, the number of RAF planes lost. The Germans had always suffered more, but that didn't make any difference. There were still British pilots being killed every day.

The sirens could be heard even here, out in the country. Every day the girls could see the planes coming and watch the dogfights going on overhead. They heard the dull thud of the bombs in the distance. Sometimes the bombers came further inland and turned to fly back over Portsmouth in an endeavour to escape the harrying of the RAF, and once or twice they jettisoned their bombs over open country. One fell at Fort Southwick, on top of Portsdown Hill, and a plume of smoke rose into the air.

The corn was dry now and ready to be brought into the yard and stacked. This time Boxer and Shandy were harnessed to a wain, which was taken out to the field and moved slowly round while Dennis and the three girls loaded it with sheaves. Jonas came with them, shaking his head at their efforts.

'My sainted aunt, you're about as handy as a cow with a musket,' he said as Erica struggled to lift an unwieldy sheaf and pass it up to Dennis, who was acting as loader on the cart. 'Don't tell me that's too heavy for you.'

'It doesn't have to be,' Yvonne said. 'It's nearly as tall as she is. P'raps you'd be better on the cart, Eric.'

'On the cart? That's bloody skilled work, that is.' Jonas passed a disparaging glance over the sheaves Dennis had piled on top. 'Here, let a man have a go, show you how it's done.'

Dennis pulled a comical face and jumped down while Betty took the horses' heads and Jonas clambered up to take Dennis's place. He stood bent-legged on top of the untidy pile and swiftly dragged them around until they were arranged round and round the cart, butt outwards. Then he looked down at the ring of expectant faces.

'That's what they got to look like, see. Tidy. Always remember that everything oughter be tidy – it'll work right then, see. And keep the middle full – you let that get hollow and it'll tip, sure as ninepence, soon's you start moving. Right, now start pitching.'

Dennis took the pitchfork Betty had left leaning against the cart and stabbed it into a sheaf. He swung it into the air and thrust it towards Jonas, who lifted it expertly from the prongs and laid it in position, then turned for the next. Dennis was just lifting it into the air.

'Well, get a move on,' the old man snapped. 'Keep 'em coming. It wastes time to keep the loader standing around with nothing to do. You girls, you oughter be pitchin' in as well, not standing idle. It's not a bloody 'oliday camp.'

Hastily, the three girls began to do as he told them, stabbing the sheaves with their pitchforks and trying to swing them up as Dennis had done. But like everything else, it was harder than it looked. The sheaves slipped off the prongs and when Betty caught on to the idea of twisting the fork to keep them on, she could barely lift it to shoulder-height, never mind up to Jonas on the cart. And when she did manage to heave one into the air, it refused to come off the prongs again. Exasperated and annoyed, sweat running down into her eyes, and irritated almost beyond bearing by the flies which had appeared from nowhere and begun to bite her neck and arms, she dropped the sheaf and stared at it helplessly.

'It's worse than stooking! I just can't lift it.' To her dismay, she felt the tears pricking her eyes and heard the tremor in her voice.

Dennis turned aside from the sheaf he had been about to lift and took her fork from her hands. 'It's not really that hard. It's just that there's a knack to it. Look.' He stood slightly behind her and held her hands over the fork, as he had done with the cow's udder. 'Hold it like this, twist it a bit – not too much – and then swing round. See?' The sheaf rose in a graceful arc straight into Jonas's arms. 'Poetry in motion.'

Betty laughed despite herself. It was a comfort just to have Dennis's arms around her, and his voice murmuring soothingly in her ear. 'Maybe we should work together all the time,' she said, and blushed. 'I mean – I didn't mean –'

'It's all right,' he said with a grin. 'But I don't think the boss'd like it. Anyway, you'll be able to do it yourself with a bit more practice.' He stepped away and thrust his fork into another sheaf.

The work went on. Gradually, the girls became accustomed to the rhythm and although Jonas still complained that they were slow they kept up a steady pace and the cart made several trips back to the yard, where it was unloaded and the sheaves built into a stack to await the thresher.

This was even harder work. The stack was to be built on a frame of poles laid between four rounded rickstones, like stone mushrooms standing about two feet high, taking up an area of about sixteen feet square. The first time that the wain, loaded almost twenty feet high with sheaves, drew up beside the framework, the girls gazed at it in bewilderment.

'How on earth are we going to get them on?' Yvonne asked. 'Does the wain tip over, or something?'

Jonas snorted. 'Course it don't! Stack has to be built proper.' He glanced at Mr Spencer. 'I dunno why the bloody 'ell you 'ad to ask for Land Girls. This lot'd be better off pickin' flowers.'

'Give them a chance, Jonas,' the farmer said. He turned to the girls. 'It's a fairly simple job, but like everything else there's a knack to it. You have two men on the stack, see, one at each end, and two or three up on top of the load pitching down to them. The stack's built from the outside into the middle, with the heads inside so they're protected, and that's all there is to it.'

'All there is to it?' Yvonne stared up at the sheaves towering above their heads on the cart. 'You mean we have to stand right up there, on top? With nothing to stop us from falling?'

'Don't have time to fall,' Jonas said with what they suspected might be an attempt at humour. Yvonne gave him a withering glance.

'But how do we get up there in the first place?'

'You climb up,' the farmer said tersely, and indicated the ropes that had been slung across the cart, dangling down at each end. 'I suppose you *can* climb?'

'Should've asked for bloody monkeys,' Jonas remarked, and for once Yvonne seemed inclined to agree with him. She looked at Betty and hesitated. And what about Erica? She was so small and dainty, she'd never manage a job like this.

'I think I can manage,' Betty said, remembering how she had always liked climbing trees when she'd been a child, playing with the boys. And once someone had produced a long rope which he said had been given him by his father, who was captain of the bellringers at St Mary's. They had found a tall tree to hang it from and used it as a swing until it snapped, dropping one of the boys in a pile of leaves. She'd often tried climbing that.

'Well, come on,' Mr Spencer said. 'Someone's got to be first.'

Betty stepped forwards. But to her surprise, Erica was there before her, her small hands already clasping the rope.

'We used to do this sort of thing in gym at school,' she said in her clear voice, and began to climb.

'Look at that!' Yvonne said. 'I reckon she went to a different sort of school from what we did, Bet. We never had nothing like that down Rudmore.'

'Nor at Copnor.' They watched with admiration as Erica

scrambled swiftly up the side of the load, bracing herself outwards with her feet and hauling herself up on the rope. She had some difficulty in negotiating the overhang at the top, where the load was wider, but eventually she clawed her way over the top and looked down at them triumphantly.

'Well, who'd 'ave thought it?' Jonas said grudgingly. 'Reckon you did get bloody monkeys after all!'

'Thanks for nothing.' Betty grasped the rope and began to climb, copying Erica. But the rope was not like the thin, smooth bellrope she had used years ago. It was thick and rough, scratching her hands. And as she got closer to the top, it was pulled tight by her weight and almost buried in the straw, so that she had difficulty in getting her fingers round it.

The overhang was much harder to climb over than it had looked, too. From below, it hadn't looked all that large, but when you were underneath it and trying to figure out how to swing yourself out and over the top, it looked immense. It's like climbing Everest, she thought. However did Erica manage it?

'That's it,' the clear voice came from above her. 'Pull yourself away – well, not like that.' She heard Erica giggle.

I'm glad you're enjoying it, Betty thought crossly. In swinging herself away from the lower part of the load, she had lost contact with it entirely and was now swinging helplessly in mid-air. Jonas was cackling below, and even Mr Spencer and Dennis were chuckling. She had a sudden picture of what she must look like, and felt her own giggles begin.

Giving up, she let herself cautiously down the rope and stood getting her breath back before having another go. This time, she managed to clamber out under the overhang and scrabble her way over the top. She plonked herself down beside Erica and looked over the side.

'We're as high as a house!'

'I know.' Erica grinned at her. 'It's rather fun, isn't it?'

Fun! Betty looked down at the others. Their faces were upturned and they looked small and distant. 'Do we really have to stand on this thing and pitch sheaves?' she asked dubiously.

It was soon apparent that this was exactly what they did

have to do. As soon as Yvonne, looking rather green, had managed to clamber up beside them, Dennis came up with the pitchforks and they stood up rather shakily, trying not to get too close to the edge as they pitched their first sheaves down to Jonas and Mr Spencer on the frame. Once again, as the farmer had warned them, there was a knack to be discovered. Pitch the sheaf wrong and you felt the rough edge of Jonas's tongue. Pitch it just right, and the two men could be kept busy, working rhythmically to arrange the bundles of corn neatly on the poles, rapidly building up the stack.

'At least it gets easier as we go,' Betty remarked, for the load was lessening in height all the time and the stack growing bigger. But it didn't stay easy for long. All too soon, they found themselves lower than Jonas and Mr Spencer, pitching upwards, and their arms and shoulders ached.

In the middle of the afternoon, Mrs Spencer came out with a jug of tea and then Jonas went back for afternoon milking. The girls and Dennis continued to work, with Dennis now back in place on top of the cart. They were out in the field, loading up the last few sheaves, when the siren sounded, and a few minutes later a dogfight began a mile or two away.

They looked at each other and hesitated. It was safe enough out here, surely? They'd heard of people being strafed by enemy aircraft, but these weren't interested in a few farmworkers down on the ground, they were too intent on shooting at each other, and saving their own lives. And then Yvonne gasped, grabbed Betty's arm and pointed.

One of the planes was out of control. It was spinning crazily and diving towards the earth – towards the very field in which they stood. Its engine screamed and little puffs of smoke were appearing in its sides. It was low enough to see the swastika painted on its wings, and above it, harrying it like dogs after a hare, were three RAF planes.

'It's going to crash,' Yvonne whispered as they stared.

The plane's engine stuttered, almost failed, then stuttered again. Betty could see the cockpit, see the movements of people inside it. She lifted both hands to her face, staring in horror. There was fire there – fire in the cockpit, where the people were. She saw the hood lift, saw a man struggling to climb out, saw the flames.

The horses were going wild. They reared in their harness, almost turning the cart over. Dennis rushed to their heads and began to unfasten the straps, shouting for help as he did so. Trembling with fear, Betty went to the other horse, terrified of his hooves as he plunged. His eyes were rolling with panic. She knew that if they were left in harness, they could easily kill themselves. Sobbing with frustration, she fumbled with buckles and collars, thankful when Dennis came round to her side and loosened the last strap. The horses bolted from between the shafts and galloped madly round the field, neighing with terror.

Overhead, the plane was still veering crazily about the sky, the three Spitfires still firing at it. She could see the rips in the sides as the bullets struck. The man who was trying to climb from the cockpit suddenly stopped and hung helpless, half in and half out. The plane's engines stuttered again, then suddenly appeared to come back to life, jerking the aircraft out of its downward spin so that for a few seconds it looked almost as if it might recover and level out of its twisting descent.

But it was too late. It was roaring towards them now, pursued by the Spitfires, and from close by they could hear the violent rattle of fire from the anti-aircraft gun emplacement. Almost mesmerised, they stood staring as the aircraft swooped across the fields, little higher than the hedgerows, with the crew clearly visible, their mouths wide open and their fists pounding at the hood of the cockpit.

'It's coming down!' Erica screamed, and they dived for cover under the haywain and crouched together on the rough, prickly stubble. Betty could feel Dennis's arms around her. She turned and buried her head against his chest.

The plane's engines had stopped. They could hear only the rush of air as it hurtled by directly overhead. Then a tremendous explosion blasted their eardrums, and the ground shook.

There was a moment's silence.

'He did crash, didn't he?' Yvonne whispered.

'It must be almost in the next field,' Dennis said. 'We'd

better go and look.'

Betty's ears were still ringing. She didn't want Dennis to let her go. She looked up at him and he met her eyes. His own were grave.

'We'll have to go,' he said. 'The crew might be needing help.'

'They need capturing,' Erica said sharply. She crawled out from under the cart and brushed herself down. 'They're the enemy. They'll have to be handed over to the authorities.'

Dennis let go of Betty and they followed Erica. Yvonne too had scrambled out and was already halfway across the field. Beyond the hedge they could see the tail fin of the plane, sticking up into the air. Suddenly excited, they broke into a run. The stubble cracked and broke beneath their feet and Betty felt it scratch her legs. It was difficult to run on and she felt as if she were in a dream, urgently needing to get somewhere yet unable to make it.

'It's got the swastika on it,' she exclaimed as they reached the gate. They could see the machine now, a crumpled heap of broken wreckage strewn across the stubble of the corn they had gathered yesterday. Its back was broken, its tail torn away and its fuselage a mass of twisted metal. One of its wings was crumpled. The men inside were dragging back the hood. Only two of them were moving; the other still hung over the side, limp as a rag doll.

'Of course it has,' Erica said scathingly. 'It's a Jerry, isn't it?' She scrambled over the gate. 'I'd just like to get my hands on them –'

'No!' Dennis reached out and grabbed her arm. 'Don't go near it.'

'Why not? They won't shoot now. They'll be too scared –'

'Stay here,' he commanded, and at the note in his voice Erica stopped and stared. But Dennis had let go of her arm and was running towards the plane. The three girls started after him, but he turned his head and yelled at them again to stay where they were. They hesitated.

'Who does he think he is?' Erica demanded, obeying him nevertheless. 'Ordering us about like that.'

'He doesn't want us to get hurt.' Betty's hands were at her

mouth again, watching as Dennis approached the aircraft.

'They're not doing anything. I bet they're injured,' Yvonne said suddenly. 'He's going to try and help them out.'

'He ought to leave them where they are.'

'That one who tried to get out – he looks as if he's dead.'

'Good thing too. The only good German's a dead German,' Erica said spitefully. But they're *people*, Betty thought.

She began to run forward again. Dennis was now almost there. And then, appalled, she saw its outlines blur in a haze of blue vapour. Before anyone could speak again, the whole plane seemed to shiver slightly, as if it were a mirage seen on a hot day, and then with a roar it was enveloped in a burst of orange flame.

'Oh, *no.*'

Yvonne turned away, her hands over her face, but Erica stared as if transfixed. Slowly, she lifted both fists to her mouth, biting on the knuckles. Her eyes widened and glittered, almost as if in elation.

Betty screamed and raced towards the flames, only to find their searing heat too much for her. She tripped and fell, screaming again as she felt them reach towards her as if eager to devour her too. Desperately, she clawed at the stubble, trying uselessly to get up, and then felt strong arms around her, lifting her to her feet and dragging her across the field.

'Get back,' Dennis said tersely. 'The whole of the field's going to be alight in a few minutes. This stubble's like tinder.'

She turned to him and said frantically, 'There are people in there. I saw them. We've got to help them.'

'We can't,' he said, still pulling her along. 'We'd never get near it.' And when she turned to look again, she knew that he was right. Even at this distance, the heat was scorching their faces. Dennis's skin was black with smoke, his eyebrows and hair singed. There was no possibility of rescue for the men they had seen staring out of the cockpit as the plane flew towards them.

'It's horrible,' she whispered. 'Horrible . . . There were men in there. I saw them move, Dennis, they were *alive.*'

'I know,' he said quietly. 'But they aren't now. And there

was no chance of getting any of them out. It must have been over very quickly.'

They could hear shouts now, as other people ran across the fields towards the plane. Jonas and Mr Spencer came through the gate and stood beside them, staring.

'Bloody *'ell*,' the old man whispered. 'Bloody, bloody *'ell* . . .'

'There's nothing we can do,' Dennis said. 'It'll burn itself out pretty soon. And then I suppose the souvenir-hunters will be around.'

Jack Spencer nodded. He looked at the three girls, at Yvonne's white face, at Betty's tears, at Erica's glittering eyes.

'Well,' he said sharply, 'what are you all hanging about here for? The Army'll deal with this. We've got a harvest to be brought in. Let's get on with it, before some joker lands on a field full of stooks. We can't afford to lose the crop just because of Hitler.'

The girls stared at each other. Yvonne looked shocked. 'But someone's just been killed. Don't you *care*? There's men died in that plane – burnt to death. And you want us to just go back and stack corn as if – as if nothing had happened! Don't you have any feelings at all?'

Mr Spencer opened his mouth, but Jonas butted in first.

'Feelings? Those were bloody Jerries in that plane! They'd've bombed us flat without even thinking about it. Why should we 'ave feelings for that sort o' filth, eh?' He glowered at Yvonne. 'You want to be careful, saying things like that – people'll be taking you for a bloody fifth columnist, that's what. Like *'im*!' He jerked his head at Dennis, whose skin flushed under its layer of soot.

'That's enough!' Jack Spencer said quickly. 'Leave the girl alone, Jonas. She's upset, and no wonder. And you'd better watch your own tongue, too.' He turned back to Yvonne, and spoke more quietly. 'Of course I've got feelings, girl. I don't like seeing men burnt to death any more than you do. But like Dennis said, there's nothing more we can do. It's not going to help if we sit about crying over it. And stacking corn's important. You want your families to have food to eat, don't you?'

Yvonne bit her lip. Betty remembered Mrs Marsh saying that whatever Hitler threw at you, you just had to get on with it. And Uncle Frank saying that life had to go on as normal. There was still corn to be harvested, animals to be fed. She took Yvonne's arm and said gently, 'He's right. That's what we're here for. Land Army, remember – we're soldiers too!'

Yvonne's mouth trembled into a watery grin. She nodded, and let Betty lead her back through the gate. But they were silent as they walked across the field. And Betty glanced at Dennis and wondered what he was thinking.

Erica had said he was too frightened to fight. But he hadn't seemed frightened when the plane crashed, and he hadn't run the other way when they'd thought there might be Germans still alive in it. He'd gone to help. They might have turned the plane's guns on him as he ran across the field, they might have fired at him with pistols, but he'd still gone to help.

To *help* – not to fight.

One day, she thought, I'll ask him about this conscientious objector business. I'll ask him to explain why he feels like that and what it all means.

But for now, there were stooks to be loaded, cows to be milked and pigs to be fed. And no time at all for conversation.

CHAPTER TEN

'Derek Harker! Whatever are you doing here?'

Derek grinned a little self-consciously. With the rest of 698 Unit, he had been working on Salisbury Plain, building an aerodrome. He was in uniform, tanned and fit, and Ethel Glaister looked him up and down admiringly.

'Hello, Mrs Glaister. We've got a forty-eight-hour pass. I've come home for a bit more of my honeymoon.'

Ethel Glaister bridled, as if he had said something offensive. Maybe she'd forgotten what honeymoons were for, Derek thought with a private grin. Looking at poor old George, he wouldn't be a bit surprised.

'Honeymoon!' Ethel said. 'I wonder you haven't got better things to think of, with a war on. Does that mean my George is going to be home too?'

'That's right. He stopped at the newsagent's. Buying you a nice box of chocolates, I wouldn't wonder.' He winked.

'If he is, it'll be the first time,' Ethel retorted. 'And if he's getting them from that spy's wife I shan't take them anyway. I'd rather die!'

Derek stared at her. 'Spy's wife? Mrs Brunner? What d'you mean?'

'You know perfectly well what I mean. Heinrich Brunner was a German, an alien, he was interned. Speaks for itself, doesn't it? What I don't understand is why they never took Alice as well.'

Derek felt suddenly sickened. He looked at Ethel's carefully made-up face, at her permed hair and smart blue suit. He thought of George Glaister, more like a mouse than a man. It wasn't surprising he was so nervy, with a wife like this. No wonder he hadn't seemed all that thrilled when they'd got their leave passes.

'Well, I daresay he'll be pleased to see you,' he said uncertainly. 'And I know Olive'll be pleased to see me. So if you don't mind, Mrs Glaister, I'll be getting along – forty-eight hours isn't long, when you've only had two days' married life!'

He strode on quickly. It seemed a lifetime since he and Olive had got married, and he hadn't been able to get home since. Olive would be at his father's yard now, working in the office, and with any luck he could get the old man to let her off early. We'll have a spree tonight, he thought. Wonder if I can get her mum and dad to go out somewhere this evening.

Or maybe he'd take Olive out himself. There might be something good on at the flicks. At least they'd be able to sit and have a cuddle – spending the evening in polite conversation with his in-laws was not at all what he had in mind!

He turned the last familiar corner and went straight into the yard. The little office was there, looking the same as always, he'd had a brief fear that it might have been hit in a raid and no one told him, and he could see Olive inside, her head bent over her desk. He stood for a moment, gazing in at her.

Derek had had several girlfriends before he had started going out with Olive. They had known each other slightly since childhood, for the streets where they lived were only a few hundred yards apart, but they had not gone to school together. Derek had been sent to a primary school in the opposite direction and then to the boys' Grammar School. He had stayed at school until he was sixteen and then gone to work for an accountant. His friends had moved in a different social circle from Olive, and although he was aware of the pretty, chestnut-haired girl from the bottom of March Street, it wasn't until they both went to the same church dance that he'd ever spoken to her.

From then on, they had spent every spare moment together and when the war had broken out had wanted desperately to get married. But Ted Chapman didn't approve of girls marrying before they were twenty-one, and it had taken Dunkirk to change his mind.

Unable to wait any longer, Derek pushed open the office door. Olive turned, and stared at him. For a moment there was total silence, and then she leapt to her feet, knocking over a pile of invoices, and flung her arms around him. He held her close against his rough khaki tunic, hardly able to believe that she was in his arms again at last, and bent his head to kiss her. He could taste the salt of tears on his tongue, and laughed shakily.

'What are you crying for? Aren't you pleased to see me?'

'Pleased? Oh, Derek – Derek!' She clung to him, lifting her face to his, half crying, half laughing. 'Why didn't you say you were coming? Why didn't you let me know? Oh Derek, *Derek*.'

'Ssh, ssh.' He stroked her back, disconcerted to find that his own eyes were wet. There was a lump in his throat and his lips were quivering. Surely he couldn't be going to cry. He'd hardly cried at all since he was a kid. 'Livvy, I've missed you so much.'

'Oh, Derek, it's been awful without you. Hearing about the raids, never knowing if they were getting through to you. They've been going for the airfields, haven't they? Every day I've woken up and thought, have they bombed my Derek? I couldn't bear it if anything happened to you, I just couldn't bear it . . .' She was crying now, the tears pouring down her cheeks. 'Derek, don't go away again.'

'I'll have to, Livvy. You know that. I'll have to go.' He held her away from him and looked down into her eyes, forcing a tremulous smile to his face. 'But not till the day after tomorrow. I've got forty-eight hours, Livvy two days. And *two nights*,' he whispered wickedly, making her laugh through her tears. 'So let's make the most of it, eh? And not think about the war at all.'

Olive laughed and sniffed. She felt in her pockets and Derek took out a large handkerchief and mopped her face with it.

'Forget the war!' she said. 'Chance'd be a fine thing, with the siren going off two or three times a day. Still, at least it's mostly in daylight, they don't seem to come over at night much. Frightened of being seen in the searchlights and shot down.'

They heard footsteps running across the yard and Florrie Harker burst in. She threw herself into Derek's arms.

'I couldn't believe it, I couldn't believe it was really you, but Fred Stokes just came in, he said he'd seen you walking up the street. Oh, Derek, why didn't you let us know? I'd have got something special in for supper. And your room's all untidy, it's all piled up with wedding presents and stuff. And what I'm going to give you for your breakfast, I can't think, we haven't seen bacon for weeks and as for eggs –'

'You don't have to give me anything for breakfast, Mum,' Derek said gently. 'I'll be staying with Olive, won't I?' He kissed her. 'Remember, we arranged that we'd be stopping with her parents until all this is over?'

Florrie stared at him. 'Well, yes, of course Olive's stopping with her mum and dad. But when you're home –'

'You don't expect me to say goodnight to Livvy and come back here to sleep, do you?' he said with a grin. 'We're married now. And we've got a double bed at her house.'

His mother looked flustered. 'Well, you'll be in for supper, though, won't you? You'll let us see something of you. And I know Auntie Jane and Uncle Bill will want to come round once they know you're home.'

Derek glanced at Olive. There was a querulous note in Florrie's voice. He thought of his plans for the evening, indoors alone together, if it could be managed, or else at the pictures. Not a family supper, with relatives popping in and out and everyone wanting to know what Army life was like. And there was Olive's family too, they'd want him there part of the time.

Olive said firmly, 'That's kind of you, Mrs – Mum' – she stumbled over the word, still embarrassed by having to call Mrs Harker by the intimate title – 'but I'll be cooking Derek's supper myself tonight. My mum and dad are going out for the evening, to see Charlie Kunz and Elsie and Doris Waters at the Hippodrome, so we'll be able to have the place to ourselves.' She smiled at Derek. 'That's if you'd like that.'

'Need you ask!' he said, grinning, and then turned back to

his mother. 'You don't really mind, do you, Mum? Tell you what – we'll have a bit of a do tomorrow night. Ask Auntie Jane and Uncle Bill, and anyone else you want. And maybe Olive's mum and dad can come up too. We'll have a proper party before I have to go back again.'

'Mock Duck, it's called,' Olive said. 'Mum says it's just meatloaf. But the butcher's got nothing in but sausages today, so it's all I can do for tonight. And there's Mock Apricot Flan for afters. It's carrots really, but they look like apricots and they do taste like them, a bit.' She gave him a wry smile. 'It's all pretend, isn't it? Mock this and mock that, it's like playing make-believe when I was a kid.'

'It'll be grand,' Derek said. 'Anyway, I don't want you spending all your time cooking.' He came behind her as she stood at the kitchen table, and slipped his arms around her waist. 'How long's it going to take?'

Olive spooned the mixture of sausage-meat, onion, bread-crumbs and herbs into a loaf tin and pressed it down. 'An hour in the oven. And I've already put in two big potatoes.' She turned into his arms and stood with her eyes closed while he kissed her. 'Oh, Derek . . .'

'So we've got an hour to ourselves while we wait for it to cook?' He moved his hands over her body. 'Let's go upstairs.'

'Derek! It's only six o'clock.'

'So what? I've got two nights, Livvy, that's all. And God knows when I'll get home again.' His hands were urgent now. 'And your mum and dad'll be back – what time's the show finish?'

'Well, it must finish around eight, there's another show at twenty-five past. But I heard Dad say they might go for a drink afterwards. That's if old Hitler lets us off!' The warnings were continuing to sound, sometimes several times in a day, although Portsmouth had had no major raids since Monday. People were learning to live with the 'music' playing so often in their ears. They ran for shelter when the siren's wail rose, but came out again and got on with whatever they had been doing as soon as the Raiders Passed sounded. And even Annie had been persuaded to go to the theatre when she heard that 'Gert and Daisy' were appearing.

'They're her favourites,' Olive said. 'Uncle Frank wanted to go – he thinks they're really funny – but the baby's got a cold and Auntie Jess didn't want to leave her. I told her I'd look after her, but she was a bit worried it might be a fever.'

'Well, I'm glad you didn't,' Derek declared. 'The only baby I want you looking after when I'm at home is ours.' There was a sudden silence and they looked at each other uncertainly.

'Our baby?' Olive said. 'D'you really mean that, Derek? D'you want us to have a baby?'

'I don't know,' he said slowly. 'I've never thought much about it. I mean, we've only been married a couple of months – and we've only had two nights together out of that. And what with the war, and not having our own place, and everything . . .'

'It'd be daft,' Olive said, her voice trembling a little. She stood within the circle of his arms, holding him close. 'It'd be really daft. But, oh Derek, to have our own little baby, to have something of you while you were away. We'd be a family. Our own proper family.'

Derek's eyes darkened as he looked down into her face. A baby, he thought. Our baby. Ours.

Olive, pregnant with our baby.

'Let's go upstairs,' he said with a sudden roughness in his tone. 'Oh, Livvy, I've waited so long to make love to you. Don't make me wait any longer, *please* . . .'

Derek's leave was short-lived. He was recalled the next day and on 7 September, a year and four days since war had been declared, the full fury of the Luftwaffe was unleashed on London. The East End lay helpless beneath a deluge of high explosive and incendiary bombs, and the sky was lurid with the fires that raged through the docks. In that one raid, nearly five hundred people died and three times as many were injured. It was almost impossible to count the homeless.

Even the Thames was alight as rum, sugar and paint from bonded warehouses drifted on the water and caught fire. Hundreds of people had to be evacuated, some through streets where buildings threatened to collapse on them at any moment, others by boat down the blazing river. And the blitz was not soon over, as the earlier raids had been. Instead, a thousand aircraft droned overhead, wave after wave of them. And as night fell and the city burned, they came again, bombarding people who had barely begun to put out the fires of their first attack.

In Portsmouth, people listened to the news each day and shuddered. It was clear that London was the main target now but nevertheless, the fact that Portsmouth lay on one of the Luftwaffe's flight paths to the capital, and was the home of one of the nation's most important dockyards, brought the sound of the siren several times a day and disrupted the daily lives of even the most phlegmatic.

The raids were now taking place at night as much as during the day, and families would sometimes find themselves incarcerated in their shelters for the entire night. For hours they sat on benches or lay on bunks, perhaps with only the dim flicker of a paraffin lamp to give them comfort, often in pitch darkness. Occasionally, during a lull, a brave – and desperate – soul would dash up the garden to go to the lavatory or even into the house to make some cocoa. And outside, the planes could be heard roaming overhead, and every few minutes the harsh rattle of anti-aircraft fire would break out as they were spotted in the beam of the searchlights which swept the sky.

'Night after night,' Annie said to Jess. 'I don't know how we can stand it. I'm so tired, I can hardly stand up, but the shopping's still got to be done and Ted must have his dinner.' She looked at the dish she was about to place in the oven. 'Toad in the hole we're having today, but it's more hole than toad. I managed to get a few sausages from Mr Hines, but they're poor things, disappear to nothing when you put them in the pan. And you can't make much of a batter when you have to treat eggs as if they came off the Crown Jewels.'

'How are Ted's nerves these days?' Jess too looked exhausted. Frank had to leave home at six each morning for work, and although they tried to sleep in the shelter there was little rest to be had with the roar of planes in their ears. In any case, he was usually on duty as a firewatcher too, which meant standing outside the shelter looking out for incendiaries. Jess hated to think of him out there, exposed to danger, but she knew that someone had to do these jobs, and Frank had said more than once that he felt guilty at not going to fight. He had to do his bit.

'Poor Ted,' Annie said, shaking her head. 'He looks like a man who's walking in Hell. To be quite honest, I don't know how he's going to get through. It's the blackout, you see, he just hates taking the ferryboat over in the pitch dark. And with bombs likely to drop on the harbour at any time, I don't blame him. But what can I do? I can't skipper the boat for him.'

Jess sighed. 'It's awful. It's like the whole world's gone mad. Look at what's happening to those poor souls in London. There's whole streets bombed to bits, and some of those big shops in Oxford Street are completely burnt out.'

'I don't know how they can put up with it.' Annie drew off four cupfuls of water and poured it into the kettle. Ted had worked out that she could save a shillingsworth of gas a week just by doing that. 'They're going down into the Underground stations to sleep.'

'I know. It must be terrible, never knowing what you're going to come out to in the morning.'

'Still, we're giving as good as we get,' Annie declared. 'Our boys have been over to Germany, giving them a taste of what it's like too. That might make them think twice.'

It might have done, but there was little sign of it. The blitz continued unabated, and other cities were attacked as well. Merseyside and South Wales were badly hit, and bombs fell on Buckingham Palace itself. It was said that Mr Churchill wanted the King and Queen to leave the country, or at least to move out of London, but they refused and it was reported that the Queen herself had commented that she was glad that the Palace had been bombed because 'now I can look the East End in the face'.

Portsmouth was not left undisturbed. One evening, after the Raiders Passed signal, a solitary bomber scored a direct hit on a house not many streets away from April Grove, killing a couple who had just returned to bed. Jess and Frank looked at each other, appalled, when they heard the news.

'But they ought to have been safe,' Jess kept saying, though she knew that it meant nothing. 'The all-clear had gone. They ought to have been all right. It's not *fair*.'

Frank didn't bother to tell her that this was war and you couldn't expect fairness any more. She knew that as well as he did. But you couldn't just jettison all your old values in the way that the Germans jettisoned their bombs. You had to cling to something when the world was going mad.

'Thank God we're all right, anyway,' he said, holding her against his broad chest. 'And thank God the children are safe out at Bridge End.'

But that was another worry. Edna Corner had written to say that she didn't think she could look after the boys for much longer, as she wasn't at all well.

'What are we going to do?' Jess asked. 'I'd ask Mrs Greenberry, so they could be with Rose, but I know she's got another family billeted on her now. Oh, it's such a pity, the Corners are good to the boys and they love being there.'

'Well, they can stay there a few more weeks,' Frank said. 'Edna says they're welcome until Reg has to go. And she might be feeling a bit better then herself.'

'Yes.' But Jess was unconvinced. Morning sickness might wear off after the first few weeks but there were plenty of other inconveniences to take its place. Perhaps she ought to go out to Bridge End herself and see if she could find somewhere for Tim and Keith to stay. She didn't want them billeted somewhere where they'd be unhappy – better to have them back home than that, bombs or no bombs.

Tim and Keith received the news that they might have to move with equanimity. They enjoyed living with the Corners, but since life had not yet dealt them any harsh knocks they did not expect them. It had been an adventure coming to Bridge End, and it would be another adventure to go somewhere else. Maybe they'd stay on the farm itself next time and be able to put all their new skills to good use.

'Edna says she's having a baby,' Keith said as they walked across the field to the schoolroom which they shared, turn and turn about, with the local children. 'D'you think it's true?

she hasn't got fat.'

'I expect she will. It's not going to be until next May, so there's plenty of time.'

'May?' Keith echoed. 'But that's next year! Does it take *that* long to grow a baby?'

Tim shrugged. 'S'pose it must.' The two boys had learned about babies soon after their sister Maureen had been born. The procedure of getting them had seemed far-fetched and unlikely then, but during the past year they had seen cows being serviced by the bull, and rams with the ewes, and Edna had called them early one morning to come downstairs and see Tibby having kittens by the kitchen fire, so they had come to the conclusion that it was probably true.

'I wonder how many Edna will have,' Keith remarked. 'Tibby had six.'

'Don't be daft. People don't have kittens. And they only have one.'

'Sometimes they have more,' Keith argued. 'There's twins. And triplets. And – and –' he searched his mind for the word '– squads. I bet they could have six if they wanted.'

'Well, I bet they couldn't.' Tim was bored with the subject. He began to run across the grass, his arms held out sideways. 'Yaaaaaaarh! You're a German plane and I'm a Spitfire coming to fight you off. Whee! Whee! Yaaaaaaarh! I've shot you down, you'll have to bale out or you'll get burned alive.'

'That's not fair! You didn't give me a chance.' Keith zoomed after him, and they zig-zagged across the field, making nasal noises of aircraft engines, gunfire and explosions. By the time they reached the hedge, they had forgotten all about Edna Corner and her baby, and were totally caught up in their own version of the battle that was going on over their heads each day. They clambered over the stile and tumbled into the lane almost at the feet of the Woddis sisters.

Miss Millicent and Miss Eleanor glanced at them with disgust and walked round them. The hairs growing from the mole on Miss Eleanor's chin quivered dangerously and the two boys pressed themselves against the hedge almost as if they were hoping to become invisible.

'Coo,' Tim breathed when the two elderly ladies had

passed. 'That was a near thing. They could've caught us easy.'

'D'you think it's true? About them eating evacuees?' Keith whispered nervously.

'Nah. They didn't eat Wendy and Alan, did they? They didn't even fatten them up.' But Tim's voice was less sure than he would have liked. There was something funny about Wendy and Alan Atkinson and the time they'd spent with the Woddis sisters. Something his mother and Edna knew about but wouldn't tell them. And he remembered the day he and Keith had gone to the house, when the snow was deep on the ground, and seen what they thought was a ghost at the window.

The feeling of terror that had gripped them that day had never quite departed and since then the brothers had taken care not to go down the narrow little lane where the tall, thin Victorian house stood isolated. And although Tim was *fairly* sure that the evacuee-eating story was no more than a myth, he wasn't prepared to take chances. Nothing was quite the same these days, after all. If people could start wars and make happy, cheerful men like Reg Corner go off and kill people, how were you to know what else might be true?

'Yaaaaaaaarh!' he screeched suddenly, and zoomed away down the lane, arms outspread once more. 'I'm a Spitfire. You can't catch me. *Nobody* can catch a Spitfire!' And he turned suddenly and dived at Keith, his head down and a rapid gunfire spattering from his lips. 'Bi-bi-bi-bi-bi-bi-bi-bip! I've got you. You're dead.'

'I'm not. I baled out.' Keith was a quick learner. 'I'm in the sea and you've got to rescue me. You've got to take me prisoner.'

Tim made a face. Taking prisoners was no fun at all. He wanted a dogfight, with aircraft swooping through the sky, guns blazing and parachutes opening like flowers overhead. He shrugged and turned away. It was time for school.

Erica Jones did not see much of her airman fiancé during the Battle of Britain. Although Tangmere was near enough for him to be able to visit her, the war gave him little time off, and when the airfield was bombed and almost destroyed he was moved to another a little further away.

'I hate not knowing when I'm going to see him again,' Erica grumbled. It was a Sunday afternoon, and she was lounging on an old blanket flung on the grass with a magazine open on her knee. Betty and Yvonne were up ladders picking a few plums and early apples for Mrs Spencer.

'None of us know when we're going to see our chaps again,' Betty said a little sharply. 'My boy's in the Navy, somewhere at sea, I don't suppose he'll be back for months. At least your Geoff's in England, he can pop over when he's got a few hours off.'

'That's just it, he doesn't *get* time off. They're on standby all the time. They have to fly at a moment's notice. And when they are off-duty they're so exhausted all they can do is sleep.'

Betty shrugged. She still found Erica difficult to get along with, although the three girls had settled down to an uneasy kind of friendship. You had to, living as close as they did. But Erica always seemed to have the idea she was special, somehow. As if what was all right for other people didn't apply to her.

For a while, they were silent. The only sounds were the quacking of Mrs Spencer's ducks on the pond and the clucking of a few hens in the orchard. A soft breeze rustled the leaves. There had been just a touch of autumn in the air that morning, but now the sun was hot again and Erica moved her blanket into the shade.

'Do you realise,' Betty observed, succumbing to the temptation of a ripe Victoria plum, 'there hasn't been a single plane over today? It's just like peacetime.'

'Perhaps it's all over,' Yvonne said. 'Perhaps we've won and they haven't told us yet.' She climbed down her ladder, shifted it and climbed up again. 'Maybe by this time next week we'll all be home again. Not that I'm in any hurry,' she added, thinking of Rudmore Alley. 'I like it here.'

The sound of an engine came from along the narrow lane leading to the farm. Dennis and Mr Spencer were bringing in the cows for milking, and they heard a few indignant moos as the approaching vehicle was brought to a halt. Erica glanced up without much interest.

'What's going on?'

'Dunno.' Betty craned round a branch to see. 'Looks like a sports car. It's full of men – pilots, I should think, they're all wearing flying helmets. I say, d'you suppose –'

'*Pilots?*' Erica was on her feet. 'It's Geoffrey, it must be. Oh good heavens, I look such a sight! He mustn't see me like this. Oh, what shall I do? What shall I *do?*'

'Go in through the back door,' Yvonne said. 'We'll keep them here. But don't take too long making yourself beautiful, they might only have a few hours.' She watched Erica's hasty departure and giggled. 'Wonder what she'll do to herself? She looked all right to me as she was.'

'Oh, she'll dress herself up like a doll.' Betty climbed down her ladder. The cows were now pushing their way into the milking shed, and the little green open sports car was standing in the yard. Three young men were leaping out without bothering to open the doors, each wearing a sheepskin jacket and flying helmet. They looked about them, grinning, and the tallest one accosted Dennis.

'Hey! Have you got a Land Girl called Erica Jones working here?'

Dennis nodded. 'She's about somewhere. Probably over in the orchard.' He waved across the yard to the gate where Betty and Yvonne were standing, then turned to urge the last cow into the shed. The young man looked at the girls and grinned again. He took off his flying helmet and Betty saw that he had thick fair hair and very blue eyes.

'Well, your luck's in, boys. Erica told me there were two other girls here but she never said they were beauties. I like the dungarees!' He strolled across the yard, followed by his two friends. 'I'm Geoff Martin. Is Erica around?'

'She – er – just popped indoors for a minute.' Yvonne returned his look frankly. 'I'm Yvonne and this is Betty. We came at the same time as Erica.'

'Yvonne and Betty, eh? Well, Yvonne and Betty, I've brought you a boyfriend for the afternoon. Thought we'd go for a jaunt round the lanes, didn't we, lads? These two characters are idiots but the best I could rustle up. The short one with a nose like a frog is called Duff and the ginger twerp is Sandy. They'll behave themselves as long as we tie their hands behind their backs.' He took a long look around the farmyard and orchard. 'So this is where she's doing her muck-spreading is it? Well, I never thought she'd stick it.'

'Nor did we,' Betty muttered to Yvonne. Aloud, she said, 'Erica says you'll be getting married soon.'

Geoff shrugged. 'When this lot's over. I'd say next week, but she wants a big wedding and we can't fix it with old Hitler liable to send his guests to the reception. I must say it'd be a lot easier to have her nearer the station. We could get married quarters.'

'That'd be a loss to the mess,' the ginger-headed airman commented. He gave Betty a grin and said, 'Geoff's our star performer.' He had rather a nice grin, she thought. And even more freckles than she had herself.

Betty smiled doubtfully, not sure what he meant. Was Geoff an actor or singer, or something? But before she could ask Erica emerged from the farmhouse door and the three men turned and whistled in unison.

'Wowee! You're a lucky chap, Geoff.'

'So this is what the smart dairymaid's wearing in 1940!'

'Doesn't the skirt get caught up in the machinery?'

Erica gave the other two a withering look and swept up to Geoff, holding out her arms. She looked like Ginger Rogers, about to dance with Fred Astaire, Betty thought. She was wearing a white dress with a heart-shaped neckline and tight, fitted bodice, billowing out from the waist in a full, swirling skirt. Her golden hair was pulled back into a pleat at the nape of her neck, and she had smudged blue shadow on her eyelids and smeared Vaseline on her lashes. Her lips were painted bright red.

'Talk about a glamour queen,' Yvonne whispered. 'She looks like Gloria Swanson.'

'After a bad night,' Betty giggled, but she felt envious of Erica all the same. To have a frock like that and the figure and looks to go with it! She pulled discontentedly at her own short curls and found Sandy watching her.

'You'll come with us, won't you?' he said. 'We know a little tea-place about fifteen miles away from here. We thought we'd have a run out. It's not often we get the chance nowadays.'

Betty looked down at her dungarees. 'We haven't got anything to wear. We've only got our working things and a few other bits and pieces. Nothing posh like Erica's.'

He laughed. 'You don't have to look posh. Actually, I think you look very nice as you are. I like girls in slacks and things. Anyway, there's only room for one frock like that in Geoff's old crate.'

'Yes, come on,' Duff joined in. 'We'll need a bit of company to take our minds of these two canoodling!'

Geoff looked up. His face was now liberally daubed with Erica's lipstick and Betty felt half embarrassed, half envious. Fancy being bold enough to kiss her young man like that, in full view of everyone. Well, full view of herself and Yvonne and twenty cows, anyway. She thought of Graham and felt suddenly lonely. What would he say if he knew she was going out with airmen?

Yvonne saw her hesitation. 'Come on, Bet. It's only a run in a car and a cup of tea. You're not being asked to spend a weekend in Paris.'

'Chance'd be a fine thing,' Sandy laughed. 'Not that I'd fancy a weekend there myself just now. But who knows, when the war's over . . .?' He gave Betty a friendly smile and crooked his arm. 'Come on, you sit with me and we'll leave your friend – Yvonne, is it? – to fight off Duff's advances. You'll have to watch him, mind,' he warned Yvonne. 'Last girl he took to the pictures said it was like going out with an octopus. He might be only five foot nothing, but he's got a good reach!'

They crammed themselves into the little car. Erica sat in the front with Geoffrey and the other four scrambled into the back. Betty found herself beside Sandy, while Duff and Yvonne perched on the top of the seat behind them. There was a good deal of laughter and squeals from the girls, and Betty decided to take Yvonne's advice and enjoy herself. After all, what was the point of moping around by yourself when you could have some fun? And they deserved it, didn't they?

They'd worked hard enough on the farm all week.

The little tea-shop was in a pretty village in Sussex. It was part of a flint-built house and had tables set out in a pleasant garden, with a tiny pond. Betty and Yvonne crouched down to exclaim over the goldfish that swam amongst the waterlilies and Erica draped herself gracefully on a garden seat beneath a cherry tree. A waitress in a gingham dress took their orders for tea and sandwiches.

'Plenty of 'em,' Geoffrey demanded. 'And a plate of cakes. And scones with lots of jam. I suppose you haven't got any cream?' he asked with an appealing smile.

The waitress shook her head and went back into the house, and Betty looked around at the peaceful scene.

'You wouldn't think there was a war on, would you? They don't seem to know a thing about it here.'

'Well, it's not on the flight-path, you see. They'd take either a western or an eastern route from here.' Sandy stretched and yawned. 'It's good to have a few hours off.'

Betty looked at him. All the way here, the young airmen had been laughing and joking, but they looked as tired as small boys who have stayed up too late. Their eyes were smudged with fatigue and there were lines that ought not to be on such young faces.

'What's it like?' she asked. 'Flying a plane. Fighting in the sky.'

'Oh, it's wizard fun. There's nothing to beat flying, is there, chaps?' The others shook their heads and suddenly they were all talking together, describing their exploits in the air.

'Bandits everywhere,' Geoff said, waving his hands. 'They just came out of a clear blue sky. No warning at all.'

'That was the day old Snowy came back with half his wing dropping off. He was livid. He loved that crate, darned near took it to bed with him.'

Geoff nodded, still intent on his own tale. 'There was nothing in sight, I was absolutely alone up there, and suddenly I saw it, a vicious-looking brute with a black swastika on its tail. Well, I knew then it was going to be him or me, and I was sure as hell not going to let it be me. Of course, he tried to get behind me, but I wasn't having that, I stalled and dropped below him so that I was behind, and then I started firing. He didn't know what to do. Must've been his first time out, I reckon. Pranged in a field somewhere near Brighton.'

'Was he killed?' Betty asked, and he laughed.

'What do you think? Look, you don't have to feel sorry for 'em. It's us or them. One of our chaps, a gunner he was, was caught in ack-ack over Belgium. The plane caught fire, he knew it could blow up any second, went for his 'chute and found that in flames too. The whole caboodle was ablaze, and all his ammo was going off as well. What could he do?'

'What did he do?' Betty asked, her imagination showing her the young airman, trying desperately to save his life in a blazing aeroplane while anti-aircraft guns fired from below.

'Chucked it all overboard, of course. There was a crew of four, two of them had already baled out. The pilot was still aboard and this gunner managed to get the fire out and the plane limped home. Both pretty badly burned, of course. They say he's in line for a VC. Not bad for a kid of eighteen.'

Eighteen years old! Younger than me, Betty thought. She looked at the three faces again. 'How old are you?'

Geoff grinned. 'Oh, we're ancient. I'm twenty-three, Duff here's twenty-one – got the key of the door last week, didn't you, old man? – and Sandy's the baby. He's nineteen.'

'That's not ancient,' Betty said.

'It is in our line of business,' Geoff replied, and there was a sudden uneasy silence.

Sandy stirred abruptly. 'Where the hell's our tea got to?' He jumped up and went towards the house. His uniform looked too big for him, as if he'd got thinner since it had been issued. The girl in gingham came out, carrying a large tray, and he took it from her and carried it back to the table.

'How about that, then? A teapot they must have pinched from the NAAFI, enough sandwiches to feed an army and a dirty great pile of rock cakes. *And* scones, and a pot of real live strawberry jam. I told you this was a wizard place to come.'

They spread the feast out on the table and fell to with much noisy laughter. How did the café manage to provide such a tea? Betty wondered. But it was true that in the country there didn't seem to be the shortages there were in towns, even though stocks were supposed to be shared fairly round everyone. Still, you could get food off-ration in restaurants and teashops, and if you could have a tea like this every day – or even once a week – it would certainly help the rations go round the rest of the time.

The girl came out three times to replenish their teapot, bringing them more milk and a fresh plate of scones and cakes as well. Betty looked at her face to thank her and glimpsed a strange expression as she gazed at the airmen. A mixture of pain and pity, as if she could see further than the sunny afternoon, into a darkness that lay beyond. She caught Betty's eye and her mouth twisted a little as she turned hurriedly away.

The noisy banter went on, with Yvonne joining in with gusto. But Erica sat silent, her slender body in the white dress pressed close against Geoffrey's side. And for the first time Betty felt some compassion for the girl.

We're all in this together, after all, she thought. And it's as bad for her, saying goodbye to her chap, even though he's only stationed a few miles away, as it is for me seeing Graham off to his ship. And all that daft talk of babies and big weddings doesn't mean she doesn't love him just as much.

She got up to go into the teashop and find a lavatory. The waitress met her at the door. She looked older than Betty had first thought her, about twenty-seven or twenty-eight, perhaps. She nodded her head towards the noisy group on the lawn.

'It's awful, isn't it? They're just kids. They come here a lot, them and their pals, some of 'em haven't even started to shave . . . And then there's a raid and next day there's one or two missing. They never come again. And you know what the rest say if you ask?'

Betty shook her head.

'They say "Old Buster? Oh, he bought it last night." Or he "copped a packet", or "pranged", or something like that. And then one of 'em'll make a joke and they all roar with laughter and never mention his name again.' She looked at Betty, her eyes bright with tears. 'It's not that they don't care. It's that they can't let themselves care. Otherwise it'd break 'em up. And they wouldn't be able to fly. They're all tired out as it is. They're seeing their mates die all around them, all the time. They just wouldn't be able to take it.'

Betty stared at her, appalled. Like everyone else, she had known the facts, known that pilots were being killed. She had never wondered what it was like for those who remained alive, who knew that their chances of being next were greater every time they took to the skies.

'That's why we give 'em a good tea,' the girl said. 'You never know but what it might be their last.'

Their last. Betty came slowly out of the teashop. She looked at the little tableau across the lawn, the table set under the cherry tree, the three young men still laughing and joking around it. Geoffrey was sitting back on the garden seat, his arm around Erica, smoking a cigarette. Duff had shifted his chair closer to Yvonne's and was playing with her hand. Sandy was lying on his back on the grass, his arms behind his head, gazing up into the sky. The sky that was so strangely peaceful today, but which could at any moment turn into a bedlam of fury and killing.

I don't understand it, Betty thought. And she remembered Dennis, the strange young man who had turned his back on the fighting and refused to go to war. Maybe he can explain, she thought. Maybe he's the one who can help me.

CHAPTER ELEVEN

Jess and Peggy Shaw had been in the habit of sharing an afternoon cup of tea together, often with Annie as well. Now they included Kathy Simmons in their little group. They were over at Kathy's one afternoon when they heard a knock on the door.

Kathy heaved herself to her feet and went to answer it. Jess heard her give a cry, almost a scream, and ran to see what was the matter.

'Mike! *Mike*! Oh God, tell me it's you, tell me it's really you, tell me it's not a dream!'

'It's not a dream. It's really me.' He was holding her in his arms, a tall, rather skinny man with straight brown hair and blue eyes. His face had a rubbery look about it, as if he could pull it into any shape he wanted, and as he caught sight of Jess over his wife's shoulder he twisted his mouth into a grin that must have been meant to be comical, but instead brought the tears to Jess's eyes. 'I had to ask my way to find out where I lived,' he said wryly. 'Last time I looked, it was in Portchester Road.'

'Oh, Mike,' Kathy said again. She drew herself away slightly and laughed a little self-consciously. 'This is Jess Budd, from April Grove. She just came in for a bit of a chat. Her sister and Mrs Shaw are here too.'

He nodded, but his eyes were already on Kathy again and Jess knew she and the others must make themselves scarce. They gathered together their bags of knitting and sewing and slipped out of the room and through the front door. It had closed before they were on the pavement.

Inside, Kathy and Mike Simmons were once again in each other's arms. Kathy was trembling, the tears streaming down her face, and Mike held her close, comforting her.

'It was so awful,' she wept. 'Hearing the bombs, *knowing* they were falling on our house – knowing there'd be nothing left when we came out. And there wasn't, not a thing. And our Muriel's baby doll, the one you brought back for her – oh, Mike, its face, its poor little face!'

'There,' he said softly, moving his hands over her back. 'There, it's all right now, Kathy love. It's over. It's been over a long time.'

But for Kathy, it had not been over. Unable to share her experience, having no one she could talk it over with, and having to keep a bright face for the children, she had bottled it all up inside her. Every night she had relived it, until there were times when she had thought she was going mad. And whenever the sirens sounded, the terror slid down her spine once more, sending her scurrying for the shelter where she would crouch with Stella and Muriel close in her arms, praying that the same thing would not happen again.

'Why don't you go out to the country?' Mike asked as he ate the supper she cooked for him. Her first storm of weeping over, she had pulled herself together and made rissoles from a recipe she had heard on the *Kitchen Front* programme on the wireless. There were just enough potatoes, if she didn't have any herself, and a tin of peas. There was no pudding, but Mike declared himself quite satisfied with bread and margarine and a tiny pot of blackberry and apple jam.

'Jess Budd gave it to me. She makes it. It was nice of her, wasn't it, when you think how scarce sugar is now.'

'It's good jam.' He spread it thinly on his bread. The girls, having come in full of excitement to find their father at home, had gone out to play again, with strict instructions not to go beyond the end of the street and to come back at once if the warning sounded. 'I still think you ought to be out in the country.'

'But I want to be here for you. In any case, I thought you didn't believe in it.'

'I've changed my mind.' He looked at her seriously. 'This

war's not going to be over quick, Kathy. I've seen some of it, and it isn't pretty. I'd rather you and the girls were out of it.'

'I've seen it too,' she said obstinately. 'But where would you have gone tonight if I hadn't been here? What would you have done?'

'I'd have stayed aboard ship, like I do other times.' He pushed his plate aside and took her hands in his. 'Kathy, I went and had a look at Portchester Road. They've patched it up a bit now, but I could see what it must've been like. And our house, there's nothing left of it, Kath.'

'I know,' she said, her voice trembling. 'I know.'

He came round the table and put his arms around her shoulders. 'I can't stop thinking of you and the kids in there,' he said. 'Having to manage by yourself and look after them and everything. And what about when the baby comes?' He laid his hand on her stomach and felt the kicking of unborn feet, the punch of unborn fists. 'That's three of them you've got to get down the shelter in the middle of the night. What sort of a life is that? And suppose you get bombed out again?'

'We'd have to move again, I suppose.' She shrugged, then collapsed against him. 'Oh, Mike, I know you're right, I know we ought to go away. Every time the siren goes it's like a knife slicing through me. And I'm scared stiff the girls will be out in the street and won't be able to get back. There was a woman strafed in the street the other day, just going home with her shopping she was, and a plane came right down low and fired a machine-gun at her. In the street! If they did that to our girls . . . But I just can't face it, somehow. Going away, living with strangers. And you know I'm scared of cows!'

Mike burst out laughing. 'Cows? You're scared of *cows*?' But there was more pain than mirth in his laughter. 'Kathy, if that's what it'd take to make you move I'll write to Hitler personally and ask him to send cows instead of bombs.' He held her against him again. 'Let's get the washing-up done now, love, and talk about it again later on. I want to have a bit of time with the girls.'

As he spoke, the air-raid warning sounded for the third time that day, and Kathy flew to the door to call the children from their game. Mike got his wish to spend some time with the girls, for they were in the shelter for the rest of the night after that, not coming out until after the All-Clear at six in the morning. But there was no more time to talk, for by eight he had to be back on board his ship and although Kathy waited all the next evening in the hope that he would be able to come ashore, he never arrived. The ship had sailed, and there was no knowing when she would see him again.

She touched her swollen stomach. By the time Mike came home, the baby might be born. Might be sitting up, walking, talking. Might be out at work, earning a living, she thought bitterly, and cursed the madman over the Channel who had taken her husband away from her.

She thought again about asking to be evacuated. If only Mike had been home a bit longer, if only he could have helped her, she might have agreed to go. But now that she was on her own again, she knew that she had spoken the truth. She really couldn't face it.

And still they came. That one day of peace, when no bombers approached the south coast, when no air-raid warnings sounded, when Betty and Yvonne and Erica spent the afternoon having tea on a sunny lawn, proved to be no more than a flicker of bright light; a brief, teasing reminder of what life could be, and once had been. The next day the raiders returned in force and continued their bombardment of the city of London, paying attention to other towns and cities while they did so. The sound of the sirens became commonplace and while some people remained terrified, others began to develop a defiant, almost blasé attitude towards them. Peggy and Bert Shaw, playing whist with their daughters, finished the hand before gathering up their belongings to run down the garden to the shelter. Jess's mother Mary refused to budge until she had completed a row of her knitting. 'You never pick it up at the same tension again,' she said when Arthur urged her to hurry. And Granny Kinch flatly refused to go to the shelter at all. 'I'm too old to go gallivanting at night,' she told Tommy Vickers with a wink. 'I leave that to the younger ones.'

'Like your Nancy,' he said, and then wished he could bite

his tongue. Who was to say Nancy Baxter wasn't doing a service to the young soldiers and sailors who were facing death every day? He thought of Graham Philpotts, desperate to know what sex was like before he went to sea, and of Graham's sweetheart Betty, too 'respectable' and too inhibited to share it with him. Well, you couldn't blame the girl, but neither could you blame Graham for going home with Nancy, as Tommy was certain he had. What else could a young feller do?

Granny Kinch said nothing. She knew Tommy of old, and she wasn't going to apologise to him for what her Nancy did. Of all the people in April Grove, he was the only one who might understand and make allowances. After all, he'd been in the Navy, he must have met other Nancies in his time, yes and made use of them too. He knew what their lives were like, even if he didn't know what drove them to it.

The old woman turned and hobbled back indoors. Nancy was making a cup of tea, a cigarette hanging from her lip. She had the baby Vera balanced on one hip, grizzling.

'This hot weather plays hell with my feet,' Granny Kinch said, sinking into her sagging armchair. 'Look 'ow swollen my ankles are. And there's flea-bites all up my legs. It's that cat of yours, mangy thing, it must be riddled with vermin.'

'Go on, Ma, we always has fleas in summer.'

'Only because of your cat. It ain't healthy, Nance, having it around with a baby just starting to crawl. You don't know what she's putting in her mouth. There was a dead mouse under the chair for days last week, she could've ate it any time.'

'What, our Vera?' Nancy gave a short laugh. 'It's hard enough getting her dinner down her, let alone dead mice. She wouldn't eat a Christmas dinner if she found it on the floor.'

Granny Kinch sniffed and said nothing. Nancy passed her a cup of tea and she sucked at it.

'Where's young Micky?'

'I dunno. Out somewhere. He's bin running errands for people for a bit of pocket-money.'

'Is that where this come from?' Mrs Kinch picked up a china ashtray. It had a picture of a beach on it and the words

'A Present from Brighton' printed round the edge. 'Run as far as Brighton, did 'e?'

'Oh, that's just something someone give him. Didn't have no money, see, so they give him that instead.' Nancy glanced out of the back window. 'Here he comes now. Looks as if he's got a bag full of groceries.'

Micky came in, swaggering. He dumped a large paper bag on the table and tipped it over. Several tins of fruit rolled out and his mother and grandmother stared at them in astonishment.

'That's peaches!' Granny Kinch said. 'I ain't seen a tin of peaches in a year. Where d'you get those, Micky?'

He shrugged and grinned. 'That's for me to know.'

'Micky!' Nancy said sharply. 'Don't cheek your gran. Tell us where you got the peaches. Runnin' errands, were you?'

'That's right.' He glanced at them sideways. 'Got meself a job. Errand boy at a shop. The boss said I could take whatever I liked.'

'He said you could take *peaches*?'

'Yeah. Whatever I like, I can 'ave.' He struck a nonchalant pose. 'He'll pay me too.'

'What shop's this?' Nancy asked suspiciously. 'Is it far away?' Nobody around September Street was likely to employ Micky.

'Down past Kingston Cross. You wouldn't know it.' He stood the tins upright, balancing them in a tower. 'I can go down there whenever I like. An' I got another job too, choppin' wood for a bloke down Charlotte Street. He gives me fruit an' stuff. I can get all sorts.'

He turned away and they heard him clatter up the stairs. Nancy and her mother looked at each other.

'I s'pose it's all right,' Granny Kinch said. 'So long as he gets in a shelter when the siren goes.'

'Oh, he always does that. I made him promise.'

They looked at the tins again.

'Peaches . . .' Granny Kinch said.

Micky had his little gang well organised now. As soon as the siren sounded, they were out in the back alleys, keeping a wary eye open for air-raid wardens, watching to see people run for their shelters. Nine times out of ten the back door was left open and the boys could slip inside, grab whatever was left lying about, and be gone before the Raiders Passed signal.

You had to be careful, of course – sometimes there was someone left in the house, someone too slow or stubborn to run down the garden. Jimmy Cross once had the fright of his life when he nipped through a back door and suddenly caught sight of a pair of eyes watching him as he riffled through a sideboard drawer. 'I thought it was just a pile of old clothes,' he said indignantly to the others, 'an' it was this old bloke, all huddled up in blankets and stuff. He never said a word, just looked at me, like he was a ghost or something. Didn't 'alf make me jump.'

'Too old to take down the shelter, I s'pose,' Micky said. He sorted through the day's collection. 'We got some good stuff here. Cyril found this wallet with nearly three pound in it, and Jimmy got a pot of jam and a bag of sausages, and I got this.' He held up his own booty with pride and the other boys whistled.

'Cor! A model Spitfire. That's smashing.'

'Someone's made it, see.' Micky set the aeroplane on a box they were using as a table. It was about two feet long, made from wood which had been smoothed and polished, and its wings were made of parchment. 'I bet it was a real pilot made that,' he said, touching it lovingly. 'You can see it's a proper one.'

Making model aeroplanes was a craze amongst all the boys. Comics like *Wizard* and *Beano* carried instructions almost every week, and nearly everyone had a cat's cradle of cotton and string festooned across their bedroom ceilings, with aircraft arranged as if in flight.

This one had not been made by any boy, though. It was clear, as Micky said, that an adult hand had fashioned the wood and shaped the wings; an adult who knew aeroplanes, too. The boys gazed at it with awe.

'That's our best thing.'

'It's my best thing,' Micky corrected them, pushing away their hands. 'I found it.'

'I thought we were going to share everything we found.'

'Stuff like food and money, yeah. But not this. Unless you want me to cut it up into bits?' He picked it up again and held it on his lap, stroking the polished wood. 'Here, how about making a fire and cooking those sausages? I could do with summat to eat.'

Willingly, the other two boys set about gathering wood from the debris which still littered the bombed house. They lit the fire in the middle of the basement floor – they had already tried using the fireplaces, but found the chimneys blocked – and cooked the sausages on an old tin coal shovel they had found. They were burnt on the outside and raw halfway through, but to the boys they were the best sausages they had ever eaten.

'We could live in a place like this,' Micky said, stretching back on his broken chair. 'When the Germans come, we'll hide down here and creep out at night and sabotage 'em. We could murder 'em and they'd never know who it was.'

Replete with half-raw sausages, they sat in the dank gloom of the ruined basement, gazing at the model aeroplane and contemplating a future filled with adventure and excitement. Micky's mind drifted back to the days before the war, days when he had been expected to go to school every day and sit at a desk, bored and frustrated.

'It's good, this war is,' he said with satisfaction. 'I 'ope it goes on for ever 'n' ever.'

In London, people were changing their entire day in order to accommodate the timetable of Goering's bombers.

Shops and offices closed an hour earlier to allow workers to reach home in time for a meal before taking to the shelters. There was no need for a warning – everyone was in place by eight o'clock, women with their bags full of knitting and magazines, men with their newspapers and pipes. After some efforts to prevent it, the Underground stations were now an accepted place of shelter. There was quite a party atmosphere down there, it was reported, with singing and dancing, and even a few impromptu bands composed of mouth organs, concertinas and, if all else failed, the good old comb and lavatory-paper.

The daily newspapers carried pictures of devastation. Huge piles of rubble were all that were left of the great Oxford Street stores, wrecked houses stood open to the sky, vast craters swallowed entire streets. Shops had their stocks burned or ruined by water, and people who were suffering the deprivation of rationing were galled to see molten butter flooding from a storehouse and running down the drains, or precious sugar burning like coal.

There was another rush for safety. Children who had come home from the country during the 'phoney war' were sent back again. True to her word, Ethel Glaister sent her daughter Shirley to Canada, going to Southampton to see her off on a big liner.

In Portsmouth, people found themselves spending long hours in their air-raid shelters. And even worse than the frustration and annoyance of such disruption and wasted time, they found themselves more and more often returning to their homes to find that they had been looted. The newspapers were full of such cases; even a few policemen were found guilty.

'It's kids that's the worst, though,' Frank said, sitting at the table with the *Evening News* spread out in front of him. 'And I bet I know who's one of the ringleaders. Probation! A young hooligan like Micky Baxter's not going to take notice of probation.'

'You don't know it's him, Frank.' Jess took the paper from him and studied it. 'You shouldn't paint people black without knowing the truth.'

'Paint him black! I don't need to – he already is black.'

'We haven't heard he's been in any trouble since that business with the jeweller's shop. Perhaps he's learnt his lesson.' Her eyes moved down the columns. 'Oh, listen to this. One little boy told the magistrate he'd got no school to go to and no friends to play with. "I just took things to play with," he said. "I thought the people weren't coming back." Poor little chap.' She laid the paper down. 'He was just lonely. And frightened too, I daresay.'

But Frank looked stern and shook his head. 'Stealing's

stealing. If they don't make an example of boys like him, all the little scamps'll be at it. People have got enough to put up with, without having to reckon with burglars every time the warning goes.'

A sudden violent knocking at the door startled them both. Jess gasped and reached down to pull the baby on to her lap. She looked wide-eyed at Frank.

'D'you think it's them?' The fear of invasion was a menace in everyone's minds. Already there had been reports of German landings at Stokes Bay and other south coast beaches. Nobody knew if it was true that hundreds had been killed, or if it was just rumour, but every unexpected knock on the door brought the same thrill of terror as the wail of the siren. 'Oh, Frank . . .'

'Of course it's not. They wouldn't knock.' But he went down the passage and opened the door with some caution before he looked out.

Ethel Glaister stood there, her cheeks running with tears. Before he could speak, she was in his arms, her face pressed against his shirt. She clutched him, sobbing, and he staggered slightly then held her, patting her shoulder and looking round for Jess.

'What's the matter?' Jess was at the end of the passage, staring at them. 'Who is it?'

'It's Ethel, Mrs Glaister.' He gestured helplessly. 'She's upset. You'd better come in,' he said to the weeping woman. 'Tell us what's happened. Is it George?'

Ethel shook her head. Even in her distress, she managed to convey the impression that she wouldn't have been in this state if it had just been George . . . She sank down on a chair at the table and leaned her head on her hands. Her weeping was almost hysterical.

Jess pushed Frank aside. She viewed Ethel Glaister's woe with concern but she wasn't going to have the woman weeping in Frank's arms. She put her hand on Ethel's shoulder and spoke gently.

'What is it, Ethel? What's happened? Try to tell us.'

'It's Shirley. Our Shirl.' Ethel broke into a fresh gust of sobs. 'Oh, I shouldn't never have done it, I shouldn't never have sent her off . . .'

'Shirley? But she's gone to Canada, she's gone to be safe. What's happened to her?'

Ethel raised her head. Her face distorted like a child's. The make-up she habitually wore was streaked and blotchy. Her eyes were puffed with tears.

'Safe!' she echoed bitterly. 'Safe! They've only torpedoed the bloody ship, that's all. Torpedoed a ship loaded with kids. I mean, what good does that do them, eh? Why should they do a thing like that? Little children!'

Jess and Frank stared at her.

'They've torpedoed the ship? Are you sure?'

'It was on the wireless,' she said drearily. 'They reckon there's hardly any survivors.'

'Oh, *Ethel*,' Jess said, and put her arms around Ethel's shoulders, drawing her close. 'Ethel, that's terrible. I really am sorry.'

Frank stood hesitantly beside her. He was as appalled as Jess, but had no words to express his horror. He caught Jess's eye and realised she wanted him to make Ethel a cup of tea. Thankful to have something to do, he hurried out to the scullery and put the kettle on.

Little Shirley Glaister! She was such a sunny little thing, always smiling and skipping on the garden path. She used to talk to him when he was out in the garden, chattering away nineteen to the dozen, telling him what she'd been doing at school and asking endless questions. What are you doing, Mr Budd? Why? Why is the sky blue, why is grass green, why, why, why?

It made his head buzz at times but he liked her questions. He thought they showed a bright little mind. And now that little mind had been snuffed out, the bright smile wiped away for ever, the chatter silenced.

He went back with three cups of tea. After a shock like that, they could all do with one. He looked at Jess, still standing with her arms around Ethel, and he knew that there was no need to search for the right words, for there were none. At times like this, there was nothing that anyone could say.

*

The report of the torpedoing reached the newspapers a day or so later. Jess went into the newsagent's and looked at the headlines with Alice Brunner.

'Poor little mite,' Alice Brunner said. 'I don't wish her any harm, she was a nice enough little scrap. But maybe that cat of a mother of hers has got some idea now of what I've been going through all these months.'

'Oh, Alice.' Jess hated to hear the bitterness in her friend's voice. But she couldn't blame Alice. She had suffered more than enough from the cruel remarks made by Ethel at the outbreak of war, when she had called Heinrich an enemy and a spy and tried to prevent customers from using the Brunners' shop. And she had still not heard officially whether Heinrich had died when the *Arandora Star* had been sunk. That, too, had been on the way to Canada.

'We don't even know for sure that Shirley was on that ship,' she said. 'It doesn't give its name here. I suppose they want to let the families know before they read about it in the paper. But you're bound to think it's that one, aren't you?'

'I don't know why she ever wanted to send the child that far away,' Alice observed. 'She's got relations in Devon, hasn't she? She was always on about them and talking about her holidays with them. Why not send the kiddy there? She just wanted to be better than the rest of us, that's what it was. Wanted something to be stuck up about.'

Jess didn't answer. She was growing more and more worried about Alice these days. There was a brittle nervousness about her, a sense that she was hovering on the brink of disaster. She's going to break up completely if something isn't done, Jess thought, gazing at the white face with its flushed cheeks and over-bright eyes. But what could anyone do? It was Heinrich she needed.

'I don't think it does any good to say that sort of thing,' she said at last. 'It's help Ethel needs now. There can't be anything worse than losing a child.'

Alice turned away and started to mark up the pile of evening papers. Joy came in from the back room to help her and they worked in silence for a few minutes. Jess, seeing that Alice didn't want to talk any more, picked up her own paper and went out.

'What difference does it make anyway?' Alice burst out suddenly. 'I mean, I'm sorry for little Shirley Glaister, of course I am, but it don't make any difference whether you're a little child or a grown man when you've been torpedoed. The water was just as cold for your father as it was for Shirley Glaister. It was just as bad for him, floating in hundreds of feet of water, knowing nobody was going to save him. It's as bad for everyone that gets killed.'

Joy gazed at her. 'Mum . . .'

'Everyone tells me to be brave. Everyone says we don't know for certain he's been killed, he could still turn up, stranger things have happened. D'you know something, Joy? I wish we *did* know for certain. I'd rather – I'd rather know he's been drowned than go through this – not knowing, wondering every day whether I might get a telegram, whether he might even walk through the door.' She dropped her pencil on the heap of papers and burst into tears. 'I just can't stand much more of it! I can't *stand* it . . .'

'Mum,' Joy repeated helplessly, but Alice pushed past her and ran through the door to the back room. A moment later, Joy heard her feet on the stairs.

She stood for a moment, struggling with her own tears. A few dropped on to the newspapers and smudged the print.

Alice would not come downstairs again that day, she knew. She would lie on her bed and Joy would hear her sobbing. She would refuse anything to eat and if Joy took her a cup of tea it was as likely to go cold as to be drunk. And there didn't seem to be anything anyone could do for her.

And meanwhile there would be people coming in for their papers, the delivery boys would want their satchels filled and the shop would have to be kept open until six o'clock.

Joy brushed her hand across her eyes and picked up the pencil.

CHAPTER TWELVE

'I wonder that Dennis has got the nerve to show his face when my Geoffrey comes here,' Erica said one day after they had waved the little sports car down the lane. 'I don't know how he can stand there, knowing they're risking their lives to save his yellow skin.'

'It's not easy being a CO,' Betty said. 'He's had to go to prison, you know.'

'Good thing too. Pity they ever let him out.'

The atmosphere on the farm was strained. Mr and Mrs Spencer had accepted Dennis for what he was, and provided he did his job well took the view that his principles were none of their business. Yvonne treated him, as she did everyone, with casual friendliness. But Erica made no secret of her contempt and loathing, and Mrs Spencer's sister Iris, who was married to an army captain, sided with Erica and did her best to pretend that Dennis did not exist.

'He's smarmy,' she said. 'He knows when he's well off! It's all wrong, employing men like him when there's good patriotic farmworkers being called up.'

'We've got to get the work done,' Mrs Spencer said mildly. 'Dennis is a good worker.'

'Conchie-petting!' Iris Blake said disgustedly. 'Do you know, they get *paid* when they go for their interview? *And* get a luncheon for three-and-six. I read it in the paper. And then they get a nice soft life on a farm when my husband and Erica's fiancé are risking their lives fighting for their country.' She gave her brother-in-law a defiant look. 'There's plenty of farmers who'd refuse to take 'em.'

'Look,' Mr Spencer said with some force, 'I'm not a politician, I don't know the rights and wrongs of all this, I'm just a farmer trying to do my job. I'm producing food for my country, which I love just as much as anyone else, and I'll take what labour I can get to help me do it. Aye, prisoners of war if it comes to it. Why not? And Ada's right, Dennis is a good worker and he's no trouble about the place. As far as I'm concerned, his reasons are his own affair.'

'They ought to be ours as well —'

'No!' Mr Spencer thumped his fist on the table. 'The man's been to a tribunal, he's been to prison. He's proved himself, and that's good enough for me. I thought this country believed in free speech. I thought that was what this war was all about, letting people live the way they want to live and believe the things they want to believe. And that's the way it'll be on this farm and in this house.' He glowered at his sister-in-law. 'And anyone who doesn't like that can always find themselves somewhere else to live.'

The two stared at each other and then Iris Blake got up and flounced out of the room. There was a small, embarrassed pause and then Mr Spencer glanced at his wife.

'I'm sorry, Ada, but it had to be said. We can't have her making trouble. You know what she's like once she takes against someone.'

'Oh, I know. Our Iris always did set herself a cut above the rest of us. But this is our place, and if she wants to sit at our table she has to put up with our ways.'

'And that goes for us too,' Yvonne said later, as the three girls walked across the yard to the milking shed. 'No more snide remarks about Dennis, see, Erica? Mr and Mrs Spencer don't like it.'

Erica tossed her head.

'I'll say what I like. Free speech counts all ways. And I think Mrs Blake's right — he is smarmy.'

However, there was little time for the situation to develop any further, for there was more than enough work to do and the girls found themselves up at six every morning in order to get it all finished during the diminishing hours of daylight. By the evening, they were usually too exhausted to do anything other than flop on the sagging sofas in the untidy living-room, or on their beds in the narrow attic.

'I'm growing out of all my clothes,' Betty wailed one day as she went through her chest of drawers. She had been home for the weekend to collect her winter skirts and jumpers. 'Everything's too tight.'

'Mine too,' Yvonne said. 'My mum says I'm getting fat, but I don't see how we can be, working the way we do.'

'It's muscle. We're getting stronger, that's what it is.'

Erica gave a shriek. '*Muscle*? But I don't want to get muscles. Girls don't have muscles.'

'Land Girls do,' Betty said, and rolled up her sleeve to look at her arm. It was smooth and firm. 'I couldn't have lifted a bale of hay when we came here and now I can shift 'em all day without noticing. I don't mind getting strong, if it makes the work easier.' She looked out of the attic window. Autumn was beginning to tint the trees with red and brown, and the recently harvested fields were a carpet of golden stubble. The cows were grazing peacefully and she could see Dennis walking across one of the meadows to look at the sheep.

What was he thinking? He was always friendly and good-humoured, but mostly fairly quiet, keeping his thoughts to himself. He must know what people like Erica and Mrs Blake thought of him. Did he care?

She thought of the day the aeroplane had crashed. He hadn't behaved like a coward then. But neither had he shown any hatred for the German pilot and crew. It seemed that, to him, they were just people. Young men like himself, caught up in someone else's war.

The sky was a soft haze, half blue and half gold, fading towards a pearly horizon. A creamy mist drifted between the trees. And as she watched she saw, appearing out of a glow of apricot, a formation of aircraft flying steadily north from the coast.

'Look,' she whispered, and the other two girls came over and knelt beside her, staring out.

'They're Jerries,' Yvonne said in a low voice. 'They're heading for London.'

The planes came nearer. Their shapes were clearly

discernible now. They were like a menacing cloud in the golden sky, like a dark cloak which grew larger with every second and would soon be thrown over the shimmering landscape.

'Oh, no . . .' Betty breathed. 'Oh, no . . .'

The planes were almost overhead. Dennis, walking in the meadow, was standing quite still, watching them. The cows were restless, showing signs of alarm, tossing their heads and flicking their tails. The sheep had huddled together, bleating. And then, from high in the sky, there was a sudden swoop of smaller aircraft, like wasps buzzing around the relentless advance, and the girls saw the spattering of the guns and the little bursts of fire, only seconds before they heard the sounds.

In another moment the formation had broken up and the battle was on. The girls ran downstairs and out into the yard, ignoring all the advice they had ever been given to find places of safety while such fights were taking place. They stood staring up at the turmoil, watching the Spitfires dart like mosquitoes around the marauders, watching the more ponderous Hurricanes as they marked their victim and went in for the kill.

Betty lifted her hand to her mouth, biting her knuckles. She saw the flash of fire as one of the German planes was hit. For a second or two it seemed to hesitate, hanging in the sky, and then the flames burst all around it, enveloping it in a brilliant sheet of orange light and thick, billowing black smoke as it spiralled towards the earth.

Betty gasped and shut her eyes tightly. When she opened them again, the plane had gone, but there were others filling the space where it had been, RAF and Luftwaffe all mixed up together, swooping and darting about the sky, the air streaked with flame as more aircraft were hit, some to follow the first to earth, others to lurch away in an effort to escape. And, here and there, the white puffing umbrella of a parachute as the airmen baled out.

Yvonne screamed and turned to clutch Betty's arm and bury her head in her shoulder. They clung together, staring at the sky, half crying, half laughing as the planes of the RAF finally routed the invaders, and sent them scattering and making for the coast from where they had come.

'Hurray!' Erica cried, leaping up and down in her dungarees. 'That gave 'em what for! That taught 'em a lesson! They won't come over here again in a hurry.' She caught Betty's hands and danced her round the yard. 'I bet that was my Geoffrey up there. I bet he scored some hits. He sent them home with a flea in their ears!'

Betty laughed with her, but there was a feeling of unease in her heart. Some of those planes had been shot down, and some of them had been British planes. Suppose Geoff's had been one of them? So far he seemed to have led a charmed life, but how long could anyone's luck last?

She saw Dennis come into the yard. His face was sober, his eyes veiled. He looked at the dancing girls, and for a moment she thought he was about to say something. And then he seemed to change his mind. He walked slowly past, without speaking, and went into the house.

Betty felt a sudden chill, as if another shadow had passed across the sky. She withdrew her hands from Erica's and moved away. Suddenly, laughter and dancing seemed out of place.

They were sitting round the table in the farmhouse kitchen having their meal later that evening when they heard the sound of the little car buzzing down the lane like a bee. Erica jumped up, her eyes alight. She ran out into the yard, but when she returned a few moments later the light had died from her eyes and she looked pale and frightened.

'It's Duff and Sandy,' she said, and then stopped as if her voice had stuck. She opened her mouth but nothing emerged but a queer strangling sound. She reached out blindly and gripped the back of a chair.

'They – they say –' She shook her head, and tried again. 'They –'

Betty stared at her. Her face was paper-white, her blue eyes enormous. Her whole body was quivering.

The two young men were standing miserably behind her. Betty sought Sandy's eyes but they were downcast. She felt horror brush cold across her skin and spread like a chill web

216

over her body.

Mrs Spencer came swiftly to her feet. She put her hand on Erica's arm and looked at the two airmen.

'Geoff?' All the questions that needed to be asked were in that one syllable. Betty wanted to turn her head away; she didn't want to hear the answer. But her eyes were riveted on Erica's white face.

'Was Geoff – is he –?' She couldn't bring herself to say the words. She shook her own head and tried again. 'Sandy?'

'His plane was shot down this afternoon,' Sandy said in a dull, flat voice. 'I saw it go. He didn't bale out.'

Erica's knees buckled suddenly. Her tears burst from her in great sobs and she collapsed against the chair. Sandy caught her in his arms and held her against him, then carried her through to the sofa in the living room. He laid her down and knelt beside her, stroking her hair. The others followed, Mrs Spencer settling the cushions around her and covering her with a crochet rug, Mr Spencer going straight to the cupboard where he kept a small stock of bottles. Betty and Yvonne knelt beside Sandy, stroking Erica's hands, and Duff hovered uneasily in the background. Even the Blake children were momentarily silenced, their mother's mouth a thin bitter line, while Dennis stood grim-faced beside the door.

'Here, girl, sip this.' Mr Spencer poured some brandy into a glass and held it to Erica's lips. She turned her head away. 'Come on, it'll do you good. You've had a bad shock.'

Erica sipped and coughed. 'I don't want it.'

'Another sip. Come on.'

'I don't want it, I tell you. I want Geoff – my Geoff.' She stared up at them. Her eyes were like black pits in her white face. 'Get my Geoff for me. Get him! I want him, I want him *now*!'

Mrs Spencer spoke soothingly, her voice dry with pity. 'Oh, my poor lamb, we can't get Geoff for you. He – he's –'

'He's *not*!' she cried before Mrs Spencer could utter the dreadful words. 'He's not, he's not. He can't be. He's my Geoff. It's all a horrible lie, it's a joke.' She turned her desperate eyes on the other two young airmen. 'That's what it is, isn't it? It's a joke. You've cooked it up between you, the three of you, and Geoff's outside now. He'll come in any minute and tell me it's all a joke. He *will*.' She paused, staring from face to face while they all gazed unhappily back at her, not knowing what to say. 'He will, won't he?' she whispered, and her voice sounded very thin and small and lonely in the silent room.

'Oh, Erica,' Betty said, and pushed past Sandy to pull the other girl against her. 'Oh, poor, poor Erica.'

Geoff, shot down. Geoff, killed. Was it his plane they had seen, spiralling towards the earth with smoke and flame billowing from the cockpit? Had they actually seen Geoff's last moments, had he looked down and seen them, staring up towards him, known that they were there?

Her own tears were flowing fast now. They ran down her cheeks and into Erica's hair. The fair girl felt their wetness against her neck and drew back her head.

'You're crying,' she said in a tone of surprise, and then her sobs began again, sobs of fury as well as grief, a wild and useless raging against the war that had taken her Geoff away.

At the back of the room, Iris Blake turned on Dennis, her face contorted with fury. 'Well, I just hope you're satisfied!' she blazed. 'I just hope you're enjoying yourself, watching this poor girl suffer. It ought to have been *you* up there today, getting killed. It ought to be you, giving your life to save your country. Why should you and your yellow friends be allowed to stay safe at home in the country, when better men are getting blown to pieces? What's so bloody marvellous about *you* that you get let off? Prison! You ought to have been kept there for the rest of your life. If I had my way, you'd be *shot*!'

There was a moment's silence. Erica was still sobbing. Betty knelt beside her, holding her close, sharing her tears, but at Mrs Blake's words she lifted her head.

Jack Spencer moved forwards.

'Now look, Iris –'

'Oh yes,' she retorted, 'you'll take his part, won't you. You'll stand up for him. And you with two sons of your own away fighting, risking their lives. I don't know how you can, Jack, I really don't, no, nor you, Ada. Don't you care? Doesn't it mean a thing to you, what they're going through? And this girl, her young man's been shot out of the sky, burnt to death as like as not and crying for his mother – I don't know how you can give this lily-livered milksop house-room. You ought to turn him out this minute.'

'I've told you before, Iris –'

Dennis stepped forwards. 'No. Don't argue with her, Mr Spencer. She's got a right to her opinion.' He turned to Mrs Blake. 'I know you can't understand. Not many people can. But believe me, it's not because I'm a coward that I won't fight. It's not because I'm afraid.' He paused for a moment. 'Or maybe it is. Because I *am* afraid. I'm afraid of having to do what some German did to Geoff this afternoon. I'm afraid to have to shoot another man out of the sky. I'm afraid of having to kill people I don't know and have no reason to hate. I'm even afraid of killing people I do hate. Because to me, that's the worst possible thing I could do. Because I don't believe another man's life is mine to take.' He paused again. His face was pale and there was a strange fervour in his eyes, a passion taut in his voice. 'If it came to a straight choice between doing that and being shot, I'd choose to be shot.'

He turned and walked quietly out of the room. But Betty had seen the set of his shoulders. She knew that he was deeply upset.

Erica was still weeping. Betty tightened her arms about her, rocking her gently as if she were a small child. She felt Erica's pain mingle with Dennis's passion in her own body, and her mind reeled with the confusion of it all.

Iris Blake looked around at the shocked faces. She tilted her chin in defiance.

'Excuses!' she said scornfully. 'Just nothing but excuses!'

CHAPTER THIRTEEN

The city of London exploded and burned about its inhabitants' ears. There was no doubt now that the war would not be easily won. There was doubt that it might be won at all.

'Why don't we just give in?' Kathy Simmons said miserably. She crossed her arms over her bulging stomach, as if to keep her growing baby safe. Jess remembered feeling the same when she had been expecting Maureen. But a baby wasn't any safer inside its mother than out. A mother's body was as likely to be blown up as a baby's . . . 'Why don't we just let him come and take over? We could just go back to living normal, without all this killing.'

'Could we?' It was tempting to think so, but Frank said that people who thought that way didn't realise what life would be like under Hitler. They'd already forgotten what he'd done to the Jews. Making them wear yellow stars, not letting them do decent jobs, forcing them to live like rats . . . And there had been those horrible stories about camps like Auschwitz, reported in the papers last year. And the terrible things that had happened in Poland . . . Would he let anyone live a normal life?

'We can't give up now,' she said. 'We're in it too deep.' She looked compassionately at Kathy. 'I suppose there's no chance of your husband getting home?'

'Not this side of heaven.' Kathy flinched. 'I didn't mean that! It didn't come out the way I meant. I just meant, it'll be heaven when he *does* come home, not –'

'I know. It's all right.' It was all too easy to make a casual remark and then realise what it sounded like. 'Look, you know you can come over to Frank and me any time you want anything, don't you? Day or night, it doesn't matter.' She thought of Kathy in her air-raid shelter at night, alone with two little girls. Suppose the baby started to come then? 'If you want to be with us at night anyway, when the time comes – well, you know you're welcome.'

Kathy shook her head. 'There's not room, is there? These little dugouts aren't meant to have parties in. I'll be all right. I don't have babies quick anyway, the girls both took over twelve hours. But I'll be glad of your help just to give an eye to them while I'm laid up.'

Laid up! Why, she wouldn't even be able to go to the shelter after the birth. She ought to be in hospital, Jess thought, where she can be properly looked after.

'Haven't you got any relations? Isn't there anyone you can go to?'

'Not a soul,' Kathy said with a cheerfulness that didn't fool Jess for a minute. 'I'm not a Pompey girl, you see. Mike and me, we both come from Basingstoke. My mum and dad died when I was a kiddy, I was brought up by my gran. She's over ninety now and lives with my aunty, and she hasn't got room for me as well, anyway, we never did get on very well. And Mike's mum's in a home. She don't hardly know what time of day it is.'

Jess gazed at her. How lonely it sounded. She thought of her own family, of her sister Annie who lived at the end of the street and whose family had been in and out of Jess's house ever since they'd moved to April Grove. And Frank's brother Howard, over in Gosport. She and Annie still had their mum and dad, living down North End, and she and Frank had their own four children, close as a family could be even though the war had parted them for the time being. She felt a sudden savage longing for them. Families shouldn't be apart, she thought. They ought to be together, no matter what . . .

'You come over to us any time you like,' she said warmly. 'And I'll come over and stop with you when the baby's born, if you want me to. I know our Annie'll say the same – and Peggy Shaw, and half a dozen other women round here. We won't let you be on your own.'

She went up the street, pushing Maureen's pram. *We won't let you be on your own.* But Kathy Simmons *was* on her own, wasn't she? And so were thousands more like her, young wives and mothers left to manage by themselves, with no idea when their men might be back again. And more and more of them, as time went on, having to manage for the rest of their lives, as widows.

She went into the butcher's shop. There was little enough on the slab these days, but Mr Hines was a kindly man and often had a few sausages or a bit of liver for her. He'd taken a fancy to Maureen too, and liked Jess to take the toddler into the shop with her. Jess lifted her from the pram and let her stagger in on her own legs.

'Well, if it isn't my best girl!' The butcher wiped his big red hands down his blue striped apron and bent to pick Maureen up. He was wearing his straw hat and the baby reached up and grabbed it. 'D'you want my hat, then?' He took it off and plonked it on Maureen's head. It came down over her eyes and she gurgled with laughter.

He stood Maureen on the counter and leaned across to Jess. His face was serious. 'Are you popping in to see Alice Brunner today?'

'I always do. She's been looking worse than ever lately.'

He nodded. 'The wife's proper worried about her. Seems to be losing her grip on things. It's young Joy does all the work there now. Gets up early, marks up the papers, sorts out the paper-boys. Same again in the evenings. And keeps the shop going too. It's not right for a young girl.'

'Joy's a good girl though,' Jess said uneasily. 'She's always been a help.'

'Yes, but to run the place more or less single-handed . . . She's not fourteen yet, you know, she ought to be at school by rights. And she needs her mum to be a mum to her, not lay about all day feeling sorry for herself.'

Jess sighed. It was easy enough to say that Alice ought to pull herself together, but who knew what it felt like to have had your husband torn away from you, thrust into prison and then sent overseas all because he was an 'alien' – even though he'd lived in England almost all his adult life? And worst of all, to hear that his ship had been torpedoed and not even to know whether he was dead or alive . . . Some days, Alice had told Jess, she was certain he was dead. Other times she was equally sure he was alive. And for much of the time, she could only torment herself by wondering.

'I don't know what we can do,' she said miserably. 'Except keep popping in, let her know she's got friends all around who'll help her.'

'Well, she's got those all right,' Mr Hines said warmly. 'Trouble is, she's also got a few of the other sort. Naming no names.'

He didn't need to. Both of them knew that Ethel Glaister was one of the most vociferous of Alice's enemies, never averse to making loud remarks about Germans and aliens in her hearing. Both Jess and Peggy Shaw had had sharp words with Ethel over that, but you couldn't stop spite and Ethel wasn't the only one.

'Well, I'll go in and see her,' she said. 'Come on, Maureen, say goodbye to Larry and give Mr Hines his hat back.'

Maureen had crawled along to the end of the counter, where Mr Hines kept his model lamb. It was life-size and made of *papier-mâché*, and it had been fashioned as if it were in mid-leap, with a comical expression on its face. Maureen loved it and Mr Hines had named it Larry especially for her.

'She's a cheery little soul,' Mr Hines said, giving her a smacking kiss as he handed her back over the counter. 'Keeps us all happy with her sunny smile.'

'She don't know a thing about the war, that's why,' Jess said. 'Thinks it's all a game, going down the shelter at night. Well, it's just as well. It's nice to have someone around who still thinks life's wonderful.'

She took Maureen outside and held her for a moment before putting her back into the pram. Just let's hope it goes on being good for you, she thought. Just so long as nothing happens to you. I couldn't bear it if anything happened to you.

Alice Brunner lay in bed, staring at the net curtain over the window. Her bedroom was over the shop and she could hear the sounds of the street outside, the clop-clop of the baker's horse, the rattle of the little electric milk-float. There were voices and footsteps too as folk did their shopping, and she could hear the chirpy voice of little Maureen Budd calling goodbye to Mr Hines.

That meant Jess was in the street and would be coming into the shop. She'd be asking after her, wondering why Joy was on her own at this time of day. And she'd probably been talking to Mr Hines already, discussing how she left Joy to do nearly all the work these days. Letting the girl get up at crack of dawn – after a night in the shelter, as likely as not – to heave great bundles of newspapers about and sort them all out for delivery. It wasn't right. She knew that. But she just couldn't face it.

She turned over, her face to the wall. Footsteps were coming up the stairs now, not Joy's quick, light tread, but heavier ones, coming more slowly. And the sound of scrambling which meant that a small child was coming too, heaving herself up step by step.

The door opened and Jess poked her head round it. Alice looked up at her, half ashamed, half defiant but without the energy to express either.

'There you are,' Jess said, as if she thought Alice might have climbed out of the window. 'Well, what's the matter?'

'What d'you think's the matter?' Alice's voice was bitter. Wasn't it enough that she'd lost Heinrich, her rock? Did there have to be something else the matter as well? 'I just felt like a lie-in, that's all.'

'On a weekday?' Lie-ins were unheard of in the Budd home. Even on Sundays she and Frank were up before eight, and *that* was a lie-in, for him. 'Alice –'

'I know what you're going to say. What about Joy? I'm leaving her to do all the work. Well, she's young and strong, she's got nothing else to do. The school's no good to her now, there's only a few kids there and a couple of old teachers they've dragged out of retirement. She's better off learning the trade. Anyway, she likes being in charge.'

Jess sat down on the bed, Maureen standing at her knee. Alice's voice was truculent but there was a bitter pain behind it. Poor woman, Jess thought, she doesn't know what to do with herself. She misses Heinrich like losing her right arm, and she doesn't even know whether to grieve for him or not.

'I know how you're feeling,' she said in a low voice. 'But it can't be good for you, laying in bed like this. You'd be better to get up and carry on, you really would.'

'How do you know? How do you know what'd make me feel better? You can't know how I feel, nobody could who's not going through it.' Alice stared at Jess. Her eyes were dark and hollow, rimmed with red. They looked as if they were set deeper in her head than usual. Her face was like one of her own newspapers, grey and lined. Her hair hung in rat's tails.

'It's all right for you,' she went on. 'You've got your husband at home, and past call-up age. Nobody's going to take him away and send him off in a ship to be blown up. Or die struggling in the water, hurt perhaps and not able to keep his head up.' Her voice shook. 'Heinrich never liked the water. He'd come out to Southsea with Joy and me because we liked it, but he never went into the water himself, not even to paddle. Can you imagine what it must have been like, drowning in the sea, in pitch darkness, choking on oil, maybe burning . . .' The tears came again and she turned her face into the pillow.

Jess stood up. She felt helpless, pitying and angry all at once. It seemed as if Alice was intent on wallowing in her misery, as if she'd *rather* be miserable.

'You're not the only one in this sort of trouble,' she said gently. 'There's Ethel Glaister, half out of her mind over her Shirley. It must be just as bad for her, thinking of her little girl ending like that.' Her voice broke a little. 'Alice, I know it's horrible. I can hardly bear to think of it myself. But it's no good torturing yourself. Whatever happened to Heinrich, it's over now. If – if he died, it must have been quick. You've got to think of yourself now. And Joy. She shouldn't be working all those hours in the shop, she ought to be having a bit of fun with her friends. She's getting old before her time.'

'She's always been a helpful girl. She's always liked being with me and helping.'

'But she's not with you, is she? She's down there all by herself. And you're up here moping. Look, why don't you let me make you a cup of tea while you get up? Have a wash and put on something fresh. Put the wireless on and listen to *Music While You Work*.'

'A cup of tea,' Alice said in a droning voice. 'A wash and a clean blouse. That's all it needs, is it, to make me feel better? To make up for not having Heinrich?' She turned away again.

Jess stared down at her friend and felt like shaking her by the shoulders. It might help. But it might also turn Alice against her, and that would only make things worse. She gave a little sigh of frustration and removed Maureen's hand from a silver brush that lay on Alice's dressing-table.

'I'll go and make a cup of tea,' she said quietly. 'It'll be downstairs if you want it.'

Ethel Glaister looked through her back window and saw Frank Budd out in his garden, looking at the runner beans. She went outside, walking slowly down the garden path. Out of the corner of her eye, she saw Frank hesitate then come over to the fence.

'Hullo, Ethel.' His voice was gruff and awkward. 'How're you feeling now?'

She gave him a wan smile. 'Oh, all right, you know. Bearing up. Not much else to do, is there? Someone's got to keep the home together, what with George being away.' She moved closer, looking up at him. 'I'm glad to see you. It's proper lonely with no one to talk to – *you* know.'

Frank looked embarrassed. 'I thought Jess had been popping in to see you.' Jess had told him that she'd spoken to Ethel several times, meaning to offer her sympathy or ask if there was anything she could do. But after her first desperate cry for help, Ethel hadn't seemed to want sympathy. She had withdrawn even further into herself, answering tersely as if Jess had no right to be speaking to her, making Jess feel guilty that she still had all her children safe.

'Oh, she has. But there's times, you know, when a woman wants a *man* to talk to.' Her voice trembled a little. 'I suppose my trouble is, I'm not really a woman's woman. I need a man to lean on. And with George away . . .'

Frank shifted his big body uncomfortably. 'I don't know

what I can do to help, Ethel. I mean, if there's anything you can't manage round the house or garden, you know you've only got to ask, but Jess is better than me at, well, at anything else. I know she feels really sorry about Shirley.'

Ethel drew back slightly. Frank irritated and excited her both at once. He didn't seem to have any idea how to talk to a woman, how to offer a bit of comfort. Surely it wouldn't do him any harm to unbend a bit, just once in a while! And it would help her no end. She was starving to have a man take care of her, take a bit of interest in her. It didn't have to go any further than that. She just wanted to know that they were interested, that's all. Just to make her feel a bit better about things.

'Jess has just gone up the road to see her sister,' Frank said, moving towards his shed again. 'Shall I ask her to pop in when she comes back?'

Ethel shook her head. 'No. Don't bother.' She watched him wistfully for a moment, then went back indoors.

She looked in the mirror again, trying not to see the lines between her brows, the discontented splay of wrinkles around her lips. Her eyes moved to the snap of Shirley on Southsea beach, that George had pinned up on the wall so that he could look at it while he shaved.

The sudden wave of misery struck her, just as the waves at sea must have struck her little girl. She turned away abruptly, went into the back room and switched on the wireless. Glenn Miller's music swelled through the room and she turned it up as loud as it would go, remembering how George had switched it on last time he'd been home and wanted her to dance.

Bugger George, being away just when she needed him. Bugger Frank Budd, who could have taken her mind off all her misery if he'd had a mind to. Bugger the swines who'd torpedoed the ship her Shirley was on, and left her to drown in the middle of the cold Atlantic.

Ethel stood in the middle of the room, letting the music swirl about her. Then she twisted the knob of the wireless to silence it, and stalked out of the room and up the stairs. She put on her powder-blue jacket and the little hat with the veil, found her best high-heeled shoes, and marched downstairs and out through the front door.

People didn't wait for the siren to sound now. They went to the shelters as a matter of course, taking rugs and cushions, books and knitting. Many people 'trekked' out of the city each evening, going to the countryside north of Portsdown Hill for safety. There they would stay with relatives or sleep in tents or barns.

'They ought to dig tunnels in the hill,' Tommy Vickers remarked. 'That'd be the best thing. Hide us in caves, like they're doing round Dover. Like they're doing in London, really.'

But tunnelling into the hill, even though it had already been extensively quarried for chalk, would be a major undertaking, and surely the war wasn't going to last that long?

'No,' Bert Shaw said lugubriously, 'but we might need 'em to hide from Hitler when he invades.'

'You don't have to talk like that,' Peggy said sharply. 'We want to keep cheerful, not make ourselves more miserable. Hitler's not going to invade, our boys won't let him.'

'So why are there all those notices up about what to do when German soldiers come marching down the streets?' Bert demanded. 'Shut the door in their faces? That's what one of them says, just as if a Jerry with a machine-gun's going to be put off by the likes of you and Jess Budd with a broomstick in your hands. And what about all those instructions about ignoring "false alarms and rumours" and "only obeying the orders given by the British Government"? How can you do that if the country's occupied, like France? There won't *be* any British Government, will there!'

Peggy turned on the wireless.

'I'm not listening to any more of that sort of talk, Bert Shaw. Defeatist talk, that's what that is. I'd sooner listen to Tommy Handley and Mrs Mopp. Or those Americans in *Hi Gang*. It's a laugh we want, not gloom and doom.'

It was almost the end of September when Ethel Glaister accosted Frank out in the garden again. Her face was pink and glowing, and she was waving a newspaper and half laughing, half crying.

Frank stared at her. 'What is it? What's happened?'

'It's the ship! The kiddies – they're safe. A lifeboat – they found a lifeboat.' The words cascaded from her lips. 'The *City of Benares*, that's the ship my Shirley was on. They've found a lifeboat full of kiddies, they've got them safe and *my Shirley's one of them*! She's safe, she's *safe*!'

'Your Shirley? Are you sure?' Frank snatched the paper and read it quickly.

'Well, that *is* good news.' He smiled at Ethel. Why, she looked really nice with no make-up on and her face happy and laughing. Why couldn't she be like that all the time? It was her bitterness that put him off, pulling her lips into tight folds and cutting lines between her brows, and putting a hard edge to her voice. Like this, she was altogether different. 'I'm really pleased. I know Jess will be too. She was proper upset about your Shirley.'

'Eight days they were in the lifeboat,' Ethel said, taking the newspaper back and reading it again. 'There was a woman with them, she kept on massaging them to keep them from getting cold and stiff, and she told them a story. They'd nearly run out of food when one of the boys saw a flying-boat and waved to attract its attention. When a ship finally came to rescue them, the poor little devils were too weak to climb aboard.' She looked up at Frank. 'They will be all right, won't they? My Shirley –'

'She'll be all right,' Frank said gently. He reached across the fence and patted her awkwardly on the shoulder. 'You'll get her back safe and sound now, you'll see.'

Ethel nodded. She went back indoors and wept over the newspaper, thinking of her Shirley tossing about at sea in a lifeboat wondering if she would ever see her home again.

Well, at least Jess Budd wouldn't be able to look at her now as if she'd done something wrong. Shirley had had a narrow escape, but she was still alive and just because the Germans had torpedoed the ship it didn't make Ethel a bad mother like some of the women round here would like to make out – Alice Brunner, for instance, and Peggy Shaw who was so thick with

Jess. She could stand up and look *them* in the eye again, any day!

Jess had been down to North End to see her parents. Frank told her the news when she came in and she hurried out into the garden first thing next morning to see Ethel.

'I'm so glad. I bet you can't wait to have her back again. You won't want her out of your sight now.'

Ethel Glaister looked at her over the garden fence.

'Oh no, I shan't have her back here,' she said. 'I'll send her straight down to Devonshire. I won't take any more chances with her.'

'Well, I can understand that,' Jess said. 'But surely you'll want to be with her? I know how I'd feel if it was one of mine.'

'And how can I go to Devon?' Ethel demanded. 'I've got Joe and Carol to think of too, haven't I? And George likely to be back home again at all hours. You know they're sending the unit back to Pompey, don't you, to clear up some of the bomb damage. You'd think they'd at least let them spend a bit of time at home, there's enough jobs piling up, for God's sake, but no, he says they'll be too busy, he'll just have to get home whenever he can. Drop in for a meal when he feels like it, that's what he means. Sometimes I think I'm running one of those British Restaurants.'

'You should think yourself lucky he'll be able to come home at all,' Jess retorted. She'd bitten her lip with Alice but she didn't have the patience to listen to Ethel's grumbles. 'Specially now you've heard about Shirley. Think of poor Alice Brunner, still worrying about Heinrich. You've got a lot to be thankful for, Ethel Glaister.'

'Oh yes,' her neighbour sneered. 'Bombs dropping all round night after night, and the street going downhill. That Nancy Baxter's getting worse – she's bringing sailors home quite openly now, the brazen slut. And I wouldn't be surprised if that Mrs Simmons is another of the same sort. Husband in the Merchant Navy! We've only got her word for it.'

'Ethel, how can you say such things? Kathy's husband came home last month, I was there when he arrived.'

'And how d'you know that was her husband? Show you

their wedding certificate, did they? You mark my words, once she's had that baby she'll be back on the game same as Nancy, see if I'm not right.'

Jess stared at her in disgust. 'I'm not listening to any more of this. You're a spiteful woman, Ethel, and one day that tongue of yours is going to get you into real trouble. I came out to tell you I was glad about your Shirley, and so I am, but I don't have to stand here and listen to filth. Kathy Simmons is a decent little body and she's having a bad time. And if I hear you saying things like that about her again, you'll be sorry.'

She turned and went back into the house, her blood seething. But she had too much to do to worry about Ethel Glaister. It was washing day, and the copper was just coming to the boil. There were Frank's working shirts to scrub and Maureen's few nappies to wash, though there weren't so many now that she was getting so good on the pot. And then there would be all the mangling to do before she could even hang the things up to dry.

Washing took almost the whole day, and if it wasn't good drying weather there would be wet clothes hung round the fire indoors all evening and even draped over pictures on the wall. Sometimes it was Wednesday before she could do her ironing, and that meant the whole week was put out of joint.

She sighed and bent to take the big yellow bar of Sunlight soap from the cupboard Frank had built under the kitchen sink. Arguing with Ethel had put her in a bad mood. It would be a long time before she went out to give *her* a pleasant word again!

For Alice Brunner, there was no good news.

Each morning she woke knowing that she must go through another day without Heinrich. And without knowing even whether he was alive or dead, for she had still heard nothing of him. Many of the men on board the *Arandora Star* had died, many others been saved, and yet there had been no word of Heinrich. No word of whether he was one of those taken on to Canada, no word of whether he had been deported instead to the Isle of Man. It was as if he had vanished into thin air.

He must have drowned.

There were times when Alice wished he had died before the war had even begun. At least then she could have been a widow, and respected as such by her neighbours. At least she wouldn't have had to suffer the spite of people like Ethel Glaister, who had sneered at her for being married to a Jerry and refused to buy her newspapers from a Hun. And she would have known what had happened to him. She could have shared his last moments.

But no sooner had she let these thoughts travel through her mind than they would be followed by a searing guilt. How could she wish her beloved Heinrich dead? He had been her rock. Her lover, her husband, her friend. Never strong, she had clung to him through all her periods of despondency, through the depression that had so inexplicably followed Joy's birth and which had struck her, usually without apparent reason, at intervals since.

And there was Heinrich's own family too. As soon as war was declared, all communication from Berlin had stopped. It was terrible that a man could be split apart from both his families, the German one and the British. His mother and sister in one country, his wife and daughter in the other.

It's not knowing that's the worst, Alice thought. Not knowing whether *Mutter* has been bombed by our planes, perhaps buried or burned alive like so many of our people. Not knowing whether Heinrich . . .

And there she was, back to the beginning again, in the ceaseless circle of her anguish, on a road that had no end.

As Ethel Glaister had said, in early October the 698 Royal Engineers Unit was brought back from its wanderings to Portsmouth in order to clear some of the bomb damage and demolish the shattered buildings, and Derek was able to spend time at home.

'I never thought you'd be back so soon,' Olive said, hugging Derek in the double bed that had been squeezed into her room. 'Will you be able to get home every night?'

He shook his head. 'They'll want us in the barracks. But most of the blokes are Pompey chaps so they'll have to let us off some of the time, or there'll be a riot! I'll be here every minute I can be, you can bet on that.'

'It'll be like being properly married,' Olive said blissfully, and he laughed.

'We *are* properly married! At least, I hope so, I wouldn't want to think of you carrying on this way with a man you're not married to.'

'Oh, you know what I mean,' she said, punching him. 'With you coming home every day, just like it ought to be. I'll be able to cook your supper and mend your clothes and everything. I'll feel more like your wife.'

'You don't have to worry about cooking and mending,' he said, pulling her closer. 'There's a better way than that of feeling like my wife.'

Olive laughed and nuzzled close. Her heart was alight with happiness. She and Derek had had so little time together, and although he had warned her that the Unit would probably not stay long in Portsmouth, she refused to look ahead to a time when it might move away again. There was plenty to do here, wasn't there? And more damage being done with every raid. Why should it ever be moved away?

She wondered if she should tell Derek that she thought she might be pregnant. It was a bit soon really, only a few weeks since that night he'd had at home in the first week of September. But she'd missed once since then, and been feeling a bit queasy in the mornings. It wasn't enough to be sure, but if she missed again she'd tell him, and they could go and see the doctor together.

We'll be a real family then, she thought. Mum and Dad and baby. A real family.

The Shaws were pleased with 698's return too, for they had missed Bob. They sat around the supper table on the first evening, eating rabbit pie and listening as he told them about Devon and Wiltshire, and about the aerodromes they had been servicing. Before the evacuation of Dunkirk, the Unit had been on active service in France, building advanced landing strips at somewhere called Thelus, and since their return they had been employed in repairing RAF Bomber Command runways damaged by bombs. Bob, who had been unemployed before the war, had found himself enjoying the strenuous work, and his body had filled out as a result.

'Just look at you,' marvelled his sister Gladys. 'You were just a weed when you went away.'

'Thanks for nothing, sis.' But he was grinning as he gave her shoulder a gentle thump. 'I could always rely on you for a kind word.'

'I think you look smashing,' Diane declared. 'Like Mr Universe. I think I'll join the WAACs when I'm old enough. Or maybe the Wrens.'

'Why, what d'you want muscles for?' Bob asked, and Gladys snorted.

'She doesn't. She's more interested in the blokes' muscles than her own.'

'That's enough of that kind of talk,' their father said sharply. 'Tell us a bit more about the building you're doing, Bob. Sounds as if it'll set you up in a good trade for after the war.'

The two men plunged into a discussion of different kinds of bricks and mortar and the girls made a face at each other. They looked at their mother, but Peggy shook her head.

'Let them natter. It's the first time your dad's ever talked to Bob man-to-man. It's good for 'em. Come and help me get a pot of tea.'

It didn't take three women to make a pot of tea, but when they came back into the room with the tray Bob and his father were sitting back looking pleased with themselves, and there was a new confidence in Bob's face as he took his cup. He gave Diane a wink and then turned to Gladys.

'So what've you been getting up to, then? Still learning to drive?'

This was the chance Gladys had been waiting for. She put her nose into the air and said airily, 'No, not any more. I've passed.'

'Passed? What, passed your test? Your *driving* test?'

'Well, it's not a spelling test!' she retorted, and then let her grin break out. 'I passed last week. Last Wednesday. First time.'

'Well, that's a turn-up,' he said admiringly. 'So what are

you going to do? Get a job as a bus-driver?'

'She'd better not try,' Bert said disapprovingly. 'And don't you encourage her, Bob. It's a man's job, that is. I don't approve of women driving as it is.'

'And what if there's no men to drive the buses?' Gladys demanded. 'Have we all got to walk everywhere? Anyway, I don't want to drive buses. I'm going to drive ambulances.'

'*Ambulances*?'

'Yes, ambulances. I've joined the Red Cross, along with Mum. We go to the First Aid post whenever there's a raid and look after casualties. And some of 'em need taking to hospital, so that's what I'm going to do.'

Bert looked annoyed. 'I've heard nothing of this.'

'What's the point of telling you?' Gladys said. 'You'd only tell me I couldn't. And I'm going to, so there's no point in arguing.'

Bert's face reddened. He leaned forward, laying his arms on the table, and raised one hand to jab his finger at Gladys. 'Now, you listen to me, my girl –'

'No,' Gladys said. 'You listen to me. There's a war on, isn't there? They're crying out for people to help, and that means *people*, not just men. They're sending all the men away to fight, aren't they? So who's going to run things here? We've all got to look after ourselves in this lot and it's time you men realised that you're not the only ones capable of doing a job of work. There's not much a woman can't turn her hand to, just as good as a man. We proved that in the last war, that's why they had to give in and give us the vote.'

'More's the pity too,' her father retorted. 'It gave you all big ideas, that's what that did. Women doctors! Women drivers! Women this, women that. Who's looking after their homes, that's what I'd like to know, who's getting their husbands' dinners for them? Well, I'll not have such goings-on in *my* house.' He glared at his wife. 'I'm still master here, even if *your daughters* don't seem to think so, and you needn't think *you're* going to go gallivanting off at all hours driving ambulances and such capers!'

'Oh, for God's sake,' Gladys began, but her mother cut in sharply.

'That's enough of that kind of language, our Glad. And you don't have to annoy your father more than you already have done, specially not on our Bob's first night home.' She turned to her husband. 'As for you, Bert, you're just getting silly. I've never said a word about driving ambulances, nor anything like it. All I do down the First Aid Post is put a few bandages on, as well you know. And Gladys is quite right, we all have to pull together in this war and if that means changing our ideas a bit about what we do, well, that's all there is to it. D'you think our Bob *wanted* to go off and and risk getting killed being a soldier? But he's had to do it all the same, and –'

'Get away,' Bert said, 'it's done him the world of good. Given him a trade and made a man of him. Hasn't it, Bob?'

They looked at the young man sitting there, his skin tanned with fresh air, his body filled out and strong. He looked awkward and self-conscious, as though not certain which parent to support, then shrugged and said, 'Well, it's a pretty good life, but I wouldn't say it was much fun in France.'

'No,' Peggy said, 'you were lucky to get back alive from that. So don't try to make it out to be better than it is, Bert. It's a muddle, the whole thing, and we just have to do our best and not start quarrelling amongst ourselves, all right?'

Bert Shaw pushed out his lower lip. He had grown up believing in certain traditions, and every day it seemed that a new one was upset. And he was alarmed by the rate at which his children were growing up – especially the girls. It seemed only yesterday that they had been in pigtails, running to him with their dolls, climbing up on his knee and, most important of all, behaving as he wanted them to behave. Being seen and not heard. Keeping their opinions – if they had any – to themselves. Playing quietly in a corner, and not arguing with their elders and betters.

Now, it seemed as if they wanted to rule the roost, as if they thought they could do as they liked, and they were altogether too free with their opinions. Learning to drive, indeed – and driving *ambulances*, of all things! Why, his Gladys would be in the thick of any bombing if she did that, just when he wanted her safe in a shelter. He'd rather she was driving buses after all.

'All right, Bert?' Peggy repeated, and he scowled.

'I suppose it's as all right as anything is these days. I don't pretend to understand anything. But there, I'm getting old and old men aren't wanted these days, not when there's bits of girls can do their jobs better than they can.'

'Oh, Dad!' Gladys jumped up and came round the table. She put her arms round her father's neck and pulled his head back against her. 'You're just being silly. Of course you're not old! And if there were more men like you, well, maybe girls wouldn't have to do the jobs. But we're *needed*. And we can do them – some of them, anyway. And anyway, why should we have to spend our time in shops and offices when there's so many more interesting things to do –'

'Because men are the ones who have to work!' For a few moments, Bert had seemed to be mollified by her words, but her last question had touched a nerve that many men, and women too, were still finding raw. 'It's *men* who have to provide homes for their families, men who have to earn the money. Women should stay at home and look after their families, not take away the jobs men need just because they're "more interesting". That's the way it is and it's the way it always has been. And the way it always will be, if there's anyone left with any sense after all this is over.'

'Oh yes,' Gladys said, moving away. 'And it's the men who start wars, isn't it, and land us in messes like the one we're in now.'

There was an uncomfortable silence. Bert was breathing heavily, his face suffused with anger. Peggy looked exasperated and anxious. Diane was watching with suppressed enjoyment and Bob was staring at the tablecloth. Gladys stood by the fireplace, her expression sulky but her eyes full of tears.

'Let's drop it,' Peggy said at last. 'You're both getting overheated, and all over nothing. I don't know what you wanted to say that for, Gladys, setting him off all over again. You ought to have known better. And Bert, you've got to realise the girls are growing up. They know their own minds. And things are different from when we were young.'

'You don't have to tell me that,' he returned sullenly. 'I can see it for myself. It doesn't mean to say I have to like it.'

'No, but you've got to put up with it,' she said sharply. 'Same as we all have. And just remember that it's men and women younger than our Bob and Gladys, no more than boys and girls really, who are fighting this war, and getting killed or maimed for life doing it. And if they're old enough to do that, we can't turn round and tell our Glad she can't drive an ambulance, now can we?'

There was another silence. Then Bob lifted his head. He glanced around the table. It's always been like this, he thought. Dad claiming to be 'head of the family' and 'master in his own house', laying down the law and getting us all in a knot. And then Mum, only half his size, putting us all right with a few sharp words. And the girls in tears and me wishing the earth would open . . .

But it didn't have to be like that now. As Mum had said, they were growing up. They didn't have to be treated like kids, and they didn't have to behave like them either.

'Well,' he said with a grin, 'I must say it's good to be home again and find nothing's changed. D'you know, for a while I was afraid you were going to treat me like a visitor. It don't seem like home when you're all on your best behaviour!'

They all turned and stared at him. For a moment, he was afraid that his joke had fallen on stony ground or, worse still, caused even more offence. Then Diane began to giggle and Gladys's face relaxed into an unwilling grin. Peggy gave him a wry smile and they all looked at Bert.

'Come on, Bert,' Peggy said cajolingly. 'Don't let's have a row on Bob's first night home in months.'

'I didn't want to have a row,' he muttered righteously, but he picked up his cup and looked at it. 'I suppose this has gone cold after all that shenanigan.'

'Maybe it has,' Peggy said equably, 'but we can soon make another pot. I don't think the rationing's that bad we can't afford another spoonful of tea to celebrate. And then I suppose Bob'll have to be getting back to the barracks and we'll be off down the shelter for the night. It's nearly time for the warning to go, isn't it?'

Bert nodded. He didn't want upset in the family any more

than the rest of them, but he felt scared and uncertain by the way things were changing so fast. The whole world was upside down, he reflected as Peggy filled his cup with fresh tea. And maybe he was just too old to keep up with it all.

I just wish I could go and fight too, he thought, and clenched his big fist on the table. I'm as fit and healthy as any of these youngsters, and got the experience too – yet because I'm over forty, I'm chucked on the scrap heap and left to do the jobs that young girls like our Gladys think they can do better! Why, me and Frank Budd, we've already been through a war – we know what it's like. Why can't *we* go and sort 'em all out?

Instead, they were reduced to being firewatchers. Or members of the Home Guard – parading with broomsticks instead of guns, playing games like kids in the street.

Broomsticks instead of guns! Aeroplanes made out of old saucepans – ships from iron park railings. And now they were even asking for people to hand in their old binoculars because they didn't have enough to give sailors at sea.

A proper home-made war this is, he thought in disgust. How can we ever win it this way?

CHAPTER FOURTEEN

Tim and Keith were building themselves a cart with a set of old pram wheels and a couple of planks of wood that Reg Corner had given them.

'It'll be smashing,' Tim declared, tying the wheels on with bits of string. They were all short bits, collected over a period of some weeks and forming a tangle of ends and knots in his pocket. 'We'll be able to go all over the place on it.'

'Not up hills,' Keith pointed out. 'We'll have to pull it up hills.'

'Well, I know that. But there's lots of hills to go *down*. None of the others have got a cart as good as this.'

'Brian Collins says he's making one.'

'Well, he would, wouldn't he? He's always got to be best.' Tim looked up as Reg came down the garden path and stopped beside them. 'Look, isn't it a smasher? We'll be able to help you on the farm with this.'

Reg squatted down beside them. His face was grave. He looked at the cart and nodded.

'It's a good one. You've done well. But you won't be able to help me on the farm. Not for much longer.'

The boys stared at him.

'Why not?'

'Because I'm not going to be there. I've got my papers.'

Tim and Keith knew what that meant. Reg had been called up. He'd be going away, to fight in the war. They sat back on their heels, the cart momentarily forgotten.

'What are you going to be? Will you be a pilot?'

'No, I'm going in the Navy.'

'Oh.' Tim was momentarily disappointed. 'I'd rather be a pilot. That's what I'm going to be, when I'm old enough, if the war lasts long enough.'

'Let's hope it doesn't,' Reg said soberly. 'We just want it to be over as soon as possible.'

'Don't you want to go and fight?' Keith asked curiously. He and the other boys talked about the war incessantly, discussing aeroplanes, ships and tanks. They were all convinced that if the enemy invaded and penetrated as far as Bridge End, he would meet his match in the children who were prepared to defend it. They had built dens in the woods, ready to go into hiding if the need arose, and were constantly on the lookout for spies.

'I'm no fighter,' Reg answered. 'I'm a farmer. But it seems you can't be what you want to be, these days.' He stopped. He and Edna had always tried never to grumble in front of the boys. As they saw it, they had a duty to make their disrupted childhood as normal as possible. But now it looked as if they weren't going to be able to do that either.

Keith looked at him and saw something of his feeling in his face. He got up and leaned against Reg's big body.

'Don't worry,' he said. 'We'll look after Edna.'

'And the baby,' Tim added. Keith wasn't so sure about the baby, but he nodded anyway.

Reg grinned but the grin faded quickly, leaving his face more serious than ever.

'That's just it, kids. You can't. You see, if I'm not working on the farm any more, we can't stay in the cottage. It belongs to Mr Callaway, and he'll want it for someone else.'

'But what about Edna?'

'She's going to go and stay with her mum.'

The boys digested this in silence. They knew Edna's mum. She was all right, but they didn't think they wanted to go and live in her little cottage. There wasn't really room, not like where Reg and Edna lived now.

'What will we do?' Keith asked at last. His voice was slightly wobbly and Reg put his arm round him.

'We'll have to find you somewhere else, won't we? Somewhere you'll like just as much as being with us.'

Tim frowned. 'There isn't anyone else in the village who could take us.' A sudden fear gripped him. 'We won't have to go and live with Miss Woddis, will we?'

Reg shook his head firmly. 'You won't have to go there, don't worry. I'm sure we'll find someone.'

'I'd rather stay with you,' Keith said, his voice rising a little.

'I know, son. But you can't. Not if I'm going away and Edna goes to her mum's. And with a new baby, too . . .' He looked at them. He and Edna had talked it over night after night, trying to see how they could keep the boys, but there was no solution to the problem.

What he was really worried about was that they might not be able to find Tim and Keith a billet together. Most of the houses in the village were already taken up, with one or two children, and he couldn't think of anyone with enough room.

'It's no use,' he'd said to Edna at last, the previous evening. 'You'll have to write to Mrs Budd. It's for her to decide what to do, not us.' And Edna had agreed and got out the writing pad, her tears dripping on to the pages as she wrote.

Jess read the letter next day and saw the marks of the tears smudging the ink.

'Not many people want two lively boys,' she said as she read the letter to Frank when he came home from work that evening. 'And most of those who've got space for evacuees are already full. I don't like to think of them being split up, Frank.'

'Well, they're not coming home,' he said firmly. 'Not with all these raids. And it's not just the raids – you know what boys are, they'd be wanting to go and look at all the bomb sites. I've seen young Micky Baxter and his gang, clambering about all over ruined houses, collecting shrapnel and bomb cases. One of them's going to pick up something live one day and get blown to pieces. Or get buried by a wall falling on top of them. It's not safe, but you wouldn't be able to get those two young scallywags to see that.'

Jess nodded. She remembered the first raid, when the boys had been out playing cowboys and Indians. There was the problem of school, too. A few schools were open again because so many children had come back, but since the bombing had started a lot of them had been re-evacuated and it was difficult to know which schools were working and which weren't. And nobody seemed to be checking that the children were actually attending.

'I know they're better off in the country,' she said. 'But I want them to be happy there. And I do miss them so much.'

Frank nodded and put his hand on her shoulder. 'I know you do, love. So do I. Look, we'll go out to Bridge End on Sunday and see them. We'll have a talk with Mrs Corner and see what she's got to suggest. And perhaps Mrs Greenberry will know of somewhere they can go.'

Perhaps she would. But Jess wasn't too hopeful. Tim and Keith had fallen on their feet with the Corners, and you couldn't expect that sort of luck twice. And when she remembered what had happened to some of the other children who had been evacuated, it made her shiver.

Better to have the boys at home, facing the dangers with their own parents, than living miserably miles away. But it wouldn't be easy to get Frank to see that.

Mr Churchill had changed his War Cabinet and Mr Chamberlain, whom so many blamed for getting Britain into the war, had resigned. Egypt was demanding the abdication of the King of Greece, and Japan had attacked the Burma Road. Portsmouth set itself to raise a million pounds for weapons in one week, and people began to talk of rebuilding the city when the war was over. But when would that be?

The raiders were still coming, and still being fought off by the RAF. But the pretence that it was no more than a game had been replaced now by a brittle, feverish lightheartedness that was very near hysteria.

Duff and Sandy missed Geoff desperately. As long as the three of them had been flying together, it had seemed as if their luck would hold. Now the leader of the trio had gone, and each time they flew the other two strapped themselves into their seats with a sick fear that they would be next.

Duff had taken over Geoff's little sports car, and they continued to visit the farm whenever they could manage a few hours away from the station. But without Geoff they seemed incomplete. The group of six which had careered so gaily around the countryside was now unbalanced.

'Why not ask Dennis to come with us?' Betty suggested one evening. There was a village hop in the church hall and the girls had dashed up to their room as soon as milking was over to get ready. Erica was standing on a chair where the sloping ceiling was highest, while Betty drew a line down the back of each leg with eye pencil to make it look as if Erica was wearing stockings. 'I bet he can dance all right.'

Erica moved so abruptly that the pencil jerked across her calf and drew a zigzag from knee to ankle. She jumped down, inspecting the damage crossly.

'Now look what you've done! It'll never rub off. I shall look a proper fool.'

'Well, you shouldn't have moved. Just because I said we might ask Dennis –'

'I've told you before, I wouldn't walk to the end of the street with that conchie!' Erica exclaimed. 'I'd rather stay here. I never wanted to go to the dance anyway, not really.' Her face twisted suddenly and she turned away, clenching her arms across her body. 'I know what it'll be like. Stupid girls wrapping themselves round any man they can get hold of, kissing and slobbering all over each other – it'll be disgusting. Well, you can do that if you want to, but I –' She sat down suddenly on her bed and stared at the photograph of Geoffrey that she kept on the little chest of drawers '– I'd rather stay here.'

Her voice broke on the last words and Betty bit her lip. Since her first outburst of grief when Geoffrey had died, Erica had refused to talk about her feelings. She had gone home for a few days and visited his parents, returning with tight lips and glittering eyes, apparently determined to get back to her normal life as quickly as possible. It had been her idea that the girls should go to the village dance.

'I thought she was getting over it,' Betty said as she and Yvonne went out to meet the two young airmen. 'She hasn't said a word against Dennis since she came back.'

'She hasn't said a word *to* him, either,' Yvonne pointed out. They climbed into the little sports car and gave Sandy and

Duff a quick rundown on what had happened. 'She hates him more than ever.'

'He seems a decent enough bloke,' Sandy remarked later, when he and Betty had stepped outside the hall for a breath of fresh air. 'He's entitled to have his own ideas.'

'Erica doesn't think so. She thinks he ought to be in prison if he's not going to fight. I tell her he's helping his country more by working on the farm than picking oakum in jail, but she doesn't see it that way.'

'Erica's still in a state. You can't blame her.' Sandy climbed up to sit on top of a gate and threw away his cigarette butt. 'I shouldn't tell you this, but we're going on a big raid over Germany tomorrow.'

'*You* are?' Betty turned her head to look at him. He was staring into the darkness and frowning. 'You mean – bombing?'

'That's right.'

'But I thought you and Duff flew Spitfires.'

'We do. We're going as escort. We've done it before.' He was scowling. 'Look, Betty, there's something I want to ask you.'

She gazed at him, feeling uncomfortable. There was something odd in his manner, something she hadn't encountered before. If it had been Graham, she'd have thought he was about to make a pass at her. But Sandy wasn't like that. He'd never touched her, never even tried to kiss her. He and Duff had just started coming over as company for Geoff, and then the six of them had had fun together. There had never been any more to it than that.

'Don't look so scared,' he said. 'Look, I know you're engaged to this sailor bloke. But – well, I think a lot of you, Betty. And I'd just like to know if – well, if ever things – you know, went wrong or something between you and him – well, if you might think of me a bit, that's all.'

He finished with a rush, his face scarlet, looking away from her into the trees. Betty gazed at him, feeling suddenly touched. She reached out and laid her fingers gently against his sleeve.

'I do think of you, Sandy,' she said in a low voice. 'You're one of the best friends I've ever had. But I can't break faith with Graham, not when he's away at sea. It wouldn't be fair.'

'Oh, I'm not asking you to do that,' he said quickly. 'It's just – well, I'd like to know there was a chance – you know?'

Betty looked at his open face. He wasn't as ginger as Graham, but his fair hair had a definite reddish shine to it. Funny that she should pick up with two boys with red hair. Maybe that was why she liked Sandy, because he reminded her a bit of Graham.

Immediately, she knew that was wrong. Sandy wasn't a bit like Graham. He was shy where Graham was cheeky, reserved where Graham was bold. He'd never once tried to go 'too far', he'd never even tried to kiss her, except for a quick peck on the cheek when he arrived and one when he left. Well, no more should he when she wasn't his girlfriend, but Betty knew very well that that wouldn't have stopped Graham in similar circumstances. Taking a girl out to tea, or just for a run in a car, would have seemed to him quite sufficient excuse to ask for, and expect, a few kisses in return.

She thought of Graham on that last evening, demanding that she let him make love to her, almost trying to force her. As if the fact that he was going to sea tomorrow, and might never know what it felt like, gave him a *right*. But Sandy went flying every day, fighting in the sky, risking his life with every minute he was in the air. And he had never so much as suggested . . .

If she had met Sandy first, would she have fallen in love with him? And what about Bob Shaw? And Dennis . . .?

Sandy climbed down from the gate. His frown was gone and he grinned, put both hands on her waist and swung her high in the air.

'Well, it's back to the 'drome now. See you next weekend, eh? And then I can tell you all about the raid.'

'Oh, I can't,' Betty said in dismay. 'I'm going home next weekend. But I'll see you the week after that. That's if you want to come,' she added, feeling suddenly shy.

'Oh, I'll want to come. You don't know what it's meant to me and the others – I mean, me and Duff – coming over here to see you girls. It's been a lifeline.' He looked at her, his eyes serious again. 'It's pretty lonely up there in the sky, Betty.'

He took her hand to lead her back into the hall for the last dance. But Betty lingered for a moment to look up at the empty sky.

For once, there were no aircraft to be seen. It rose overhead like a smooth blue dome of glass, unmarked, impregnable.

It's pretty lonely up there in the sky.

For Sandy, the loneliness was the worst part of flying. He hadn't minded it at first. It had been a joy, the first time he flew solo, to have the sky to himself, the eternal blue all his own, the clouds to play with. But there had been no marauders then, no vicious black Heinkels or Dorniers to appear suddenly from the sun, no Messerschmitts on his tail.

Like all the young airmen, Sandy tried not to think about death. He ignored the possibility that he might be shot down, that he might not return from the next mission. When other airmen failed to return, he said they'd 'bought it' and turned away from the knowledge of what had really happened. One day, he would have time to let himself feel, but not now, not yet. Now, it was vital to remain cool, not to feel, to be as much a machine as his aircraft.

But now he had seen too many of his friends and colleagues nose-dive to their doom to be able to ignore it any longer, and when he had watched Geoff's plane spiral out of control into the sea, his coolness had departed and he had felt the shock and horror of it throb like a knell through his body. He had relived it a hundred times a day, feeling himself there with Geoff in the cockpit, injured and in pain, struggling with a harness that wouldn't unfasten, watching the flames leap around him, feeling his skin scorch, his eyeballs swell and burst, his lungs on fire.

It wasn't a joke. It wasn't something to dismiss casually with a flippant remark. It was real and it was unbearable, and it had happened to his friend and could happen to him.

Would happen to him . . .

He had never spoken of it to anyone except Betty. Nobody in the mess talked of such feelings, although you could sometimes see the same fear in another man's eyes, before he turned hastily away. Anyone who showed the slightest trace of fear was suspect, a danger to the others. You could be taken off ops, grounded, the ultimate shame. You would be treated as a pariah, as a leper who might spread the deadly virus of panic amongst the others.

The loneliness would follow you down from the sky and be with you all the time.

It was a greater fear than the fear of being shot down, and its effect was to produce an addiction in Sandy. The greater his fear, the more he wanted to be in the sky, shooting down enemy planes, wiping them out of existence. Every one shot down was one less threat. Every one destroyed brought the end of the war a fraction closer. He longed to be up there all the time, destroying, destroying, destroying.

His dreams that night were a turmoil of burning aircraft, of the sharp rattle of machine-guns, of screams and yells, of explosions. Through it all, Betty's face floated like a talisman, but he could never quite see her clearly, never quite hold her expression in his mind. She drifted past and away from him, elusive and unattainable.

He strapped himself into his cockpit the next day in a daze. Duff and the others were noisily exuberant. They ate a huge breakfast, clapped each other on the back, sat about playing cards until it was time to set off. The squadron set off across the Channel, in neat formation.

Nobody was surprised when they were intercepted. Somewhere over Belgium, the expected cloud of enemy fighters appeared before them. And behind them. Above and below; all around. The squadron was suddenly on the defensive, breaking away to tackle them, to force a path for the bombers.

Sandy was still half in a dream. He thought of Geoff in a nose-dive. He thought of his friend, of all his friends who had died, whose lives had been shorn by these very planes, by these men who were shooting now at him. His hatred swelled and burst like a red flame inside his skull and he attacked savagely, blasting about him in the sky, swooping and diving, gunning the planes that swarmed about him, yelling with triumph as one by one they fell away, their sides ripped by his bullets, their engines ablaze.

He never felt the bullets that hit him. He scarcely understood the meaning of the sudden sheet of scorching orange that exploded around him. His brain was lit by white light, as searingly brilliant as if he had flown straight into the eye of the sun. His ears were filled with the screaming of his own blood.

The plane turned slowly over in the air. In his last few dying moments, he knew that he was experiencing what Geoff had experienced, Geoff and a thousand others. But he could not care now, about Geoff, or about anyone other than himself.

He knew the ultimate terror, the awareness of imminent and agonising death. Amongst the crackling of the flames around him, through the frying of his own skin and the boiling of his welling blood, he heard his voice screaming, screaming for the mother who had once kept him safe and who was now too far away ever to hear his voice again.

And then his eardrums burst and he heard no more. He could only feel. And the plane tumbled slowly, too slowly, out of the sky.

Betty knew the moment she saw two strange young airmen drive the little sports car into the yard that Sandy and Duff were dead.

She came out of the cowshed with Yvonne. They looked at the two pilots in silence. For a moment, it was as if time had run backwards and Geoff was arriving again on that first Sunday afternoon when they had all gone out to tea together. But Geoff had been killed, and there was no merriment in these two young faces. They were white and haggard, old before their time.

'You don't have to tell us,' she said to the misery in their eyes. 'It's over, isn't it? Sandy. And Duff. They're –'

'No!' Yvonne gripped her arm so tightly that the nails dug into Betty's skin. 'Don't say it! It's not true. It's not true.'

The young men looked at her wretchedly. Betty felt the tears in her eyes. *It's pretty lonely up there in the sky*. She looked upwards, as if to see him above, and when she lowered her head the tears ran over and down her cheeks like rain. Sandy dead. Sandy, dead.

'It was pretty quick,' one of the boys said. 'They couldn't have known much about it, either of them.'

They'd said that when Geoff was killed. But how could anyone know?

Erica came out of the house. She was looking pale, her mouth taut. She glanced at the car and the two men.

'So that's another two bought it,' she said, her voice hard. 'Well, I daresay there's plenty more where they came from. That's all that matters, isn't it?' Her gaze moved across to the cowshed, and Betty saw through her tears that Dennis was standing there, grave and still. Erica's voice rose suddenly to a shout, harsh with pain. 'You see? There's another two gone, gone to save your yellow skin. I hope you're pleased with yourself. I hope you're bloody *pleased* with yourself.'

She turned on her heel and stalked back into the farmhouse and, through the open door, they heard her voice again.

'I won't stay here another minute with that bloody conchie! I *won't* . . .'

Erica wasn't the only one to take her grief out on Dennis. Iris Blake, too, issued her brother-in-law with an ultimatum.

'Either he goes or we do. It's bad for the children, being influenced that way. He was talking to them again yesterday. I told you, I won't have it.'

'He was helping them thread their conkers,' Mr Spencer said wearily. 'Look, Iris, I've talked it over with him and I don't think he is a bad influence. He's promised me he won't mention the war or his ideas to them. He's a decent chap and a good worker –'

'And that's all that matters to you, isn't it!'

'Well, what else is there, for God's sake? I've got to keep this farm going, haven't I? I've got to have help to get the food produced. I reckon I'm lucky to have a strong young chap about the place, especially one as willing as Dennis. And he's quiet and decent, and not off down the pub every night.'

'They wouldn't have him. They know better.'

'The man's entitled to his ideas,' Mr Spencer repeated.

'They're none of our business.'

'Of course they're our business! He's a traitor and a coward. He ought to be shot.'

'It's the law, Iris.'

'Then the law's daft,' she said. 'Well, if you won't listen to reason, we'll pack our bags and go. Our Primrose has offered to have me and the kids for the winter and I think we'll go there. I reckon we'll be a bit safer up north anyway.'

She gave her brother-in-law a defiant glare, as if expecting him to change his mind and beg her to stay, but Jack Spencer said nothing. He put on his wire-rimmed glasses and began to sort through the pile of papers on the dresser, and after a few minutes Mrs Blake made an exasperated noise and flounced out.

Mr Spencer sighed with relief. Neither he nor his wife had welcomed the intrusion of Mrs Blake and her two badly-behaved children, but they were family so what could you do? But if his other sister-in-law, who lived in Lancashire, was willing to do a turn having them, that would be fine by him. He was more worried about the Land Girl, Erica, wanting to leave. He hadn't thought all that much of her to start with, with her yellow hair and toffee-nosed ways, but she'd settled down and turned into quite a good little worker. If she left, he'd have to get someone else, and that meant an upheaval. Jack Spencer didn't like upheavals.

Dennis had his own solution to the problem.

'Look, maybe I ought to be the one to go,' he said as he and Betty finished the milking one evening. 'It's because of me Mrs Blake and Erica are leaving. It'd be better if I asked for a transfer somewhere else, where I won't cause any trouble.'

'You don't cause trouble,' Betty said. 'They're the ones who cause trouble. We'll be better off without them, specially that Mrs Blake. Just because her husband's an army captain, she thinks we're dirt.'

'Well, I've been thinking I ought to do something else anyway,' Dennis said. 'It's too safe on the farm. Plenty of COs do other jobs, medical orderlies, Red Cross, things like that. I'm not a coward, Betty.'

'I know you're not,' she said soberly, thinking of the day the aircraft had crashed. She hesitated, then said, 'Why did you decide to be a CO, Dennis? I've never really understood what it's all about.'

He smiled slightly. 'Not many people do. That's the trouble.' They walked down the lane towards the little river. He pulled a piece of dry grass from the hedgerow and swished it back and forth as they strolled along. 'I don't think I ever actually decided. It was always there, a part of me. My dad was a CO in the last war and he went through hell for it. But I always thought he was right. He said it was wrong to kill other human beings, whatever the reason, and I agree.'

He looked at her with the hazel eyes she had always liked. They were often merry and laughing, but now they were serious.

'That plane that crashed in the field – the men in it were just like me, and Geoff and Sandy and Duff. They'd been called up and sent to fight and maybe they enjoyed it, because it must be fun to fly a plane and exciting to dodge about in the sky with other blokes in planes – like a game of tag. But it's not fun when you're burning to death or falling to earth without a parachute. It's not fun when you're being bombed or machine-gunned or stabbed through with a bayonet. How can you do that to other people, people you've never even met? How can anyone justify it?'

'But Hitler was taking over the whole of Europe,' Betty said. 'He'd take us over too.'

'I know. I can't tell you the answers to that. All I can say is, to me it's wrong to kill. It's not that I'm not prepared to die for my country, Betty, I am. But I won't kill for it. Nor for anything else.'

Betty sighed. It was difficult to understand. 'But if everyone did the same thing –'

'There'd be no wars,' he said.

She hadn't been going to say that. She'd been going to say *We'd all be overrun.* But in her mind, 'everyone' had meant simply the British. In Dennis's, it had meant everyone in the world.

And he was right. There *would* be no wars. But how could you persuade a whole world to think that way?

'So what happened?' she asked. 'When you decided to register?'

'I had to go to a tribunal. I had to explain why I felt the way I did. Sometimes they accept that and give you exemption, without any condition. Sometimes they say you've got to do something, stay in the job you're in, or work on the land, or go as a stretcher-bearer or something. And sometimes they won't exempt you at all, and they say you have to join up. If you refuse, you go to prison.'

'Is that what happened to you?'

'I was given conditional exemption. I was working in the City Council offices in Portsmouth and I was exempted on condition I stayed in my job.' His mouth twisted a little wryly. 'Actually, I wasn't all that keen on conditional exemption, I thought if the law said COs should have exemption for matters of conscience, there shouldn't be any conditions at all. But as it happened, the City Council decided that for me, they made their own rule that any COs on the staff would be sacked. So I was out anyway.'

'But they were going against the law,' Betty said indignantly.

'That's right. There was quite a rumpus about it, the Free Churches had a lot to say. But it didn't make any difference. So I couldn't fulfil my condition and I refused to accept any other.'

'And was that when they sent you to prison?'

He nodded. 'Yes. Not a lot of fun, prison, especially when the warders treat you worse than the criminals. I was put to sewing uniforms the first day, army uniforms. Well, that was against the law too, they weren't supposed to force us to do anything towards the war effort. So I refused, and that didn't help me much. They gave me other jobs instead.'

Betty wanted to ask what jobs, but the look on Dennis's face warned her to leave the subject alone. Clearly, prison had been a painful experience. He was silent for a moment, then grinned at her.

'Cheer up. It's over now. I was only in for a few months anyway. And I spent the last couple in Wormwood Scrubs, they had a better attitude there. It wasn't too bad, not when you think what my old man went through in his time. And when I came out, I volunteered to work on the land.' He smiled again. 'Daft, I know, but I don't mind volunteering, I just won't be forced. And now I think maybe it's time I volunteered to do something more. I don't like being safe here, when there's people being bombed back in Pompey.'

They had reached the little river. It wasn't much more than a stream really, running through the fields with willow trees hanging over its banks. Dennis sat down on the trunk of a fallen tree and looked down into the water.

'There's only one thing bothers me about going away,' he said quietly. 'I'd miss you, Betty.'

There was a little silence. A few rooks cawed as they made their way home across the chilly fields. A cloud of gnats danced above the surface of the stream.

She looked at him, sitting there on the fallen trunk. He had had his curly brown hair cut short and his face and neck were tanned. His body was lean and hard. Suddenly, Betty felt a powerful urge to hold herself against that body, to feel his warmth on her skin.

'I'd miss you too,' she said wonderingly. 'I don't want you to go away, Dennis.'

There was a catch in her voice. She heard it with surprise, and felt another flood of emotion. What was the matter with her?

Dennis lifted his head. His hazel eyes looked straight into hers and he reached out his hands.

'Betty . . .'

'Oh, *Dennis*,' she said, and moved blindly into his arms.

His body was warm and hard, just as she had known it would be. She could feel his heart beating against her breast. His cheek was slightly rough against hers, and his lips were firm as he kissed her. He held her closely but not tightly, and she felt safe and secure within the circle of his embrace.

For a few moments they stayed close together, and then he let her go.

'I'm sorry. I shouldn't have –'

'No. It's all right. Please, Dennis –'

'You've already got a boy. You're engaged –'

'Not properly,' she said. 'It's just a game really. To make him feel better while he's away.'

Dennis stared at her. 'What d'you mean?'

Betty reddened. 'It wasn't serious at all at first. We just went out together a few times. And then he got called up and he wanted me to – to wait for him. He wanted to know I wouldn't go out with anyone else. So that he could think of me when he was away, you see, knowing I'd be there when he got back. And I sort of thought it would be nice to be engaged, only I knew my mum and dad would never agree, so he gave me this little ring – she fished it out of her collar, where it hung round her neck on a thin chain – and when we're by ourselves I wear it on my engagement finger. But it doesn't mean anything, not really.'

'Doesn't it?' Dennis asked gently. 'Are you sure?'

Betty's blush deepened. 'I don't really know,' she said honestly. 'I thought it did, for a while. But since I've been here . . . I'm not sure, Dennis. And the last time I saw Graham –'

'Yes?' he prompted, and she looked away from him.

'Well, maybe I shouldn't tell you this, but he wanted – he wanted –' She shook her head. 'I can't say it.'

'All right,' Dennis said. 'You don't have to. I can guess what Graham wanted.' He sighed. 'I can understand it. Having a girl like you, and going off to sea, not knowing whether he'd ever see you again. How did you feel about it?'

Betty looked at him. Her face was still scarlet, but suddenly it was easy to talk to him. His eyes were calm and warm, full of understanding. She said, 'I wanted to a bit, but it was wrong. I knew it was wrong. In the end, he kept on so much that I promised I would after supper, and then Mum made us all play cards till it was time for him to go.' She glanced at him sidelong, still a little embarrassed. 'She knew perfectly well what was going on, she did it deliberately. And Graham knew too. He was furious but there was nothing I could do about it.'

Dennis laughed. 'So a game of whist saved you from a fate worse than death!'

'Actually, it was rummy,' she said seriously, and then laughed with him. 'Would it have been worse than death?'

'I don't suppose so,' he said, 'but you might have been in a difficult situation now.'

'I know,' she said with a shiver. 'That's what scared me. Well, partly. But it just didn't seem right.'

'Perhaps Graham wasn't the right one,' he said lightly. 'It has to be the right one, Betty. And you have to really want it. It's no good giving in just because a chap keeps on. That's not love.'

'No,' she said. 'I know.'

She looked at him again. His eyes were grave. He reached out a hand and she took it and let him draw her close. The warmth of his skin radiated and enfolded her, and she rested against him, her head against his chest, his cheek against her hair.

'I'd like to think I might be the right one, Betty,' he said quietly. 'But I won't keep on at you. I want you to be sure. I want us both to be sure.'

Betty looked down at the stream, flowing gently at their feet. She and Dennis seemed to have come a long way this afternoon. Or perhaps they had been moving slowly towards each other for a long time – ever since that first afternoon, when she had stepped off the bus and looked into his hazel eyes for the first time.

I love you, Dennis, she thought experimentally, as if tasting the words. And then, more strongly, with a power that surged through her body: *I love you*.

The words tasted right. They sounded true and honest in her heart. She knew now that what she had felt for Sandy was friendship. Now, with Dennis, she felt a flowering of joy within her, an opening and blossoming that she had never experienced before, with either Sandy or Graham.

Graham . . .

Her heart sank. What in heaven's name was she going to do about Graham?

CHAPTER FIFTEEN

Graham was back in Portsmouth. His ship was in dock again and its crew employed in helping to clear up the devastation in the city. He spent his days shovelling debris and helping to demolish buildings that were considered dangerous.

'It's a respite,' Elsie Philpotts told her son when he went to Gosport for some home cooking. 'I'm thankful to know you're safe here and not at sea. The longer it takes, the better, as far as I'm concerned.'

Graham pushed away his plate. He had packed away a huge mound of fried potatoes and his parents' entire week's ration of bacon. He was accustomed to eating large amounts on the ship, but it wasn't like Mum's cooking. He gave a sigh of satisfaction.

'That was smashing . . . It's all right, I suppose, but I wish Betty was home. There's not much to do when you haven't got a girl to go with.'

'Not much to do? In *Pompey*?' Elsie gave a little scream of laughter. 'And you a sailor? Still, I suppose you're right. It's all right going to pubs with your mates in strange places, but when you're home you want something different. You want your own sweetheart. And with Betty out on that farm, you're bound to feel lonely.'

Graham nodded. He'd been annoyed to come home and find Betty away, even though he'd known it would happen. It was what he'd foreseen when she'd first announced her intention of volunteering for the Land Army, and he'd told her then he didn't approve. Her father hadn't liked it either, but she'd gone ahead and done it just the same.

Maybe we ought to get married, he thought, remembering how she'd let him down that last evening he was home. She'd have to do what I say then, and she'd have to let me make love to her as well. There'd be none of this 'mummy wouldn't like it' nonsense then.

She'd been wearing his ring long enough, after all. Last Christmas, he'd given it to her. It was nearly Christmas again now. That was plenty of time to be engaged. They *ought* to be thinking about getting married.

'She's coming home this weekend,' he told his mother. 'I'll talk to her then. It's time we got things sorted out.'

He went to Betty's house at the weekend, filled with determination. This time, there would be no games of cards, no hiding behind her mother's skirts. Betty was his girl, and if she wouldn't give him what a man needed, they'd just have to have a showdown. They were getting married, he'd tell her, never mind her dad's objections. There were ways of getting round that.

'What d'you mean, ways?' she asked when he said this. They were in the front room as usual, holding hands after their first reunion. He'd have gone straight ahead then, he was ready enough for it, but Betty had held back, as he might have known she would. In fact, her kisses weren't as enthusiastic as he'd expected and he already felt annoyed. He wished they'd gone out for a walk, so that they could talk properly, without her family in the next room, but it was pitch dark out there in the blackout, and raining too, and there was no chance her mum would let her go out with planes liable to come over at any moment.

'We could fix it so he had to let us get married,' he said. 'Plenty of people do.'

She stared at him. 'Get me in the family way, you mean? Deliberately?'

'Better'n doing it by accident,' he said flippantly.

Betty snatched her hand away. 'I don't know what you think you're suggesting, Graham Philpotts. I'm a decent girl –'

'Oh, for crying out loud!' he broke in. 'I'm not asking you to do anything unnatural. I'm asking you to get married. Don't you know a proposal when it hits you on the nose?'

'It'll be you that gets hit on the nose if you go on talking like that,' she retorted. 'My mum would die of shame if I had to get married. She's always told me what would happen if I got into trouble.'

'I'm not talking about getting into trouble. I'm talking about a wedding. You know? White dresses, bridesmaids, a cake? Isn't that what you want, Betty?'

She looked at him. They seemed to have had this conversation before, but last time she had been the one dreaming of the day that was supposed to be the best day in a girl's life. Now, the glitter seemed to have faded. There was more to life than that one day.

'I don't want it all in a rush,' she said quietly. 'Getting married – it's serious. It's not just an excuse for a pretty frock and a party. Anyway, how could I get married in white if – if –'

'Well, that's all right – *I* don't want to wear a pretty frock, and it doesn't matter a tinker's cuss what colour yours is. It can be sky-blue-pink for all I care. And I couldn't care less about the party. We'll just keep it simple, all right? A quick dash into the church, or the registry office, it's all the same to me, and then a pint or two up the pub and home to bed.' His face was flushed and he grabbed her hand again. 'How does that sound, Bet?'

'It sounds horrible!' Again, she pulled away. 'Graham, what's all this about? Why are you so keen to get married all of a sudden? What's the point, when you'll be going away again?'

'That *is* the point! Don't you understand? I'm fed up with going away and not knowing you'll be here waiting for me when I get back. I'm fed up with coming back to Pompey and finding you're out grubbing about on some farm miles away. I'm fed up with taking second place to a spud!' He glared at her, his blue eyes hard and angry. 'You were keen enough before. You wanted to get engaged. Well, now I want to get married, and I want to know why you don't.' His eyes narrowed with suspicion. 'Is there some other bloke, is that what it is? Some country yokel you've gone and fallen for?'

'No!' The word was out before Betty could stop it, and she turned scarlet. Oh dear, she thought despairingly, what can I say? I ought to tell him things are different now, I don't feel

259

the same. But I didn't want to tell him like this. And I don't even know if I do want them to be different, not really. I don't know *what* I want!

I only know I don't want to hurt him. But he's hurt anyway. And now I've gone and told him a lie, and I don't even know how much of a lie it is.

'All right, then,' Graham demanded, 'so tell me why you *don't* want to get married, all of a sudden.'

'But we never did say we wanted to get married,' Betty said, trying to remember if this was true. Her mind was so confused, she could hardly recall what had happened. 'We just wanted to get engaged, so you'd know I was here waiting for you.'

'Right. And you're not, are you? You're cavorting round the countryside with a lot of farmers –'

'Graham, I'm not! I'm not cavorting. I'm working, working hard.' She showed him her hands, the skin roughened and calloused by toil. 'I'm working as hard as you.'

'Yes, and I don't like it. I don't want my girl slaving away in all weathers, spoiling her looks. You've got hands like a navvy's. What sort of a welcome is that for a bloke when he comes home, to find his girl's got hands like sandpaper? If we were married, you'd come back and act like a woman again instead of trying to pretend you're a man. You'd have my supper on the table and you wouldn't be too tired or too strait-laced to give me what a man wants.'

'Yes, that's it, isn't it,' Betty flashed. 'That's what it's all about. You just want me here, ready to wait on you hand and foot the minute you step through the door. And ready to go to bed with you. It's all for you, isn't it – never mind what *I* want to do. Never mind that it's *my* life we're talking about.'

'I thought it was *our* life –'

'So did I. But you want it all your own way.'

'And don't *you*?' he shouted. 'Don't you want everything *your* own way? First you want to get engaged, so I've got to buy you a ring. Then you want to go off and work on a farm so I never know where you are and you can't be around when my ship comes back to Pompey. God knows what you're doing out there or who you're going with, you could have a different bloke every night for all I know –'

'Graham! That's disgusting!'

'Well, and how do I know it's not true?' he demanded. 'You don't tell me everything in your letters. Do you?'

His eyes were on her face and Betty looked away, biting her lip. It was true that she'd never mentioned the outings in Geoff's car, the walks with Sandy and the others. She hadn't even said much about Dennis. Most of her letters had described her work on the farm. It wasn't surprising Graham had found them boring.

'Do you tell me everything?' she asked, and was surprised to see him flush in his turn.

There was a brief silence. Then Betty touched his sleeve gently.

'Don't let's quarrel, Graham. It's the first time we've seen each other for weeks. We ought to be happy.'

'That's what I want.' He pulled her roughly against him. 'That's what I thought it'd be like. But you seem different. You're harder. You've got more selfish –'

She sighed. 'I haven't got more selfish, Graham. I've just had to grow up a bit, that's all. Life's changed for me. I've been living away from home, I've had to make up my own mind about things. I'm bound to seem a bit different. You're different, too.'

'I'm a man,' he said. 'I've got to go away. But you're a woman, you're supposed to stop at home.'

'It's wartime. That sort of thing isn't true any more.'

'Well, it bloody ought to be!' he exclaimed, losing his temper again. 'For Christ's sake, Betty, isn't there anything you could do at home? Knit balaclava helmets, or work in the canteen like my mum does, or something like that? Do you *have* to go miles away and wallow about in the mud?'

'No, I don't have to. But I want to.' She looked at him, her head on one side, trying to make him smile. 'Can you see me knitting balaclava helmets or making cauldrons of soup, Graham? Can you honestly?'

'I don't see why not. Plenty of other people do. Oh hell, you can do what you like, so long as you're *here*. Don't you understand?'

Betty moved her eyes slowly over his face, taking in the ginger hair, the sandy eyebrows and freckled face. The merriment she had once found so attractive had vanished, leaving his mouth petulant and his eyes sulky. She thought of his mother, jolly and untidy, letting the whole house revolve around her son.

'The trouble with you, Graham, is you're spoilt,' she said. 'You think everything's got to be arranged to suit you. You don't seem to think I'm entitled to a life of my own at all, it's all got to be organised so that I'm here when *you* want me, doing the things *you* want me to do. You think you own me, and you want to get married so that you can own me all the more.'

'That's stupid. I don't want to own you. I just want to know you're my wife.'

'And if I was?' she said. 'Would you let me go on working on the farm?'

'Well, of course not! I'd want you back here, behaving like a wife should. Haven't I already said so?'

'Yes, you have,' Betty said. 'I just wanted to make sure I'd heard you properly. I'm sorry, Graham, but I don't want to give up my life like that. I'm enjoying being on the farm. I'm doing something worthwhile there. I'm not prepared to give it all up and come back here and knit.'

'You don't have to knit. You could go back to the dairy.'

'Thank you very much. I left the dairy, remember?' She looked at him. She hadn't wanted to hurt him, but she was wondering now just how much he really did love her. Wasn't it just his own idea of himself he loved? 'Graham, I'm sorry, but I don't think this is going to work.' She pulled the chain which held her ring from inside her blouse. 'You'd better have this back.'

He stared at the ring, with its tiny glittering stone. 'What are you talking about?'

'Us being engaged. It isn't working.'

'It isn't getting a chance to work!' he shouted. 'You're not giving it a chance. Look, I've been back five minutes, all I wanted to do was hold you in my arms and kiss you and love you, all the things a bloke wants to do when he gets back home with his girl. But you don't seem to care any more.' He was

262

holding her tightly, rubbing his cheek against hers, covering her face with kisses. He put his hand over her breast and squeezed it. 'Last time I was home, you said you'd let me love you properly, and then you never did. Don't you realise how I've been feeling? Don't you realise what it's been like? And all I wanted, all I've ever wanted –'

'Graham, stop it! You'll have Mum in here, making all that noise.' Betty pulled away and sat panting, her hair dishevelled, her blouse half out of her skirt. 'I'm sorry it doesn't seem the same. I'm sorry. But I can't help it. I can't let you do what you want. I don't want to get caught –'

'I've told you it doesn't matter. We'll get married. They'll have to let us get married.'

'And I've told you it *does* matter! I won't do it that way, Graham, and the way you've been going on tonight I don't think I want to do it at all.'

He stared at her, bewildered. 'What way I've been going on? All I've wanted –'

'All you want is to get me tied down,' she said. 'You don't give a damn what *I* want. I'm to live my life the way you want me to live it, which is sitting at home night after night doing sweet Fanny Adams, just on the off-chance that you'll show up. Well, I won't. I'd be bored stiff.'

'Not if you had a baby,' he said. 'You'd have plenty to do if you had a baby to look after.'

'But I don't *want* a baby! Not yet. Not for years. And I'm certainly not having one just so my mum and dad'll have to let us get married. They'd never forgive me. They probably wouldn't ever speak to me again.'

'Well, that's all right,' he said. 'There needn't be one, not really. We can tell 'em it was all a mistake, or you could say you'd had a miss –'

'Tell *lies* about it?' Betty stared at him. 'You'd want me to tell lies, just so we could get married and you could make me stay at home and knit woolly hats? Is that really what you want me to do? Never mind that it'd break my mum's heart and Dad would probably turn me out.'

'You could go and stay with my mum. In fact, it'd probably be better that way. I wouldn't have to –'

'You wouldn't have to come up this way at all when the ship was in Pompey,' she finished for him. 'You don't understand anything at all, do you? You just want the whole world to revolve around you.'

'Oh, for Christ's sake, Betty –'

'And you needn't bring your language here!' she shouted. 'Just because you're in sailor's uniform you needn't think you can come here laying down the law and swearing –'

'Look, I'm asking you to *marry* me, that's all! What's so bloody wrong with that? Most girls *want* to get married, don't they? They *want* to have kids. You're bloody unnatural, you are. I just want to love you, like any bloke wants to love his girl, I don't see anything so criminal about that. And you'd want it too, if you really loved me. You'd *want* to marry me and be my wife.'

'Well, I don't want to,' she said flatly. 'I don't want to be anyone's wife, if that's what it's all about. I'd rather live an old maid.'

'And that's what you'll be,' he sneered. 'Because I can tell you this, Betty, nobody else is going to want you, with your face getting all lined and weatherbeaten, and your hands like sandpaper, and muscles like a brickie's. Shall I tell you something else? You don't know *how* to be a proper woman. You never did. You always wanted to be a boy, out in the street playing football and cricket. And you're no different now. That's why you won't let me touch you, you've got no proper feelings at all. I reckon there's something wrong with you!'

He came to his feet and stood glowering down at her. Betty sat quite still, shaken by his words, wanting to refute them but too overcome by her own guilt to hurl back any more accusations. Her eyes filled with tears and Graham saw and seized upon them.

'That's right, start piping your eye. Isn't that what girls always do, when they start to lose an argument? Well, cry all you like, Betty, it won't bring me back. I've had enough of your prim and prissy ways and I've had enough of waiting for you to finish the milking before you can spare me a minute or two of your precious time. I'm off!'

'Graham, don't go like that –'

'And how do you want me to go?' he demanded, wrenching open the door. 'In a Rolls-Royce? Or maybe on a carthorse, like you're used to?'

'I didn't mean that. You know I didn't. I just –' She gazed helplessly at him, unable to express what she was feeling. 'Graham, we've had some good times together. Can't we still be friends?'

'Oh yes,' he said bitterly, 'that's the next line, isn't it? Let's stay friends. They all say that, in the "Dear Johns". *I can't love you any more, there's this other man who's the love of my life, but let's stay friends*. Friends! Who wants to be friends? Being friends doesn't get you anywhere.'

'If you think that,' Betty said, 'I'm sorry for you. Really sorry.' She stood up. Her knees were shaking but she tilted her chin and looked him in the eye. 'I didn't mean it to be this way, Graham. But I don't see what else we can do. Thanks for the good times, anyway.'

He stared at her, baffled. Then he swung on his heel and wrenched open the door. In another moment, he was out on the street, the front door crashing behind him.

Betty stood quite still. She put her hands up to cover her face, feeling the tears overflow from her eyes to fill her palms and squeeze slowly out through her fingers.

I really didn't mean it to be like that, she thought. I meant it to be gentle. I didn't want all that argument and bitterness.

But perhaps she'd been fooling herself. Perhaps you couldn't, after all, break up with someone without pain and bitterness. Perhaps Graham was right, and it was impossible to stay 'friends'.

From the other room, she could hear the voices of Olive and her parents. It was almost supper-time. They'd be expecting her and Graham to come through at any minute.

She heard her mother knock on the door and took a deep breath, preparing herself to go through and tell them that Graham wasn't, after all, staying to supper.

CHAPTER SIXTEEN

The news from London was worse each day. It became a dreadful commonplace to pass dead bodies in the street, and even small children developed a casual indifference.

'That's our baker. He's lost his hat.'

'I wonder who'll get his horse . . .'

Huge craters appeared in the roads, and cars, taxis and trolley buses were reduced to smashed wrecks of twisted metal. So many London buses were destroyed that the city appealed for help from other towns, and the streets were suddenly brightened by buses of all colours, taking the place of the familiar red.

The blitz was spreading to other cities. In November the Germans attacked some of Britain's most famous cathedral cities. Nine days later they tore the heart from Coventry in one of the worst raids yet, nearly five hundred bombers, dropping over five hundred tons of high-explosive bombs and nearly a thousand incendiaries. And before the nation could draw breath, they were back again, hurling an apparently inexhaustible supply of red-hot fury at the capital city.

'It's coming closer,' Jess said, sitting in the air-raid shelter and listening to the planes passing overhead. 'It'll be our turn soon.'

Southampton was next. Only three days after the crushing of Coventry, the planes were thundering up the Solent and over the docks which had sheltered some of Britain's most famous ocean liners. A week later they came again, and then again. The flames could be seen for miles around, lighting the sky all night.

They could be seen from Bridge End, where the Budd children and their friends were evacuated. Tim and Keith watched from their bedroom window, excited and only half afraid, while their sister Rose stared in panic, imagining it happening to Portsmouth, imagining her parents and baby sister Maureen, burning alive in the holocaust.

'It's all right, love. It's not Portsmouth. Your mum and dad are all right,' Mrs Greenberry tried to comfort her. But Rose shook her head, her eyes fixed on the brilliant glow.

'They'll go to Portsmouth as well. I know they will. They keep on getting raids there.'

Mrs Greenberry held her against her bosom and sighed. What could she say to the girl? Rose wasn't a child any more, she was thirteen years old and intelligent enough to know what was happening. You couldn't tell her everything would be all right, when you knew it wasn't true. Nothing was all right.

'We'll just have to trust God to look after them,' she said. 'He knows they're there, Rose. He'll take care of them.'

But the girl looked up at her, her brown eyes dark with despair.

'Why should he? He's letting other people be killed. He's not looking after *them*.'

And there wasn't anything you could say to that either. She could only go on holding Rose tight and stay with her, watching the fires that raged over Southampton, thinking of London and of Coventry and waiting for the same thing to happen to Portsmouth.

It began only a few days later, when Portsmouth suffered what was described as 'the most violent attack yet carried out by the Luftwaffe'. Hospitals and cinemas were damaged, property destroyed and fires started all over the city. Gladys, still nervously learning to handle an ambulance, found herself racing along crumbling streets, her way lit by flames, while her mother crouched in the back trying to staunch the bleeding of terrified victims.

'Oh God, it's awful, it's awful,' she kept repeating to herself. 'I can't stand it. I'll go mad. I can't stand it.' But there was no time to give in, and it had to be withstood, for there were people dying and only she and Peggy and a few others to help them in a world that had gone sickeningly mad.

For many, there was no help. They lay buried beneath huge heaps of shattered brick and plaster, pinned down by heavy beams of wood and concrete, blood and breath slowly crushed from their smashed bodies, and they died with the taste of the dust and smoke filling their lungs, and the screams of other victims in their ears.

And in the midst of it all, Kathy Simmons, huddling in the damp little Anderson shelter with her two small daughters, went into labour.

She had been feeling strange all day. Yesterday the baby, which had been riding high, had begun a frenzied burst of activity. It seemed to be kicking itself down her body, like a swimmer diving energetically to the bottom of the sea. Her shape changed by the hour, until the bulge was lying low on her thighs and she felt exhausted.

She called the midwife, but after an examination Mrs Frame told her that she didn't think there was any hurry. 'You say the other two took a long time. I don't reckon this un'll be born for a day or two yet. Head's not properly engaged, see, and nothing can happen till it is. You just get some rest and I'll look in again tomorrow.'

Kathy watched her go, feeling uneasy. Mrs Frame wasn't the best midwife in the district, but she was all Kathy could afford until some more money came through from Mike. And she couldn't ask the baby to wait! She wondered whether to go over to Jess Budd and ask if she could stop the night in their shelter. She looked at her daughters, who had finished their tea and were playing by the fire.

'Put your coats and shoes on. We're just going round the corner to see Mrs Budd.'

Muriel looked up. 'Mrs Budd's out. I saw her with Mrs Chapman, pushing Maureen's pram up the street.'

Kathy felt blank. 'She might have been just going shopping. I expect she'll be back by now.'

Stella shook her head. 'No, she said they were going to tea with her auntie.'

Her auntie. That must be the one who lived half a dozen

streets away, the one Jess and Frank had lived with for a while when they first got married. That meant Frank would go there too, straight from work, and they might stop on for supper.

Kathy chewed her lip, wondering what to do. She knew most of the other women in the street now, by sight if no more, and she knew that most of them would help if she needed it, but she was reluctant to bother them for what might be only a false alarm. After all, Mrs Frame had said the baby couldn't be born until the head was engaged, and if that hadn't happened yet she ought to be safe enough. Why not wait till morning, and then ask Jess if she could go over to them at night until the baby was born?

She tried to settle down to some knitting, but she felt heavy and uncomfortable. The baby's head was like a hard rock pressing against her pelvis. The girls were uneasy too, looking at her and whispering to each other. Kathy had told them a baby was on the way – she knew most mothers wouldn't have done, thinking they were too young to know about such things, but you had to take a different view when you were on your own.

She went to the front door and peered out, careful to ensure that no light was showing. The street was very dark. The worst of the air raids had taken place during the full moons which had occurred during the middle of October and November – Bombers' Moon, they'd called them. Tonight, there was no moon at all, but the air was clear and the sky prickling with stars. Was that enough to show German aircraft the route to England? For the first time, Kathy wondered how they found their way through the night skies. During the day, they could follow roads and railway lines, but what did they do at night? She gazed up, thinking how peaceful it looked, and how false.

Footsteps sounded on the pavement and she drew back a little. Her eyes had grown accustomed to the darkness and she could see the figure of a man walking down from September Street.

He caught a glimpse of her movement and stopped.

'Is that Mrs Simmons?'

'Yes. It's Mr Vickers, isn't it?'

'Tommy,' he said cheerfully. 'I've never liked being called "mister". It makes me want to look round to see who's standing behind me.'

Kathy smiled. She had heard a good deal about Tommy Vickers. He was well known for his cheekiness and good humour. He'd do anything to help anyone too, Jess had told her, and didn't make a lot of fuss or noise about it either, like some people did. He'd leave bundles of kindling on the doorsteps of old people, for instance, or go round collecting odd bits of shopping for anyone who found it difficult to get out. He wasn't above a bit of fiddling – he always seemed to know where to lay his hands on a few eggs or a pound or two of potatoes – but he wouldn't have anything to do with real black marketeering, and he'd never do anyone down.

She supposed he was on his rounds now. He'd become an Air Raid Warden soon after the war broke out, but he wasn't one to go around yelling 'Put that light out!' Instead, he'd be more likely to knock on the door where a light was showing and chaff the offender into being more careful.

'What are you doing out here?' he asked. 'It's a bit cold to be standing admiring the view.' He stood gazing up at the glistening sky. 'Not but what it's not a view worth admiring. Look at all those stars. You can see the Milky Way as plain as a main road tonight.'

Kathy nodded. 'It doesn't seem possible it could be full of planes, dropping bombs on us. It's like a – a –' she searched for the right word and remembered something the vicar had said in church once '– a desecration. What's it all about, Mr Vickers? What are they doing it for?'

He shrugged. 'I know why *we're* doing it. So people like you and me can stand at their front doors of an evening and look at the stars without being afraid of being bombed out. But don't ask me why Hitler started it all. I wonder if anyone knows now. It's like a stupid kids' quarrel that's got out of hand, and they've all been home and fetched their dads to fight it out for them.'

Kathy knew exactly what he meant. She had often heard the boys in the street threatening each other. *I'll get my dad to fight your dad . . . Well, my dad's bigger than your dad . . .* The difference was that the fathers usually had more sense than to get involved, and the boys couldn't do that much damage anyway. With the countries of Europe, it was a different matter.

And it wasn't just Europe. It was spreading like a canker, all over the world. Japan and China at each other's throats. Italy, Egypt, Greece. Only America was holding herself aloof and, like most people, Kathy wished they would join in too. Surely with a mighty nation like that on their side, the Allies could finish off Hitler and his cronies for once and for all . . .

The baby gave a sudden violent squirm and she gasped and put her hand on her stomach. Tommy turned his head sharply; she could see the gleam of his eyes in the starlight.

'You all right, love?'

'Yes. It's just the baby – been restless all day.' She gave an embarrassed little laugh, but Tommy didn't seem bothered.

'It must be due around now, surely?'

'Yes, I wondered if it might be on its way but Mrs Frame says not for another day or two.' She sighed and crossed her arms over her chest. 'I wish it'd come and get it over with. I get scared at night, what with all these bombs and wondering when it's going to get born . . . And I'm so *tired*.'

'I know, love.' Everyone was tired, bone tired. Night after night in the shelter, hearing the planes pass overhead, listening for explosions and wondering what had been hit now. And still you had to get up in the morning and go to work. Or see to the kids, get breakfast, do the shopping and housework. Sleep came in snatches these days, like a precious jewel that was handed to you only to be plucked away again just when you thought you had it in your grasp.

'I just want to lean against the wall,' Tommy's wife had said to him a few days ago, and he'd smiled and pulled her close.

'Lean against me instead, love.' But he couldn't be there for her all day, and sometimes he needed to lean on something too.

Now it was Kathy Simmons who needed someone to lean on, and her need couldn't be ignored.

'Look,' he said, 'it's a fine night and I reckon there'll be raiders over any minute. Why don't you get yourself settled down in your shelter with the kids? I'll see you settled and then I'll look in again later on to make sure you're all right.'

'That's good of you, Mr Vickers,' Kathy said gratefully and he gave her arm a little shake.

'I told you, it's Tommy. Now, what d'you usually take down there with you?'

He came into the house and helped her collect together the nightly bundle – blankets, pillows, the mattresses of the two camp beds Kathy had managed to buy. You couldn't leave things there during the day because of damp. He made a big pot of tea and brought that down too, covering it with cushions to keep it warm as long as possible. He made sure the hurricane lamp had enough fuel and that no light showed through the thick curtain Kathy had hung over the door.

'There, that's you all serene.' He'd kept the two little girls laughing as they paraded up and down the garden path with all their belongings. 'Now, I don't want to hear a peep out of any of you till morning.'

'You can't hear peeps,' Stella said cheekily. 'You can only see peeps.'

'You'd be surprised what I can see and hear. I'm like Father Christmas, I am, I know everything.' He pretended to growl and the girls shrieked and scuttled into the corner of the shelter. 'And what I know now is that you're both going to go fast asleep till morning.'

'Even if the bombs come?'

'Even if the bombs come,' he said firmly. He looked at the two little faces and felt a spasm of anger, sharp and hot inside him. Why should little scraps like these two have to worry about bombs? And Kathy, sitting there white-faced and obviously uncomfortable. She ought to be tucked up in bed, with someone to look after her, not facing the night all alone.

He wished he could get Freda to come and give an eye to her. But Freda had developed flu yesterday and he didn't even like the idea of her having to go down to their own shelter, let alone come round to Kathy's. And it wouldn't help the young woman to catch flu at a time like this.

Well, it was only a few hours till morning. He'd poke his

head in now and then to reassure her, and –

The wail of the siren splintered his thoughts. He gave a swift look round the dank little cave, and said, 'I'll have to go. You sit tight and don't worry. And you two little uns, remember what I said. Look after your mum and go to sleep.'

How they were to do both at once wasn't clear, but Stella and Muriel nodded, their faces suddenly fearful. They were old enough to be frightened of the bombs, old enough to see and understand the destruction around them even if they couldn't understand its causes. And they still had nightmares about the day their own house was bombed. As Tommy ducked out through the curtain, they drew together on their camp bed, staring up at the flickering shadows on the corrugated iron roof.

'It's all right,' Kathy said, pressing them gently down on the mattress and tucking the blankets around them. 'It's all right. You know we're safe in the shelter.'

She looked at them, huddled together, their eyes huge in white faces. Why don't I just give in and take them out into the country? she thought. They've been through enough. They deserve to sleep safe in their beds at night.

But if she gave up this house and went out to the countryside, there would be no home at all for Mike to come back to. There would be nothing for him to picture as he worked at sea, no family base to give his thoughts security. No roots for any of them.

Kathy hardly knew how to express these feelings. All she knew was that without a home of their own, their marriage would no longer have its firm foundation, a foundation to which they both – *all* of them – needed desperately to cling. In a world that was teetering on its axis, some things just had to remain secure, however dangerous it might seem.

It was less than half an hour after Tommy had gone that she felt the first savage pain.

There had been no possibility of sleep. The raid was a fierce one, beaten off at first by a heavy barrage of anti-aircraft fire, and then followed by a wave of planes that burst through the defences, flying low overhead and scattering bombs all

273

over the city. Kathy and the girls crouched together, feeling the earth shake, remembering that terrible afternoon when their own house had been bombed, wondering if it was about to happen again. The explosions sounded closer, louder – was that one their home, gone again? Or that one, or that?

Kathy felt ill. Pain had been circling round her back and pelvis for hours, pushed away until it became too bad to ignore. The baby could not be born tonight. Not in an air-raid shelter, in the middle of a raid, with no one to help her. It could not. It would have to wait till tomorrow. She set her jaw and concentrated, as if by ignoring the steadily increasing contractions, by trying to pretend they weren't happening, she could postpone it till morning. Why not? Why shouldn't it be possible? It *had* to be possible.

It was not possible. As the agony gripped her, starting in the small of her back and spreading like an iron band around her swollen stomach, she knew that nothing now could delay the forces of nature. She could feel the body of the baby, forcing itself along the canal, punching at the walls that had sheltered it for nine months, thrusting its head against the muscles whose strength had carried it and now made their own protesting stand against its assault. Her whole abdomen was clenched in the vice of the most severe contraction she had ever experienced, wave after wave of pain grinding through her until she could hold back the groan no longer and it burst from her lips and swelled like the pain to a scream. And then that was all she was, a scream, a white-hot, searing shriek of anguish that pulsed with the frenzy of flesh and blood and bone that was trying so desperately to escape from the prison of her womb.

Slowly, the waves of pain receded. Kathy opened her eyes, her head swimming, and saw the two little girls sitting bolt upright on their camp bed, staring at her in terror. Shaken, dreading the next contraction, she held out her hands and tried to smile.

'It's all right. It's just the baby, wanting to be born. It'll be all – oh!'

It was coming again, starting low in her back, spreading its grip like a web over her whole body, tightening and strengthening its grasp until she was once more helpless and could only lie on the flimsy bed, the blood roaring in her ears as the enemy aircraft roared overhead and Portsmouth exploded about her.

Tommy Vickers hurried along the darkened streets. The stars above were dimmed now by the brilliance of the searchlights. The unearthly light filtered down into the city, but he was too anxious about Kathy to be either grateful for its help or anxious about the bombs that would follow.

What a time to be having a baby! What a *place*. And all on her own too, with two other kiddies scared out of their wits. It wasn't right that women should have to put up with such things. And it was dangerous.

Tommy didn't know a lot about childbirth. Freda had told him a bit but mostly it was something women talked about between themselves, in hushed voices. But he did know that women could die if they weren't properly looked after. Kathy Simmons needed someone to look after her. And it ought to be someone who knew what they were about.

Who could he ask? He racked his brains. If only Freda wasn't laid up with flu, he would have fetched her. Jess Budd or her sister Annie were the next who came to mind, but he'd seen them going out earlier on. They'd probably be stuck now in someone's shelter. What about Peggy Shaw? No, she'd have gone to the First Aid post, and her daughter Gladys with her.

There must be other neighbours who'd help. But Mrs Minns who lived next door to Kathy was old and frail, and anyway she'd never had any babies. Vi Redding from number 12 had had plenty of kids but she wasn't all that bright. And a lot of the others had started 'trekking' every night, going over the hill to Denmead or Cowplain to escape the bombs.

The snarl of approaching planes could be heard quite clearly now. He stood irresolute for a moment, and then caught a glimpse of light, flickering momentarily from a front door. Ethel Glaister.

'Here!' he shouted. 'Mrs Glaister! I want you.'

The light disappeared. He heard the click of the door and

ran down the pavement. There was no sign of life now in the house and he guessed that she was probably going down to the shelter in the back garden. He lifted his fist and pounded on the door, found the letter-box and shouted through it.

'Mrs Glaister! Ethel! Open the door.'

The blackout curtain hung heavily against the letter box. He tried to thrust it aside with his hand. The planes were almost overhead.

'Ethel! It's Tommy Vickers. There's an emergency – for God's sake, open the door.'

'Go away,' a voice called from inside. 'We're going down the shelter.'

'No – open up Ethel, please!'

'There's a raid on –'

'I know that, for crying out loud!' He tried to force the exasperation from his voice. Ethel Glaister was too touchy to offend now. 'Look, I need your help. Open the door a minute.'

There was a pause, then he heard the click of a light being switched off and the door opened slightly. He could see the pale oval of Ethel's face peering out.

'What is it? Has someone been bombed?'

'No, it's –'

'If you got me out here,' she said, beginning to sound haughty, 'just so you could tell me off for showing a light for about half a second –'

'It's nothing to do with that.' He was beginning to feel desperate. 'I just want to ask your help.'

'Help?' Her voice was suspicious. 'What sort of help?'

'It's young Mrs Simmons. The woman who got bombed out – lives in number 16, October –'

'I know who she is. What's the matter with her?'

Her tone wasn't encouraging but Tommy plunged on. 'She's having a baby –'

'Well, anyone can see *that*, too. What's it got to do with me?'

'She's over there all by herself.' The sky was filled now with the roar of enemy aircraft. 'I'm worried about her – I think the baby might be on its way.' His words were drowned by the whistle of a bomb and the crash of its explosion. He ducked

276

involuntarily. The first explosion was always the worst – after that, you were expecting it. 'I said, I think the baby –'

Ethel had jumped back inside the house. She looked up nervously at the sky and said, 'I'm going down the shelter. I ought to have been there already. You'll get us all killed, Tommy Vickers, standing here gossiping when there's a raid on.'

'I'm not gossiping. I'm worried about young Mrs Simmons. She needs someone with her.' There was another explosion somewhere in the city, and another. 'She shouldn't be there on her own –'

'Look,' Ethel Glaister said sharply, 'we're all having to manage on our own. All us women. Isn't my George away, in the Army? Ask someone who's got her husband at home, someone like Jess Budd next door or Peggy Shaw. I've got my own children to think of. I can't go out gallivanting about having tea with the neighbours in the middle of an air-raid.' Another *crump* sounded, nearer at hand this time. 'Anyway, Kathy Simmons wouldn't want *me* popping over to pass the time of day, as good as turned me out last time, she did, when I tried to be friendly. And now I'm going down our shelter, where I ought to have been ten minutes ago.'

She drew back and slammed the door in Tommy's face. He stared at it for a moment, feeling helpless. Then he thrust his hand through the letter-box again and put his mouth close against it.

'Ethel, she needs your help. She's having her baby, she might be having it this very minute. Ethel, she could *die* over there, with no one who knows what to do . . .'

But there was no reply. And as the bombs fell thick and fast all over Portsmouth, Tommy Vickers knew that there was only one thing he could do.

'My God!'

Kathy scarcely heard Tommy's voice as he ducked back into the shelter, hardly knew he was there, only knew that suddenly a hand was in hers and she was clutching it with all the desperation of a woman drowning and almost beyond help. He slipped his arm under her shoulders and held her hard against him, sharing the anguish with her, waiting until it receded. At the same time, he reached out his other arm and the two frightened children slid across their bed and pressed themselves against the warmth of his body.

'Is Mummy dying?' Stella asked in a small voice as Kathy relaxed again and lay panting, her eyes closed, in the circle of his arm.

'No, of course she isn't. She's just having a baby. You knew you were going to have a baby brother or sister, didn't you?'

'Brother,' Muriel stated firmly.

'Well, we'll soon see. It's going to be born tonight. That's what's happening now, see, it's been living in your mum's tummy all this time and now it's coming out, that's all.'

'But it's hurting her,' Muriel whispered as Kathy began to tense again. 'Why is it hurting her so much?'

'It just does sometimes.' Tommy sought for words to explain but Kathy was groaning again, and her body was thrashing about on the bed. He caught her against him, letting her clutch his hands until he feared she would break all his fingers, and rode the storm with her. His mind echoed the little girl's words. Why was it hurting so much? Why did it have to be like this?

'Does the baby have to make a hole to come out of?' Stella looked fearfully at her mother's body as if expecting it to rip like a paper bag. 'Is that what it's doing now?'

'No, there's a place for it come out.' He looked doubtfully at the swollen body. Should he get some of her clothes off? Surely it would be easier for her. If only there were another woman here. Surely one of the neighbours would help, if he could only let them know they were needed . . . Even that bitch Ethel Glaister . . . He glanced towards the doorway, then swore under his breath and hesitated. Kathy was resting again, but the contractions were coming too quickly for him to go for help. And he couldn't send the children out into the bomb-spattered streets, not even to hop over the fence to next-door's shelter. No, he would have to stay and just do the best he could.

Hot water. Wasn't that what was needed, lots of hot water? He'd never known exactly why. Perhaps it was just to make tea. He looked at the teapot, covered with cushions to keep it hot. Well, at least Kathy could have a drink when she needed it.

Kathy's body bucked and twisted in his arms. He held her tightly, feeling the waves of pain shudder through her body. How long would it go on like this? How long could she *stand* it like this?

'Listen, love,' he said when the contraction had passed, leaving her weak and trembling against him. 'I think we ought to get some of your clothes off. Don't worry – I won't look at you. But the baby's got to have room.'

'It's all right. I don't care what you do.' She managed a twisted grin. 'There's no modesty when you have a baby, Mr Vickers. Just – don't go away.' Her face contorted and she grabbed his hand again and screamed through gritted teeth. 'Oh God! Oh God, oh God, oh *God*!'

The two girls began to cry. 'Mummy, Mummy. It's hurting her, she's going to die, oh Mummy, Mummy, *Mummy* . . .'

'It's all right,' Tommy panted, himself far from sure. 'It'll be over soon and you'll have a lovely brother. Or sister.' It didn't matter a row of buttons which it was, he thought, so long as it didn't take too long. But Freda had been over eighteen hours in labour with their Eunice. Had it been like this all through every one of those eighteen hours? No wonder she'd never wanted any more.

What were you supposed to do? Was it enough just to hold her, or was there something else he ought to be doing? He pulled the blanket down and undid the laces on Kathy's maternity skirt. It fell away, a big rectangle of material. If he could get it out from underneath her, he could lay it over her body. She had knickers on too, huge bloomers with elasticated legs. Blimey, he thought, they're like a ruddy barrage balloon. He tried to ease them down but they were trapped beneath her heavy body. They were soaking wet and sticking to her skin.

'Kathy, you'll have to help me. We've got to get your knickers off.' I hope to God nobody's outside listening, he thought with grim humour. Not that anyone would hear anything, over the cacophony that was going on out there, with planes still droning overhead, ack-ack guns firing and bombs whistling and crashing to the ground. What a time to be having a bloody baby!

'I can't – oh God, no. *No*!' Her head twisted in useless rebuttal. She clutched his hands, her nails digging into his skin. 'It wasn't like this with the other two. Oh God, Mr Vickers, it's killing me!'

'It's not. It's not.' He tried to keep the fear from his voice. Suppose it *was* killing her? Suppose she died here in the shelter, in his arms, in front of her two little girls? 'It's going to be all right, Kathy. Your baby's being born and everything's all right. Just don't panic.' And you're a fine one to talk, Tommy Vickers, he thought. You're on the verge of panic yourself. What in hell's name should I *do*?

Between them, and between the contractions, they managed to get her knickers off. Stella helped, once he'd told her that this was where the baby would come out. She looked at him with some doubt at first, but her mother nodded weakly and said, 'It's right, Stell. You do what Mr Vickers tells you,' and she put her small hands to the waist of the garment and tugged when Kathy, panting hard, lifted her body an inch or two to allow it to be pulled down.

'That's better.' Tommy felt relieved. He pulled the blanket quickly back over the distorted body. If only it wasn't so cold down here. But it was December and the shelter was half underground and damp. Not that Kathy seemed to feel it. She was streaming with sweat.

The labour went on, and overhead the roar of planes and the reverberations of the bombs continued in accompaniment. I ought to be out there doing my rounds, Tommy thought. I ought to be making sure everyone's in shelter and not showing any lights, and I ought to be looking out for fires and parachutes and giving a hand wherever it's needed. But that's what I'm doing, isn't it? You can't say it's not needed here. If only I knew what to do.

'Kathy, love,' he said urgently, 'you're going to have to help me. Tell me what I should be doing. I mean, I've never done this before. You've had babies, you must know . . .'

'Just stay here. Don't go away – for Christ's sake, don't go away.' She was clutching him again. The contractions were coming almost in one long wave now, wrenching at her body, twisting her to and fro. Her heavings had tossed off the blankets and he could see the rippling of the muscles, actually see the pain that threatened to split her in half. Bloody hell, he thought, if this is what women go through it's a wonder any of them ever has more than one kid. But then he remembered his Freda saying that you forgot, somehow, once it was all over. You'd need to, he thought.

The shape of Kathy's body had changed. The bulge was much lower now, right down to her thighs. She was lying with her legs splayed and he could see a gaping black cavern between them, with red lips stretched far apart in a parody of a grin. And just inside the cavern, just visible, something else. Something smooth and dark that approached the mouth of the cavern and then receded, and then, as Kathy gave a shout of pain and her whole body contorted, came almost to the entrance and almost, *almost*, pushed its way out.

'The baby!' he shouted in sudden realisation. 'Kathy, it's the baby! I can see it. Look – Stella, Muriel, look – there's the baby, it's almost born.'

As the contraction passed, it slithered back in again. Once again, Tommy was racked by doubt. Should he help? Put his fingers in and give a bit of a tug? Almost as soon as the thought had entered his mind, he dismissed it. He stared, fascinated, as the space widened and the head emerged a little more. He could see it pulsating. He could almost see its face. Surely it had got to be born now. He remembered the term Freda had used when talking about Eunice's birth.

'Bear down, Kathy! You've got to bear down.' He gripped her hand and lifted his arm so that she could brace her feet against it. 'That's it. Now – next time it starts, bear down. Hard. That's it. That's it. A bit more. A bit harder. Don't stop now – give it all you've got. *Now*!'

'I can't!' Kathy shrieked, kicking so hard that he almost toppled over as her body shot along the bed. 'I can't, I can't, I *can't*!'

'You can! You *have*!' The baby was thrusting from her body, virtually elbowing its way out, in a gush of blood and water and God knew what else. Tommy grabbed it as it came, and almost dropped it on the cold earthen floor. It was covered in grey slime, as slippery as a fish squirming in his grasp, tiny arms and legs flailing, face screwed up and mouth wide open in a yell of fury. He held it in both hands, staring down at it. It's born, he thought dazedly. It's born. A baby. A new baby. No one's ever seen it before, no one. I'm the very first . . .

Kathy had subsided. She lay suddenly flat and exhausted. He looked at the baby and then at her. What did you do next? Weren't you supposed to hold newborn babies up by their feet and smack their bottoms or something? He stared again at the slippery, grey little being who was glowering back at him. It seemed cruel. And what about the cord, which was quite different from anything he had ever imagined – a thick, purple rope leading from the baby's navel back into Kathy's body? What were you meant to do about that?

'What is it?' she whispered. She sounded drained, as if every ounce of strength had been beaten out of her. And no wonder, he thought. 'Is it a boy?'

'A –?' He looked hurriedly, feeling guilty that he hadn't noticed at once. 'Yes. Yes, it's a boy. What – what should I do next?'

'Give him to me.' Her voice was soft. She held out her arms and he laid the baby in them, across her breast. In the tumult, her smock had got rucked up around her neck, and her heavy breasts were bare. She cuddled the naked, slimy little body against them and to Tommy's amazement the small head turned as if already seeking milk.

'Blimey, he's a hungry little bugger,' he said. 'Look at that!'

Kathy smiled at him and he marvelled at the sudden luminous quality of her smile. It was as if the agony of the past hour was already forgotten, just as Freda had said. Then she said, urgently, 'You've got to cut the cord, Tommy. Have you got scissors? And some string or something?'

He shook his head helplessly. The situation was once more desperate. Babies could die – mothers too – if their cords weren't treated properly. Freda had said so. She'd known someone who'd died because of that. He glanced anxiously around the little shelter, lit so dimly by the hurricane lamp. What could you find here to tie and cut a baby's cord with?

'Here, Mr Vickers, I've got a ribbon.' Stella was already untying it, a blue ribbon that held a hank of hair on one side of her head. She handed it to him and he thanked God that she'd been here after all. Sensible kiddy.

'Tie it in two places,' Kathy instructed. 'Near the baby, and then nearer me. Tie it tightly. I don't think it matters about cutting it straightaway, so long as it's tied.' Her voice began to fade. 'Oh God, here comes the afterbirth. Here – take him, quick.'

'The what?' Tommy stared in dismay as her body began to contort again. He snatched the baby and handed him to Stella. 'Kathy, what's happening now, for God's sake? Don't tell me you've got another one in there!'

She laughed in spite of her discomfort. 'I hope not! It's the afterbirth – it's what the cord's attached to. It's a bit mucky, I'm afraid . . .' Again, her body contracted and she closed her eyes and tensed herself. And then it came, gushing out between her legs as the baby himself had come. An almost black mass of flesh and mucus, like a grossly deformed liver, which squirmed as if it had a life of its own and lay on the bed, pulsing like a slowly dying creature.

'Ugh!' Muriel exclaimed. 'It's horrible!'

Tommy thought so too, and he would rather that the little girls had not seen it. But children were seeing a good many things these days that it would be better they didn't see, and birth had to be better than death. He wondered what to do with the squidgy-looking mass. Was having a baby always as mucky as this?

Suddenly, he became aware of a change. He looked up at the roof, almost puzzled, and then grinned.

'Here,' he said, 'the planes have stopped.'

Kathy lifted her head. The baby was back on her breast now and the two girls were close to her, gazing down at their new brother. They all listened for a moment, scarcely able to believe the sudden silence.

'D'you think it's over?' she whispered.

Tommy made up his mind.

'Over or not, I'm going to get you some help. Annie Chapman's girl Olive, she might be home, she'll come across. And I'll go for Mrs Frame as well.' He hesitated. 'There's – er, there's nothing else likely to – er – well, you know . . .?'

Kathy laughed weakly. 'No, the afterbirth's the only thing. But it ought to be attended to.' She smiled down at the baby lying across her bosom. 'And so should this little chap. He badly needs a bath!'

So that's what the hot water was always wanted for. There was certainly a lot of clearing up to do. Tommy surveyed the mess on the floor, the blood-soaked bed. It looked as if there'd been a murder in here rather than a baby being born.

'I'll go and get someone to come and look after you,' he said, and turned towards the doorway.

Kathy reached out a hand and brushed his leg with her fingers. He looked down at her.

'Thanks, Tommy,' she said quietly. 'Thanks a lot.'

Tommy nodded, suddenly unable to speak. He pushed aside the curtain, taking care not to let the slightest glimmer of light escape, and climbed out into fresh, cold air. He gazed up at the stars.

A few minutes ago, death had been raining down from that dark, star-pricked sky. But all the death the Germans hurled down couldn't stop new life being born. Kathy's baby had been determined to live, determined to survive. And if a newborn baby could be that tough . . .

You'll never beat us, he told Hitler silently. You'll never, never win.

CHAPTER SEVENTEEN

Christmas was coming. The second Christmas of the war. Last year, they had all been waiting, wondering if anything was ever going to happen. Now, they were in the thick of it and nobody could pretend it would soon be over.

Micky Baxter and his gang were still running wild. There were a few teachers in Portsmouth, mostly retired, who were attempting to run a school of sorts. They gathered children together in front rooms, giving them lessons one or two days a week and setting them homework to do the rest of the time. Some of the children bothered, some didn't. Some rarely attended.

'He ought to come to lessons,' an elderly schoolmaster said, knocking on Nancy Baxter's door one day. 'When this war's over, it's people with education who'll be needed to get the country back on its feet. Your Micky's bright enough to do well if he puts his mind to it.'

'Go on,' Nancy said cynically, 'education won't do my Micky no good. Teachers've always had a down on him. He'll have to look out for 'imself, same as I've 'ad to. That's what it's like for people like us.'

The teacher looked past her along the narrow passage with its dark brown, peeling wallpaper and cracked linoleum. A stale, sour smell wafted through from the back room. He sighed.

'But it doesn't have to be like that. He could pass exams, get a good job. He could better himself, don't you see?'

'Better himself?' Nancy echoed. She removed the cigarette end that hung from her lip and sneered. 'Yes, that's just it, ain't it? We're not good enough as we are, we've got to *better* ourselves. An' we've got to do it your way. My Micky's got to waste his time sitting in school listening to a lot of fat-arsed teachers with posh voices tellin' 'im he's got to learn bits of poetry and draw maps of China. What good's that sort of thing to a boy like my Micky, eh? What good's it ever done you to learn poetry and draw China? It didn't stop a war startin', did it? It didn't stop Hitler tryin' to take over the world.'

The schoolmaster gazed at her blankly and Nancy put the cigarette back between her lips.

'My Micky's 'elpin' me at 'ome,' she said dismissively. ''E's got a job workin' in a shop, errand boy. 'E's doin' more good there than 'e'll ever do in school. Anyway, 'e's not far off fourteen, so you might as well save your breath and your shoe leather.'

She slammed the door and went back inside. Her mother was sitting by the fire, holding out her hands to the small pile of smouldering coal. The baby Vera was playing with a couple of battered saucepan lids.

'Silly old fool,' Nancy said scornfully. 'Comin' round 'ere trying to get our Micky to go for lessons. 'Tain't natural, tyin' a boy like 'im down to a desk all day. Stands to reason 'e won't do it.'

'Still, 'e does have a point, Nance,' Granny Kinch said. 'People do get on better now with a bit of education. You couldn't get it when I was young. I learned to read but your dad never did, and 'e always wished 'e 'ad.'

'Micky can read, and add up too. That's all a boy like 'im wants. The rest is just rubbish.'

'It'd keep 'im off the streets a bit,' Mrs Kinch said. 'We never know where 'e is these days.'

'I don't need to know where 'e is,' Nancy replied, lighting another cigarette. 'Not so long as 'e keeps bringin' stuff 'ome the way 'e does.'

The three of them kept up the fiction of Micky's job as errand boy, although he came home less frequently now with food or ornaments and clothing. People were becoming more careful, keeping their doors locked when the siren sent them running for the shelter. But there were still enough careless ones to bring in a steady supply, and the store-room in the basement of the bombed house was filling with things the boys kept for themselves.

Shrapnel was the latest treasure to be salvaged from the air-raids. They vied with each other to find the largest, most jagged pieces and arranged them around the cellar. Cyril found a large shell case and stood it in the middle of the ramshackle table, where Micky gazed at it enviously.

'I'll get a better one than that,' he said. 'I'll get a proper bomb. An unexploded one. There's plenty around after a raid.'

'What, and blow us all up?' Jimmy jeered. 'Fat lot of good that'd be.'

'A dud one, then. Or I'd take out its fuse. That's easy. I saw a bit about it in my comic. I bet I could do that.'

'Bet you couldn't. Proper soldiers get blown up doing that.'

Micky leaned back and put his feet up on the table. He was smoking a fag-end he'd found in the gutter. Sometimes he pinched cigarettes from his mother's bag, but she kept a sharp eye on them and gave him a good clout if she thought there were any missing.

'I'm goin' to be a proper soldier one day. A Commando. That's what I'm goin' to be – creepin' about round the enemy's camps, layin' mines and blowin' things up and that. And killin' sentries with one blow.'

'I'd rather be a bomber pilot,' Jimmy said. 'Fancy dropping a bomb and seeing a whole city go up in flames. I bet that's really good.'

Micky said nothing. His mind had drifted away to a fantasy of dark woods surrounding the perimeter of a German army camp. He was crawling on his belly, wirecutters in his hand. He had already killed two sentries when he was accosted by a third. One chopping movement with the side of his hand, and the third lay dead as well. From there, it was a simple matter to slice his way through the wire fence and stalk silently to the hut where Hitler, Goebbels and all the rest sat in conference. He took a grenade from his pocket, tugged out the pin with his teeth and lobbed it through the window . . .

Micky Baxter, world hero.

*

Jess and Frank could not decide whether to bring the children home for Christmas. Frank was against it. The bombing was getting worse, he said, and it was crazy to bring kids back from safety just for the sake of a few days' celebrations. What was there to celebrate anyway? There was almost no food in the shops, nothing much to give them for presents, and any party games they might be playing would probably have to be played in the air-raid shelter.

They were better off where they were. And the Government agreed with him, he pointed out. They were urging parents to leave the children where they were.

'But we're losing their childhood,' Jess argued miserably. 'We hardly know what the boys are doing now. They'll never be this age again. And Rose is making herself ill.'

Frank sighed. He knew Jess was becoming really anxious about Rose. Mrs Greenberry had written twice to say that the girl was worrying herself sick over the bombing. She woke each morning, terrified that her home and parents had been blown up in the night, and listened desperately to the News on the wireless, avid for any mention of Portsmouth.

'I still think they're better off where they are,' he said. 'I'd rather they were alive and miserable than dead.'

'But they wouldn't be. It's safe enough in the shelter. We're still alive. We haven't even had any bombs round here.'

'What about St Alban's church? What about the railway? Look, you don't know where the next bomb's going to fall – nobody does. They just drop 'em wherever they feel like it. And even Anderson shelters can't survive a direct hit. Look at that one in St Mary's Road, a whole family killed.'

Jess knew he was right. But she longed for her boys and her daughter. It wasn't natural, families being split up. Sometimes she thought Kathy Simmons was right and you ought to stay together and keep the home going no matter what happened.

She went over to Kathy's every day to give a hand, feeling guilty that she hadn't been on hand when the baby was born. Fancy the poor young woman having to go through that with no woman beside her! But the baby was thriving despite his dramatic arrival, and didn't even seem to notice the noise of the bombs, Kathy said. Hardly any wonder, when they'd been the first things he'd heard in this world.

Everyone in the street knew now the story of how Tommy Vickers had delivered the baby, and he was a bit of a hero, though he shrugged it off with his usual grin and a joke. All the same, he'd obviously been proud as Punch when Kathy had said she was going to name the baby Thomas after him.

'He was going to be George, after the King,' she said, 'but it wasn't the King who came into the air-raid shelter and brought him into the world, was it!'

Kathy seemed to have recovered well enough too, though Jess knew she was worried about Mike, facing danger at sea every day in the Merchant Navy convoys.

But everyone had someone to worry about. There was Annie, fretting over her Colin, and Alice Brunner still creeping about like a shadow and leaving almost all the work of the shop to Joy.

At least some of the other men were at home now. Derek Harker and Bob Shaw, both in Portsmouth's own 698 Unit, were able to come home at weekends, and so was George Glaister. Not that that seemed to give either him or Ethel much pleasure! Jess could hear them arguing sometimes, through the adjoining wall of the little terraced houses.

'I suppose you think just because you're a soldier now, you can rule the roost at home,' Ethel remarked sarcastically. 'Well, that khaki uniform doesn't cut any ice with me. I know it's still George Glaister inside it, just as much of a mouse as he's ever been.'

George didn't answer. He didn't want to argue with Ethel, and tried to keep silent when she started nagging, but somehow that seemed to make her worse. She'd go on and on, her voice rising all the time, and if he didn't give her any answers she'd provide them for herself, just to give herself something to argue about.

'I know what you're thinking. You think being trained to kill people makes you better than the rest of us. Well, it doesn't as far as I'm concerned, it just makes you a worse brute than ever.' But just now I was a mouse, he thought, staring at the fireplace where a few coals lay sullenly glowing.

'You think you're God's gift to the Army. You think you can win the war with one arm tied behind your back. Well, why not? You do everything else as if you'd got one arm tied behind your back!'

'Oh, for goodness' sake, Ethel, shut up,' he said, goaded at last. 'The way you go on, I wonder why I bother to come home at all. Aren't you a bit pleased to see me?'

'Not much. It's been nice and peaceful here these past few months. And it's a change to have a bit of room in bed and not have to listen to you driving pigs to market.'

'Look,' he said, 'I know you've had a lot on your plate lately, specially with all the worry over our Shirley. But she's safe now and down in Devon with her auntie. Why not relax a bit, Ethel? Let's go out somewhere. The pictures. Or maybe dancing at Kimball's. You used to enjoy a spot of dancing.' He moved over to her and put his arm round her waist. 'You were good at it, too. The belle of the ball, I always said, didn't I?'

Ethel shrugged, but she didn't bite his head off. She let him take hold of her hand, as if they were about to waltz. George reached past her and switched on the wireless. It gurgled and spluttered a bit, then warmed up and they heard the liquid notes of Louis Armstrong's trumpet.

'Hear that?' George said, delighted. 'That used to be one of our favourites. Remember?' He pulled her closer and rubbed his cheek against hers. 'A few smoochy dances and then a bit of a cuddle outside before I walked you home. And then a bit more of a cuddle at your front door. You were a lovely little armful then, Ethel. Still are.' His hand slid down to her bottom. 'How about slipping upstairs for half an hour before our Joe gets home from work?'

Ethel snatched his hand away and jerked herself out of his arms. 'George Glaister! Oh, you men are all the same. It's all you think about. In the middle of the afternoon, too. If that's what being in the Army does for you, you can go right back to your barracks this minute!'

George stood quite still. He felt as if he'd been doused with icy water. He'd been looking forward to coming home – not because he'd expected any special welcome, but because it was his home and he'd had enough of living in a barracks. He wasn't a real soldier after all, only a Territorial. He liked a quiet life, looking after his garden and doing a bit of woodwork in the shed. And somehow he'd forgotten what Ethel had become, and remembered her as she used to be, full of life, thrilled with their home, always ready for a bit of kissing and cuddling even if she'd never been all that keen on what went with it. Somehow, he'd expected to find the old Ethel waiting for him.

Ethel had flounced out to the scullery and he heard her run the tap. Perhaps she was making a cup of tea. He'd been home an hour and not had one yet. He sat down heavily in his armchair and picked up the paper. Joe and Carol would be home soon. Perhaps it would be better when they came in.

The day after the big raid when Kathy Simmons' baby was born, the *Evening News* carried advertisements for Christmas presents alongside its reports of the damage done. The Landport Drapery Bazaar was going to town on silk stockings, thousands of pairs, at prices from three shillings and sixpence up to six-and-three. That was a lot of money when you could get cardigans and jumpers for the same price, but it would be almost impossible to get stockings at all soon and many women would be pleased to receive them amongst their Christmas presents.

There were also notices about Christmas rations. Lord Woolton, the Minister for Food, had announced a 'Christmas box' of an extra four ounces of sugar and two ounces of tea for each person during the week before Christmas. But there was little other festive fare. No cargoes of fresh or tinned fruit were coming into the country, except for a small number of oranges, and although bananas were supposed to be available until Christmas, when their import would be banned, none had been seen around September Street for months. Molly Atkinson shook her head when anyone asked for them, and there were a few mutters about 'black market' and suggestions that the Atkinson children didn't go short of a banana or two. To such comments, Jess Budd was very sharp indeed. She didn't believe Molly was keeping anything back, but if she did give her own children first choice of anything special, who could blame her? They hadn't had much of a Christmas last year, after all.

Turkeys too were in short supply, not that most of the inhabitants of April Grove and its surrounding streets normally bought such grand fare. A big chicken did most of them for Christmas dinner. Annie Chapman usually had one, but Jess and Frank chipped in with the cost of that and it fed both families, together with Jess and Annie's parents. The advice of the Ministry was not to pay any more than two shillings and tenpence a pound for birds up to eighteen pounds in weight, and two and sixpence a pound for bigger ones. (What sort of ovens did people have? Jess wondered.)

Milk was another problem. In order to keep up the supply to those who needed it most – nursing mothers, babies and young children – the rest of the population had to accept a reduction. There was talk of re-introducing the half-pint bottle, but there were difficulties enough in getting people to return their pint bottles for refilling. Unless they did, a number of areas would have to go back to the churn and bucket method, taking their jugs out to the roundsman to have them filled as he came round the streets.

'We don't want that,' Jess said to Kathy. 'It's not nearly so clean. People ought to wash their bottles out and give them back every day.'

'They must lose a lot through the bombing,' Kathy said. 'People put them at their front doors at night, and by morning there's no front door, let alone any milk bottles.' She grinned. 'Someone wrote No Milk Today on one of the doors in Portchester Road. There was practically no house left! I had to laugh.'

Jess smiled. She was feeling better today, for a letter had come from Edna Corner to say that the billet she'd found for Tim and Keith wouldn't be able to take them after all. The woman's son was in the Army and he'd been wounded and sent home for her to look after, so the room was needed. And Edna herself was definitely going to her mother and would be there for Christmas, so the boys would have to come home.

Jess was sorry they wouldn't be able to be with the Corners

any more, but she'd known that was going to happen, and she was too pleased at the idea of having them home to worry about what was going to happen next. She'd told Frank she wanted Rose home too, and to her relief he had agreed.

'We can't leave her out there by herself when the rest of the family's all together,' he said. 'But the minute Christmas is over, back they go.'

'Of course. As soon as we find somewhere for them to stay.'

'The billeting officer will do that,' he said, but Jess made a face.

'I've seen some of the places they send the kids to. I want to be sure my boys are going to be looked after properly.'

Frank sighed. 'You can't even be sure they'd go to the same village again. With half the schools back in Pompey, they're sending youngsters all over the place. They might finish up in Yorkshire – we can't go all the way up there to look at billets as if we were the king and queen of England!'

'I wouldn't let them go that far,' Jess said obstinately. 'I want them near enough to be able to go and visit, like we do now.'

Frank looked at her. He knew she still wept for the children every night, and especially for Rose, who was really unhappy despite Mrs Greenberry's kindness. Rose had always been close to her mother, following her about the house as a toddler, pretending to sweep and dust, rolling out bits of grey dough and stamping out biscuits with a teacup, standing up beside her at the sink with a tiny washboard Frank had made her. And as she'd got older, she'd turned into a real mother's help, especially with baby Maureen. He knew Jess missed her a lot.

She missed the boys too, of course. You didn't have a family around underfoot all the time, especially in a house as small as number 14, without noticing the difference when they weren't there. And Tim and Keith were so lively, always up to something but not a scrap of real mischief in them. They might scrump a couple of apples from the orchard in Carlisle Crescent, though if Frank caught them at it, he'd give them a walloping, but they wouldn't go tramping about on other people's allotments or out-and-out stealing like young Micky

Baxter. And of course Jess wanted them at home. He did, too. He wanted to see them growing up, to watch them change from babies to boys, to young men.

And that was just it. He wanted to see them grow up. And he was desperately afraid that if they came back to Portsmouth they might be killed.

Frank had still not really recovered from that first raid, when he had come round the corner of Farlington Road and seen the mess the bombers had made of Drayton Road School. He couldn't forget the pall of dust and smoke, the acrid smell that hung over the still trembling streets. He couldn't forget the sight of the smashed buildings, the debris of brick and wood and concrete that had been hurled everywhere as if by some mad giant. Worst of all, he couldn't forget the bodies, ripped to pieces by the blast. The foot he had tried to match up with its mate. The head, gazing at him from a pile of blood-soaked bandages.

Sometimes in his dreams, it was Tim's head, or Keith's. He couldn't bear it when the faces of his sons stared at him like that, in nightmare. And he couldn't tell Jess about such horrors. They were things he had to bear alone.

Well, there were plenty of people having to suffer worse for this war. It wasn't what they'd wanted from life, but life had a way of only giving you part of what you wanted. And you just had to be thankful for that part.

He went down the garden path to his shed. He was making Keith a toy fort for Christmas, with bits of hardboard cut with jagged edges to look like a palisade, and little wooden turrets. Luckily, the boys already had some model cowboys and Indians, and Tim even had a couple of Mounties of which he was very proud. You couldn't get much of that sort of thing now.

Making things for his children was something Frank had little time for these days. But he'd started in good time and he enjoyed tinkering with something that, for once, had nothing at all to do with the war. With so much of his time and attention taken up with it, from his work in the Yard to his firewatching and warden's duties, he didn't get much relaxation at all these days.

He wished there was something he could make for Jess too. She was a wife in a million, his Jess, and she deserved the best. But he knew there was only one present she really wanted this Christmas.

And that was to have her children home around her once more, and to know that this time it was for good.

Jess too was thinking about Christmas presents.

There were a few bits and pieces she could make for Keith's fort, flags sewn from scraps of material, wigwams for the Indian camp, and she had managed to buy a second-hand football for Tim. For Rose, she was knitting a jumper out of an old cardigan of her own that she had unravelled. It was just the shade of green that Rose liked best, and it suited her dark hair and brown eyes.

Maureen, at eighteen months old, was still happy with simple toys. She would play for hours with a few cardboard boxes or some newspaper, and Tim's old building blocks were still her favourites. Her grandmother and various aunts had all made or knitted her things, she had an assortment of woollen animals and dolls in the most unlikely colours, including a fair isle cat knitted by Howard's wife, Nora, who fancied herself with the needles. But it was difficult to know what else to give her.

She went up the street to do her shopping. Kathy Simmons' pram was outside number 16, with little Thomas fast asleep inside. His eyes were fringed with long, dark lashes that curled at the ends and seemed to have been tipped with gold-dust. It's not fair, Jess thought. Boys always get the most gorgeous lashes. And when he opened his eyes, she knew they'd be a dark blue, as if they were going to stay that colour, not the milky colour new babies' eyes often were before they changed to brown or hazel. He was a lovely baby, and Kathy was quite rightly thrilled with him.

'I don't know why I bother to do the shopping every day,' Jess remarked to Mr Hines. 'There's almost nothing about. But you have to keep coming, on the offchance that someone's actually had a delivery.'

Mr Hines stood Maureen on the counter. He winked at

Jess and laid his finger alongside his nose.

'Don't tell anyone, and I'll let you have a pound of liver. Came in just this morning. I thought you might be in.'

'Oh, that's good of you.' She watched as Mr Hines weighed it out. There was nothing underhand, or under-the-counter about the transaction – liver wasn't rationed anyway – but there were still enough spiteful people around to make comments if they saw you getting something they didn't. 'I don't know why they don't ration liver. It's so good for you, and there's only one in each animal, isn't there?'

Mr Hines smiled. 'That's right. And kidneys too, twice as many of them, of course, but they're much smaller, they make a real tasty pie or stew. But people don't seem to make the use of 'em.'

'Well, I do, and I make sure this little one eats her share. It's good for her blood.' Jess went to scoop Maureen from the counter. The little girl was kneeling by the *papier-mâché* lamb, her arms around its neck. 'Say goodbye to Larry now, Maureen. She really loves that lamb,' she said to the butcher. 'I wish I could get her something like that for Christmas. But there's just nothing in the shops for kiddies now.'

'I know,' he said. 'The toymakers are all working for the war effort. God knows what they're making, soldiers never took teddy bears to war with them in my day, but there it is. It's like furniture makers, they're all doing different things now. Nothing's the same as it was.'

Jess lifted Maureen off the counter and took her outside. She was getting almost too big for her pram now, but she'd go on using it till she was past two, for you couldn't expect a toddler to walk all the way up the street and round the shops. Besides, it made carrying the shopping so much easier. Jess would miss it when she finally stopped using it.

Alice Brunner was looking whiter than ever. Jess tried to persuade her to come down to number 14 for a cup of tea in the afternoon, but she shook her head. It was as if she were afraid to leave the house.

'She won't go out in case there's a telegram from Daddy,' Joy told her afterwards, coming out on to the pavement on the pretext of cleaning the windows. 'She's got really superstitious about it, as if it would bring bad luck. She's certain that the minute she steps out of doors, they'll tell us he's dead.' The girl rubbed her face tiredly. 'Sometimes I wish they would, then it would all be over. That's an awful thing to say, isn't it?'

'It's an awful thing to feel,' Jess said gently. 'It's been hard on you too.'

The girl's face crumpled. 'I miss Daddy too. But we can't go on as if he's only just died. We've got to carry on, haven't we? That's what everybody says.'

'Yes,' Jess said, 'we've got to carry on.' She hesitated, then said on impulse, 'What are you and your mum doing for Christmas?'

Joy made a face. 'Christmas! We don't even talk about it. We'll only know it's happening because there won't be any papers that day. At least we'll get a lie-in, that'll be our only Christmas present, I reckon.' She bent and swilled her rag about in the bucket of water. 'I got Mum some of those chocolates she likes, and a book. I can't afford any more than that.'

'I'm sure she'll be pleased. But what I was going to say was, why don't you both come down to us for your Christmas dinner? We'll probably be at my sister's, but there's room for another two at the table. We can always squeeze round a bit. It might be better than being on your own.'

Joy paused in her polishing and stared at her. 'Oh, Mrs Budd. Could we really? Will Rose be there too?'

Poor kid, she's lonely, Jess thought. Stuck in this shop all day and all by herself with her mum in the evenings, no time to have fun with her own friends. And she's missing Rose. She's always asking how she is, out at Bridge End.

'You tell your mum that's what you're doing,' she said firmly. 'And as soon as Rose gets home, I'll send her up to see you. It's time you had a bit of companionship of your own age.'

She looked at Joy's face. There were lines that shouldn't be there, a frown of worry on her brow. The girl was growing old before her time.

There were more ways than one of being injured in the war.

297

CHAPTER EIGHTEEN

'Will you be going home for Christmas, Bet?'

Yvonne was sitting on her bed, cutting her toenails. The girls had had their weekly bath and Erica was drying her hair. She had had it all cut off the week after Geoffrey had died, almost as short as a boy's and it had curled just like Betty's. It clustered like a golden halo all over her head and created much envy in Yvonne's breast.

'Look at her. She doesn't even *care* what she looks like now, and she still manages to look like a film star! I thought having all her hair cut off would make her look – well, not ugly, but more ordinary. What chance have you and me got, Bet?'

'I don't know that I want any chances,' Betty said with a sigh. 'Seems to me you've only got to put a skirt on and it causes trouble.'

'It causes even more when you take it off!' Yvonne said with a giggle. 'But you never answered me. Are you going home?'

'I don't know.' The arrangement was that two of the four farm workers – the girls and Dennis – should have Christmas, while the other two had the New Year. Betty wanted to go home, of course, she'd had a letter from Olive only yesterday which hinted at some news she and Derek would be breaking to the family, but she also wanted to be on the farm while Dennis was here. And she hadn't plucked up courage to ask him. 'What are you doing, Yvonne?'

'Oh, I'll go home. Mum's got enough on her plate as it is, with all the kids round her feet.' There were five younger than Yvonne, and her sister Clarice's two who were looked after by their grandmother while Clarrie worked in the Dockyard.

'And Mrs Spencer told me she'd give me a few bits and pieces to take home with me. That'll make a lot of difference in our house.'

'What are you doing, Erica?'

'What?' The blonde girl turned from the photograph she was gazing at. She looked at it every night for hours, as if trying to memorise every line of Geoffrey's face. In fact, she was trying to remember it. In her memory, his face had blurred and become indistinct and it was only when staring at his photograph that she could recall clearly what he looked like. She was bewildered and upset by this, thinking that it meant she hadn't loved Geoffrey after all – and I did, I *did*, she thought despairingly.

'I asked what you're doing at Christmas? Staying here or going home?'

'Oh, I don't know. It doesn't really matter, anyway. My parents don't even know I'm there, half the time.'

'Oh go on, they must do.'

'No, they don't. It was all right while I was little, my mother could dress me up like a little doll and show me off to her friends. But now, she doesn't want me around. It doesn't matter how nice I look – sometimes, I think that makes it worse.'

The other two stared at her, fascinated.

'How could looking nice make her worse?'

Erica shrugged. 'She doesn't want me around when she's got her friends in the house. Her men friends,' she added with slight emphasis.

Betty felt her cheeks turn scarlet. Yvonne smothered a giggle of embarrassment.

'You mean she has – has – you know, lovers?'

'I don't know what they are,' Erica said. 'All I know is, there are always people at our house, men and women. It's like one long party. And if one of the men takes a fancy to me, she doesn't like it. All the same, when I took Geoff home, well, you'd have thought he was *her* boyfriend, not mine!'

She turned back to the photograph. Betty picked up the sock she was darning. Erica's home life sounded so different from her own, she could scarcely believe it. She tried to picture her mother having men friends at home, and failed. Nor could she imagine her father treating life as 'one long party'. As for Annie behaving as if Graham was *her* boyfriend – well, Betty's mind couldn't take that in at all!

Not that Graham was her boyfriend now. She hadn't heard from him since the night he'd walked out and didn't really expect to. She felt sorry that they'd parted bitterly, but relieved to be free of his possessiveness.

She hadn't told Dennis yet about that last quarrel. She wasn't ready yet to start a new relationship. She wanted to get to know him slowly, to try to understand the way he thought about things, the different attitudes he seemed to possess. She asked him about them as they worked together.

Dennis was willing enough to talk.

'I've always believed in peace,' he told Betty. 'It's all any of us want. Well, except for a few madmen who've got the power to send other men to die for what *they* believe in. I think that's what I've got against it mostly. Why should anyone have that sort of power? Why should anyone have the power to send thousands – millions – of people to fight other people they haven't even met?'

Dennis was a Quaker too. He explained this to Betty as they worked together, milking the cows. It was warm and cosy in the byre in the early mornings, with the cows breathing steamily and the lamp flickering gently. Betty pressed her head against the solid flank and squeezed the teats between her fingers. The milk squirted into the bucket and made a white froth.

'We don't really call ourselves Quakers,' he said. 'We're Friends. The Society of Friends.'

'That sounds nice.'

'I think so, too. We believe that every man has the seed of God within him.' Betty blushed, feeling almost as embarrassed by the reference to God as she felt about sex. 'That means Germans and Japanese and Russians, you and me – everyone. And you can't kill someone who's partly God, can you?'

'No. But . . . even Hitler?'

'Even Hitler,' Dennis said firmly. 'And Rommel and Goering and Mussolini and all the rest of them. Not that I mightn't forget about being a Friend and a pacifist if I had *them* there in front of me,' he added thoughtfully, eyeing a pitchfork that was leaning against the wall.

Betty laughed soberly. 'I can see what you meant about the pilots, the ones who crashed in our field. They were just young chaps, like Sandy and the others. But Hitler and those people, they've got to be stopped.'

'Oh yes. But killing young men and girls and children and old people, and people who've got nothing to do with the war, isn't going to stop them.' Dennis finished milking Bluebell and came round the other side to start on Dewdrop. 'Look at what they're doing. They're just getting together as many soldiers and sailors and airmen as they can and setting them against each other, like spiders in a jar. In the end, it'll all come down to who's got most men and most bombs. Why not just count them all in the first place? Or better still, why not just sit down and talk about it?'

Betty shook her head. It sounded so simple when Dennis said that, but could it really be so easy? If it was, why hadn't people tried it?

'Because they're not reasonable people,' he said. 'They're mad. But that doesn't mean everyone else has to go mad as well.'

'But if there's one man like Hitler who goes mad, what can you do about him? He's got so much power, he controls everything. How can people go against him? And if they did – if the whole army rose up against him – he'd still have enough people to take his side. There'd still be a war.' She gazed at Dennis with troubled eyes. 'D'you really think there'll ever be enough people to stand up and say war's wrong, and refuse to fight?'

'I'd like to think so,' Dennis said. 'But I don't suppose there ever will be. But that doesn't mean that those of us who do think that way should be forced to go against our beliefs. And more in this war than ever before, because this is supposed to be a war for free speech. The Archbishop of Canterbury himself said so.'

He finished Dewdrop and stood up. Betty gave Buttercup a pat on the flank and the cow turned large, mild brown eyes on her and blew softly. Dennis came to stand beside her.

'You never told me, Betty. What happened when you went home the other weekend?'

'About Graham and me, you mean?' She looked down at her hands. She still missed Graham's little ring, even though she'd rarely worn it on her left hand. She had felt as though she was wearing it. 'We've broken up. He wanted us to get married so that I'd be there waiting for him whenever he came home. And I didn't want to, so we called it a day.' She looked up into Dennis's eyes. 'I'm not sorry, not really. We shouldn't ever have let it get that far. He wanted to own me, that's why he wanted to get married. That and –' she blushed. 'He never did like the idea of me working on a farm.'

'I see.' Dennis said nothing for a few minutes. Then he said quietly, 'I won't rush you, Betty. You need a bit of time when you've just broken up with someone. But when you feel ready to think about someone else, well, you know I'll be here.'

Betty turned her head to look up at him. He was tall, an inch or two taller than Graham, and his body was lean and strong. Graham had filled out since joining the Navy but there had always been a hint of flabbiness about him, as if he had muscles he didn't bother to use much. He had cheeky eyes and a grin that had caught at her heart for a while, but he didn't really have much sense of humour. He got most of his fun out of teasing, or even taunting, other people.

She remembered the day she had first met him, walking down Queen Street with Bob Shaw. Bob had been friendly but a bit shy and Graham had seized his opportunity to ask her out. If he hadn't, she'd have gone out with Bob, because he'd asked her too, on the bus on their way home, but by then she'd promised Graham.

Well, it was all over and no harm done. And now Bob was in the Army, though he was back in Pompey now, and she'd met Dennis instead.

He was looking down at her, his eyes smiling and serious all at once, and his mouth was slightly curved. Suddenly, she wanted nothing more than to put her arms around him; to feel those smiling lips touch hers.

'I feel ready now,' she said quietly. 'That's if you are too.'

'Oh yes,' Dennis said, 'I've been ready for a long time.'

He slid his arms around her and drew her close. Betty went willingly, feeling the excitement leap like a flame in her body. She closed her eyes, savouring his warmth, the steady beat of his heart. She felt a strength flow from him, a strength that had to do with more than mere physical muscle. There was a power in Dennis that Graham hadn't had, a stamina and courage that she hadn't known before.

Dennis bent his head and laid his lips gently upon hers. She felt their tension, an emotion that quivered very slightly against her mouth. It drew from her an instant response and she tightened her arms about him and opened her mouth to his.

'Betty, I love you.'

The words came from his lips as if they had been born there. She heard them with wonder, heard the truth in each syllable, and felt her answer like a warmth inside, like a flower opening to the sun.

'I love you, Dennis.'

It was like a vow, spoken there in the byre with the cows shifting gently around them and the smell of warm milk in the air. They looked into each other's eyes and smiled gravely, and Dennis lifted one hand and traced the contours of her face with his fingertips.

'You're beautiful, d'you know that? Has anyone told you before?'

Graham had, at least, he'd told her she was a 'smasher'. But it hadn't been the same. Dennis was talking about a beauty that was more than skin deep, a beauty that arose from the love they had just expressed for each other. It was a beauty that shone only for him, and had nothing to do with perms and make-up and silk stockings.

'So are you,' she said, and he laughed.

'Nobody's ever said it to *me* before!'

'No, but you know what I mean.' She gazed at him, noting the straight brows, the golden flecks in his eyes, the firmness of his mouth. 'When I first saw you, I thought how good-looking you were. But I don't mean that. It's not looks, it's something else. Something in your eyes, in the way you look.

Oh, I don't know how to explain it but –'

'It's all right. I know what you mean.' He kissed her again. 'And I'm glad you see what I see. It's something between us, isn't it? Something important.'

'Yes.'

They stood quietly for a while, holding each other close. Then Dennis gave a little sigh and said, 'We'd better get on with our work, Betty. Mrs Spencer'll have breakfast ready soon.'

'I know.' She remembered what she had been meaning to ask him. 'Dennis, what are you doing at Christmas? Will you be going home?'

He grinned a little. 'I thought I'd wait and see what you were doing.'

'I was waiting for you!' They both laughed, and she said seriously, 'I suppose we'd both like to be with our own families at Christmas. But Yvonne wants to go home then too, so one of us'll have to stay.'

'What about Erica?'

'She doesn't care much. It doesn't seem as though she's very happy at home.'

Dennis was silent for a moment, then he said, 'Well, suppose we both stay here at Christmas, and then Erica and Yvonne can be here at New Year. I can't see Erica wanting to be here on her own with me. She can barely tolerate being in the same room these days.'

'Oh, Dennis.' Betty held him close again. 'I can't understand why she hates you so much. Anyone can see what sort of person you are, but she treats you like a criminal.'

'No,' he said, 'like a traitor. Don't blame her, Betty. A lot of people feel like that. And when she's lost her own fiancé . . .'

'I know.' Betty thought of the young pilots, so carefree and light-hearted, buzzing around the lanes in their little car, singing at the tops of their voices. But they hadn't been carefree at all, had they? Every day they'd seen more of their comrades killed, shot down, burned to death, drowned. Every day they'd seen their own doom approach a little closer. *It's pretty lonely, up there in the sky.* Every time they'd scrambled for their planes, they'd known this might be the last.

No, it wasn't surprising that Erica and others like her should hate the young men who had refused to fight.

She held Dennis a little tighter. I'll never hate them, she thought, never. And aloud, she said, 'I love you, Dennis.'

'I love you . . .'

At the beginning of Christmas week, families began to arrive home to spend Christmas together.

The Budd children had arrived on Sunday, fetched home by their father who had cycled out to Bridge End and brought them back by train. After Christmas, he would take them back and then ride his bike home again.

'Let's hope there isn't a blizzard like there was last year,' he commented, but at the moment the weather was quiet enough, though cold.

The boys came in with bright eyes and glowing cheeks. Jess had a fire burning in the grate ready for them, and some lentil soup simmering on the stove. Maureen was sitting on the floor, playing with Tim's coloured blocks, and he immediately got down to play with her, showing her how to build a castle. Maureen watched and chuckled, hitting the edifice with her fist the moment he had completed it.

Rose went straight to her mother and buried her face against Jess's breast. Jess held her warmly, feeling the ache in her throat. She had missed Rose's company, for the girl was growing up as a friend as well as daughter and they'd begun to share a good many interests. She held out her hand to Keith and looked at Tim, still kneeling on the rug playing with Maureen.

'Oh, it's good to have you all back,' she said shakily, and looked at Frank. 'This is how things ought to be. The six of us, all together at home. *Nothing* should come between families, Frank, nothing.'

He nodded. He knew what Jess meant and he agreed with her. But even as he agreed, he saw again in his mind the vision of a head, torn from its body, resting on a pile of stained bandages and looking at him with his son's eyes, and he knew that he would have no peace of mind until Christmas was over and he could take them back.

*

At Annie's house, just up the street, the celebrations were slightly muted by Betty's absence.

Derek was in the front room with Olive, helping to hang up paper-chains and trying to find out why one of the Christmas tree lights didn't work. There was no tree of course, but the lights could be hung round the wall and look just as good. He traced the faulty bulb at last, then arranged them in the pattern of a tree and stood back to admire the effect.

'That's lovely, Derek. Really artistic.' Olive came over and gave him a kiss. 'I like the way you've put those coloured balls round the lights. It makes them really glitter.'

'Maybe I'll set up in business when the war's over,' he said. 'Your room decorated by Harker and Son.'

Olive caught her breath and they looked at each other, smiling with excitement.

'It's really true, isn't it,' she said wonderingly. 'We're having a baby. You and me. A baby all of our own. Oh, Derek . . .'

He kissed her again. 'I can still hardly believe it. I thought when it didn't happen in September –'

'Well, it didn't have much of a chance then, did it?' Olive remembered the day she had waved goodbye to Derek at the station, running along the platform, wondering when she would see him again. Their time together had been so brief. And then he'd been back only a month later! The Unit had stayed in Portsmouth then and looked likely to be here for a while. The longer the better, she thought, laying her head against his chest. Long enough, she hoped, for Derek to be home when their baby was born and hold it in his arms. But perhaps the war would be over by then anyway.

'July,' she said. 'It's due on July the fifteenth. That's St Swithin's Day. If it rains then, it'll rain for forty days, and if the sun shines it's going to shine for forty days.'

'Gosh,' he said, 'I hope that doesn't apply to babies too. I don't know that I want forty kids!'

Olive giggled. 'Neither do I. One'll be enough for the time being.' She hugged him again. 'I hope it's a boy and looks like you.'

'I don't. I hope it's a girl and looks like you.'

'One of each, then. Only not both at once, though I wouldn't mind twins, really. It'd be fun if they were identical and no one could tell them apart. I like seeing twins dressed the same, they're cute.'

'They wouldn't be identical if they were one of each,' he pointed out, and Olive laughed again.

'Well, we'll settle for one, and take whatever we get. I don't care, so long as it's all right. And so long as it's not born in an air-raid shelter, like poor Kathy Simmons'.' She shuddered. 'That must have been awful. She had just Tommy Vickers with her, no woman at all, and those two poor little girls seeing it all.'

'She was lucky to have Tommy.'

'I know. She says he was marvellous. I wouldn't want it to happen to me, all the same.'

They went back to their decorating. Derek had managed to get some holly, and they stuck it behind the mirror and pictures.

'D'you think your mum's got any idea?' he asked.

'About the baby? I don't know, I've caught her looking at me a bit funny once or twice. But there's nothing to show yet, it's only just eight weeks, after all. The doctor said I might get some morning-sickness but I haven't so far. I think she suspected before, I missed after you'd been here in September. But then I came on again, so it was a false alarm.' She sighed contentedly. 'It isn't this time, though. This time it's real.'

'But we'll tell 'em, won't we? At Christmas dinner?'

'Oh yes,' she said. 'We'll tell them then.'

Christmas dinner was going to be different this year, she thought. Me and Derek married – last year, we'd only just got engaged. And our Betty away on the farm. And Alice Brunner and Joy, invited because Auntie Jess was so sorry for them.

It would be different. But for Olive it would be perfect, because Derek would be with her and because they would tell the family that their first baby was on its way.

And next Christmas will be different again, she thought. The baby will be here – six months old. And Derek?

A shiver passed across her skin and she turned towards him

and then laughed, forgetting everything as he held up a tiny sprig in his hand.

'Mistletoe! Oh, Derek!'

The Germans had promised a truce over Christmas, although it was not official and nobody could be certain they would keep their word. On Monday, the day before Christmas Eve, everyone went about their preparations with one eye on the sky and one ear ready for the alert. It was quiet, but tense. Nobody knew if it would last.

'If they can call a truce for Christmas, why not call it for the rest of the year? The rest of our lives?' Jess asked, but nobody could answer her and she did not expect them to try. The war had turned into a machine that, once set in motion, could not be stopped. It must, like some terrible disease, run its course.

'Let's be thankful for small mercies,' Annie advised. 'Enjoy our Christmas, with the kids around us.' She sighed, thinking of Betty. The first Christmas in nineteen years without her bright face at the table. But next year, if her suspicions were correct, there'd be another kiddy sitting up in a high chair and banging a spoon on the table. As Kathy Simmons had proved, life must go on.

Jess went up to September Street to do her shopping, accompanied by the whole family. She was proud of them as she watched the boys running ahead and felt Rose's fingers on the handle of the pram. Four lovely children. Two bright, lively boys, a daughter who was all any mother could wish for, and a baby who never stopped smiling. She was spoken to half a dozen times by neighbours who wanted to look at them, to ask them about their life in the country, to talk about Christmas. And there were other mothers with their children too, boys and girls who had been out at Bridge End with Rose and Tim and Keith, and some who had been sent to the Isle of Wight or Salisbury.

'It's good to hear the children's voices in the street again,' Peggy Shaw said. 'You forget what it's like. I've only just realised how quiet it's been all these months.'

'It's going to be harder than ever to let them go again,' Jess remarked wistfully. 'Specially as we don't even know where

308

the boys'll be going. The billeting people have got to find them somewhere else.'

'That's a shame. They were all right where they were, weren't they? It's a pity to move them.'

'So long as they don't split them up,' Jess said. 'It won't be so bad if they can be together. And near Rose.' In fact, the boys saw very little of Rose. Edna Corner invited her to tea once a week and Mrs Greenberry had the brothers over, but apart from that they didn't bother much. She was only their sister, after all. They could see her any time.

Rose went into the newsagent's and Jess left the boys on the pavement with Jimmy Cross and Cyril Nash while she went into the butcher's. Mr Hines was waiting for her, a broad smile on his face.

'I've got something for you.'

'Liver? Sausages?' She smiled back. There wasn't much else a butcher could have for you these days. But to her astonishment, he handed her a large, oddly-shaped brown paper parcel.

'What on earth –?'

'Sssh.' He winked and put his finger to his lips. 'It's for the nipper.' He looked significantly at Maureen.

'For Maureen? But –' Jess looked at the parcel again. 'Whatever – oh . . . Of course. It's L –'

'Sssh,' he said again. 'We don't want her knowing before Santa, do we? I thought it might keep her amused a bit over the holiday.'

'Keep her amused! She'll love it.' Jess looked at him, her eyes bright. For goodness' sake, she scolded herself, fancy wanting to cry because a butcher gives you his *papier-mâché* lamb! 'It's very nice of you, Mr Hines. I'm really touched.'

He waved a hand. 'It's all right. I was getting a bit fed up with it on the counter anyway. And the kiddy's fond of it. Like you say, there's not much about in the way of toys just now.'

'Well, I still think it's really nice of you. And the baby'll be thrilled.'

She went next door to the newsagent's. Alice was there, serving behind the counter. Her face was pale but she managed to summon up a wan smile and nodded as Jess asked if she and Joy were still coming down to Annie's on Christmas Day.

'So long as you don't mind looking at my long face,' she said. 'I can't feel much like Christmas, Jess, and that's the truth of it. But you're right, I've got to make an effort for Joy's sake. She deserves a bit of fun, and I know she won't come without me.'

'I should think not. Families ought to be together at Christmas,' Jess said, and closed her mouth abruptly. There she went again, saying exactly the wrong thing! It was so easy. But there was one thing you could say for Alice, she never took offence where there was none meant. And she really did seem to be pulling herself together. Look at her now, smiling at the boys and giving them a toffee each out of a jar. And Joy looked happier too, with Rose to talk to again.

It really seemed as if there had been a truce declared. No bombers came over all day that Monday, the day before Christmas Eve, and there were no warning sirens. The short December afternoon drew into evening and blackout curtains went up. Fires were lit and families who had been parted for months clustered about them. They made toast and ate scones and doughnuts and lardy cake. They played games and listened to the wireless. They almost forgot to listen, to wait, to be afraid.

But the Luftwaffe had not forgotten them. At ten minutes to seven, one bomber came unannounced. It flew over Portsmouth, a single droning note in the empty sky and, before anyone could lift a finger, dropped a bomb packed with two and a half thousand pounds of high explosive. The detonation shook the whole city, and in every home families stared at each other and then raced for their shelters.

'Blimey!' Frank exclaimed. 'That sounded like the whole Yard going up.'

'What about the truce?' Jess was clutching the baby, who was screaming in terror. 'What about Christmas?'

They snatched up the things they kept ready to take to the shelter, the old blankets, the cushions, the biscuits and bottle of water, the tin box that contained all the insurance policies and family photographs. Rose was in a panic, urging them to hurry, the boys were pale, half scared, half excited. They crammed through the half-sunken doorway and found themselves places on the bunks, staring up at the corrugated iron roof and waiting for the next explosion.

'Coo,' Tim breathed. 'That was a whopper. But I can't hear any more planes.'

'Well, there's no need to sound disappointed,' Jess said sharply. 'We don't want any more. And stop trying to peep out through the curtain, Keith, we'll have Mr Vickers down here telling us off for showing a light.'

'I only wanted to see the searchlights.'

'And the Germans'll see you.'

Frank looked at them and thought again of the head. They ought to have stayed at Bridge End. Christmas or not, they ought to have stayed there.

Even Granny Kinch had been scared into taking cover with her daughter Nancy and the two kids. Ethel Glaister was in her Anderson with Joe and Carol, furiously berating the absent George for not being there to take care of them. Annie, at the top of the street, was thinking anxiously about Ted, skippering his ferryboat across the harbour. But in number 13 Peggy Shaw and her daughter Gladys were setting off for their First Aid Post, ready to deal with whatever casualties the raid might bring.

But there were no more raids that night. The plane had come alone, dropped its bomb and departed.

'It was Conway Street caught it,' Peggy told them later, when the All-Clear had sounded and everyone was back indoors. 'We got the message at the Post. They reckon there was at least a dozen killed. All the houses in the street smashed to rubble, with everyone inside. They're still trying to get 'em out. That young Dr Mulvaney's there of course – she's a marvel, always in the thick of it all, brave as a lion, and only a slip of a thing too. They reckon it was a plane loaded with bombs that got shot down.'

The stories of what had happened in Conway Street abounded. A plane – two planes – three or more, crashed on the houses with their full cargo of explosive. A land-mine.

One huge bomb, of a kind never used before. Whatever it was, it shattered the flimsy old houses packed up against the Dockyard wall and left a scene of devastation yet unrivalled by any of the raids.

'There's a crater big enough to get Portsmouth Cathedral into.' 'It blew out every window for miles around.' 'They'll never repair all the damage, never.' 'They'll never get all the bodies out.'

The stories started Christmas Eve off on a sombre note. Nobody could have any faith now in the 'truce'.

It was as if one man had decided to bring terror instead of peace to their Christmas truce. *This is what we can do. This is what you can expect as soon as the truce is over.*

CHAPTER NINETEEN

'We can't let it spoil the children's Christmas,' Jess said. 'I know it's terrible, all those people killed and others with no homes. But we've got to think of the children.'

She set Rose to peeling vegetables, making jellies and helping to decorate the cake. She had saved enough dried fruit during the past few months to make a reasonable fruit cake, and had carefully hoarded a bag of icing sugar for the top. And on Christmas morning she took all the children except Maureen to church. Indeed, it would have been impossible to take Maureen anywhere that morning without taking Larry along too.

Alice was there, in the Deniston Road church where she and Heinrich had so often worshipped. She looked pale but determined, as if she'd made up her mind to cope. That's better, Jess thought, seeing that Joy too looked brighter, and she was glad she'd invited them to Annie's. As soon as the service was over, they walked down the street to the house with the little turret and arrived to a scene of rejoicing.

'We were going to tell you all at dinner,' Olive said, her cheeks flushed. 'But I couldn't keep it back any longer. I just had to tell Mum first.'

'And so you should.' Jess gave her niece a hug. 'A new baby! Well, that's really lovely. And our Annie a grandma! How d'you feel about that, Annie?'

'I daresay I'll get used to the idea.' But Annie's eyes were bright and her cheeks wet. Her smile broke through and she gave both Olive and Derek a kiss. 'Mind, I still think you ought to have waited. It's no time to be bringing a baby into the world. But since it's on its way, there's not much we can do but give it a welcome.'

'Go on, our Annie, you're as pleased as Punch.' Jess glanced through the window at the children, who were out in the garden playing with Tim's new football. 'We won't say anything to *them* yet, of course. They don't need to know. We don't want any awkward questions.' She knew nothing of Reg Corner's sex education lessons to the two boys, nor of Tibby's kittens. Even Rose hadn't mentioned that she now knew 'all about' babies from helping Mr Greenberry with the sheep.

'Well, let's drink to it anyway,' Ted said, producing a bottle of sherry and filling Annie's best glasses. 'To Olive and Derek's baby, and to a happy Christmas for everyone!'

'To the baby – and a Happy Christmas,' they repeated, and held up their glasses and drank.

Jess looked across the room and caught her husband's eye. Sherry was the one alcoholic drink he would take, and Christmas Day the one day he would take it. She toasted him silently with her eyes, trying to tell him all that she was feeling about this day, like a precious jewel with all her family about her. And she knew from the softening of his gaze that he understood.

And then her glance moved slowly over the rest of the people in the room. Her sister Annie, still defiantly scrubbing her step every morning, still keeping up the 'standards' her time in domestic service had instilled into her. Olive and Derek, starting their family after such a short married life, deserving so much more. Alice Brunner, who looked shy and as if she felt out of place in this family gathering.

Poor Alice. She must be missing Heinrich more than ever this morning. And there were others who were absent too – Colin, still at sea. Betty, away on the farm.

She looked at Frank again, and he must have seen the message in her eyes, for he cleared his throat, so that everyone stopped talking and listened to him.

'Another toast,' he said quietly, and lifted his glass. 'To absent friends.'

And again, they all echoed the toast, in voices that trembled with the emotions they shared.

'To absent friends . . .'

With Iris Blake and her children gone, and Erica away at home, the antagonism that had prevailed towards Dennis evaporated. Mr and Mrs Spencer had never been hostile towards him and old Jonas cared about very little provided his beer and tobacco came regularly and his plate was full at mealtimes. He did his work and spent his evenings in the village pub, sitting in a corner by the fire and making a pint last all evening. He had been more hostile towards the girls than to Dennis, but now that they had proved themselves able to do whatever was asked of them, he had relented far enough to give them a grunt of a morning and even, occasionally, a gap-toothed travesty of a smile.

'He's all right really,' Dennis said. 'He's just like a lot of old people, can't take the changes so he pretends they aren't happening. You can't blame him, he's been through one war already, why should he have to suffer another?'

'He must have been through more than one,' Betty said. 'He's seventy if he's a day. He's seen a lot.'

Erica and Yvonne departed on Christmas Eve, just before afternoon milking and, without them and the Blakes, the farm seemed very quiet. Betty wondered what it would be like to sleep by herself in the long, narrow attic. Dennis too had moved into the house; until now, he had slept in a sectioned-off part of the barn but now that there was more room indoors Mrs Spencer had decided he ought to be offered a proper bed. Betty thought of him, lying in the room below hers, and felt a quiver of excitement. It seemed almost indecently intimate, somehow, even though there would be a floor and several walls between them.

Christmas was to be a real holiday. Only essential chores such as milking and feeding were to be done, and the rest of the time was free. On Christmas morning, the Spencers would be going to church, and Dennis and Betty decided to go along too.

'I'd go to Meeting at home,' he said. 'But there isn't one near enough here. We don't have hymns or prayers or anything like that, but I like the carols.'

'What do you have, then? Bible readings and sermons?'

He laughed. 'No, not unless someone feels like it. We just sit quietly together and wait.'

Betty stared at him. 'What d'you wait for?'

'For God to speak through one of us. Then whoever it is gets up and says what he feels he should say, and sits down again.'

'And that's all?'

'Unless anyone else feels called upon to speak, yes. Sometimes several do, sometimes no one at all. It doesn't matter. It's a very peaceful, happy feeling to be sitting there all together, meeting in God.'

Betty tried to imagine it. She was accustomed to the Church of England services, busy all the way through with prayers and hymns and catechists and psalms. There wasn't a moment of quiet, except at the beginning, when you arrived and knelt to say your own private prayer, or at the end. Never a moment when God might 'speak' through an ordinary member of the congregation. In fact, when she came to think of it, he would have been hard put to it to get a word in anywhere.

'Isn't it boring?' she asked doubtfully.

Dennis smiled. 'Depends what sort of mood you're in. Sometimes I've had a job to sit still at all. But usually I find it very soothing, and afterwards I feel as if I've been, well, sort of *re-created*. It's not often you can sit with a lot of other people and not be overwhelmed with chatter. It's as if we give each other strength, even if nobody says a word.'

But this Christmas he came to church with Betty and the Spencers, and as they entered to the strains of the little organ Betty felt her own peace and joy in the warmth of companionship. She sat in the pew, looking about her at the faces which had become familiar to her over the past few months; the little woman with white hair, pinned into a bun, who ran the post office, the stout butcher, the greengrocer and the publicans. There were farmers and their wives who were friends and neighbours of the Spencers, and there were a few families who had been evacuated from Portsmouth and Southampton

316

and were slowly becoming a part of the village themselves.

The note of the organ changed and stopped. There was a hushed silence and then the high, clear treble of a boy soprano began to sing. And Betty felt her throat ache with the beauty of his singing.

> *'Once in Royal David's city, stood a lowly cattle shed*
> *Where a mother laid her baby, in a manger for his bed.'*

She turned and looked up at the man who stood at her side. And Dennis returned her look. He laid his hand over hers and clasped it tightly, and they stood together, lost in the tremulous joy of simply being together, and in the joy and peace that was being expressed all over Britain at that very moment in village churches, in great cathedrals, in tranquil villages and even amidst scenes of utter devastation.

It was Christmas, and Christmas could not be ignored.

Later that afternoon, when they had finished the milking, they strolled together down the lane and leant over a gate, watching the twilight steal gently over the sleeping fields.

'Everything seems so much quieter on Christmas Day,' Betty said softly. 'Even the animals are gentler, as if they know it's special. And it really does seem as if there's been a truce. A whole day with no bombs.'

'And if there can be one, why not two? Why start again at all?' Dennis sighed. 'If only they'd get together and talk. But Hitler will never see reason. He'll go on and on.' He stirred restlessly. 'Betty, I've been thinking about what I should do –'

'Oh, Dennis, no, not now!' she exclaimed impulsively. 'Don't let's talk about the war now. It's Christmas Day. Let's just think of happy things.'

He nodded and laid his arm across her shoulders. 'All right, sweetheart. We'll leave it for now. But we've got to talk seriously, you and me. You know that, don't you?'

She nodded, feeling suddenly shy. Her relationship with Dennis, which had grown and ripened so slowly, seemed to have shifted into a faster gear and she was half excited, half afraid, and totally unsure as to what should happen next.

In some ways, it had been easier with Graham. Their

romance had followed a set of rules. Their meeting had been flirtatious, with Betty responding saucily to Graham's boldness, and when he'd asked her out it had been to the pictures, which was the accepted venue for any first date. He'd kissed her goodnight that time, after a faint-hearted struggle from Betty, and on subsequent evenings out the goodnight kiss had been taken for granted, lasting a little longer each time and accompanied by caresses which grew ever more daring. It had been all part of the game that Graham should attempt what Betty would forbid, and until the night of the card-game there had never been any serious risk of his demanding more.

Perhaps it was part of the game too that they should be possessive of each other. Betty would have been furious if she had seen Graham looking at another girl, and he was sulky when she announced her intention of joining the Land Army. But war made everything different, and Betty had always been an independent spirit. In the past few months, she had learned a different set of values, and the naive boy-and-girl games she had played with Graham no longer held any appeal.

With Dennis, nothing was the same. There was no place for sauciness, none for teasing. There was a seriousness about Dennis that brought response from a part of Betty she had never known existed. And there was a depth to the love she felt for him and the love she sensed in him for her, that had never been present when she was with Graham.

Yes, she knew they would have to talk seriously, and soon. But this was Christmas. A time for peace. A time for standing still.

Dennis pulled her a little closer and she leant her head on his shoulder. The moon was a sliver of brightness in the sky, rolled on its back amongst the stars. The trees were dark shapes above the huddled hedges. No lights showed from neighbouring farms or villages, but despite the truce – for it was only unofficial and could not be wholly trusted – the thin pencil beams of searchlights played in the sky over Portsmouth. They moved across the heavens like a web of silky light, tracing a silver lattice in space. Closer at hand, an owl hooted and Betty felt the velvet brush of its wings as it flew past her head.

'There are some things we have to talk about,' Dennis said quietly. 'You know what it's like, Betty. Tomorrow might not come. I can't risk leaving it. I've waited a long time to tell you I love you.'

'Dennis, I love you too.' She turned in his arms, seeking his lips with her own. They clung together, their bodies pressed close, feeling their warmth in the cold night air. She felt the firmness of his arms about her and knew that his strength came from deep in his heart, that he would always keep her safe. Her heart spoke to him, making its own vows, but she knew that Dennis needed to hear her voice. With more time, the heart could be given its chance, but did they have that time? She imagined the sound of a bomber droning through the silence of the night and her arms tightened around him.

Dennis pressed his lips against her hair, against her temple, against her cheek and her neck. He found her lips and laid his own gently upon them, but the gentleness turned swiftly to passion and he caught her hard against him, his mouth suddenly fierce. Betty gasped, swung momentarily into terror, for she had never been kissed in this way before, and then her whole body responded, melting against him, her lips soft and yielding, her breasts swelling against his chest. Briefly, she glimpsed the stars wheeling above, and then her eyes closed as Dennis lifted her in his arms and then laid her gently on the icy ground.

'No. It's too cold here.' She felt his strength as he drew her up again into his arms and looked down into her eyes. She could see the stars reflected in his wide, dark pupils, shimmering through the tears that lay bright on her lashes. Gently, he kissed each eyelid, and traced a line of tenderness down her neck to the hollow of her throat. His hand curved about her breast, his palm shaping itself to her softness, and she felt the leap of her heart beneath his touch. 'Betty,' he whispered, 'Betty . . . I want to love you . . .'

Betty clung to him. Her body was surging with desire. She had barely noticed the iciness of the ground, would willingly have opened herself to him there and then. She was shaken with a torrent of feeling more powerful than any she had known before. Graham's fumblings and her own half excited, half irritated response were no more than a pale shadow in comparison with this almost violent rush of emotion. It was like stepping from a familiar room into a jungle, where everything was new and nothing certain.

'Love me now, Dennis,' she whispered, pressing her body against his. 'Oh please, please, love me . . .'

He held her tightly and groaned. Then he lifted his head and pushed her away from him. His arms were strong but she could sense the reluctance in him, the desire to pull her close again, and she laid her hands on his shoulders and tried to draw him back. But Dennis shook his head.

'Not now. Not here. This isn't how it should be between us. We should think, be sensible –'

'*Sensible*!' The word was jerked out of her body. 'Dennis, there's nothing sensible about the way I feel – sense doesn't come into it. Not that sort of sense, anyway.' In fact, all her senses were reeling and she knew it, knew that he was right, but refused to acknowledge it. 'We love each other. What else matters?'

'You know what else.' His voice was ragged. 'Betty, I love you, and because I love you I want to take care of you. I don't want to do anything that might hurt you. Do you know what I mean?'

A little subdued, recognising his emotion, she said, 'Yes.'

'I can't take any risks,' he said. 'I want to marry you, but it's got to be done right. I don't want any shotgun weddings.'

She thought of Graham. He'd said he loved her, but he'd been talking about a different kind of love, or perhaps it wasn't love at all. What sort of love was it that would use a baby to get him what he wanted?

'I don't mind what happens,' she said, 'as long as we can be together.'

He looked down at her gravely and she saw the shine of his eyes in the starlight.

'There's a war on, Betty,' he said. 'We might not be able to be together.'

'So love me! Let's love each other while we can, while we've got this chance. It's Christmas night, Dennis.' She looked up at him, pleadingly. 'There doesn't have to be a risk, does there? Aren't there things you can use? Or – or are Quakers like Roman Catholics and don't believe in it?'

She saw him smile. 'No, we're not at all like Roman Catholics. But there aren't many places open on Christmas night to buy those kind of things, Betty, and I don't keep them in my pockets.' He kissed her again and held her close. 'Besides, you haven't had time to think about it. I told you, I won't rush you. You've got to be sure.'

'I am sure,' she said quietly, but he turned away from the gate and took her hand.

'Let's go back now, my darling. Let's go back, and have our tea, and spend the evening by the fire with Mr and Mrs Spencer and that old grump Jonas. Let's be just like a married couple, sitting on the settee and holding hands and knowing that all our loving is there to be taken later on, a part of us. It won't be any the less for waiting.' He kissed her once more, his lips lingering on hers, his cheek cold against her skin. 'Let's make this Christmas a Christmas we'll always treasure, one we'll look back on when we're old and grey, one that will always shine in our memories because it was the Christmas we fell in love.'

Betty could not answer. With her hand in his, she walked back towards the darkened farmhouse. Inside, she knew, it would be warm and bright, filled with good smells and cheerfulness. Outside, it was black with the shadows of war.

A Christmas to be treasured. To shine in their memories for the rest of their lives.

Would it be really be any more treasured because we didn't make love, because we took no risks? she thought. Wouldn't it shine even more brightly if we had the memory of a sweet loving to carry with us through the years? Perhaps even a child, not used to get them their way as Graham had wanted, but conceived of their tenderness for each other, born of their passion. And shouldn't such a conception be left to the God in whom Dennis believed so steadfastly?

Tea was ready when they went back indoors, a spread of sandwiches and salad, cakes and jelly. Betty thought of the family at home. They would all be there, except herself and

Colin. Olive and Derek would have told their news, which had been conveyed to Betty in a slip of paper included with her present (a pair of mittens knitted by Olive). They would have eaten their Christmas dinner and had a walk in the afternoon and after tea they would be making a party of the evening, with games like Family Coach and the Jelly Race and Alibis. By now they would be singing, all the old songs like *Tavern in the Town* and *Molly Malone*, and some of the newer ones too – *A Nightingale Sang in Berkeley Square*, and the one the popular young singer Vera Lynn had made so famous, which brought tears to everyone's eyes, *We'll Meet Again*.

There were tears in Betty's eyes too as she thought of them, enjoying the first family Christmas she had ever missed. Did they notice the empty chair at the table, or had it been filled by someone else? Her mother had told her Mrs Brunner and Joy were coming to spend the day. They had never had 'strangers' in the house at Christmas before. Had it made a difference?

'What sort of Christmas do you usually have?' she asked Mrs Spencer, realising that she and Dennis were 'strangers' at the farm. 'You must be missing your Gerald and Dick.'

'I am.' The older woman looked sadly into the fire. 'It don't seem right without them, and that's the truth of it. And when I think of where they are and what might be happening to them . . .' The Spencer boys were in the Army, fighting the Italians in the Libyan desert. 'I know they say we're winning there, but our boys are still getting killed, aren't they? Perhaps at this very minute . . .' Her eyes filled.

'Now then, Ada,' Mr Spencer said. 'This is Christmas night, remember? There's a truce on. Nobody's getting killed now and our two aren't going to be anyway. They've got hides like crocodiles, the pair of 'em.' He refilled her glass with ginger wine. 'Drink up now. Dennis wants to hear about the old days on the farm, when we were young.'

'Ah, it were different then,' Jonas said in his gravelly voice. 'We 'ad to *work* in them days. None o' this lazin' around 'alf the day suppin' tea. And never did us a mite of 'arm, either. 'Ard work never killed no one.'

Dennis smiled at Betty and squeezed her hand. And for the rest of the evening, they listened to tales of life in the country, of Christmases past, of summers when the sun never stopped shining, and of a time that was almost forgotten, when families were together and peace ruled the land.

It was a Christmas that was different, she thought after she had said goodnight and gone to bed, but it had been a happy one after all. Happiest of all because Dennis had said he loved her. But now, alone in the empty attic, she felt a great desolation wash over her. And she knew that she could not sleep without feeling his arms around her.

This is our Christmas, she thought. Our first. We ought to be together.

Quietly, she slipped out of bed. She found the old coat she used as a dressing-gown and pushed her feet into the slippers her mother had sent her for Christmas. Cautiously, she lifted the latch on the attic door and crept down the stairs to Gerald Spencer's room, where Dennis was now sleeping.

The door opened without a creak. She pushed it gently and slid through the narrow gap. The room was uncurtained and lit faintly by the stars, and she could see the bed and the shape that was Dennis lying in it.

Betty stood for a moment with beating heart. What if he should send her away? What if he were angry, or rejected her? What if he despised her for being so brazen?

Dennis moved. He lifted his head from the pillow and whispered, 'Who's there?'

'It's me. Betty.' Her voice was strained, almost inaudible. 'I – I couldn't sleep.' She came forwards and dropped on her knees beside the bed, her hands reaching out for him. 'Dennis, let me stay. You don't have to do anything. Just let me stay here with you. Just let's be together, please.'

'Betty –'

'You said it yourself,' she whispered. 'Tomorrow might not come. We have to take what chances we have. Hold me in your arms, Dennis, and love me. Let's have this Christmas to remember.' She lifted her face to his and touched his lips with her own. 'I love you, Dennis. I love you so much.'

His arms slipped around her body and she felt the warmth of his skin beneath the thin fabric of her nightdress. Her blood surged and she felt the answering leap of his heart. He drew back the bedclothes and she shrugged the coat from her shoulders and lay beside him.

'You're sure about this?' he whispered. 'I don't want to do anything you'd be sorry for.'

'I'll never be sorry for loving you.'

'Betty,' he breathed. 'Betty . . .'

His lips were gentle on hers. Slowly, delicately, as if uncovering the most fragile of spun glass, he pushed aside the folds of her nightdress. Betty shivered as his fingers touched her skin and a tremor of desire shook her body. She touched his bare chest and felt the warmth of his heart. With a sudden need to feel closer, she pressed her body against his and then drew away to sit up and drag her nightdress over her head.

Dennis watched the movement of her arms as she lifted them, saw the shape of her breasts silhouetted against the window. He lifted one hand and traced the shape, and Betty slid down again and allowed him to twine his arms about her. She felt his legs hard against hers, and the trembling desire deepened to a burning excitement.

Dennis caressed her body slowly, covering her breasts first with his hands, then with his lips. With the tip of one finger, he drew a line between her breasts and a curve in the crease beneath each one. He slid his fingers down her arm, lingering in the crook of her elbow where he planted another kiss. He stroked her waist, her navel and the crease of her thighs.

Betty felt the tenderness of his hands spread like a warm flame, enveloping her body. She was weak with desire and helpless in his arms. She lay soft in his embrace, as dizzy as if she were falling, and felt his touch slide from thigh to knee and back again, into the deepest crease of all.

She felt a sudden flare of sensation and twisted against him. With a gasp, Dennis came into her and suddenly Betty's languor departed and she moved with him, responding to his sudden force with a strength she had not known she possessed. She lay beneath him, her hands on his shoulders, and then Dennis rose high above her, bracing himself on his hands, and threw back his head. In the pale shimmer of starlight, she could see his face, taut and concentrated in the shadows. She felt her own desire tingle through her body, felt the tremor reach to each outflung fingertip, felt the shudder of fulfilment lift her to a momentary peak of delight.

The few seconds were an eternity. And then eternity came to an end and Dennis lowered himself to lie close to her, once again enfolding her with his warmth and whispering his love in Betty's ear.

CHAPTER TWENTY

It was a strange Christmas for many that year.

For Gerald and Dick Spencer, it was blisteringly hot. From the gentle scenery of a Hampshire farm, they had come thousands of miles to North African desert sand. From ploughing and harrowing, from milking and shearing, they had come to a battle to the death, with the roar of guns and mines and tanks in their ears. From rainstorms they came to desert storms, with sand driving merciless needles against their faces and into their eyes and throats, so that they almost preferred the threat of bombshells and the menace of the hidden mines.

For Colin Chapman, it was a Christmas at sea. His ship, the *Exeter*, had been active ever since the outbreak of war, and was still in the forefront of the battles of the oceans. But Mike Simmons was home. To Kathy's almost unbelieving joy, his ship had docked in Southampton on Christmas Eve and would be there for at least a week, perhaps more. In the bare little house at number 16 October Street, furnished with other people's cast-offs, there was rejoicing and a happy Christmas, with the new baby Thomas the centre of everyone's attention.

Graham was home too, and made much of by his mother, though he was still smarting over the split with Betty. By now, he had expected a letter of apology and a humble request to 'start again'. But no such letter had arrived – not even a Christmas card – and he sat glowering at the fire. What was the use of Christmas without a girl? And you couldn't even go out and find one, everyone was stuck indoors with their families. He didn't even think there would be a welcome for him at Nancy Baxter's.

'Come on, Gray,' his mother urged him. 'There's plenty more fish in the sea. She wasn't never good enough for you, anyway.'

'I liked the girl, myself,' her husband said in his dry, papery voice. 'Always had a smile and a pleasant word, not like some young people these days.'

'Oh, you're just a pushover.' But Elsie was sorry that Betty wouldn't be coming over any more. She'd liked the girl too, in spite of what she said to Graham, and she'd hoped they'd stick together. Chances are it was his fault, she thought, trying it on when he ought to have known Betty wasn't that sort. But men were all the same in that department.

The men of 698 Unit had a peaceful Christmas too. The victims of the latest raid, in battered Conway Street, had all been found homes with relatives or taken away to rest centres or hospital, and the soldiers who were helping to demolish unsafe buildings or repair those less damaged had been given time to be at home with their families. Derek Harker, George Glaister and Bob Shaw were among them.

For the thousands now homeless, it was a time of confusion. Their houses had been bombed, often relatives killed. There were men without wives, women without husbands, children without parents. There were old people who scarcely knew what had happened, babies who knew nothing but turmoil and saw no face for long enough to recognise the features. There were children who had no home and no relatives and who did not know where life would take them next.

And amidst all these were the people who were trying to help them, the Red Cross, the WVS, the Civil Defence, the Salvation Army, the volunteers, the foster parents and the nurses. For all of them, the problem was so immense that they could do nothing but live from day to day, nothing but lend a hand wherever it seemed needed most. 'Carrying on' was the order of the day, and 'smiling through'. And the bulldog tenacity of Churchill, exhorting them to greater efforts. '*We shall never surrender.*'

The spirit took root and grew. From fear and despair, from the misery of loss, rose a determination that the bombed cities would live on. Buildings could be destroyed, cities razed and people killed, but Britain would never be beaten.

The truce had given the country a short respite. But the peace did not last. Two days were all that Hitler allowed. On 27 December the Luftwaffe was back in force, with a hundred bombers attacking London and leaving over six hundred people dead. And two days later the city suffered its worst raid yet, with nearly a hundred and fifty bombers forcing their way past the barrages to drop more than twenty thousand firebombs and something like a hundred and twenty tons of high explosives.

The ensuing blaze was said to be worse than the Great Fire of London. It raged all night, destroying the Old Bailey, the Guildhall and eight of the historic churches of Christopher Wren. Thousands of homes were in ruins, thousands of people homeless. Yet still the spirit of 'carrying on' prevailed. Those who still had homes, left them to go to work. They left early, knowing that they would have to find a new way through the devastation of the streets. They left knowing that they might have no place of work to go to, that everything familiar to them might have been blown away in the night. And as they made their way they gazed at the destruction that had been wrought by the bombs and the fires, and lifted their eyes to see the dome of St Paul's Cathedral still proudly dominating the scarred skyline. And once again the words echoed in their hearts. *We shall never surrender* . . .

In Portsmouth the respite continued, though the nightly warnings still sounded and the removal to the shelters persisted. And the uneasy dread still filled people's hearts as they looked at the wintry sky, hung with barrage balloons like heavy clouds of foreboding.

Annie Chapman was growing more and more worried about Ted. Ever since Dunkirk, he'd been getting more and more jumpy. He picked at his meals and he couldn't sleep. When the siren sounded, he went straight up the stairs to the top of the little turret and stood there, watching for fires, and only Annie knew what an effort it was.

'You feel like everyone can see you up there,' he told her. 'You feel like every Jerry's looking down from his plane and aiming his bombs straight at you. Same as when I'm on the ferry, the old *King* feels as big as the *Ark Royal*.'

'You don't have to go up there, Ted. Let me take a turn. I can watch for fires as well as you.'

But he shook his head. 'I've got to go, Annie. I've been to Dunkirk, remember. I've seen things I don't want to talk about, never. There's men living through worse every day than you and I can even imagine. I can't hide meself while all that's going on.'

There was no more for Annie to say. She could only do whatever she could to give him comfort, the warmth of a mug of cocoa to take up with him, or when he came back down, white and shrammed with cold. The warmth of her arms on the rare nights when they dared sleep in their own bed.

She was more thankful than ever now that Betty at least was safe in the country. The girl had seemed happier when she was home last, though it had been a shock to her when the young Air Force boys had been killed. Annie had wondered a few times whether she wasn't fonder of one of them than she'd admitted. But there'd been a sort of glow about her when she came back for her weekend after Christmas.

Betty hadn't mentioned Dennis to her parents, but Mr and Mrs Spencer had soon realised the situation. They said nothing, simply accepted it as a natural development. The other two Land Girls reacted differently.

'You seem to get plenty of boys,' Yvonne said with envy. 'That sailor, and then Sandy and now Dennis. I wish I could be easy-come, easy-go like that.'

'I'm not easy-come, easy-go,' Betty said sharply. 'It was never really serious between Graham and me. And Sandy was just a friend.' Her voice trembled a little as she remembered him on that last evening, asking if there might be a chance for him. Poor, poor Sandy . . . 'It's different with Dennis and me.'

'Well, I don't know how you can do it,' Erica said. 'Going with a traitor. I'd be ashamed.'

'He's not a traitor,' Betty said, but her voice was quiet.

Dennis had already taught her to react without aggression to such taunts. And she felt genuinely sorry for the blonde girl. Suppose she lost Dennis now . . . The pain was unthinkable. But it was the pain Erica was suffering. Betty touched her arm.

'Don't be angry,' she said. 'I know how you feel about Dennis, but he really isn't a traitor, or a coward. He wants to help his country just as much as the rest of us, he just wants to do it a different way. He's just as upset as we are about Geoff and the others.'

'Nobody's as upset about Geoff as me,' Erica said, but she allowed Betty to put her arms around her, and she turned her face into Betty's shoulder as the tears came. And they sat, the three of them close and unspeaking; trying, failing, to understand, yet mourning together.

Tim and Keith Budd were back in the country too. Jess had been reluctant to let them go without knowing where they would be sent, but at the last minute she had heard from Edna Corner that the vicar had room for them. Would she like them to go to him? Jess had agreed at once, though the boys had made faces, protesting that Mr Beckett was an old man, that they'd have to go to church twice every Sunday, that they'd have to say Grace at every meal and never be allowed to play games.

'You'll be safe,' she said firmly. 'And I'm sure it can't be that bad. Mr Beckett's a very nice man.'

'But he's a *vicar*,' Tim said in outraged tones, and Jess snapped at him in irritation.

'For goodness' sake, Tim! You're behaving as if he's a man from Mars. He's no different from anyone else, and if he makes you behave and teaches you the manners you seem to have forgotten, I'll be grateful to him. I know Mr and Mrs Corner were good to you but you seem to have changed since you went out to Bridge End, and not for the better.'

Tim pushed out his lower lip and went to sit on the floor and stroke Henry the cat. He would have preferred it if Mr Beckett had been a man from Mars. That would have been fun. But a vicar . . .

Rose flatly refused to return to Bridge End.

'I don't want to go back. I'm worried all the time about what's happening here. I'm frightened you'll get killed and no one will tell me. I'd rather be here with you and help with the cooking and the baby and everything.' She clung to her mother. 'Don't make me go back, Mum. Please don't make me go back.'

Jess held her and looked helplessly at Frank. They had both known Rose was unhappy, but had been shocked by her appearance when she came home. She was pale and thin, and not developing as she should. At almost thirteen, she ought to have been beginning to round out, but instead she was hollow-chested and gaunt. Jess had been convinced she was ill and wanted to take her to the doctor, but had agreed to wait until after Christmas.

'She's pining,' Annie had said. 'That's all that's wrong with her. She's always been your girl, Jess, and she's missing you.'

Jess repeated her words to Frank after Rose had gone to bed. 'Girls do pine at her age, Frank. They can just stop eating and fade away, what my mother used to call a "decline". We can't let that happen to our Rose.'

'You'd rather she was killed, is that it?'

'Of course not! Don't say such things. But who knows what will happen to any of us? And if she's as miserable as that, she might as well be back here with us. We can look after her. She's not like the boys'd be, wanting to get out and play, and messing about on bomb-sites. Anyway, she's nearly the age you were when you left school. She can make up her own mind.'

'Make up her own mind? She's under my authority till she's twenty-one, that's another seven years. And I don't want her leaving school yet. I want my kids to have an education.'

'Well, they're not getting much of that, wherever they are. I reckon Rose would do as well at home, having lessons with Joy Brunner. And that's another thing. Joy and her have always been friends, and it'd be good for them to be near each other. Joy hasn't got anyone else round here.'

'Joy's a nice enough girl,' Frank acknowledged. 'But I don't see why our Rose has got to be brought home just because there isn't anyone else for Joy.'

'I'm not saying that.' Jess sighed. 'Look, if you want my opinion, our Rose'll be ill if we make her go away again. She's worrying herself half out of her mind. And I tell you straight, I wouldn't be a bit surprised if Mrs Greenberry refused to take her back. She won't want the responsibility.'

In the end, she won. Frank was never easy to persuade but he would, eventually, see reason. And even he could not withstand Rose's distress at the idea of leaving home again.

'All right. She can stay. But not the boys. They go back to Bridge End and they stay there till there's no chance of any more bombing, all right?'

No chance of any more bombing.

December drew to a close. For the second year running, there were no bells rung to mark the passing of another year, no sirens sounded or ships' hooters blown. New Year's Day came in silently, slinking through the storms as if afraid to be seen, and 1941 began with an air of apology for not promising better things.

In bitter cold, Cardiff was raided and Bristol attacked on three separate nights. Manchester too was blitzed. Fires raged everywhere, buildings toppled, families were buried. Fire engines raced through the streets, sometimes never reaching the fire they had set out to deal with. Ambulances were driven by young women like Gladys Shaw through streets lit by flames, while bombs and shrapnel rained about them, to hospitals that were themselves destroyed before they could get there. There were fear and panic, lawlessness and looting, never reported in the newspapers for fear of lowering the already fragile morale, and later buried in people's memories as so many of the injured and dead were buried beneath the ruins of the shattered cities. It could not be acknowledged that the war of terror might be having its effect. It could not be admitted that the bulldog tenacity, the will to carry on, the determination that this was a people who would never surrender, might be faltering at last.

Portsmouth had not been raided again, but nobody could dismiss the possibility that their turn would come. They went into the new year with trepidation, spending each night in the shelters just in case. Each day without bombing brought relief that they had still escaped, and a greater fear that it must come soon.

On 8 January a huge party was held for the children in the Guildhall. Tim and Keith were already back at Bridge End, but Rose went to it with Joy Brunner, though neither of them now thought of themselves as children. Joy had barely attended school since the war began, and had been virtually running the shop for months as well as looking after her mother for much of the time. Rose, out in the country, had been receiving only half-day schooling, and not much of that, for the older girls were expected to help with the younger children and she had spent a lot of her time reading to the little ones and assisting them with their sums.

It seemed strange to them to go into the big, grand building down in the main square of the city, up the wide steps and between the two majestic lions, to attend a children's party. Strange to sit at long tables with a thousand other children, eating jelly from small cardboard bowls, with coloured lamps and balloons festooned above their heads. At one end of the room was a platform, piled high with wrapped gifts, and in front of the platform stood a tall Christmas tree, glittering with tinsel and twinkling fairy lights.

The presents came, the Lady Mayoress explained, from British people who lived in a country called Uruguay, six thousand miles away. They had sent a hundred and fifty pounds to give the children of Portsmouth a treat, and this was it. For three hours, they could forget the war and enjoy themselves.

For three hours, they did. Led by the Lady Mayoress, they marched around the hall, roaring out songs like *Pack Up Your Troubles in Your Old Kit Bag* and *Smile – Smile – Smile* and *There'll Always Be An England*, accompanied on the big Guildhall organ by the city organist. They played games. They watched a dancing display and a conjurer and were commended for their courage by the Commander-in-Chief himself, a real Admiral in full uniform, who told them they were helping England in her task of winning the war.

'You deserve a prize,' he said, and the children cheered. 'And I shall give you one. A pound note to the first boy or girl of school age who puts out an incendiary bomb. What do you think of that?'

'Hooray!' the children cheered again. 'Hooray! Hooray! Hooray!'

They cheered again as the Lady Mayoress announced that the presents so enticingly displayed on the platform would be handed out, and waited in line, some more patiently than others, as the gifts were handed out. It took an hour, but at last they were all provided for, and when their parents came to take them home each child was well supplied with a stick of rock, a present and a balloon.

Rose and Joy took their leave of the Guildhall in silence. Neither had ever been in such a grand place before, and they looked around the glittering walls with awe. The high ceiling, the white paint, the gold leaf and the gleaming, polished floor – it was like a royal palace to the girls who had known only terraced houses. They looked at the Christmas tree, decorated just for them, at the glowing colours of the Christmas lights. They looked at the walls where portraits of previous Lord Mayors and dignitaries, clothed in rich, fur-trimmed robes, gazed down at them, and wondered if they would ever come here again.

They would not, and nor would many others. For only two nights later, the Luftwaffe's attention turned once again to Portsmouth and the blitz began. The proud Guildhall was almost totally destroyed.

CHAPTER TWENTY-ONE

It began at seven o'clock in the evening. It was a Friday.

Jess had just put Maureen to bed. She slept in her cot in the back bedroom, where Rose also slept now that the boys were away. She tucked the baby in and was halfway downstairs when the siren began.

Instantly, she was back upstairs and lifting Maureen from the cot, blankets and all. Holding her close, she ran down the stairs. Rose was already gathering together the things they would need, the cushions and old blankets, the thermos flask Frank had bought for Christmas, which was filled with hot water every night, the basket which held packets of cocoa and sugar, a small bottle of milk, a tin of biscuits. They might be in the shelter for only half an hour, they might be there all night. You had to be prepared.

'Quick, Mum, oh, please be quick.' Rose was crouching under the stairs, her face white as Jess quickly thrust Maureen's feet back into the socks she had taken off only twenty minutes earlier. 'Put them on when we get down there. The planes'll be here, oh hurry, hurry.'

Frank was still at work, or more likely on his way home. Jess thought of the first raid, last July, when he'd got caught in the streets. He'd never said much about it, but he'd changed that night, as if he'd seen sights that couldn't be talked of. She prayed that he would come home safely tonight. Frank, Frank . . .

He was right, she thought, looking at Rose's ashen face. The girl would have been better off out in the country. She was terrified. But she'd been just as frightened out there, so

Mrs Greenberry had said, and at least if she was here she knew what was going on, knew that her mother and baby sister were safe. As they would be, as soon as they reached the shelter.

The planes could be heard now, droning overhead. It was high time they were in the shelter. Jess wound Maureen up again in her blankets and grabbed the tin box that held all the papers. She made for the back door and, with Rose at her heels, scurried down the garden path.

They had just ducked through the low doorway and scrambled down the steps when the sky turned suddenly red.

Olive Harker had been cooking Derek's supper when the warning went.

'Oh, drat!' she exclaimed. 'I was just looking forward to a nice cosy evening listening to the wireless.'

Her mother came into the kitchen and turned out the gas. 'Down the shelter, quick!'

'But the supper –'

'It don't matter about the supper. You can finish that later on. Derek won't be home anyway, not till it's over.'

'Oh, they do it deliberately,' Olive wailed. 'Just to spoil things!'

'D'you expect them to send us a timetable?' Annie grabbed the bundle of cushions and rugs they kept by the back door and hustled her out. 'Look at those flares. They're going to hammer us tonight, mark my words. Why, it's bright as day out here.'

Olive hung back. 'I promised to look in on Kathy –'

'Kathy'll be going to her own shelter.' The two young women had become friends since Kathy's baby was born. Olive, suddenly passionately interested in babies now that she was expecting her own, had been a daily visitor to admire little Thomas. She spent hours stroking his firm little limbs and trying to make him smile. Yesterday, he had done so for the first time and she had been enchanted.

'But she's there all on her own with those two little girls and the baby.'

'It's what she chooses,' Annie said. 'I don't want to be

unkind, Livvy, but she could have been evacuated if she'd wanted.' She pulled Olive's arm. 'Come on, for goodness' sake, do you want us to be bombed on our own doorstep? Look at the way they're lighting us up.'

Olive glanced up. The sky was now almost entirely red, the glow of the flares stretching from sunrise to sunset. The roar of the planes was directly overhead. It could be no more than moments before the first bombs began to drop.

In sudden fear, she ran down the garden path after her mother and scrambled into the shed. Together, they ducked through the doorway and dragged the old woollen curtain across. Annie found the blackout frame and pushed it into place, and then groped for the matches.

'Not that it matters if we show every lamp we've got, the way they're lighting up the whole city,' she said. 'But we don't want Tommy Vickers round here shouting the odds.'

The hurricane lamp flickered into life and they sat back on the bunks and looked at each other.

'Maybe it's just a false alarm,' Olive said, without much hope. 'Maybe they're just passing over, like other nights.'

Annie shook her head. 'I don't reckon so, love. I reckon this is something worse. We've never had flares like that before. They're lighting up their targets, that's what they're doing.' She paused for a moment, then said quietly, 'Tonight they're going to smash Pompey right down into the ground . . .'

Kathy Simmons acted calmly enough. The things they needed to take down to the shelter were kept in a basket close to the back door, blankets and cushions, an old cot mattress for the baby, a thermos flask and cups. There were a couple of books for the girls and one for herself, from the library. There was a hurricane lamp, though she didn't like to use it for too long in case the paraffin ran out. You never knew how long an alert might last, it might be only half an hour before the All-Clear sounded, it might be hours, even though nothing seemed to be happening.

Tonight, as she ran down the path in the red glow of the flares, it looked as if it might be a long time.

*

Frank Budd and Ted Chapman were on a trolley-bus together, coming up to North End. Both had finished work for the day and were anxious to get home. Frank had boarded the bus to find his brother-in-law sitting in the seat by the door, and he'd nodded and sat down beside him. The bus was dark and gloomy inside, with only the lowest possible lights to show passengers their way, and it crept slowly along the unlit streets.

The two men said nothing for a while. Both were tired from the week's work and from the alerts that sounded night after night. Both were firewatchers and had to stand outside, looking at the sky, waiting for incendiaries to drop and set Portsmouth ablaze. Both were suffering from broken nights and the dread that hung over the whole country.

'They're doing it to scare people,' Ted said at last, breaking the silence. 'They're trying to wear us down. Bombing London, night after night . . . Hitting places like Bristol and Manchester . . . They think if they keep on hammering us, we'll give in and let Hitler walk all over us.'

'They've got another think coming, then,' Frank said grimly, and they relapsed into silence again.

When the siren sounded, they did no more than sigh and wait for the bus to reach their destination. But when the flares began to light the streets, they looked at each other in dismay. And when the trolley-bus came to a halt, they rose from their seats in real alarm.

'That's as far as we're going,' the conductress called out, her face reddened by the glow. 'You'd better get yourselves to a shelter. There'll be no more service tonight, by the looks of it.'

No more service tonight! 'But I've got miles to go,' one woman exclaimed in despair. 'I live right up Cosham.'

The conductress shrugged. 'Sorry, love.' She was already gathering up her bag and coat, ready to get off the bus. 'You'd better forget about getting home tonight. There won't be no more buses running.' She turned her face up to the sky, and Frank followed her gaze and saw the mass of flares drifting from the sky. 'That's incendiaries comin' down, that is,' she said tersely, and leapt to the pavement and ran.

The street was filled now with hurrying figures. People

338

running for the shelters, people running for home. People just running, with no real idea of where to go. Sheltering in doorways, pressing themselves against walls. Looking up, up at the crimson lights, up towards the ominous drone of the planes. Calling to each other, to lost children, to elderly parents, calling with fear in their voices, whimpering, crying.

Where had they all come from? Frank wondered. It was well after dark, surely most people were safe at home by now. But it seemed that there were plenty who weren't. Or maybe they'd been driven from their homes by the siren, driven out to seek shelter. Not everyone had an Anderson; there were plenty who must go to the public shelters, and if there wasn't room in the first must look for another.

'What're we going to do?' Ted asked, and Frank turned to look at him. His brother-in-law's eyes were scared.

'What *can* we do?' Frank replied. 'Go home, of course. We're on duty there, aren't we? At least we can see to find our way.'

He set off up Stubbington Avenue, striding fast. They could, he knew, have sought shelter. They could have gone to a public one, overcrowded though it might have been, or they could have gone to Jess and Annie's parents who lived nearby. Perhaps they should do that. Nobody would expect them to walk halfway across Portsmouth in the middle of a raid.

But he couldn't do that. He didn't want to spend another night searching through rubble for bodies and bits of bodies, when Jess was there by herself with Rose and the baby, when she didn't know whether or not he was safe. If a bomb fell before he got home, if people needed help, he'd do what he could. Of course he would. But he'd do his damnedest to get home first, and so would Ted.

He looked up again at the sky, listening to the drone of the aircraft, watching the fearsome descent of the parachutes. In God's name, what was going on? Could there possibly be men on the end of those parachutes?

The first stick of bombs, falling on the electricity station, shook the ground with their explosion. And Frank knew that this was no invasion. This was the blitz over Portsmouth.

*

'There it goes!' Gladys said, and reached for the bag she always kept near the door, containing her First Aid kit and gas mask. 'I'm off.'

'Wait for me.' Peggy too caught up her bag. 'Blimey, they don't give you much warning, do they? I can hear the planes already.'

Diane stared at them, her eyes almost black in her white face. 'What about me? You're not going to leave me here by myself.'

'Oh lor',' Peggy said, stopping, 'she's right, Glad. We can't leave her on her own.'

'Where's Dad?'

'I don't know, up the pub, I suppose. He'll go to the street shelter.'

'Well, he shouldn't,' Gladys said crossly. 'He knows we've got to go when the siren sounds.'

'He knows, and he doesn't like it. He'll expect you or me to stop behind.'

'For God's sake! Don't he know there's a war on? Anyway, he ought to be on duty himself, he's a firewatcher, isn't he?'

Peggy shrugged helplessly. 'That won't help our Diane. There still won't be anyone to stay with her in the shelter.'

'Well, she'd better come with us, then,' Gladys said. 'She can help at the First Aid post. She's helped us practise our bandaging often enough, she must know what to do.'

Peggy opened her mouth to protest. The girl would be in the way, she'd see things she shouldn't. There'd be blood, broken limbs, people crying and shocked. And then she looked at Diane and thought again. She was sixteen, no longer a child. There were plenty of youngsters her age doing war work already – Boy Scouts acting as messengers in raids, girls helping in canteens, lads too young for call-up joining the Home Guard. Diane could easily make herself useful, keeping the kettle and teapot on the go if the rest were busy, and it would be better for her than staying here on her own.

'All right,' she said. 'Get your coat on, Diane. We'll leave a note on the table for your dad.' She found a scrap of paper and scribbled on it while Gladys waited impatiently. 'Here they come.'

The drone was directly overhead. It sounded as if there were planes all over the sky. They looked at each other in sudden fear. They had suffered raids before, they all knew the sound of the planes, but this sounded different, louder, more menacing, as if Hitler had sent the whole of the Luftwaffe to obliterate their city and all within it.

Gladys thought of the blitz on London, of the merciless raids on Coventry, on Bristol, on Plymouth.

She jammed her tin hat on her head, switched off the light and opened the front door. Cautiously, they looked up at the sky, criss-crossed with its web of searchlight beams. The planes could be heard snarling high above, but now they could hear the different note of RAF night fighters flying to intercept them, and the sharp rattle of ack-ack fire. Maybe we're fighting them off, she thought. Maybe it won't be a bad raid after all.

Suddenly, high above her head, she saw a red light. It dropped silently through the darkness, falling like the red balloon young Rose next door had brought home from the Guildhall party. And then, as she stared, it opened out like a flower, like a blood-red rose or a poppy, blossoming as it fell and lighting up the sky around it, and the city beneath.

Before she had realised what it was, she saw another and another, until the sky was full of them. A shower of poppies, scattering over the darkened streets of Portsmouth, casting a warm glow as they descended. A bouquet of death.

'Flares,' Peggy muttered. 'Parachute flares. They're making sure they can see us before they drop their bombs.'

'Gosh,' Diane said, her voice awed. 'It's like firework night.' Her voice quivered a little. 'It's like the biggest rockets you ever saw.'

Gladys gave her arm a shake. 'It's no good being frightened. If you're coming with us you've got to make yourself useful. Otherwise, you'd better go back home.'

'Frightened?' Diane said. 'Who said anything about being frightened? I wouldn't miss this for the world. Look at it! Look at that one!'

Gladys stared at her sister. Her face was reddened by the glow of the flares, her eyes glittering with excitement. She had been drying her hair in front of the fire when the siren sounded, and now it flew loose and tangled about her head. She looked as wild as a gypsy.

'What's got into you?' Gladys said. 'This is a raid – and it looks as if it's going to be a bad one. It's not a bonfire night party.'

'I know. I can't help it, I think it's marvellous. Look at the sky. Look at the colour. It's better than a sunset. Better than a rainbow. *Look*!'

Gladys turned her face to the sky. The flares were dropping thick and fast now, and in their light you could see that each was on its own parachute, drifting slowly down on the city. All around them were the silver searchlights, like a spider's web woven against the velvet darkness. And between the blossoming blood-red of the flares and the shimmering filigree of the lights could be seen the brilliant white sparkle of bursting shells from the anti-aircraft guns. She watched them, bemused. How many did they actually hit? Weren't they just firing at random, hoping to strike something up there in the limitless black sky? But even as she wondered she saw, here and there, a sudden spiralling orange flare as a plane was hit and corkscrewed downwards to the earth.

'Look at that,' Diane whispered, and as she spoke there was a tremendous explosion from somewhere deep in Portsmouth. The ground shook and a huge, billowing cloud of black and red and orange filled the sky.

Gladys was filled with sudden fury. For a moment or two she had been swayed into something very like wonder as she stared at the strange kaleidoscope of colour drifting above her. Now she was reminded forcibly of what it all meant. Her fear flooded back and she shook her sister's arm savagely.

'Marvellous? There's nothing *marvellous* about bombs and people getting killed. If you think it's so bloody marvellous, you'd better come with us and see what it really means. And do something to help. You'll soon see how *marvellous* it is. Well?' Another shake. 'What's it to be? Make up your mind, quick.'

'I'll come with you. I don't want to be home on my own.'

'You could go in with Mrs Budd –' Gladys began, but her

voice was drowned in the sudden burst of another explosion. The sky flared with searing white light and another great cloud of smoke and debris rose into the air, turning rapidly red as the flames began. It was followed immediately by a third, and then a fourth, and then it was as if all hell had been let loose on the city as bombs were hurled one after another into the tortured abyss, exploding on every side so that it seemed that there could be no escape.

The sky was brilliant now with the burnished glow of flames, the brightness of new fires added at every minute to those already burning. The stark white beams of the searchlights turned to red as the enemy showered bombs like deadly rain upon their target. And all the time, in a chorus of menace, the drone of the planes overhead sounded in their ears and the sharp rattle of the ack-ack guns gave a bitter commentary on the enemy's progress.

'Well, we don't have to worry about not finding our way.' They had paused, cowering back against a wall as the first explosions shook the ground, but now Gladys was off again, running. So far, it seemed that no bombs had been dropped on this part of Portsmouth but the streets were lit by the orange glow that was now spread over the whole sky. It seemed as if the supply was inexhaustible.

They reached the school which was serving as a First Aid post. It was in semi-darkness, lit only by a few hurricane lamps. Casualties were already coming in and the superintendent looked relieved to see Peggy and her daughters.

'Thank God you're here. This looks like being the big one. We think they've hit the electricity station, all the lights went out with the first bomb. Who's this?'

'My other daughter, Diane. She's come to give a hand.'

'We can do with all the help we can get. Can you put a bandage on? Go over to Mrs Jenkins, she'll tell you what to do.'

Diane nodded. Her strange exhilaration had passed and her face was pale, but she set her mouth firmly. She went over to one of the long tables which was piled high with bandages and dressings. A big, florid woman in a brown coat was already attending to a man with a bleeding head and Diane picked up a roll of bandage and held it out to her.

'She'll be all right,' Peggy said. 'Old mother Jenkins is a bit of a tartar but she won't give her a chance to get frightened. Now what d'you want us to do?'

'Get in the ambulance on stand-by. The way they're hammering us, it won't be long before you know where to go. Anyone not too badly hurt, take 'em to the nearest post, if it's too bad for us to deal with, get 'em to the hospital and then come back. Just do whatever you've got to do.' The superintendent looked up as another bomb whistled above their heads. 'They all sound so near. God knows what it's like when they're really on top of you.'

'They say you never hear the one that hits you,' Peggy remarked, intending to sound cheerful. But it didn't come out like that, somehow. She followed Gladys to the old van that had been converted to an ambulance. Bunks had been fitted inside so that it could carry several casualties, and there were benches for Peggy and less badly hurt people to sit on. A locker had been screwed inside the door and was filled with bandages and bottles of iodine and Dettol.

The explosions were coming thick and fast. Every second, the ground shook with fresh detonations and it seemed impossible that any part of the city could survive unscathed. Gladys sat in the driving seat of the ambulance, her fingers twitching with impatience. There must be people out there needing help.

A figure suddenly skidded into the playground and Gladys realised it was a boy on a bicycle. He was wearing Boy Scout uniform. His face was ruddy in the glow and there was a smear of black across his forehead. He gave her a quick, slightly wavering grin, and ran through the door, leaving it ajar. It hardly mattered about blackout now, she thought, with all this blazing light showing everything up. You could see to read a newspaper in this.

The super ran out and she leaned from the window. 'Where do they want us?'

'Palmerston Road. It's going up like a torch. The whole place is alight, there's buildings collapsed, people buried, it's chaos down there. They need all the help they can get.'

Gladys was already starting the engine. She jammed it into gear. 'Take this kid with you and drop him off at the ARP Control Centre.'

The scout scrambled into the back with Peggy, dragging his bike in after him. Gladys drove the van out through the wide gates and on to Copnor Road. Palmerston Road! That was right out at Southsea. Surely there must be people nearer at hand needing help. She sped through the reddened streets. They looked as if they were already running with blood, she thought. And, with a flash of wry gratitude, at least you could see where you were going . . . She had always been terrified of running someone over in the blackout.

The blitz was still going on. There were explosions on every side, and long before she was anywhere near Palmerston Road Gladys was flagged down by a warden and sent down a side street. She pulled the van into the side of the road and jumped out.

'Over here!' A bomb had fallen on a row of houses, demolishing at least two and leaving the others badly damaged. Two more were on fire and a crowd of people were trying to douse them with stirrup pumps and buckets of water. The flames were already flickering through the roof and, as Gladys watched, a huge orange tongue bellied out through a window and licked up the wall. The roof collapsed amidst a gush of fire.

'There's people in there!' Someone was screaming loudly near her. 'There's my Gramp and Granny in there. They wouldn't come down the shelter – they're burning alive in there.'

'Oh, my God.' Peggy was beside her. 'They'll never get them out . . .'

'Where's the fire engines? Where *are* they? Why don't they come, oh God, why don't they come?' The woman was in a frenzy. 'Gramp and Granny, they're in there, burning alive, they're burning alive, oh God, oh *God* . . .'

'Where's our Joan?' An elderly woman, her hair in curlers, staggered along the pavement. 'Where's our Joan? 'Ave you seen 'er?' She peered into Peggy's face. 'Our Joan, 'ave you seen 'er?'

'Gramp, Gramp . . .'

'Over 'ere.' A man tugged at Gladys's sleeve. 'You're the doctor, ain'tcher? Over 'ere, there's people buried, we can't get 'em out. They're hurt.'

'Our Joan, Joan . . .'

'Oh, Grampy, poor old Grampy . . . Why don't they come, why don't they come?'

'Over 'ere,' the man urged, pulling Gladys's arm.

'I'm not a doctor,' Gladys began, but he was dragging her across the road. She reached into the van as she passed and grabbed her First Aid satchel. She wasn't a doctor, but she had trained for this and would have to do what she could. But suppose there was nothing . . .? She thought of the other raids in which she had worked and bit her lip.

'Down 'ere, look, we've got a tunnel through. They're in the cellar.'

The man pushed her down and Gladys saw a huge pile of debris. Splintered wooden beams, shattered bricks, plaster, laths, all were stirred together and heaped high in what had once been someone's sitting room. Only half an hour ago, people had been sitting here, having a cup of tea, listening to the wireless. But there was no time to think of that. The warning had gone and they'd dived down the cellar steps. And now they were buried.

'We can 'ear someone calling,' the man said urgently. 'A kiddy. We've managed to get through so far but we don't dare go any further, it might bring the whole lot down. If you could just get through, see if she's hurt, like . . .'

Gladys stared in terror. I'm not a doctor, she wanted to say, I'm just supposed to drive an ambulance. I can't go down there. I won't know what to do. I might make it worse . . .

'Give me a torch,' she said, and lay down flat on her stomach.

The ground was covered with broken bricks and other rubbish. She could feel something sharp digging into her thigh. She pointed the torch down the hole and crawled forwards, praying that the structure would hold up, praying that no more bombs would fall.

'That's it, love. Keep goin' . . .'

I can't, she thought, I can't . . .

She was inside the rough tunnel now, pushing herself forwards with her toes, dragging herself with both hands. She clawed at rough stone, at bricks and mortar, feeling their sharp dust under her nails. Something sliced along her arm and she felt a sudden warmth on her skin. She was halfway along the tunnel now and the light of her torch showed a small, dark cellar just beneath her.

It was only two or three feet away, but it might as well have been a hundred miles. In the torchlight she could see the dankness of it, the water running down the walls, the blackness of the floor. One corner was piled with coal. She squirmed a little further, heard an ominous creak from above, felt the whole of one side of the tunnel shift a little. Oh God, if it collapsed now . . .

I can't be buried alive, Gladys thought, I can't. I'm not ready to die yet. I'm too young. I haven't done anything, I haven't had any life yet, I haven't even had a proper boy . . . Please God, don't let me be buried alive, not before I've done anything . . .

But other people got buried alive. Other people got blown up and burned to death and shot. And maybe most of them hadn't done anything either . . .

She found that her hands were working, as if they had decided to go ahead without the rest of her. They were pulling at the bricks, dragging at bits of wood. They were making the hole larger, carefully, almost tenderly. She watched as if they belonged to someone else and admired their sureness of touch. What a good job she'd brought them with her.

Blimey Glad, she thought, you're going barmy. Talking to your hands like that. You're going off your head and no wonder. It's enough to send anyone round the bend, down here.

She could hear voices. The man from above, encouraging her, urging her on. Her mother, asking anxiously if she were all right. And another voice. That of a small child, a girl probably, calling for help, calling for her mummy.

'It's all right, love,' she said, watching her hands as they scraped busily away at the debris. They didn't seem to care about getting hurt, about being grazed or tearing the fingernails Gladys had been so proud of. 'It's all right, I'm coming, I'll get you out.'

'Mummy,' the child said. 'Where's Mummy?'

'She's all right.' Gladys could see further into the cellar now. There was a bench along one wall, with three people sitting on it, unmoving. 'She'll be here soon.' Her hands went on scrabbling, lifting out bricks, scraping at the thick dust.

The ground was shaking with the unceasing roar of explosions as bombs continued to fall. With every one, a shuddering rumble went through the foundations of the houses and the walls shook. Part of the cellar roof fell in and a shower of brick dust pervaded the air, filling Gladys's lungs and prickling in her eyes. She coughed and retched, and her eyes streamed. She wanted to rub them but could not bend her arms back to do so and the irritation grew worse. I'm not going to get out of here, she thought. I'm going to die here, choked with brick dust, buried in muck and dirt.

But if she died, so would the little girl. And she'd done even less than Gladys. She hadn't even had a chance to grow up.

'What's your name, love? Tell me what your name is.' There was silence. The three figures were still motionless. She tried again, her voice shaking. 'What do they call you?'

'Ruth.'

Thank God. 'Ruth. That's a nice name. I've never known anyone called Ruth before.' The walls shook again and she heard a rumble as something heavy fell not far away. Very carefully, afraid that it might bring everything crashing about her ears, she pulled out a brick and dropped it into the cellar, then knew a different fear. 'That didn't hit you, did it? You're not sitting just underneath?'

'No. I'm in the corner. I can't get out.' A querulous note entered the voice. 'Why doesn't Mummy come and get me out?'

'I expect she's got caught somewhere else. She'll come as soon as she can.' Gladys pulled out another brick. The hole was getting wider. 'I'll come and get you, Ruth, and then we can find Mummy.'

'But I can *see* her. She's sitting there, just *looking* at me.' The voice began to rise in fear. 'Why doesn't she say something? Why doesn't she *come*?'

Gladys looked at the three on the bench. She could see them more clearly now. They were slumped against the wall, their bodies toppled together.

Don't let them be dead, she prayed. Oh God, please don't let them be dead . . .

'How're you doing, love?' She became aware of voices calling down the tunnel. For a moment or two, she had been conscious of nothing but the cellar, nobody but herself and Ruth and the three silent bodies. She answered briefly, almost irritably.

'I'm all right. I'm getting into the cellar now.' She had made the hole wide enough to scramble through. She pushed her head and shoulders into it and found herself about two feet above the cellar floor. She squirmed a little further, reached down with both hands and took the weight of her body, pushing with her feet, clawing with her hands. I'm going to bring the whole lot down with me, she thought, hearing the creaks and crashes, feeling the shudder of each new explosion. I'm going to bring down the whole bloody lot.

The edge of the tunnel gave way and she fell forwards on to the floor. It was littered with debris, and she lay still for a moment, her whole body shrieking in protest. But there was no time for pain. Within less than a minute, she was pulling herself together, looking around for the little girl.

'Oh, *Ruth* . . .'

The child was about eight or nine years old, and she was almost completely covered in dust, plaster, coal and bricks. From her shoulders down, she had been buried as the corner of the cellar had collapsed. Her face was scratched and smeared with blood, her eyes wide and frightened. She stared at Gladys and her mouth trembled.

'It's all right, love,' Gladys said quickly. 'We'll have you out of there in no time.' She looked round at the other three occupants of the cellar, still huddled together as if fast asleep.

'I can't breathe properly,' the little girl said. 'There's all bricks and stuff on me.'

'I know. I'll get it off.'

'Mummy . . .'

Gladys hesitated. The girl was frightened, in pain and might be hurt. The debris that had fallen on top of her was crushing her. She had to be released. But the others might need help even more badly. They might be unconscious, bleeding to death. There were pools of dark liquid at their feet. It was impossible to tell whether it was water or blood.

She looked up at the mouth of the tunnel. I can't do this on my own, she thought. I need help.

Another crash shook the little cellar and she dropped her torch. It went out and the hole was plunged into darkness. The little girl screamed and Gladys gasped with fright and groped frantically for the torch. If the house came down on top of them now . . . But the walls held and after a moment her fingers found the torch and pressed the switch. The beam of light shone out again and she sighed with relief.

'Stay still, Ruthie.' As if the poor little mite could do anything else! 'I'm just going to look at the others. Is – is this your mummy?'

The child nodded. Her eyes were enormous. Gladys crawled across the floor, the thin liquid mud like ice about her legs. She peered at the three huddled bodies. An old man – Ruth's grandfather? – and two women. Their eyes were open, fixed and staring.

Without any hope, she felt the limp wrists and touched the lolling necks. No pulses. No sign of breathing. No heartbeat.

She crawled back to the child. Voices were calling down the narrow shaft and she shouted back. 'The little girl's half buried. I'm going to try to get her out. The others . . .' Her voice trembled and failed. How could you yell the news that a child's family were dead, when she was listening and watching you with those huge, terrified eyes?

'It's all right, Ruthie.' How could she sound so calm? Inside, her heart was like thunder and her nerves were jumping like jags of lightning. Every few moments there was another crash, sometimes at a distance, sometimes almost overhead. The earth trembled and the walls of the cellar shook.

'It's all right,' she said again, and she lifted one hand to the child's head and stroked the matted hair. 'It's all right. We'll have you out of here soon. You'll be safe . . .'

Over the Hill, Betty and Dennis heard the noise and looked from the farmhouse windows to see the glow. Yvonne had gone home for the weekend and Erica was in bed with a heavy cold, but Mr and Mrs Spencer joined them, staring out at the red and orange sky. They could hear the planes roaming overhead, see the web of the searchlights, the flash of ack-ack. They could hear the dull thud-thud-thud of the explosions, their eyes were scorched by the searing blaze of the fires.

'The whole bloody city's in flames,' Jack Spencer said, his voice thick and slow with horror. 'The whole bloody city's going up in smoke . . .'

Betty covered her face with her hands, and Dennis put his arms around her. 'Oh, Mum,' she whispered. 'Dad . . . What's happening to them? And our Livvy, she's going to have a baby. Oh God, what's happening to them?'

'Ssh, ssh,' Dennis said, holding her close. 'They'll be all right. They've got a shelter, haven't they? They'll have gone into that. They'll be safe.'

'They might not. They might be out somewhere. Dad could be at work, on the ferry. Livvy might – Mum might –' She shook her head, staring at the flame-lit sky. Dennis hugged her close and looked helplessly at Mrs Spencer.

'Come on downstairs, love,' the farmer's wife said briskly, though her own voice was trembling too. 'We'll make some cocoa. It don't do no good, standing here watching it. There's nothing we can do. Come with me.'

Betty shook her head, her eyes fixed in terrible fascination on the glowing sky. Gently, Dennis urged her towards the stairs. 'Go on, darling. Mrs Spencer's right. We can't do anything to help by standing here on the landing getting cold.'

Again Betty shook her head, but this time she allowed them to shepherd her down the stairs. In the kitchen, she sat at the big table in one of the settles while Mrs Spencer moved the kettle on to the hottest part of the range to bring it to the boil, and busied herself spooning cocoa into large cups. She mixed it with sugar and a little milk, then filled the cups with boiling water and set one in front of Betty.

'There. That'll warm you up. You're shivering, girl, come a bit nearer the fire. I'll take one up to Erica too, she never got warm all day.'

Betty shook her head. 'I'm not cold.'

'It's shock,' Mrs Spencer said to Dennis. 'Look at her shivering there. And no wonder, poor duck, seeing that out there and thinking of her mum and dad.'

Dennis pushed Betty's cup a little nearer to her. 'Drink your cocoa, sweetheart. It'll do you good.'

'Drop of brandy in it'll do her more good,' Mr Spencer said suddenly and went to the cupboard in the corner. He brought over the bottle, kept for 'medicinal purposes' and poured a generous measure into Betty's cup. 'Do us all good,' he added, treating each cup the same.

Dennis lifted Betty's cup to her lips. 'Come on, darling. It'll warm you up.'

'I'm not cold. I'm not cold. It's Mum who's cold, down there in that shelter. And Dad, on the ferry. And Yvonne, at Rudmore. Oh, what's happening to them?' She lifted her head, looking at them with desperate eyes. 'The whole of Pompey's burning, you can see it. They're being burnt alive, all of them, and me not there. I ought to be there, with them. I shouldn't never have come out here to the farm. Dad never wanted me to.' The words poured from her in a torrent, as the tears streamed down her cheeks. 'He always said I ought to stay at home. Graham did too. None of them wanted me to come out here, and now they're all getting bombed and burnt and killed and I'm – I'm *safe*. And I *shouldn't* be!'

'Betty, Betty. You're talking crazy. D'you think they'd *want* you to be bombed?' Dennis shook her shoulders gently. 'They must be thankful you're safe. They must be glad you came here. They didn't want you to stay at home just so you could be in danger, you know they didn't.'

'Dennis is right,' Mrs Spencer said, coming back down the stairs. 'Why, your mum's probably thanking God on her bended knees at this very moment, knowing no harm's going to come to you. And none's coming to them either,' she added staunchly. 'They'll have got into their shelters at the first peep of the warning, and there they'll stop till the All-Clear. And as soon as one of them can get out to the phone box, they'll be ringing us up to let you know they're all all right, you see if they don't.'

Betty sniffed and nodded. She sipped her cocoa and choked a little. Mrs Spencer did the same and wiped her eyes, looking at her husband.

'You put enough brandy in there to get a regiment drunk! Now, let's get the cards out and have a game of something. It's not a bit of use sitting here worrying ourselves silly, but I can see none of us is going to get any sleep till it's over. And we're not going to sit up all night waiting for a phone call either. There's cows to be seen to in the morning, they won't stop making milk just because Hitler decides to call.'

'Cards!' Betty exclaimed with a flash of hysteria. 'It's always cards. Whenever something happens that shouldn't, we get out the cards. Your boy wants to make love to you, the Germans send their bombers over and set fire to everyone you love, and what do we do? We play cards!'

She turned again into Dennis's arms and buried her face against his chest. He held her close, his hands moving slowly over her shoulders, his voice murmuring in her ear, and after a while her sobs diminished and she lifted her face.

'I'm sorry,' she said shakily. 'I know you're right. Crying doesn't help anyone. Maybe a game of cards would be the best thing.'

She thought of the great historical figures she had been told about at school – Drake, playing bowls on Plymouth Hoe as the Spanish Armada sailed up the Channel. Nero, fiddling while Rome burned.

Perhaps it wasn't so very different, playing cards.

'Why doesn't Mummy speak to me?' The little girl's eyes were fixed on the huddled bodies on the other side of the cellar, only a few feet away. 'Why won't she wake up?'

'She's been hurt, love.' Gladys worked steadily, pulling the rubbish away from the little body. There was no point in hiding the truth. The child would have to know, and sooner rather than later. But Gladys could not quite bring herself to break it so baldly. 'We'll get her to hospital as soon as we've got you out. She won't mind waiting.' She would never mind waiting again. 'Don't worry, Ruthie. Everything's going to be all right.'

She heard her own words with a bitter cynicism. Everything was not going to be all right. It would never again be 'all right' for this little scrap for, no matter what her life might become, she would never be able to escape from the memory of this dreadful night, and the knowledge that her mother had been killed before her eyes. She would never lose the picture of that staring face with the blood congealing to a black scab on the white skin. If she lived to be a hundred, it would still be with her. She would take it with her to her own death.

Everything was very far from 'all right'.

CHAPTER TWENTY-TWO

There was no time for grief. No time for pain. As one casualty was freed from the smoking, dust-clouded ruins, so a hundred more were in desperate need. As one fire was doused, so another ten broke out.

And the water was never in the right place. Fractured water mains gushed uselessly in the roads and the fire brigade could do nothing but simply let the fires burn until the mains could be hastily repaired and water pumped through.

Sometimes the flames were put out by local firewatchers and neighbours. As soon as the bombs began to fall, people rushed out of their shelters and on to the streets, ready at the risk of their lives to give whatever help might be needed. With buckets of earth and sand, with pumps attached to their own kitchen taps, with blankets and old mats, heedless of shrapnel raining about them, they donned tin hats and battled together to save their city. As buildings crumbled and fell, they fought to tear away the rubble and release those who had been buried.

In all too many cases, there was nothing to find but a few bloody fragments. But in others, there were people, injured but alive, waiting to be released and some of them were even able to joke with their rescuers.

'I'm really sorry about this,' one young man, buried almost to his neck, whispered faintly to Gladys. 'I bet you were going out with your boyfriend tonight, weren't you?'

'Haven't got one,' she said cheerfully, scraping mud away from his mouth. It would be a nice smile when he got himself cleaned up a bit. 'So I wasn't going anywhere, see? Glad to have something to do.'

'No boyfriend? A pretty girl like you?' His voice was slurred, almost as if he were drunk, but Gladys knew that it was really the effect of the morphia injection the young woman doctor had just given him. 'Well, why don't we make a date? A night at the flicks, how would that suit you?' His voice faded, as though speaking was becoming too much of an effort, as if he needed all his energy just to keep breathing.

'It'd do me fine.' She looked at him with pity. A few moments ago, before the injection, his face had been contorted with agony, his voice a thin scream. Goodness only knew what injuries he had sustained when the building had crashed about him. They would find out soon enough, but the doctor had shaken her head. Some of them die as soon as the weight's taken off them, she'd said, and Gladys knew that she half expected it to happen to this boy.

'You can take me out the first day you get out of hospital,' she said. 'And don't think you can get out of it, I'm the one who'll be driving you there, so I'll know just what ward you're in and everything.' That's if you ever get that far, she thought, and felt the tears come to her eyes.

No time for crying. Casualties were being loaded into her ambulance all the time and she must leave this boy for others to dig out, and drive to the hospital again. By now, the Royal had been bombed and the Eye and Ear, their own patients being rescued by the nurses and doctors. That meant a long drive through the streets and over Portsbridge to the Queen Alexandra, right out at Cosham and on the flanks of Portsdown Hill. And suppose the bridge got bombed? Apart from the railway line, it was Portsmouth's only link with the mainland.

Once at the hospital Gladys saw nurses, some of them hardly any older than her sister Diane, dealing frantically with one patient after another. Staunching blood, cleaning off the incredible dirt that flying dust and grit had poured into every wound, bandaging, splinting broken limbs . . . And all by the light of hurricane lamps, emergency lighting or the red glare of fire which permeated every street in the city that night and would burn for ever in the memories of its people.

*

After two hours of consistent bombing, the sky fell silent and the bombers seemed to depart. People who had spent the time cowering in their shelters crept out and gazed on the destruction of their homes.

'Stay down in the shelter, Jess,' Frank ordered. 'The All-Clear's not gone yet.'

Frank and Ted had arrived home half an hour after the raid had begun. Running along the streets, ignoring the harried bellows of wardens who were as scared as the rest of the populace, they had dived into their shelters to comfort their wives, and to reassure themselves that their families were safe, and then had strapped on their helmets and taken up their own firewatching duties. And firewatching was the right word for it tonight, Frank thought, standing up on top of his own Anderson, staring at the blazing sky. There was nothing to watch *but* fire. God knew what was burning down there, it might be easier to say what *wasn't* burning. And although most of it couldn't be nearer than Commercial Road, you could smell it from here, that all too familiar stench of burning dust, of oil and soot, of metal and stone – could stone burn? – of bricks and mortar and roasting flesh. The smell of death.

'The whole place is going up,' he said in awe. 'There's not going to be anything left . . .'

Along the street, Ted was saying much the same to Annie and Olive. But Olive had ignored his injunction to stay under cover. She scrambled out and stood beside him, a tin helmet jammed over her head, gazing in horror at the billowing clouds of black smoke, their swirling bellies lit with orange flame. Unconsciously, her hands moved over her stomach in the age-old gesture of a pregnant mother protecting her unborn young, and the movement reminded her of Kathy Simmons.

'I'll just pop over and see if she's all right,' she said, turning swiftly. Her father grabbed for her arm, but caught only her sleeve and Olive darted up the garden path. 'I won't be long.'

'Livvy! Come back, the All-Clear's not gone, they could be back any minute, they could be up there now.' There was too much noise from the city to be able to tell if the planes were still above. The *crump* of explosions was still going on, if not bombs, it could be gas-mains, oil tanks, anything. Cars could explode, buses, lorries, anything with oil or petrol, anything with pressure, could go off. Smoke itself made a noise as it billowed about, carrying with it the crackle of flames, the rush of air in a storm of its own making. In such conditions, fire could spread from one end of the city to the other in a matter of minutes, it wasn't safe anywhere. 'Livvy!' he shouted again. 'Livvy! Come back, for God's sake, come back!'

But she was gone, running away from him down the bright-lit street, and he could only stare helplessly after her.

It took Olive no more than two minutes to reach Kathy Simmons' back garden and dive into the damp little shelter. She found her friend as she had expected, huddled in the dark on a flimsy camp bed, cradling her baby against her, with a little girl crouching against her on either side.

'Kathy! Kath, are you all right? I came as soon as I could –'

'Olive? Oh, Olive, is that you?' The young mother reached out a hand. 'Oh God, I've been so frightened. What's been happening out there? It sounds as though the whole of Portsmouth's going sky high.'

'It looks like it too,' Olive said soberly. 'Look.' She held back the old curtain Kathy used as a door. 'Never mind the lamp. That little bit of light won't show anyone the way in this lot.'

Kathy stared out at the crimson sky. 'What is it?'

'What d'you think? Fire. Fires all over Pompey.' Olive's voice shook and she let the curtain fall again. 'They've been dropping flares, bombs, incendiaries, God knows what, and Dad reckons they've not stopped yet. Just gone home for another lot, he says. The All-Clear's not gone and he don't reckon it will. I just slipped over while there's a lull.' She turned the lamp up and studied her friend's face. 'You look done in, Kath. Have you got anything to eat or drink down here?'

Kathy shook her head. 'I had a flask, but the girls needed some cocoa. And I have to save some water for Thomas. Poor little mite, he's slept through it all, can you believe that?' They looked down at the peacefully slumbering baby. One fist was curled like a bud under his chin, and his lashes lay like dark fans on his creamy cheeks. Olive touched him gently with the tip of her finger and again laid her other hand over her stomach. Soon, her own baby would quicken and she would feel its tiny feet pressing against the walls of her womb. A boy like Derek, or a girl like herself? It didn't matter. All that mattered was that it should be born safe and kept safe, away from bombs, away from war and terror.

'I wish I'd brought you something,' she said. 'We've got two or three flasks, we could've spared you one. Or you could come over to us.' Her voice brightened. 'Why don't you do that, Kath? Come over to us and stop the rest of the night. It'd be better for you to be with company, and better for the girls too. We could have a sing-song like they do in the big shelters.'

Kathy hesitated, then shook her head. 'There's not enough room. It's cramped enough as it is.'

'Don't be daft. There's only Mum and me, and Dad when he pops in for a few minutes off firewatching. We'll keep each other warm.' The spatter of ack-ack fire broke into her words. 'It looks as if they might be coming again. Come on, Kath.'

Kathy bit her lip and looked at the girls. They were pale and frightened. Olive watched her, seeing the thoughts chase each other across her face. *Perhaps it would be best. Better for the children. And better for me.* She saw Kathy make up her mind, as clearly as if a light had been switched on, and gripped her hand.

'You are coming, aren't you? Only I think we ought to be quick.'

'Yes. I'm coming. Only – will you take the girls first? I just want to pop indoors and boil a kettle to fill up the flask again. It won't take more'n a minute. I'll come across straightaway then.'

Olive looked at her doubtfully. 'D'you think you ought to? Go indoors, I mean? Suppose they come back . . .?'

'I'll be quick as a flash,' Kathy promised. She drew back the curtain and looked out. 'It's quiet enough now, look. And they've never dropped anything round these streets yet . . .'

They never had. And Kathy had been bombed once, and

ought to have been immune from further disaster. After all, they said lightning never struck twice in the same place, didn't they?

But Kathy wasn't in the same place. And the Luftwaffe did not follow the rules laid down for lightning. The bomb fell in the gardens of October Street, close to the shelter where she had been taking cover. It fractured the gas main at the moment when Kathy had just lit a match in the kitchen to boil her kettle. The gas gushed out and exploded, throwing her and the baby son she had wanted so much clear through the shattering wall.

Olive and the girls were halfway back to the turret house at the end of March Street when it happened. They too were knocked over by the blast, and when Ted Chapman came racing across to help them, found to their dismay that every stitch of clothing was ripped from their bodies. The girls scrambled up, crying and terrified, shuddering with the sudden rush of cold air on their skin. But Olive lay still, racked with sudden agony, and the blood spread in a pool around her body.

There was not a bruise on her body. The blast had torn away her clothes as cleanly as if she had taken them off herself, yet she was quite unhurt.

But there would be no baby for her in July. No baby son who resembled Derek, no daughter who looked like her.

And for Kathy Simmons, no babies ever again. Nothing, ever again.

Twice on that terrible night, the raiders returned. For seven hours they bombarded Portsmouth without relief, until it seemed that the city must have been totally destroyed by their frenzy. And when daylight finally came, to show what could not be seen even by the light of the flames which had consumed so much, so greedily, during the hours of darkness, it revealed just what havoc had been wrought.

The main shopping centres – Palmerston Road, which Gladys had never reached, Commercial Road and King's Road – lay in ruins. At Southsea, Handley's and Knight &

Lee's, two of the grandest department stores in the city, were burned, and other buildings dynamited to prevent the flames from spreading. In Commercial Road, the Landport Drapery Bazaar, which was not a bazaar at all but another large department store, was burned down and Woolworths, which had only just been rebuilt after the previous year's fire, C & A and the Royal Sailor's Rest destroyed. At Fratton the big Co-op was little more than a crater.

Six churches and the Salvation Army Citadel had been destroyed. The Eye and Ear Hospital had gone, so had part of the Royal. Clarence Pier, at Southsea, had been reduced to rubble. Gone too were three more cinemas, and the Hippodrome, where Annie and Ted had gone to laugh at Elsie and Doris Waters, was in tatters.

Houses had been smashed by the street, craters left gaping in roadways, roofs torn off and walls blasted away. In one front bedroom, the passer-by could see nothing but destruction, yet still hear the tick of an alarm clock balanced precariously on the remains of a mantelpiece. In another, the ceiling had collapsed on a double bed, killing the occupants who had refused to go to the shelter, but leaving the cot containing their baby son unscathed. In a third, there was no damage at all, only a wall removed as neatly as if it were the front of a doll's house, lifted away for display.

But worst of all for the city and its pride, was the destruction of the Guildhall, that great and gracious building so dear and familiar to them all. Standing at the edge of its square at the end of Commercial Road, it had symbolised the heart of Portsmouth; the deep tones of its bell, ringing out the hours before it was silenced by war, had echoed in the breast of every man and woman who had lived with its sound. And now the bell tower was ablaze, burning like a great torch as if in defiance of the enemy, with flames surging into the sky like crimson plumage. The copper plates of the cupola shimmered in the heat and fell away, the flames spread through the interior and the great hall where only two days earlier a thousand children had eaten jelly and marched to the tune of *There'll Always Be an England* was destroyed for ever. The organ would never play again.

'I don't want to see anything like that again, ever,' Peggy Shaw said to Jess next afternoon. She and Gladys had arrived home late in the morning, filthy and dog-tired. They had had a quick wash and then, weary as she was, Gladys had gone off to Commercial Road to report for work at the ruined shop. Diane too had come back exhausted, her brief exhilaration crushed by a night at the First Aid post. But she had not given way, Mrs Jenkins had remarked to Peggy as they left. She'd been a real help and would be welcome any time to give a hand.

'Our Glad's been a real heroine,' Peggy went on. 'Took her an hour to get that kiddy out from the cellar, and there was bombs falling round our heads all the time. But she never give way. The little un wouldn't hardly let her go when they brought her up. Broken leg, she had, poor little mite, scratched and grazed all over, and her mum killed in front of her eyes. We put her straight in the ambulance and Glad drove round to the Royal. I didn't think she ought to, she was shaking like a leaf when she come up, but she wouldn't hear of letting someone else take the van. That's my ambulance, she said, and I'm responsible for it. So they had to let her do it.'

'She's a good girl. They both are.' That hadn't always been Jess's opinion, privately, she'd thought Peggy a bit too lax with her daughters, though Bert was strict enough. But you couldn't complain about youngsters who'd worked like Gladys and Diane had, even if they were a bit flighty. 'Did she go on driving after that?'

Peggy rolled her eyes. 'Jess, we went everywhere with that van last night! You didn't have to ask where to go – you just left the hospital and there was another street afire or someone flagging you down for help. It was bedlam. I thought we were going to have an accident, I did straight, the times we nearly crashed into fire engines and such. They had the lot there, City firemen, auxiliaries, soldiers, sailors, Marines. There must've been thousands of fires burning. And half the time, they had no water, the water mains were hit, see. What could they do?'

Jess knew all too well that the water mains had been hit. Parts of the city were still cut off, and even those who still had some were asked to be extra sparing with it. And there was still no electricity. When darkness fell, you had to use candles, and there weren't all that many of them, either. What with the coal shortage and problems with the gas supply as well, there was precious little comfort to be had anywhere this bitter January.

'*I don't want to see anything like that ever again . . .*'

She and thousands of others echoed Peggy's words that morning, as they stared at the ruins of their city, as they picked disconsolately through the rubble to salvage what few belongings they could, as they trudged away along the littered streets carrying a few pathetic bundles to find shelter with friends and relatives, or in the emergency centres that had been set up by the council.

What was left for them, now that so much had been taken away? For some, there was still a family; others had lost everyone they loved. For some, there was still a job; others had lost even that. For some, there was comfort; for others, nothing but despair.

The *Evening News* printed a special edition, with a message from the Lord Mayor set squarely in its front page. He himself had been bombed out, for he had moved into the Guildhall some months previously, declaring that since he spent all his waking hours there he might as well be on hand at night as well. He had left the building only minutes before the incendiaries struck. Now he paid tribute to the people of his city.

'*At last the blow has fallen. Our proud City has been hit and hit very hard by the enemy. Our Guildhall and many of our cherished buildings now lie a heap of smoking ruins . . . We are bruised but we are not daunted . . . we shall persevere with an unflagging spirit to a decisive victory . . .*'

'It's as good as Churchill,' Jess said, when Frank read it out to her. 'It gives people heart when they read things like that. And they need it, too.' Her eyes filled with tears. 'Poor Kathy Simmons. And those two poor little girls. I wonder what'll happen to them now, with no mother and their father away at sea.'

'They've had a bad time of it,' he agreed. But you know, they shouldn't ever have been here. They ought all to have been evacuated, the lot of 'em. And –'

'I know what you're going to say,' she interrupted. 'So should I and Rose and the baby. Well, maybe we *should*. But how can we? You need me here to look after you, you know that. And I couldn't bear to think of being away, not knowing what was happening to you. Annie said she tried to telephone to Betty this morning but she couldn't get through, if there are any phones working, the authorities have got 'em all. She sent a telegram instead, but that poor girl must have been going through agonies wondering how we all were. And if you want Rose to go back, you can be the one to tell her, *I'm* not going to.'

Frank sighed and tightened his lips but he knew there was no point in further argument. They'd had all this out before. Jess saw her duty plainly as being by his side, and beyond that, she *wanted* to be here. She really had been miserable when she'd gone away at the beginning of the war.

'Well, if you can stand stopping here after last night, you can stand anything,' he said. 'And don't think I don't appreciate it, Jess. I want you here, I won't deny it, but I wouldn't make you stop if you didn't want to. And talking of Annie, how's Olive?'

Jess pulled down the corners of her mouth.

'Well enough, considering. She's really cut up about losing the baby. Derek's not been told yet, he's still out helping with demolition and so on. She'll be better when he can be with her.' She sighed. 'I feel sorry for her, but like Annie says, it could be a blessing in disguise. At least the poor little mite won't be blown to bits like little Thomas Simmons.'

Blown to bits, she thought. Babies in their mothers' arms, blown to bits.

CHAPTER TWENTY-THREE

Betty opened her telegram with shaking fingers. The disruption of Portsmouth had delayed it, so that it was past afternoon milking when it finally arrived. She stared at the orange envelope with dread.

'Shall I open it for you?' Dennis asked, but she shook her head.

'I've got to do it myself.'

Her hand shook so much that the paper tore half across before she could get it out of the envelope. Dennis watched her anxiously. Her face was as white as the milk she had just squeezed from the udders, and her lips quivered. Suddenly, her face distorted, her mouth squaring like a child's, and she dropped the telegram and swayed. He caught her just before she fell.

'Betty, what's happened?'

She shook her head. The tears were pouring down her cheeks and she was making a strange, choking sound, half laughing, half crying. She let the telegram fall and it fluttered to the ground as she clung to his shoulders with both hands, beating her forehead against his chest. He gathered her close, holding her hard, rocking her and making soft little soothing sounds.

'Tell me, Betty. Tell me. What's happened?' His own voice trembled. 'Who – who's gone? Is it your mum? Your dad? Your –'

'No! No! It's none of them – none.' She gripped his collar and leaned back in his arms, gazing up at him. 'They're all right, that's what it says, all of them, Mum, Dad, Livvy,

Auntie Jess, Uncle Frank, everyone.' A sudden fear darkened her eyes and sounded sharply in her voice. 'That *is* what it says, isn't it? I haven't read it wrong?'

Dennis loosened his arms and bent to retrieve the scrap of paper. He stared at the hastily-printed words. *All safe. Love, Mum, Dad, Livvy.* He took a deep breath of relief and caught her close again.

'No, sweetheart, you haven't read it wrong. They're all right. And you'll find out any more there is to know soon enough. So now you can stop worrying and give me a hand mucking out these cows. They'll be up to their udders in it soon, and *that* won't make the milk taste very good, now will it!'

Betty laughed shakily and picked up her fork. 'I'm sorry, Dennis,' she said. 'I've been a real misery today, I know.'

'You haven't been a misery at all. You've been worried stiff, and quite right too. Anyone'd be worried about their family, after watching the fires they had in Pompey all night long.' He glanced towards the door of the byre. The smoke had been visible all day, still shot through with red and gold. 'I hope Yvonne's all right too.'

'Oh, Dennis!' Betty stopped raking and stared at him in dismay. 'I forgot all about poor Yvonne. Oh, how could I be so selfish!'

'And you're not selfish either. Yvonne's your friend, but your family's your family.' He worked for a few minutes in silence and then said, 'There's something I ought to tell you. And now that you know your family's all right . . .'

'What?' She stared at him in sudden terror. 'Dennis, what is it?'

'It's all right,' he said. 'Nothing to be scared of. It's just that, well, I've decided I can't go on working on the farm. I've got to do something more.'

Betty felt the blood drain from her face.

'You're joining up.'

He shook his head. 'Not exactly. Well, in a way. I'm going to join the Pioneer Corps.'

'But that's the Army! You'll have to kill people.'

'No. I'll be a non-combatant. I won't be killing anyone. I

won't be fighting at all.'

She looked at him. There was something more, she could see it in his face. But at the moment, all she could think of was that he would be leaving the farm.

'You're going away,' she said in a hopeless voice, and he nodded.

'I'm sorry, Betty. I don't want to leave you. I don't want to leave the farm and Mr and Mrs Spencer. It's been like a home to me.' He grinned suddenly. 'I don't even want to leave these cows, bless 'em! But it's something I've been thinking about for a long time. And after last night . . .' He moved restlessly. 'I know what people like Erica think of me, and I don't really mind about that. There's enough like you and the Spencers who can see that a man has to be able to think and decide these things for himself.'

'It's a pity there's not more of them on the City Council,' Betty said with a flash of spirit. 'I mean, they're going right against the Government aren't they, turning you off your job. They're not supposed to do that.'

'No, they're not. But there's not much I can do about that, not without making a lot of fuss.' He paused and she knew that he was trying to decide how to tell her the rest of his decision. Her heart sank.

'You're going to tell me it's all over between us, aren't you? It was good while it lasted –' her voice trembled '– but once you've gone away . . . Don't tell me that, please don't tell me that . . . I'll wait for you.' She remembered Graham, furious because she wouldn't marry him. 'I'll do whatever you want . . .'

'But of course I'm not going to tell you that,' Dennis said, staring at her in amazement. He saw her tears and crossed the space between them with two long strides, pulling her roughly into his arms. 'Betty, my darling, I'll never tell you that, never. I love you. I don't want to leave you, not for a minute. But I can't stay here with an easy conscience. I've got to do something more to help, you see that, don't you?'

She nodded speechlessly, her tears soaking his shirt. 'But you said you never would, you wouldn't even make uniforms in prison, and now you're going in the Army –'

'Non-combatant,' he said quietly. 'I won't fight. I won't even help by making it easier for others to fight. But I will help *save* lives. I'm going to be in the bomb disposal squad.'

There was a moment of silence. The cows shifted in their stalls. Somewhere out in the yard, Jonas called to his dog. In the shed next door the hens burst into noisy, excited clucking as Mrs Spencer fed them.

'The bomb disposal squad?' Betty repeated slowly. 'But that's *dangerous*.' Dennis grinned wryly. 'War *is* dangerous. Think of last night.'

'I know, but that, Dennis, it means defusing unexploded bombs, doesn't it? Poking about looking for buried mines? Going down in craters and making sure there's nothing left to go off? It's more dangerous than *anything*.'

'Not really. There's plenty of other people –'

'I'm not interested in *them*!' she cried. 'I'm interested in you. *You're* the one who's going to be taking unexploded bombs to bits to stop them going off. Dennis, you'll be killed, I know you will. You only have to *touch* some of these bombs – and mines, they go off as soon as someone lays a finger on them. I've seen them on the news at the pictures. And in papers.'

'But the ones I'll be dealing with will be the ones that haven't gone off so easily. They're duds. Look, a bomb that falls hundreds of feet from an aeroplane and hits the ground and doesn't explode isn't going to go off just because I touch it with one finger, is it?'

'Isn't it?' she retorted. 'Don't treat me like a kid, Dennis. I'm not a fool. Bombs do go off after they've fallen. Some of them are *time* bombs – they're not meant to go off straight-away. You can't tell me you won't be taking risks.'

He shrugged. 'A few, yes. Not that many. I'm not treating you like a fool, Betty. It's honestly not that dangerous. Not if you know what you're doing.'

'And do you know what you're doing?'

'No, not yet, but I will. I'll be trained. And I've always been good with mechanical things. One of the first things I remember my dad being cross with me about was when I took his alarm clock to bits to see how it worked.' He laughed. 'I

368

put it together again, but I had two or three bits left over that I didn't tell him about, and it never worked properly after that.'

'And is that supposed to cheer me up?' Betty said. 'How d'you think I'm going to feel when they come and tell me there's only two or three bits of you left over?' Her face crumpled and she clung to him again. 'Dennis, please don't go. Please stay here with me. Or do something else, something that's not so dangerous. Bomb disposal – you couldn't have picked anything worse!'

'Perhaps that's why I'm doing it,' he said slowly. 'Perhaps I want to show people that COs aren't a bunch of lily-livered cowards. The trouble is, most of the jobs they give us are too safe. They make us look like skivers, hiding away on farms, or just carrying on with our peace-time jobs. It's no wonder people turn their noses up. But I can't do it any longer,' he exclaimed with sudden passion. 'I can't stay here, looking out of windows while cities burn and people get killed. I want to be in there, helping save lives that should never be in danger. I won't fight, I won't kill, but I won't stand by and see other people killed when I could be doing something to prevent it.'

He was silent for a moment, then he said quietly, 'You're right, Betty. It is dangerous, and I shouldn't pretend it's not, especially to you. If those bombs weren't expected to go off, I wouldn't be bothered about them. If they were that safe, they could be left there or picked up by anyone who happened to be passing. But they're not. They can explode. And that's why I want to work with them, so that I take the same risks as everyone else.' He looked gravely down into her face. 'I love you, Betty. That's why there's got to be truth between us. It will be dangerous, but I've got to do it. Can you understand that?'

She met his eyes. During the past few weeks, as their love had ripened and their understanding deepened, she had come to respect Dennis's conscience and beliefs. They were not the same as hers, though she felt that with time they might come to mean more to her than the values she had grown up with. But she knew that he had already paid dearly enough to hold them. He had lost his job and many of his friends. He had served in prison. He was now working on hard and menial tasks on a farm. All these prices had been paid with cheerfulness and honesty. He had never shirked a task, but neither had he ever compromised his principles.

Now his conscience was taking him further. It would take him right to the front line, wherever that might be, into dangers and perils as extreme as any faced by a fighting man. It could take him to his death.

'Yes,' she said quietly. 'I understand.' But even while her mind said yes, she felt her heart cry out against it and she wanted to beg him to stay.

But she knew she could not say the words. She could not have said them to Graham, to Bob Shaw, to Derek Harker or her brother Colin. Nor could any woman say them to the man she loved, for this was war and the country had first hold on its men and could take them from their hearths and homes, sending them far across the world to fight battles they did not understand and did not want. They could not choose to stay at home.

And even for Dennis and those like him, who claimed the right to set conscience above the requirements of the country, there was no choice. For the demands of such a conscience were greater even than the demands of the heart, and would drive many of them into greater peril even than those who were prepared to fight. For they could not accept 'safety' and looked instead for ways to use their own brand of courage in the service of their fellow men.

Some, Betty knew, had become stretcher-bearers, ready to go unarmed into the front line of the battlefield. Some had joined the Red Cross or went with the Friends' own field hospitals to those same areas of conflict. And some, like Dennis, went to the very heart of danger and took their lives in their hands as many times a day as it was asked of them.

She held him closely and let her tears run. He was driven by something too powerful for her to do more than glimpse. But that power contained also his love for her, and this she could understand, for her love matched his own, and she would send it with him wherever he might go.

They stood close in the warmth of the cattle byre where they had first fallen in love, and she felt the cold, black shadow of war drift slowly around them.

The work of recovery and rebuilding started at once.

Water had been the biggest problem. With nearly three thousand fires burning in a single night, the fire services had been helped by the Navy, the military and by ordinary civilians, trained and untrained, who worked throughout the bombing to try to keep the flames under control.

But the water supply had never been intended for such a conflagration, and when the mains themselves were fractured people were forced to watch it gushing out and flowing uselessly away where no fire was burning. Tenders were diverted to fill their tanks, people ran hoses down the streets and through their homes to bring them where they were needed, but many of the fires could only be contained and men and women alike wept as they watched their homes burn unchecked to ashes.

Four miles of steel piping was purchased to provide an overland main and huge water tanks were built on cleared bomb sites, ready for the next attack, for nobody believed that Jerry had finished with them. They were still alive, weren't they? Still defiant. The Germans wouldn't like that. They'd come again.

The work took a long time, some of it not begun until after the heaviest of the raids were over. But no one could know whether there was not worse to come, and the City Council, sharply criticised for being unprepared, was not going to repeat its mistakes. It even began to look again at the plans for tunnels into the hills, and the proposal for the Kearney tunnel, to be built beneath the harbour, linking Portsmouth with Gosport.

But before all this, the victims of the first blitz must be buried, and many went together to a communal grave a hundred feet long, lined with Union Jacks, their coffins borne by a long procession of hearses and accompanied by the band of the Royal Marines. Soldiers and sailors marched slowly alongside and the pavements were crowded by those who wanted to pay their last respects to friends and neighbours, those who knew nothing of the ones who had died save that they were fellow Portmuthians, and even some who were there simply from curiosity.

'You don't get many chances to see summat like this,' Jess heard a man say. 'Try and get near the front, we might get a look at the grave.'

She wanted to turn and slap his face. *There are people we knew in those coffins*, she wanted to cry, *there's a young mother there who died with her five-week-old baby in her arms. There's another woman, with her little girl only nine years old, their lives snatched away from them, and an old man of ninety-two who ought to have died peacefully in his own bed. It's not an entertainment!*

But there was no point in saying anything and, suddenly sickened, she turned and pushed her way through the crowd. She had paid her respects to Kathy in a different way, by taking in her two little girls until they could be found a billet out in the country where they would be safe. That was better than standing here, watching the sombre procession go by and living through the misery all over again.

In any case, the war had not retreated. Although there were no more raids for almost three weeks, the siren still sounded nightly, and now the All-Clear rarely went until early morning. Enemy aircraft were active in the skies whenever the weather was favourable, and even sometimes when it was not. You could hear them passing overhead, on their way to London or other cities. The south coast was permanently a potential target for those aircraft who had been turned back still loaded with bombs, and you never knew when the target might again be Portsmouth.

More people now had joined the nightly 'trekkers'. Every afternoon, a crowd of mothers with children who had not been evacuated would catch buses to trek 'over the hill' and shelter with relatives in outlying villages. Fathers would cycle to join them after work, or even take their cars, using precious petrol and causing much bitterness amongst those who must queue for a bus, or trudge through the cold and dark to safety. And even those were resented by many who stayed behind to face whatever danger there was.

'They go off for a good night's sleep and expect us to look

after their houses,' Peggy Shaw said caustically. She glanced disparagingly at number 15, now left empty each night when Ethel Glaister and her two children departed for her sister's house at Denmead. 'I'd leave it to burn, but you can't let the fire spread just because it's *her* house.'

'Well, we all have to do what we think's right.' Jess had been feeling increasingly unhappy about keeping Rose and Maureen at home. She could not get the picture of Kathy Simmons' baby from her mind. She had been the one to find him, still clutched in his mother's arms, the firm little body torn like a rag doll. She had thought of 'trekking' from the city herself, just to keep them safe, but she knew no one out in the villages and couldn't afford to pay for a room. For her, it was either proper evacuation or face it out at home, and she knew which it had to be.

The *Evening News* kept the people together. Each day, its headlines kept them informed of the progress of the war. On the big map which Frank had pinned on the living-room wall, he could see how the RAF had bombed Berlin and Wilhelmshaven, how the British Imperial Forces were closing an 'iron ring' around Tobruk, how the RAF was bombing Naples, Benghasi and Messina. Places he had scarcely heard of were suddenly important strategic points, and he spent as much time as he could studying the newspaper and the map in turn, collecting together enough information to give himself a picture of what was happening.

The map of Europe was no longer enough. He needed a map of the whole world.

But it was local news for which the Portsmouth paper was most eagerly scanned, and in those days after the first blitz the city could hardly have functioned without it. As shops and offices dragged themselves out of the ruins, the paper was filled with notices telling people where to find them.

'It's like a mystery tour, trying to find places these days,' Peggy Shaw commented. 'Bits of the Co-op in Fratton Road, other bits in Kingston. As for trying to find a newsagent or a butcher, it'd be like a needle in a haystack if it wasn't for the *News*. It's a marvel there's places for them all to go.'

'There's not, for some of 'em.' Annie Chapman touched

her hair. She had it set every Friday, bombs or no bombs. 'I had an awful job to find Rene's. She's had to set up in her own front room.'

It was like living in a huge board game, where pieces might be moved at random and the player's task was to seek them out, while still living a life as near to normal as possible and snatching some sleep between the sound of the sirens and the nightly journey down the garden to the shelter or 'over the hill'.

The wireless was another lifeline. At nine o'clock every evening, Frank and Jess switched on the set and listened. *'This is the Nine o'clock News and this is Alvar Liddell reading it.'* News was like a drug, you had to have it, good or bad. And, later in the evening, the homely north-country tones of J B Priestley's *Postscripts* would roll into the room, or the quickfire jokes of Tommy Handley in *ITMA*.

'A good laugh,' Jess said, 'that's what we need most. And some nice singing. Those girls, Vera Lynn and Anne Shelton, they're lovely. They give you heart, somehow.'

It was heart that was needed most in these cold and dismal days after the first blitz. Heart and warmth, and courage of a sort that most people had never dreamed they would need, had never believed it possible to find. In the back streets of Copnor and Fratton, in the slums of Rudmore, in the tiny alleyways of Old Portsmouth, those who had been bombed out of their homes, who had lost all that they held most dear, must face whatever came next.

For many, it was too hard a task, for they were already exhausted and became more so as the winter wore on. For many, it seemed that it was a winter that would never end.

For some, it was an adventure.

'We ain't scared,' Micky Baxter boasted. 'We likes watching the planes. I'm waitin' for that parachutist. We're doin' war work, we are.'

The three boys made it their business to investigate all the bombed areas. They roamed through the littered streets and clambered about in ruined houses, keeping a sharp eye open for wardens who would chase them off. They salvaged whatever was worth taking away and filled their basement den with treasures, broken ornaments, crockery, clocks with shattered faces. But they were more interested now in finding shell cases and shrapnel.

'Look at this.' Jimmy Cross was holding up a stubby metal object. Micky and Cyril crowded round to examine it.

'What is it?' Cyril's large brown eyes were even bigger with excitement. 'Is it a bomb?'

'I reckon it is.' Micky touched it with awe. 'It's an unexploded bomb.'

'Will it go off?' Cyril retreated a few steps.

'It might. If it does, we'll all be blown to bits.' Micky gave a sudden yell, then laughed. 'Don't drop it, Jim!'

Jimmy jumped and clutched the object tightly. It had a blunt nose and fins along its side. Gingerly, he held it up to his ear.

'It's not ticking.'

'Well, that's all right then. It's a dud. Let's take it back to the den. it's our best thing yet.' Micky looked at it enviously, wishing he could have been the one to find it. Jimmy Cross had been getting too cocky as it was. He'd be wanting to be leader of the gang soon, just because he'd been lucky enough to find a bomb.

'Our best thing until I gets a parachutist,' he corrected himself, and led the way through the ruined streets.

Tim and Keith were aggrieved that they had missed the big raid. They described the attack of Christmas Eve to anyone who would listen, but a good many of the children had been in Portsmouth themselves and had their own stories to tell.

'I wish we were still in Pompey,' Tim said disconsolately as they sat in the vicarage kitchen listening to the News on the wireless. 'They're getting all the fun.' It had snowed during the night, but even that wasn't enough to make up for what he was missing.

Mrs Mudge, the housekeeper, was making breakfast. She put a bowl of porridge in front of each of them.

'You think yourself lucky you're here, out of it all. There's no fun in being bombed out of your home. It's no place for kiddies, Pompey's not. I feel sorry for the poor souls who have to stay there.'

'Our sister's there,' Keith observed. 'She didn't want to come back and Mum and Dad let her stay. And she doesn't even like it!'

'Nobody likes it. I daresay she wanted to be with your mum and help with the baby.' Mrs Mudge had known Jess when the whole family, except for Frank, had been in Bridge End during the early days of the war. She also knew, from Mrs Greenberry, just how miserable Rose had been after her mother had gone back. 'That doesn't mean you're not better off here.'

Tim made a face and started to eat his porridge. He was still disgruntled at having to stay in the vicarage. Brian Collins already called him 'choirboy' and kept making sneering remarks about saying his prayers at night. And Tim knew that many of the children laughed at old Mr Beckett for his eccentric ways. He knew, because he'd done it himself.

The vicar came into the kitchen and sat down. He'd been to church already that morning and his pyjama trousers could be seen poking out from under his cassock.

'Well, and how are you two faring this morning? I see we had some precipitation in the night. Do you intend to build a snowman?'

Keith looked at him doubtfully. Mr Beckett didn't talk like anyone else he knew. He sounded as if he was on the wireless all the time.

'Are we allowed?' he asked.

'Allowed? My dear child, I shall be mortally offended if you do not. The front lawn, I think, don't you? We can then appoint him our guardian.' For a moment, Keith had a wild idea that he meant 'guardian angel', and imagined a snowman with wings and harp. 'We shall start as soon as breakfast is over.'

'You mean you're going to help?' Tim said in astonishment.

'Help? I shall be in charge! I've wanted to build a snowman every winter but Mrs Mudge here has never allowed it. Now that we have real boys in the house, she will not be able to object. Everyone knows that boys need to build snowmen. And have snowball fights,' he added as an afterthought. 'That's if you'll allow me.'

The two boys gazed at him. They tried to imagine his spidery figure racing about the garden, hurling snowballs. They glanced at each other.

'You're not allowed to put stones in snowballs,' Keith said at last.

'Perish the thought! My snowballs will be as pure as – as – as the driven snow.' He beamed at them. 'Do you drink tea?'

'Tea?'

Mrs Mudge said firmly, 'They drink milk while they're in this house. Growing boys need it.'

'I daresay you don't use all your sugar ration, then,' the vicar said hopefully.

Tim and Keith looked uncertainly at the housekeeper. Their mother had given her their ration books and they took no further interest in them. Food appeared on the table and they ate it (unless it was cabbage). They put sugar on their porridge and in their cocoa, but that was all.

'I wondered, you see,' Mr Beckett said delicately, 'whether we might come to some arrangement.'

'Arrangement?'

'Over sugar. It's a failing of mine, you see. A very sweet tooth. I do like plenty of sugar in my tea, and Mrs Mudge says my ration won't stretch to it. So if you don't use all of yours . . .'

'You'll not take the children's sugar,' Mrs Mudge said at once. 'The idea!'

'Oh, but I'd be happy to buy it,' the vicar said at once. 'A halfpenny a spoonful, I thought.' He looked appealingly at the boys. 'You might like to discuss it and let me know later what you decide.'

'They'll do nothing of the sort –' Mrs Mudge began, but Keith was already nodding.

'I'll sell you mine. I don't mind not having any.'

'It's unpatriotic,' Mrs Mudge said. 'Why, it's almost Black Market.'

'You can have mine too,' Tim said. 'We can buy a present

for Mum. And our baby.'

'I never *heard* of such a thing –'

'You can have our tea as well if you like.'

'Such an example to set –'

'That's settled, then,' the vicar said, beaming. 'And now we'll go and make a start on the snowman, shall we?'

'That you will *not*!' Mrs Mudge said, putting her foot down at last. 'Not until you've all cleaned your teeth and put on warm clothes. You,' she said, fixing Mr Beckett with a stern eye, 'are still in your pyjamas.'

Tim and Keith scrambled down from their chairs and made for the door. The vicar followed them. He turned and gave his housekeeper a wink.

Mrs Mudge watched him go with a feeling partly of exasperation, partly of tenderness. She knew quite well what he was doing. She also knew that he was thoroughly enjoying it.

'Boys!' she said, and started on the washing-up.

CHAPTER TWENTY-FOUR

The weather was still bitterly cold. Snow had fallen after the terrible raid of the early weeks, and now it melted into icy floods. The second blitz of Portsmouth was its thirty-seventh raid, but the sirens had sounded many more times than that and people were by now accustomed to whatever arrangements they had made for sheltering.

Frank and Jess had made their Anderson as comfortable as possible. With a concrete floor and plywood fitted against the corrugated iron walls, it was dry and draught-proof. Frank had covered the plywood with cream distemper and Jess had pinned pictures from old Christmas and birthday cards all over it. They brightened up the shelter and gave the baby something to look at and, because Maureen was fond of a comic strip which featured a baby called Henry, she included some of these and added more magazine and newspaper cuttings, pictures of Mr Chad, peering over a wall and asking 'Wot – no bananas?' or 'Wot – no coal?' and photographs of the King and Queen on their visit to Portsmouth.

Winston Churchill came to Portsmouth too, and toured the bombed areas. He picked his way over streets still littered with collapsed houses and pitted with deep craters, and grunted, looking like an angry baby with a cigar stuck in his mouth.

The Royal visit had been a fillip for the city, and especially for Olive Harker, for Derek had actually been presented to them when they came down Commercial Road. 698 Unit were there with a mechanical caterpillar and hawser, pulling down a dangerous wall. Actually, it didn't really need to be pulled down at all, Derek said, and the soldiers weren't best pleased at having to do it just for 'show'. But they'd put their backs into it all the same and the Royal party, with the Lord Mayor and his wife and a crowd of VIPs, had watched until the dust had settled and then come over to speak to the commanding officer.

'O'Rorke was like a dog with two tails,' Derek told Olive when he came in that evening for the hour or two that was all that was allowed for time off. 'He puffed out his chest like a cockerel and told 'em all about how he formed the Unit single-handed and took us over to France. Pity he couldn't claim to have beaten the Germans on their own ground, but he had to admit we'd got evacuated from Dunkirk.'

'Well, that's something to be proud of, it seems,' Olive said. She was still pale after the loss of her baby, and had lost much of her old zest. But the memory of Kathy Simmons, whose baby had been born only to be killed a few weeks later, and who had herself died at the same moment, served to remind her that she was still one of the lucky ones. 'Better to have been evacuated than killed on the beach, or taken prisoner.' She rested her head on his chest. 'I'm so thankful you're still here . . . And did the Queen actually talk to you?'

'She did.' Derek looked as proud as Colonel O'Rorke. 'She asked me my name and whether I was a Pompey chap.'

'Derek! She never said "Pompey"!'

'She did. Well, I thought she did, anyway. Honest, Livvy, she was just like anyone else, only she spoke a bit posher. And she asked about you –'

'About *me*?' Olive sat up and stared at him. 'How on earth did she know about me?'

'Well, she didn't, I suppose. She just asked if I was married and what your name was, so she knows about you now, anyway. And –' he looked away, as if half uncertain as to what to say '– she asked if we had any children.'

'Did you tell her?' Olive asked quietly, and he nodded.

'I said we'd been expecting, *you'd* been expecting, but when the blitz came . . . well, I just told her what happened, that's all.' He glanced at her face and added as if in justification, 'There didn't seem to be anything else to say, Livvy. She was

380

really interested.'

'It's all right.' She took his hand and stroked it. 'It just seems funny, telling the Queen of England about us. Did she say anything else?'

'She said to tell you she was very sorry. And not to be disheartened. She said, "There *will* be a time when we're no longer at war, and you'll raise your family in peace." That's what she said, Livvy.'

'She said that to you?' Olive gazed at him, marvelling. 'The Queen said that to you? And told you to tell me she was sorry – about *our* baby? Oh, Derek.'

'I know.' He grinned. 'It makes it seem different, some-how, doesn't it.'

'It makes it seem easier to carry on.' Olive rested her head on his chest again. 'There's been times these past weeks, Derek, when I've felt, well, that it just wasn't worth the effort. All the struggle to get up every morning and get through the day. Never knowing what's going to happen next. Waiting for the next raid, waiting for the bombs. Sometimes I almost wished Hitler would come himself, and bomb us out of it all, because there don't seem any other way. I can't see that it's ever going to stop, not until there's just nothing left anywhere.'

'Livvy –'

'And then you come and say the Queen's been talking to you, and told you to tell me she's sorry. About our baby! And says that there *will* be peace, and we *will* be able to have our family and bring them up without having bombs dropping on us. Well, somehow it seems possible again. After all, she ought to know. It's not as if they haven't been bombed themselves. They know what it's like.'

Privately, Derek wondered if they did. Buckingham Palace was rather different from the houses in April Grove and March Street, and the King and Queen did not spend their nights in an Anderson, or in a damp, overcrowded street shelter. But he did not say so. It had been a real pleasure – a 'tonic', as more than one man had called it – to see the King and Queen at such close quarters, and to talk to them just as if they were ordinary people. And if it made Olive feel so much better, then it was worth any amount of red tape and show.

Yvonne had come back from that first blitz on Portsmouth subdued and anxious, her careless gaiety dimmed. Her own home had not been bombed but many others had, and she had seen the waves of destruction and heard the screams of the injured. The memory haunted her dreams and she worked with a forlorn doggedness where before she had danced laughing through the days.

'I know we're doing good work out here,' she said to Betty, 'but it don't seem enough, somehow. When I saw what other people are having to put up with, what they're having to do, I ought to be doing more.'

'I know what you mean,' Betty said. 'It doesn't seem right to be safe and comfortable when all the people we know are having such an awful time.' She looked around the fields. Spring was coming rapidly and the trees were beginning to unfurl their buds. One corner of the orchard had been white with snowdrops all through February, and now primroses were beginning to star the banks, and violets throw down a velvet cloak. She had never seen so many birds, nor heard so much liquid song, and would have spent hours watching their busy nest-building. Soon the sheep would begin to lamb.

There was plenty of work on the farm, and it was hard. The girls were fitter now and could keep up with all that Jonas and Mr Spencer asked of them, but there was still a lot to learn and they fell into bed dog-tired at night.

'You don't have to be in danger to be helping the war,' Mr Spencer said. 'People have got to have food. We're feeding Servicemen as well as civilians. If it wasn't for us, the country would starve and Hitler would walk in and take the lot.'

'Anyway, they won't let us change now,' Erica observed. 'The Land Army's a service just like the WAAFs and the rest. We're in it and we've got to stay in it, unless we can give a good reason for getting out.' She thought for a moment and then added, 'Not that I want to get out, as it happens.'

The attic room had become home to the three girls. They pinned up snaps of their families and pictures cut from magazines. Erica had brought a bright quilt from home for her bed, and had given Betty and Yvonne cushions. When Dennis left the farm, Mrs Spencer offered her his bedroom, but she shook her head. 'I'd rather stay here.'

'She's nicer than I thought,' Yvonne said, and Betty heard her creep across the attic floor in the night to comfort Erica as she lay weeping for Geoffrey.

The three girls had drawn closer together, and Betty knew that the deaths of the three airmen had forged a bond between them. She knew that their work was valuable. But it was still hard to stand at the window and watch the glow of fires blazing in Portsmouth. It was hard to wait for the telephone call or telegram that would tell her everyone was safe.

I ought to be there, sharing it, she thought. It doesn't seem right to be safe, these days.

Graham was polishing his shoes and brushing his hair before going ashore for a jaunt round Portsmouth's pubs with Arnie and Knocker White. They'd done this quite a few times now and found plenty of girls who weren't actually tarts yet were more than willing to accommodate a lonely sailor for the price of a few drinks. And why not? 'It's my bit of war work,' one fluffy little blonde had giggled as she squirmed suggestively on Graham's knee. 'And I can tell you're a nice boy, just a bit lonely so far away from home.'

Graham had hidden a grin at that. Gosport wasn't exactly a million miles away! But he'd let her believe he came from London, and she'd listened wide-eyed to his tales of the blitz there, and made no objection afterwards when he took her into a dark shop doorway. Why did I want to waste so much time with Betty? he thought, swaggering back to the ship afterwards. Why bother about little prudes like that, when there's fun and games to be had for the cost of a port and lemon, and no worries afterwards?

All the same, he couldn't help wondering how Betty was, out on the farm. And he missed her bright chatter and the way she would look at him so adoringly with those big hazel eyes of hers. And he missed sitting in her mum's front room with her, holding hands and listening to *ITMA* or *Band Waggon*. It hadn't really mattered all that much that she would never give in to him, it was all part of the game. And now he'd never know what it was like with her.

With Betty, it would really have been making love. With these other girls, the fluffy blonde, the toffee-nosed brunette, the dozens of others who haunted the pubs ready to go walking off arm-in-arm with any man who would buy them a drink, it was no more than sex.

Well, there was nothing to be done about that. Sex was pretty good after all, and who wanted a steady girlfriend worrying about whether she'd got 'caught'? Time enough for that when the war was over. For now, best to enjoy yourself, make the most of what was on offer and get yourself a few pin-ups to look at while you were at sea.

The siren went just as he had finished slicking Brylcreem on his hair.

Everyone in the mess groaned. Most of them had been looking forward to a few jars, and now their evening was gone, unless the raid proved to be a short one. They had to be ready, on stand-by, to go wherever help was needed in the city. They might have to man stirrup pumps or hoses, render First Aid, dig through piles of newly-fallen masonry to find people buried by exploding bombs. They might have to save their own ship, for the bombers would surely aim for the Dockyard, or go to the help of one of the others tied up at jetties or moored in the harbour. Any of these and more they might be called upon to do. And until they were called, all they could do was wait.

'*Bugger* it!' Graham said in disgust. 'Bugger, bugger, *bugger* it!'

For Derek, Bob Shaw and George Glaister, the raid signalled action.

All three had been preparing for an evening of relaxation. Unless there was a raid, the men of 698 Unit were allowed to go home for a few hours at weekends and Derek had been looking forward to eating supper with Olive while her parents went down April Grove to spend the evening with Jess and Frank. Bob had no wife or girlfriend to occupy his evening, but had been cheerfully anticipating an hour or two in a chair by the fire, and the ministrations of his mother and sisters. And even George Glaister had been hoping for a few home comforts at number 15.

But for 698 Unit, the orders were constant. If a raid was expected, all leave was cancelled and they must stand ready to go out into the city. From that point, there was a difference between the part they must play and that demanded of the Navy. The sailors could give real help. The Army's duty was to stand guard.

'Guard against *looters*!' Derek had exploded when he first heard the command. 'Pompey folk don't loot!'

'They're not getting the chance,' the sergeant-major said. 'We'll be at every doorway, armed and with fixed bayonets. It's no good looking at me. I didn't issue the order.'

'Well, who did?' Derek wasn't the only one disgusted. George Glaister was equally annoyed and less frightened of saying so to his sergeant-major than he would have been to his wife. 'We want to be out there *doin'* summat. We're soldiers, aren't we? Fighters. Well, that's what we oughter be doin', tannin' the Huns' backsides for 'em. Standing guard! *Looting*. It's a bloody shame.'

But there was nothing to be done about it. Orders had come from somewhere on high, and such orders must be obeyed. The Unit would be sent out as soon as it was known what damage had been done and where. And yes, they could give a hand to people who'd been injured and dig out any who were buried, and do whatever else they thought necessary. But their prime function was to prevent looting, and they'd better remember it.

The first stick of bombs landed and in the barracks of 698 Unit, as in every home in Portsmouth, the lights went out.

'They'll kill us all,' a woman moaned as Gladys Shaw worked to free her from the rubble of her home. 'Oh, why don't they do it and get it over with? I can't stand this any longer, I just can't.' A bomb whistled as it fell in the next street, and everyone cringed as the explosion brought more debris raining about them. 'Oh no, no, no . . .'

'Here, love, shift out of the way and let me do it.' A navy-clad arm pushed Gladys as she struggled with a heavy beam. 'Little scrap like you can't move that.' The sailor thrust his shoulder under the wooden shaft and heaved. 'There she goes. *The-e-ere* she goes . . .' The beam groaned and creaked, then rose just enough for Gladys to pull the woman free. 'There you are. Takes a man to do a man's job, eh?'

Gladys was half grateful, half annoyed. She said sharply, 'I'd have got it up in a couple more minutes.'

'Daresay you might, but a couple of minutes saved means a couple of minutes to use somewhere else.' The sailor grinned cheekily and reached out to ruffle her hair. Gladys jerked her head away and he stared. 'Here, don't I know you?'

'I dunno. Do you?' she retorted waspishly, already turning away. It was no place to start making up to a girl, in the middle of an air-raid. Trust a sailor! But his next words brought her turning back, startled.

'Yes, I do. You're Gladys Shaw, old Bob's sister. You live down April Grove.'

Gladys stared at him. His cap was gone, his hair covered in dust and soot, but she could see traces of ginger. 'Graham Philpotts! What are you doing here?'

'Having tea with her Majesty, of course,' he retorted, grinning, and ducked as another bomb whistled and crashed a few streets away. 'See you later, Gladdie.'

Gladdie. Ginger Philpotts had been the only person ever to call her that, she thought as she slammed the door of her ambulance and set off once again. They had patched up the Royal Hospital and casualties were being taken there again, but she'd been told to take this lot to the Queen Alexandra. It was a longer drive, and all the way Gladys found auxiliary fire engines passing her on their way from other districts into the city. They must be bringing in thousands, she thought. What in God's name were they expecting?

They were expecting bombs. And bombs they got. All that night and the next, the incendiaries and high explosives rained from the sky. For Gladys, there seemed to be no respite from the ceaseless journeying to and fro through streets that rained with shrapnel and roared on every side with flame. She could feel the heat of it through the sides of the van, her eyes were seared by the blaze that billowed from the houses she passed. Sometimes every house in an entire street was on fire, sometimes a huge building created an inferno. She saw walls, great panels of flaming masonry with each window a scorching glimpse of the fury within, topple slowly outwards across a road she had just been about to enter, and jammed on her brakes violently, swerving to avoid the scattered gobbets of burning debris.

She set her bell ringing, with little hope that it would be heard in all the turmoil, desperate to get her load of injured bodies to the hospital, despairing at having to ignore the pleas of those who flagged her to stop.

There must have been times when she slept, times when she ate and drank and rested. But she could never recall them afterwards, or if she did saw them too as a blur, a vague memory of sandwiches and mugs of tea thrust into her hand, a faint recollection of an hour or so of oblivion on a camp bed, somewhere in a corner of a noisy room.

From time to time, she thought of Ginger Philpotts. She'd known him at school before his parents moved over to Gosport. He'd been in her brother Bob's class and had come round to their house a time or two. Now he was mucking in with the rest of them, giving a hand wherever it was needed, shifting rubbish, crawling into burning buildings, facing danger every minute. And so was Bob, working with the 698s. And so were Betty's brother Colin, somewhere at sea, and George Glaister, and Uncle Tom Cobleigh and all.

She wondered if she would see Graham again. He'd been working in Peterborough Road when she'd come across him, where a bomb had scored a direct hit on an Anderson. Eight bodies there'd been in there, all dead when they'd got the rubble off them. Eight dead, when they'd thought themselves safe. It just showed . . . And where was Graham now, with his ginger hair and his cheeky grin? You couldn't keep track of anyone in this mess.

Graham had been one of the rescuers who had found the Anderson with the family killed inside it. He'd gone at the rubble like a madman, scraping away at torn and jagged corrugated iron until his hands had bled and an ARP man had dragged him off. 'You won't help nobody by getting yourself hurt as well, son.'

Graham knew he was right, but the sight of those poor broken bodies huddled together in the damp little dugout had touched him on the raw. A whole family wiped out, just like that. And what sort of a shelter had they had? A pathetic little hole in the ground. What had the Government been thinking of, to get them all into a mess like this?

The past few weeks had shaken Graham more than he had realised. From being a bit of a game, the war had turned into something serious. At first, he'd felt the same kind of exalted patriotism that many young men had felt as they queued outside the recruitment offices to volunteer. When he'd swaggered down the street in his uniform and gone straight round to Betty's house to show it off, he'd felt important, a sort of hero even though he hadn't done anything yet. Perhaps that was why he'd got so annoyed when she wouldn't do what he wanted. She'd made him feel ordinary again, a chap who wasn't anything special after all, trying to take advantage of his girl.

He went back to the shelter, working more carefully now, but it wasn't long before he was needed to help where someone was buried alive. And then there was another, and another . . . It wasn't until dawn was breaking that he was able to walk slowly back to the ship, through the littered and still burning streets, and remember Gladys.

Gladdie Shaw. He'd known her when they were kids, of course, but he hadn't seen her for years now. She was a bit of all right, though – not very tall, and even though her hair had been covered up with some sort of hat or scarf, he'd been able to see that it was yellow. He liked small girls. They made him feel protective. And he liked yellow hair too.

Mind, Gladdie Shaw didn't seem to need much protecting. She looked as if she knew just what she was doing, helping to get people into the old van she was driving as an ambulance. And she'd been pretty cool with that too, backing it away and then tearing off up the road like a bat out of hell . . . She was quite a girl, was Gladdie Shaw.

I wouldn't mind seeing her again, he thought as he reached the ship and reported aboard before going below to crash out on his bunk. Maybe I'll go up Copnor one day and see how she got on last night . . .

Micky Baxter and his gang had given up searching ruined houses for whatever broken oddments might have been left behind, and looked for bombs instead. Their first one was kept carefully in the basement den. None of them was quite sure whether it was a dud or not and they were half scared, half thrilled to possess it.

They had almost managed to retrieve another from a crater a few streets away, but a policeman caught them just as they were scrambling down the rubble and jerked them roughly back to the road. He banged Micky's and Jimmy's heads together.

'You stupid little twerps! D'you want to get killed? Dragging a little 'un into it, as well.' He looked at Cyril's angelic face. 'You shouldn't be running around with these boys, sonny. Get off home to your mum.'

'Mum's at work.' Cyril watched as a truck arrived and several soldiers jumped out. 'Are they going to explode it?'

'Never you mind about that. You get off home like I said, and you two go with him, see he gets there all right.' The policeman released Micky and Jimmy and gave them a parting cuff. 'And don't get playing round bomb craters any more, it ain't safe.'

The three boys scuttled down an alleyway and then doubled back, flattening themselves against the wall to peer round the corner. The crater had already been roped off and the soldiers were climbing carefully into it. One or two stayed on the rim, peering down. The policeman had retreated to another corner.

'They're going to blow it up,' Cyril breathed. 'We'll be able to get bits for souvenirs.'

'I'd rather have a bomb.' Micky was disgruntled. Jimmy was beginning to challenge his position. Possessing a bomb gave a boy automatic rights and Micky still hadn't found one of his own. If he didn't look out, Jimmy would be trying to take over.

The soldiers scrambled out of the crater. They were moving more easily now and one of them was carrying the bomb. The policeman came out of his shelter and the boys stared in disgust.

'They didn't even blow it up.'

'It musta bin a dud.'

'They defused it, that's what they did.'

They wandered away, feeling let down.

I've got to get a bomb, Micky thought. I've got to.

Betty worked her way slowly down the field, setting the seed potatoes in their rows.

The days on the farm seemed long and hard now that Dennis was away. He had been accepted immediately for bomb disposal work in the Pioneer Corps and had been shifted somewhere up in the Midlands for training. He wrote every other day, and Betty spent hours writing back, but the farm was lonely without him and she lay awake night after night, longing for his touch, for the feel of his arms about her, for the warmth of his body.

She knew that she was not, as she had been with Graham, in love with love. Engagement rings and outward symbols had never figured in their conversation. And Dennis had made no demands, had never assumed that he had rights over her in any way. She was free – free to love him as she wished, free to give her body or to withhold it.

But that freedom brought its own price, and the price she must pay to love Dennis was to give him his own freedom, the freedom to walk into danger, knowing that he might not walk away.

Night after night, Betty lay awake listening to the bombers passing overhead. Nobody was really safe. In the darkness, you could see fires burning, often over the hill in Portsmouth or Gosport, occasionally in another direction.

'We're giving as good as we get,' Mr Spencer said, reading the newspaper reports of RAF attacks on German cities. 'Our lads are flattening them, just like they're trying to flatten us.'

'Good job too,' Erica said. 'The sooner we wipe every German off the face of the earth, the sooner we can get back to normal.' Her lips quivered.

'And how many more of our boys are getting killed while we do it?' Betty demanded. 'I'm sorry, Erica, but what's the point of boys like Geoff and Sandy being killed? They're gone for ever –'

'You don't have to tell me that!'

'Betty, don't,' Mrs Spencer interposed.

'Why not? She's not the only person who's lost someone. We're all going to lose if this goes on.' Betty stared at them. 'You've got two boys out in Libya. I've got a brother in the Navy. And Dennis, you know what he's doing. You can't call him a coward now. But what good is it going to do if they all get killed? What sort of "normal" is there going to be when it's all over?'

'It's not for us to think about. We've just got to do our bit.'

'And let other people drag us into an even worse mess? Look, it's right what Dennis says. We're just killing by numbers. Why can't they sit down and *talk* about it? Or kill the ones who're causing all the trouble? Hitler and Goering and all them.'

'It's not as simple as that,' Jack Spencer said. 'There are more and more countries joining in all the time. The whole world's in a muddle.'

Betty sighed. It was like a tangle of differently-coloured wools that must be sorted out before they could be made into something useful. And perhaps the tangle was so bad that some parts would just have to be cut out . . . But that would spoil the rest, leaving some colours too short to be used at all . . .

It had to be left to the people at the top, even if they were the ones that had got the world into it in the first place. And meanwhile, men were fighting each other on land, sea and air and Dennis was training for one of the most dangerous jobs of all, so dangerous that even the training could kill him.

Erica touched her arm and Betty turned. Her blue eyes were serious.

'I'm sorry, Bet. I know I'm not the only one. We're all

worried half out of our minds. And I'm sorry for the things I said about Dennis, too. I never did think he was a traitor, not really.' She smiled waveringly. 'Don't let's fall out. We've all got to pull together now, whatever we really think.'

CHAPTER TWENTY-FIVE

'I'm thankful our Betty's out in the country, anyway,' Annie Chapman said. 'At least I know she's safe.'

Soon after the first blitz she had volunteered to work in an Emergency Centre for those who had been bombed out. Like Elsie Philpotts, she worked day and night, serving out cocoa and hot soup to those who no longer had a home.

'There's hardly space for them all in those schoolrooms, but we have to cram them in somehow. And at least there's a good store of clothes in Pompey now, since the Lady Mayoress set up that collection. But what most of 'em wants first off is just a shoulder to cry on. And a bit of a joke to cheer 'em up.'

She sat back in Frank's armchair and sighed. She had called in for a cup of tea, worn out after a morning at the Centre, cleaning floors on which children had been sick and washing sheets from beds that had been wet or soiled. Yet, exhausted as she was, her own house was kept as spotless as always, for Annie refused to let her standards slip 'just because of Hitler'.

Jess could not help in Emergency Centres or canteens because of Maureen. But she had her own war work, making sailors' square rig collars and stitching on the rows of tapes whenever she had time to spare from her housework.

'It's just as well I've got this to do,' she observed. 'There's precious little dressmaking to be done these days, what with hardly any materials in the shops. And they're talking about putting clothes on ration too. I reckon we're going to have worn out every frock in the England by the time this lot's finished. I'm already cutting down my old jacket to make a winter coat for Rose, and some of Rose's things are going to have to do for the baby. I don't know how women who can't sew are going to manage.'

Annie went back to get Ted's supper ready. She had been gone only ten minutes when a knock brought Jess to the front door. Mike Simmons was there, looking grey and tired. He had come home a few days ago, not that there was a home for him to come to, and had called over to see his two little girls, who were staying with Jess.

Jess brought him into the back room and sat him down in her own armchair. She could sense the shock he'd had in seeing the ruins of his house. She still felt it herself, every time she went up October Street and saw the gap, like the hole left by a rotten tooth.

'I'm ever so sorry, Mr Simmons,' she said. 'It's a terrible thing to have happened. But she couldn't have known anything about it, you know.'

He shook his head. 'I know. Everyone's told me how quick it was. But – she *shouldn't* have died, Mrs Budd. She was too young. And the baby, little Tom, I only saw him the once, at Christmas.' His face twisted and the tears ran down his cheeks. 'I'm sorry,' he mumbled, wiping them uselessly with his hands. 'Letting myself blubber like a kid. I don't seem able to stop, somehow.'

'Don't try. If you can't cry when you lose your wife and baby, when can you? It'll do you good.' She gave him one of Frank's handkerchiefs. 'Stay there and I'll make you a cup of tea.'

He did as he was told. Jess could see he was just about at the end of his tether, all his strength gone, like a little boy again. Well, perhaps the best thing was to treat him like one, be a mum to him for a little while, give him something hot and sweet to drink and let him have his cry out. He'd have enough to face from now on, what with two little girls to think about, and being away at sea most of the time. It was a miracle he'd been able to get home now.

'What am I going to do?' he asked later, when he'd drunk two cups of tea liberally laced with Jess's sugar ration. 'I'm

394

really grateful to you for looking after the girls, but I'll have to do something about them. I suppose they'll have to go out to the country somewhere, but the ship's only in for a day, I'm not going to have time –'

He was sounding desperate again and Jess spoke quickly.

'You needn't worry about the girls, Mr Simmons. I know somewhere they can go, that's if you'd like them to. My boys are out in the country, at Bridge End. It's a nice village and they've been there nearly eighteen months.' She bit her lip, thinking how much she had missed of their boyhoods. 'They're really enjoying themselves,' she went on determinedly, 'and the place they're staying at has got room for some more children. Your Stella and Muriel could stop with them.'

'With your boys?'

'That's right. Tim and Keith, they're eleven and nine. Just a bit older than your two, so they'd be able to look after them a bit. They're good boys,' she added, thinking that he might be doubtful about his daughters staying in the same house with the two young Budds. 'I mean, they get into a bit of mischief now and then but they wouldn't do anything, well, anything you wouldn't like.'

'I reckon any kid of yours'd be a good friend to my girls,' he said. 'But what sort of place is it? A farm? A big house? I don't know as they'd like anywhere too posh.'

Jess smiled. 'I suppose you could call it posh, but not the way you mean. At least, I don't think so. It's a vicarage.'

'A *vicarage*?'

Jess laughed. 'That's right. There's just the vicar there, he's quite old, and a housekeeper. She looks after the boys mostly, sees to their meals and their clothes and that. But Mr Beckett takes quite an interest. He's never had any children of his own, you see, and I think he quite enjoys having youngsters about.'

Mike looked worried. 'But, well, we've never been much of a family for church. I don't know if the girls –'

'Oh, that doesn't matter,' Jess said cheerfully. 'He likes the boys to go to the morning service on a Sunday, but he always lets them out before the sermon. And then Mrs Mudge cooks them a proper Sunday dinner. They have their supper with him every night, and their breakfast in the mornings.' She laughed again. 'The last time I saw them, Tim told me they sold him their sugar!'

'Sold him their sugar?'

'That's right. He's got a sweet tooth, you see, and they don't drink much tea or anything like that, they've always liked plain water best, and a cup of cocoa at bedtime, so they sell him their sugar ration at a halfpenny a spoonful. Mind, I think myself he does it just out of kindness, but it did my heart good to see them measuring it out and adding it all up. It was a sort of *family* thing, if you can understand what I mean.'

Mike found that he could. He listened while Jess told him more about Bridge End and its vicar. Mr Beckett was in his sixties and had always lived alone, it seemed. He was as thin as a spider, in spite of all the sugar, and went everywhere on an old sit-up-and-beg bicycle. He was forgetful and more than a little eccentric, but he was kind and although it was very different at the vicarage from the Corners' house, Tim and Keith were happy with him.

'I was a bit worried when the boys first went there,' Jess confessed. 'I thought they'd hate it. I thought he'd be strict and make them read the Bible all the time – not that there's any harm in that, I read the Bible myself when I'm in church, but boys wouldn't like it. But he seems more like a boy himself. Second childhood, Frank calls it.'

'And you think he'd have room for the girls? You think he'd take them?'

'I know he would. The last time I was there Mrs Mudge said they would probably have to take more children anyway – people are sending them away again, after the blitz. If I were you, I'd take them out there straightaway.' She hesitated, then said diffidently. 'As a matter of fact, they're almost expecting you. I wrote last week and said you might be looking for somewhere for the girls.'

She left Mike to think about it for a few minutes while she went out to the coalshed to fill up the scuttle. Coal was scarce again and the pile she'd got in during the summer had almost gone. She scraped about with her shovel and lifted out something that wasn't coal at all.

Puzzled, Jess carried it out to daylight. It was black with coal dust and a bit damaged, but she brushed it off and saw that it was a donkey, made of wickerwork. She stared at it.

Mike came out through the back door.

'Let me get the coal in for you. And I was thinking, I'd like the girls –' He stopped, his eyes on the wickerwork donkey. 'Where did that come from?'

'I don't know. I've just found it in the coal. I've never seen it before in my life.'

Mike Simmons reached out and touched the dirty, broken ornament. His fingers traced it gently. They began to shake and Jess looked at him in surprise. His eyes were full of tears.

'Mr Simmons, Mike, what's the matter? What is it?'

'We had a donkey just like this,' he said, his voice cracking. 'I brought it home from Gib one time. Kathy kept it in the front room, on the mantelpiece. It got lost in the bombing.'

Jess looked at it again. 'Our Annie's got one too. I thought for a minute it might be hers, but I know she's still got it. I don't know where this one came from.'

'I could swear it's the one I gave Kathy,' Mike said. 'One of its feet was a bit broken, just like this one. But I know it can't be, not really. How could it have got into your coalshed?'

He took the donkey and held it, his hands trembling. Jess saw his shoulders begin to shake and knew that he was on the verge of breaking down again. She took his arm and led him back indoors.

'Sit down there,' she said gently, and he sank back into the chair with the donkey on his knee. Jess sat with him, listening to the voices of the children outside, thinking of Kathy and the baby Thomas, thinking of her own children at Bridge End and of all the friends and neighbours who were facing pain as Mike was facing it now, a pain that ate into their hearts and would never go away.

Would anyone ever be able to forget the things that were happening in this terrible war?

Gladys had begun, almost without knowing why, to see more of Graham Philpotts. She hardly looked upon him as a boyfriend – she was still writing to Colin Chapman, still hankering after something more than friendship there, and in any case Graham was a year or two younger than she was, and had always been her brother Bob's mate. But she liked his cheery, freckled face, and the way he always had a joke on his lips, and it was nice to have a boy to go about with a bit, when there was time, which wasn't often these days.

All the same, she probably wouldn't have given him much more thought if he hadn't arrived on the doorstep one Sunday afternoon. Peggy had answered the door, surprised to see him there, but had let him in without comment thinking he had called to see Bob. But although the two lads had looked pleased enough to see each other and had chatted for a few minutes, it was only when Gladys had come downstairs that she'd seen his face light up and realised why he had really come.

'Hullo, Gladdie,' Graham said, rather self-consciously. 'I just thought I'd look in to see how you got on in the raid the other night.'

Gladys shrugged. She was blushing to the roots of her hair, Peggy noticed with some surprise, and wasn't that lipstick on her mouth? Had she heard Graham's voice from upstairs and hastily done herself up a bit before coming down?

'I was all right. Bit tired, that's all. And I wish they'd give me a better van.'

'It looked a bit past it,' Graham agreed. 'Still, you drove it pretty well. I didn't know you could drive, Gladdie.'

'No reason why you should, is there?' She sounded a bit sharp – didn't know quite how to take it. Obviously she hadn't expected him to come. Still, Peggy thought, there was no harm in it. Why not encourage them a bit, let 'em have a bit of fun? Gladys hadn't had a boyfriend for a while now, not since she'd started carrying a torch for young Colin Chapman. It'd do her good to have a boy who wasn't always away at sea.

'Why don't you two go in the front room and have a talk?' she suggested. 'I lit the fire in there after dinner, seeing as it's a Sunday. And then you can stop and have a bit of tea with us, Graham, if you'd like to.'

Gladys sat down on the settee and patted the cushion beside her. 'Well, don't just stand there, Graham, you make the place look untidy. Tell us what's been happening.'

Graham sat down awkwardly. Now that he was here, he wasn't sure what to do. He hadn't sat in a girl's front room since the night he'd walked out on Betty. He'd almost forgotten what you did with a girl who wasn't a tart.

'Not much,' he said. 'Been working on bombed houses, mostly. You wouldn't think I'd joined the Navy, more like a flipping builder's yard.'

'That's what our Bob says. He's down in Wiltshire or Dorset or somewhere, putting up huts for the RAF. Why can't the RAF build their own huts?'

Graham shook his head. 'I dunno. Seems a daft way to run a war to me. I don't reckon any of them know what they're doing.' He glanced sideways at her. 'You – you don't mind me coming to see you like this, do you, Gladdie?'

'Mind? Why should I mind? You were lucky to catch me in, that's all.'

'I suppose you get plenty of boyfriends,' he said wistfully.

'As many as I want, I s'pose,' she answered. 'Don't have much time for that sort of thing these days, what with the ambulance and First Aid classes and all that. Why d'you want to know?'

Graham shrugged. 'No reason, really. Well –' he hesitated, then blurted out, 'I just wondered if you might go to the pictures with me one night. I mean, ever since me and Betty broke up, I've been a bit, well, you know. I won't try anything on,' he added anxiously. 'I know you're a decent girl. I just thought – well, if you hadn't got anyone to go with . . .'

He stopped, feeling the blush run up his neck and flood his cheeks. He had never felt so awkward with Betty. He'd always been sure of himself with her, taking every opportunity to kiss her or let his hands rove over her body. Maybe that was why he was in such a state now, because in the end she'd turned him down. Since then, he'd not been with any girl who wasn't a whore, and whores never turned you down.

But whores didn't go to the pictures with you either and sit holding hands, and when you left them they forgot you. They didn't write to you and wait for you and talk about getting married. They didn't care.

'It doesn't matter,' he said, starting to get up. 'Perhaps I shouldn't have come round here. I'd better go. Tell your mum thanks but –'

'Here, hold on,' Gladys said. She grasped his sleeve and pulled him down beside her again. 'You asked me a question. Don't you want to know my answer?' She looked into his flushed, freckled face and smiled. 'I'll come to the pictures with you, Ginger Philpotts,' she said. 'And you can forget all that malarkey about not trying anything on. I might be a decent girl, but I'm not made of stone!'

Graham turned to look at her in surprise, and she laughed, leaned towards him and kissed him full on the mouth.

'There,' she said. 'Thanks for asking me. No –' as he moved to slide his arms around her – 'that's all for now. It's teatime.'

She felt in his pocket and found a handkerchief. She wiped his lips with it and handed it back to him. It was red with lipstick.

'There,' she said. 'Sleep with it under your pillow tonight, Ginger. Shall I tell you what I think?'

He nodded, still dazed, uncertain but elated.

'This war's going to get worse,' Gladys said, her voice suddenly serious. 'You've seen the raids just like I have. People getting buried, blown up, killed. It could be us next time. We've got to take every chance we can of having a bit of fun. That's what I think.'

Derek and Olive Harker had not been able to be together much more after the momentous day when the King and Queen had come to Portsmouth. Once again the Unit had been moved, this time to Warminster where they were to build hutted camps. It seemed that their brief period of action in France was to be their only journey abroad. Olive was deeply thankful, but for Derek and Bob Shaw it was frustrating. They were soldiers. They ought to be fighting.

Even George Glaister, who was glad enough not to have to go and fight, was irked by the mundane jobs he had to do. He had enough trouble with Ethel as it was, without having to confess that his Army career was turning out to be not much different from being a plumber's mate. He'd been looking forward to writing home letters that spoke of gunfire and trenches and 'going over the top', without stopping to think that these were images he had gleaned from stories about the Great War of 1914–18, and that those conditions were far more cruel and savage than any he was likely to endure on the plains of Wiltshire.

'It's just a rest cure, that's all that is,' Ethel said scornfully. 'Going for a soldier! They saw you coming, knew you wouldn't be any good with a gun in your hands, so they gave you a bloody monkey-wrench instead. Just the right tool for you, and all.'

'Well, at least it gets me out of your way,' George retorted. 'The way your face drops every time I come home, you'd obviously rather I never came at all. I suppose you'd be happy if I was sent overseas and got blown up.'

'Don't be stupid! I don't want to be a widow, do I?' Ethel tossed her head. 'If you can't talk better sense than that, you'd be better off not talking at all.'

She stalked out to the greenhouse George had built by roofing in the yard outside the kitchen. Through the door, she could see Frank Budd working in his garden. She watched as Jess came down to say something to him and saw Frank put his hand on her shoulder.

What he saw in that mouse of a woman, Ethel had no idea. Irritated and jealous, she turned and went back into the house to harangue George again.

'I've found one! I've found a bomb!'

The boys were in the cellar, eating cold sausages which Micky had filched from his grandmother's larder. The dimness was lit by a paraffin lamp they had stolen from an air-raid shelter. It stood on the rickety table, close to Jimmy's bomb. Around them, on the floor, was scattered the booty they had gleaned from their forays into other bombed houses, or from their own swift raids when the siren had sounded.

Micky looked up from his sausage. He and Jimmy had arrived first and when Cyril tumbled in ten minutes later, his normally pale face was flushed with excitement.

'Where? Where is it? You sure it's a bomb? I bet it's not.'

'It is.' Cyril stopped his capering and stared with shining eyes at Micky. He had never dreamed that he would be the lucky one. The other two boys were older than he, and Micky was the leader, it had been taken for granted that the next bomb would be his. 'It's a whopper. It's *huge*.'

'Where is it?' Jimmy was playing with an old mouth organ. It had been rusty and full of dust when he found it, but he'd cleaned it out and oiled it and now he could play tunes on it. He was practising *Run, Rabbit, Run*.

'Down Powerscourt Road. Where the first bombs fell last July.'

'Last *July*! Go on, there can't be no more bombs there, they cleared all them houses out.'

'There are,' Cyril said stubbornly. 'I found one. It's down in a cellar, like this one, only it's all full of dirt and stuff. I went down to see if there was anything there and I saw it sticking out. It just wants digging out, that's all. I'm going to take my mum's coal-shovel down.'

'Well, it can't be a time bomb,' Micky said. 'It'd have gone off by now. It must be a dud.'

'It's a good bomb, anyway. It's bigger'n Jimmy's.'

'How much bigger?' Jimmy demanded jealously.

'Twice as big. Three times as big.'

Micky scowled. The other two were arguing now over the sizes of their bombs and the likelihood of their exploding. He felt his leadership slipping away and spoke loudly.

'We'll go down and look at it. We're not digging it out this morning.'

'Why not?' There was a belligerence in Cyril's voice that had never been there before. His large brown eyes met Micky's challengingly. He grabbed a sausage and stuffed it into his mouth.

'Because we'd be seen, stupid. There's people all over the place, they'd never let us carry a bomb through the streets in broad daylight. It'll have to be at night.'

'I'm not allowed out at night,' Cyril objected through a mouthful of sausage.

'You'll have to get out. Or it won't be your bomb.'

'It *is* my bomb. I found it.'

'Finding ain't everything,' Micky said grandly. 'It's gettin' it out and gettin' it back to the den that counts.'

'It's my bomb. You don't know where it is.'

'We can find it. You told us.'

'You don't know exactly. You'll never find it without me. And I won't tell you unless you say it's my bomb. I can dig it out on my own. Or I'll keep it there and have that for my den.'

The three boys stared at each other. Cyril stopped chewing. Jimmy laid down his mouth organ. Micky glowered.

'This is my gang. If you go off, Jimmy'll stay with me. You can't have a den without a gang. You won't be able to come back here. An' if we catch you, we'll torture you.' He put on his most fearsome expression, and Cyril flinched. 'We don't even know for sure it *is* a bomb. I bet it's not really. Anyway, it's only a tiddler, I bet.'

'All right, we'll go and look at it now.' Cyril got up and made for the steps, then turned back and snatched up another sausage. 'You'll see.'

They ran through the streets. Some were untouched by the raids, others ruined. Boarded up windows had graffiti chalked on them, or the new addresses of their occupants. One had a sign that read 'We still live here'. But mostly, the only occupants were a few scrawny cats or stray dogs with their ribs showing.

Cyril led them along the back alleys and through a broken fence into a scruffy garden. There had once been a lawn and flowerbeds, but all were overgrown now with weeds and scrub grass. The house had been bombed. The roof was torn away and every window had been smashed.

Under the back window there was a hole. Cyril ducked into it and scrambled down. He flashed the torch he had stolen around the walls.

'Coo,' Jimmy breathed, gazing at the damp walls and slimy floor. 'It's smashing.'

'Go on,' Micky said disparagingly, 'there's loads of places like this. It ain't nothing special.'

'They don't all have bombs, though.' Cyril shone his torch into a corner. 'See?'

The bomb had fallen nose-down, slicing a path for itself through the rubble wall, and come to rest a foot or so above the basement floor. It was about two feet long. Its sides were half buried and streaked with rust.

'It *is* a bomb,' Jimmy whispered in awe.

'It's a beauty, isn't it,' Cyril said proudly. He reached out a finger and touched it tentatively, then stroked it as gently as if it were a kitten. Jimmy backed away slightly, his eyes goggling.

'It looks live to me.'

'Don't be daft,' Micky said loudly. 'How can a bomb *look* live? Anyway, it can't be, it'd have gone off by now. It musta bin there months.'

'Why don't we tell the warden?' Jimmy suggested. 'They're giving rewards for bombs. The Mayor said so at that party in the Guildhall.'

'That was for putting out incendiaries, and they only give it to the first one. Catch them paying out for every one! Anyway, if we told a warden he'd just pretend he'd found it hisself. This is our bomb.'

'My bomb,' Cyril corrected him.

'It's ours if we dig it out and take it back to the den. It's ours if you want to stay in our gang.' But it was time to give Cyril a little praise. 'It's a smasher. You done well.'

Cyril looked pleased. 'Shall we dig it out then?'

'Yeah, but not now. We'll come back tonight. We'll bring the paraffin lamp and torches and spades or shovels. We'd better bring some grub as well.' He gazed at the bomb, wishing again that he had been the one to find it. 'We'd better be careful in case it is still live.'

They turned to go, creeping warily out of the hole in case anyone saw them. But there was no one about in the trampled gardens or the smelly alleyway and they ran swiftly home through the streets.

'Tonight,' Micky said as they parted. 'We'll go and get it out tonight.'

CHAPTER TWENTY-SIX

That night, the exhausted city suffered its third heavy blitz.

Thrusting away his fears, Ted Chapman went straight up to the little turret from which his son Colin had fired arrows at the neighbours' cats, and which was now so good a lookout post, while Annie hurried up the road to the school. Frank Budd saw his wife and daughters into the shelter and then climbed over the fence on to the allotment with his stirrup pump. Tommy Vickers started on his rounds, looking into each Anderson shelter in the three streets to make sure that everyone was present, or accounted for. And Peggy, Gladys and Diane Shaw ran to join Annie Chapman.

'Looks like another bad 'un,' Annie commented as they arrived panting at the school gates. Already bombs were whistling down and could be heard exploding in different parts of the city. 'I can tell you, I'm sick of this. If I had Hitler here I'd knock his block off.'

'Not till after I'd finished with him, you wouldn't.' Peggy marched in to register with the superintendent. 'You get that urn on the go, Annie – we'll be glad of summat hot later on. It's going to be a long night.'

Gladys had been hoping to see Graham that evening. She signed her name in the book and went out to her ambulance. It was looking battle-scarred and weary, almost leaning against the school wall, and seemed to heave itself to its feet with a sigh as she started to swing the crank-handle. It's as tired as I am, she thought, and no wonder. We've been on duty together through half a dozen raids in the past fortnight. It's had punctures by the score from broken glass and nails

405

and God knows what lying about in the road, it's had its headlamps smashed, not that you can see much with most of the glass blacked out, it's lost its horn that nobody can hear for the noise of bombs and ack-ack, and I'm tired of having to scrub it clean of blood every morning. And Mum's just as exhausted, riding in the back with the casualties night after bloody night when she ought to be sitting safe at home by the fire, listening to Arthur Askey and Tommy Handley, or down the Hippodrome laughing at Elsie and Doris Waters.

But there wasn't a Hippodrome any more. And at this rate there wouldn't be much of a Portsmouth. And as long as Hitler kept sending his planes over, so they'd have to turn out to fight him with whatever weapons they had. And if a battered old van, done up as an ambulance, was her way of fighting, she'd bloody well *fight*. So put that in your pipe and smoke it, Adolf!

Back and forth she drove, from one raging fire to another, from the town railway station and the main post office, both damaged by the blast which destroyed the big Maddens Hotel, to the inferno of McIlroys, yet another of Portsmouth's big department stores. She'd been shopping there herself only a few hours ago . . . All along the way there were bombs falling all about her, debris flying from their blasts, shrapnel raining from the sky. The pitted sides of the van were dented further by red-hot metal, sharp and jagged as a saw, and half a brick came through her windscreen like a cannonball, landing on the seat only inches from her thigh. Swearing, she snatched up the cushion Peggy sat on when she rode in the front, and thrust it through the shattered glass, brushing the fragments impatiently away. The night air blew cold on her face and she shrugged angrily when a warden waved at her to stop. She could still see to drive, couldn't she?

Anger drove her that night. She had been angry from the beginning, when she was torn away from the fireside to go out yet again. She had been angry to see the flares, as red as the fury which consumed her. She'd even been angry to see her poor little van, looking so woebegone and weary, and the destruction of its windscreen was the last straw. From now on, her feelings about the war and Hitler had condensed into one intense spot of white-hot fury. He was hurting her van! Well, *she* would show him.

'Gladys,' her mother remonstrated. 'Let up a bit, girl. You're like a mad thing. Take a coupla minutes off for a cupper tea.'

'Tea? I haven't got time for tea.' Gladys was fidgeting, impatient to be off again. 'There's bombs coming down everywhere. People are getting hurt. We've got to be out there, helping –'

'It won't be no help if you pass out yourself. You've got to get something hot inside you. You're out on your feet.'

'I'm not. I'm all right.' She grabbed the mug Peggy was holding out and gulped down its contents, hardly knowing whether it was tea, cocoa or cabbage-water, and well beyond caring. 'There, I've drunk it, now can we go?'

Peggy sighed and climbed back into the van. 'Look, I want to help as much as you do –'

'Right, let's go then.' They were off once more, tearing through the chaotic streets. It was worse than ever, she thought. It wasn't just tonight's damage, it was all the houses that had been knocked down in the past weeks, through raid after raid, all the holes in the road, not yet patched up, all the streets you couldn't go down, all the blackened and burned-out buildings. Even with the Navy and the Army helping too, there hadn't been time to fence them all off, to make them safe. Something ought to be done, but there wasn't time, there weren't the people to do it, not when other jobs had to be done too, not when the city was struggling simply to keep going.

A bitter despair rose inside her. When would there *ever* be time? Did Hitler know what he was doing, was he keeping up this relentless barrage deliberately so that they would be worn down by the hopelessness of it all, by the impossibility of simply staying awake? She'd seen her father going off to work in the morning, scarcely able to keep his eyes open, and her uncle Frank stumbling down the street half-dead after a hard day's labouring in the Yard. How long could they keep going? How long could it last?

I *will* keep going, she swore to herself as she battled

through the streets on the way back from yet another trip to the hospital. I *won't* let him beat me.

She braked sharply as a bomb screamed down from the sky and scored a direct hit on a house less than a hundred yards away. She ducked her head and, through the gap in her windscreen, felt the hot, choking blast. The ambulance shuddered as the tremor raced outwards through the earth like ripples on a pond, and Gladys clung to the steering-wheel.

'My God,' Peggy called out from behind her, 'that was a big un.'

'It's hit a house just down the road.' Miraculously, the engine was still running. Gladys slammed it into gear and moved forwards. The air was still full of dust but already people were running about near the site of the explosion, and a fire engine had appeared from nowhere. 'There'll be injuries. We'll have to go and see.'

'But we're supposed to be going back to the post –'

'We can't. You know we can't.' She drove as near to the bombed house as she could get and dragged the van to a halt. The air was filled with thick, choking dust, but there didn't appear to be any smoke yet. As soon as the van stopped, she was out, thrusting her way through the little crowd that was already gathering.

'I'm a First Aid worker. Are there people inside?'

One of the women turned to her. She was enormously fat and wrapped in an old coat. Her grey hair was scraped back from her big, coarse face and her eyes were like buttons. But there was real anxiety in her gravelly voice.

'It's Marge Jennings' house.' She turned to another woman who had just run across the pavement. 'Was she inside?'

'Well, she never goes down the shelter, not since her mum was killed in one. She always gets under the stairs, reckons it's safer.'

The fat woman looked at Gladys. There was a small cluster of people around them now, mostly women with one or two old men hobbling on sticks.

'Well, we'd better look for 'er then, 'adn't we? 'T ain't no good standin' 'ere talkin' about it.' She glanced around at the neighbours. 'An' it's not much use you lot standin' 'ere, makin' a target for the next one. Get back in yer own shelters.' She looked impatiently up and down the street. 'Where's old Bertie Hicks, he's supposed to be warden round 'ere, ain't 'e? Just like coppers, never around when you want 'em, but you just let a glimmer of light get out round the blackout and 'e's on the spot right away . . .' Her button eyes came back to Gladys. 'Well, get on with it, poor old Marge could be dyin' in there for all you know.'

Gladys was already jamming on her tin helmet and reaching for her First Aid kit. With Peggy beside her, she made for the front door. There was no problem in getting into the house – the door had been blown off its hinges. Every window was blown out, and when they shone their torches inside they could see that the ceilings had collapsed, turning each of the downstairs rooms into a pile of rubble.

'Think she's got a chance?' Peggy muttered.

'I don't know. I'll see if I can get through. If she's under the stairs, she might be all right.' Gladys peered through the darkness. It was never easy to know exactly where the stairs were in a house. Even in two-up, two-down terraces, there were half a dozen different designs. Sometimes the stairs went straight up from the front door, sometimes they led from the scullery, right at the back of the house, sometimes from one of the rooms. And when a bomb had hit the house and virtually demolished it, it was almost impossible to tell. She stared at the piles of debris. Could anyone have survived a hit like that?

'Mrs Jennings?' she called. 'Marge? Are you there?'

There was no answer. Her heart sank. It didn't look as if she'd survived. Or maybe she'd gone to the shelter after all.

'She might be unconscious,' Peggy said. 'She might be buried.'

'I know. I'll have to go in, Mum.'

Peggy looked at her. 'Glad, you've been working all night. You're just about done in. Why don't you let the warden or someone do it?'

'The warden's not here, is he. Or anyone else. Only a few

women and a couple of old men. And the only one who seems to have any sense is that fat one, can you see her crawling through this lot? I'll have to do it.'

'But –' They heard the fat woman's voice again. Peggy went back and then returned to Gladys's side. 'Someone's looked in her shelter. She's not there. And – they told me summat else.' She looked miserably at Gladys. 'There's a baby. Six months old. Her hubby's in the Navy and she lives here by herself.'

'Well, that settles it. I'll have to go in. You stop here, Mum, and be ready if I shout.' Gladys settled her tin helmet more firmly on her head and stepped gingerly on a broken plank. It tilted. She waited a moment, then edged her way along it, supporting herself with her hands on the wall.

Somewhere else in the house she heard a rumble and then a crash. Something had given way. There was still no sound of people. Was Marge Jennings alive or dead? And what about her baby?

Something wet dropped on her cheek and she wiped it away. A waterpipe burst, probably. Or maybe a bottle broken, or a teapot smashed. Or the upstairs lav cracked . . .

I hate this, she thought, I just want to go away somewhere, somewhere nice and peaceful where there's no war and the sun shines and people can do what they want with their lives. I don't want to be crawling through a bombed house, with more bombs falling all over the place, looking for a woman and her baby who are probably dead. I don't want to find them. Why do *I* have to be the one? I never asked to do this.

She flashed her torch. She could get an idea of the layout of the house now. It must have three bedrooms, and there was a long passage from the front door to the stairs. To get to the space underneath it, you had to go through both downstairs rooms to the little kitchen at the back. There'd be a door there, leading to the cupboard that had been made in the space, but when she edged gingerly through she found that the kitchen had collapsed entirely under the weight of the bedroom above, and the door was blocked by piles of masonry and broken furniture.

I can't move all that, Gladys thought, gazing at it in despair.

I can't possibly move all that.

She shifted what she could, tearing nails and skin as she wrenched at splintered wood and jagged bricks. A piece of broken glass cut a thin line down her arm but she scarcely noticed it. She propped her torch up on a shelf that was hanging precariously from one wall, and worked on, heaving and pulling, trying to make a way through to the cupboard door.

'Here, love. Let me do that.'

There was a man beside her, a burly man who also wore a tin helmet. He had big hands with big, strong fingers, and he pushed Gladys out of the way and shifted a beam with which she had been struggling. He was wearing a dark blue uniform. A warden, she thought dully, they're never about when you want one. But there was one here now, and they worked together, heaving the rubbish away, staggering as they pulled at beams which were wedged under piles of smashed bricks and mortar, coughing as fresh clouds of dust rose around them.

There were other people too. She was aware of them as a dimly lit crowd, moving in the shadows. Bodies, voices, faces, hands. They came and went before her vision, blurred and reeling. She was grateful for their help. But it was her task really . . .

They seemed to understand this, and when the door was at last free, they drew back, letting her set her hand to the knob, letting her be the one to turn it.

She opened the door and looked inside. Nothing.

'They're not here,' she said, and her voice rose and wavered. 'There's nobody here.'

For a few seconds, there was complete silence. It was as if even the bombs had ceased to fall. From somewhere in the shattered house, she could hear a dripping sound, slow and measured. And then there was a crash from somewhere else in the city and, as if it had touched a button to set them moving again, the rest of the neighbours gathered round, staring into the dusty space.

'Not here?'

'Where is she, then? Where's Marge?'

'She never said she was goin' away. I saw her yest'day and she never said.'

'They must be there.'

Peggy was at Gladys's side.

'Come on, Glad. There's nothing more we can do here. If there's no one hurt we ought to be getting back to the post –'

'No.' Gladys shook her head. She could not believe it. Marge Jennings should have been here with her baby, Gladys should have found them. It was her job. It was what she was supposed to do. 'They've got to be here.'

'Glad, you can see they're not. Come on. There's other people –'

'Listen!'

'Glad –'

'*Listen.*' Gladys turned to her mother and shook her arm, she turned to the others and blazed at them. 'Can't you hear it? Listen. It's the baby!' She dived forwards into the deepest recess of the cupboard, the part where the stairs came right down to the floor. 'Give us a torch, quick.'

She could hear it clearly now, a muffled whimpering, no louder than the mew of a newborn kitten. She scrabbled with her hand, finding the usual kind of rubbish – few old boxes, a rag-bag, a broom . . . A rag-bag! Was that really what it was? She felt Peggy thrust the torch into her hands and shone it on the soft pile under her hands. It cried again and she flashed the light and saw the face screw up, the eyes closing in protest at the sudden brightness.

'I've got it! The baby – it's here!' Cradling it in one arm, she scrambled backwards through the space, hearing the exclamations. 'Look, it's safe, it's alive, it's the baby.' She was out now, in the place that had once been the kitchen. 'I've got the baby, I've got the baby.'

'Oh, *Glad –*'

'The baby! She's got the baby. But where's Marge?' The neighbours passed the word back into the street and Gladys could hear the cheer that went up. But the warden was beside her, urging her out. 'It's not safe in here, love. The whole place could come crashing down round our ears. Get out of it, quick.'

Gladys stumbled out into the street, the baby still held in her arms. It was yelling with rage and fear. She stopped and looked at it more carefully. There seemed to be no injury at all. No blood on its little face, none seeping through its clothing. It had survived unhurt. But where was its mother?

Gladys looked around. She saw the warden go back into the house. She saw the other neighbours gather round, waiting until he came out, and she saw the look on his face when he emerged again at last.

He came over to where she stood, still holding the baby, and touched the little cheek with a dirty forefinger.

'Poor little bugger. Poor little sod.'

'Have – have you found her?'

His mouth twisted and he looked away. 'There wasn't much left to find. Just enough – enough to know it was her.' He drew in a ragged breath. 'She musta put the baby in the cupboard before the raid ever started – did it every night, most like. And she was upstairs. The bomb blew everything apart. Everything.' His whole body shuddered with the memory of what he had seen. 'We'll 'ave to go in and get 'er out, but not tonight. Not tonight.'

Gladys thought of the dripping sound she had heard. She remembered the drop of wetness that had touched her cheek. She put her hand up to her face and saw the stain on her fingers.

She looked at the baby in her arms. He had stopped screaming and was gazing peacefully at the reddened sky. She wondered how soon he would begin to miss his mother.

Burdened with shovels, spades and paraffin lamp, the three boys were halfway down Powerscourt Road when the siren sounded. They stopped and looked at each other.

'I'll have to go back,' Cyril said. 'I'm not supposed to be out.'

'What's the point? They'll know by now. You can't pretend you was in the lav all the time.'

Cyril considered. If he stayed out and went on with their plan, his father would take the strap to him when he got home. But he'd do that anyway, so Micky was right, there was no point in going back now. Besides, he had never been out in a night raid.

The planes were already overhead. The boys watched the shifting white beams of the searchlights criss-crossing the sky and stared at the bursting orange flowers. The sudden riot of noise and colour was like a gigantic firework display. They jumped and capered whenever a bomb exploded somewhere in Portsmouth, looking like demons from hell as they waved their shovels in the gory light, their yells drowned in the shattering blast of bombs and the rattle of gunfire.

'Come on!' Micky shouted. 'Let's get over to the den. No one'll take any notice of us in all this, an' if they see us with the bomb they'll think we're heroes!'

Fired by this new idea, they scurried through the streets. Some were empty as their inhabitants sheltered, others were a noisy confusion of people and vehicles. The fire engines were already out, followed by the vans and old buses that were being used as ambulances. Buildings were already in flames, their walls tottering and collapsing. The boys slid like shadows amongst it all, caught up in the excitement, only half aware that it was real.

'It's better'n the pictures,' Micky breathed as he slunk along a wall, watching a house opposite suddenly burst into flames as the roof was torn away by the inferno within. 'It's like being *in* the pictures . . .'

He was totally enraptured. Like the others, he had never been out in a night raid, and this was the best yet. He felt like a film star, running unscathed through streets that rained with bombs. Anything might happen, but nothing could touch him. He waved his shovel at the sky, yelling at the Germans, sneering and challenging. He was invincible.

They were in Powerscourt Road, climbing through the back fence. The house still stood in ruins, jagged walls in spectral silhouette against the flaming sky. The hole was a black shadow against the wall.

Cyril switched on his torch and climbed down the broken steps.

'It's still here.'

'What d'you expect?' Micky jeered. 'Think it might've

walked away by itself?' He scrambled down to stand beside Cyril, gazing at the bomb. The rotting wall in which it was embedded shook with each explosion. Jimmy retreated.

'It could go off any minute.'

'Go on, it's a dud. It must be.' Micky set the paraffin lamp on a pile of bricks. 'Let's get it out.' He looked at Cyril. 'You start.'

Cyril hesitated. He glanced at his shovel, then at the bomb. It looked bigger in the flickering light, more menacing. There was quite a lot of rust along its side.

'You can if you like.'

'It's your bomb,' Micky said with a shrug, and leant his own shovel against the wall. Cyril looked at him again and bit his lip. He advanced slowly upon the bomb.

'I thought you said it was only his if he got it out,' Jimmy said craftily, and Micky scowled. He saw his leadership slipping again.

'All right, then, I'll do it if you're scared.' He pushed Cyril aside and approached the bomb himself. There was another explosion close by, and a few stones and some earth were dislodged around it. They rattled down the wall and the boys jumped back.

'Bombs don't have to be duds just because they haven't gone off,' Jimmy said. 'There was one down Fratton the other day, bin there weeks, suddenly exploded.'

Micky scraped some more rubble away, exposing the bomb's smooth, rounded sides. 'It won't take much more before we can lift it out.' He scraped again.

There was another explosion outside, even nearer. The blast shook the little cellar, bringing down a shower of bricks and plaster over the entrance. The bomb seemed to shiver and Micky leapt back.

'I'm getting out of here!' Jimmy's voice rose in panic. 'We'll get buried alive. Or blown to bits.' He scrabbled at the mound of broken bricks and earth on the steps. 'I can't get out . . .'

The bomb was forgotten. Gripped by sudden terror, the three boys clawed at the debris blocking their exit. Behind them, the paraffin lamp guttered and flared. Outside, through the narrow gap, they could still see a glimmer of fiery light.

Desperate now to reach it, to be away from the hole, they pushed and shoved each other aside, each intent only on his own survival.

Another explosion. The ground shook. More debris collapsed above them. Cyril cried out, a gargling scream that sounded as if he were being sick. Micky and Jimmy tore at the bricks and earth, forcing their bodies up the steps. Hair, eyes and mouths were filled with dust and they choked and retched.

Another explosion. There was a roar from above as the entire house began to collapse. Floorboards shattered and plaster rained down into the basement. There was nothing in Micky's mind now but the sheer desperate need to breathe. Jimmy, Cyril, the bomb, all were forgotten in the frantic necessity to fill his choked lungs with air instead of dust, to relieve the intolerable pressure, to silence the roaring of blood in his ears and the terrified screaming of his mind.

He thrust his way through a pile of splintered laths, fell over a heap of bricks, knew without feeling it that he had sliced his arm across a jagged shard of glass. He half rose to his feet, tried to force his trembling legs to run, could manage no more than a crawl. Behind him, the house was toppling; all around, the sky was glaring red, and fire lit the wrecked garden with its angry flicker.

Another explosion. And this time it was the bomb itself, the bomb they had thought to be a dud, the bomb that had lain unexploded for months, awaiting its time. Its rusted sides gave way, the unstable contents stirred into life and it tore a hole in the collapsing house, sending bricks and wood and plaster flying into the sky. The blast shook every house left standing, shattering several more windows and bringing down a hundred or more slates. Like all bomb blasts, its effects were strangely erratic. A plaster gnome in a nearby garden was unaffected. A chimney-pot two streets distant toppled and fell.

It cleared the steps of their debris and blew it away in a fine dust, which became a part of the heavy, choking cloud that shifted and hung over the shattered houses.

There was no movement from the boys. They lay quite still,

Micky on top of a pile of bricks and plaster, Jimmy half buried. Of Cyril, there was no sign at all.

Ted Chapman leaned against the low wall of the turret, his hands clutching the rough stone. His body shook with each blast as a bomb whistled down from the sky and burst into a shower of flame somewhere in Portsmouth. He stared at the orange glow that lit up the sky, at the white pencil beams of searchlights. He heard the rattle of anti-aircraft fire, the wild clanging of firebells, the shouts of wardens in the streets, and it was as if he could hear every cry, every scream, that sounded in the city of Portsmouth that night. They shrilled in his ears and battered at his skull; they stabbed into his body, and his head whirled and sickened with the sheer terrible force of it.

He sank to his knees. He had been at Dunkirk and had seen the men standing neck-deep in the water, waiting for rescue. Thousands of them had died there on the beaches before he and the other boats could get them away.

Thousands were dying now, in Portsmouth, in London, in every major city, in towns and villages, at sea and in the sky.

The screams echoed in his head.

By dawn, Gladys was moving in a daze. She scarcely knew what patients were being loaded into her van, scarcely registered the journeys along the chaotic streets. It was as if the ambulance knew its own way, as if something outside her own mind directed the functioning of her body. Down this street, along that – no, you can't, it's blocked. Try the next one – fire engines – well then, the next – yes, this one's clear – no, there's a crater at the end, reverse, watch out for that old woman – this way's OK – which way is the hospital now – down that way – no – yes, there it is at last, drive to the door, stop, get out, see the casualties in, get back in the van, start again . . .

'You ought to give it up,' Peggy said. 'You're done in. We both are.' But she knew they could not give up. As long as the bombs kept falling, as long as there were people to get out of shattered buildings, so the ambulances must keep going, and so their drivers and their attendants. People like Gladys and

Peggy, all equally worn out, all forcing themselves to keep going, operating in a dream.

They'll win, Gladys thought, driving to yet another bombed building. If they keep this up, they'll win. We just can't go on for ever.

She pulled up and looked hopelessly at the familiar sight, the cloud of dust, the smoke and flames, the firemen with their hoses, the people huddled on the pavement. Another family homeless.

'*Gladdie*!'

She turned, her heart leaping. Only one person had ever called her that. She saw his face, smeared with dirt but grinning the same as always, his ginger hair almost black with soot under the cap that was still somehow perched at a rakish angle.

'Graham! Oh, Graham . . .'

'So this is where you've got to,' he said cheerfully. 'I thought we had a date tonight.' He looked at her with concern. 'Here, are you all right?'

'Me? .Yes, I'm all right. I'm always all right.' Gladys frowned slightly, then swayed a little and Graham caught her in his arms. 'I'm just a bit tired, that's all, a bit fed-up. All these planes coming over all the time, all the bombs . . . I just wish they'd stop, don't you?'

'We all do.' Graham held her up and looked closely into her face. 'You're all in, Gladdie. You ought to have a rest.'

'Can't,' she mumbled. 'Can't rest, got to drive the van, keep going. Too many people, too many bombs . . .' Her knees buckled and Graham tightened his arms and looked round for help.

'Here, what's up with our Glad?' Peggy was at his side, staring anxiously at Gladys's white face. 'Passed out, has she? I'm not surprised, bin driving that van like a mad thing tonight, I told her time and time again she oughter have a rest. Trouble is, there's no one else can drive the bloody thing, they've all got their own jobs to do and *I* can't drive it.' She chewed her lip. 'There's a bloke here hurt bad, we oughter be getting him to hospital. I dunno what to do.'

'I do,' Graham said firmly. 'Get him in the back, Mrs

418

Shaw, and I'll see to Gladys. She can ride with you for a change. I'll drive the van.'

'You?' Peggy stared at him and felt suddenly reassured. He looked tall and capable in his matelot's uniform. She wondered irrelevantly whether Jess Budd had sewn that square collar . . . 'Can you drive?'

'Well enough. I've been learning anyway.'

Gladys moaned and struggled a little in Graham's arms. She put her hand to her head. 'What's happening? The ambulance – I've got to drive the ambulance –'

'You're not driving anywhere,' Peggy said firmly. 'You're coming in the back with me. Graham's going to drive.'

Gladys stared at him. 'You? Ginger? But you can't – it's my job –'

'That's all right,' Graham said. 'You just get in the back with your mum.'

'But –'

The local warden appeared beside them, his arm supporting a man who was hobbling and clutching an obviously broken arm. There was blood oozing from a jagged cut on his head. His clothes were badly torn and there were dark wet stains, as if he was bleeding in several places. His face was grey under its coating of dust.

'This bloke needs to get to the hospital. What's going on here? What's up with her? She's the driver, ain't she?'

'She's not fit to drive,' Peggy said. 'This sailor's taking over. We'll get him there.'

'There's another coupla women ought to go too.' The warden stared at them doubtfully. 'Think you can manage? Perhaps I oughter –'

'It's all right. I know him,' Peggy said, omitting to mention that she had known Graham Philpotts best when he was eight years old, a mischievous small boy who knocked on respectable folk's doors and then ran away . . . 'He'll get us there.'

Another bomb shrieked to a crash a street or two away and the warden looked harassed. 'All right, then. Take 'em, and then come back, we'll have a few more for you by the looks of it. I've gotta go –' He turned and hurried off along the street, shouting for help as he went.

Gladys was standing now, still looking dazed. She turned and made for the ambulance, pulling open the driver's door. 'We've got to get these people to hospital –'

'In the back.' Graham grabbed her arm and led her to the back door, where Peggy was already helping the injured man inside. Two women were leaning against a broken lamp post, one crying weakly. 'You get in too. Come on, Gladdie. You're going to ride in style this time.'

He slammed the back doors and clambered into the driver's seat. In fact, he had never driven anything other than his boss's old van, just up the street and back when the old man wasn't looking. And there was an old car someone had abandoned once on a bit of waste ground in Gosport. He and a few other boys had got hold of a can of petrol and managed to get it going. It had accomplished a few hundred yards in kangaroo hops before finally spluttering to a halt, and that had been that.

But there wasn't really anything to driving, if you knew the principles and after a couple of false starts and a startled leap or two the van set off up the road with Graham holding tightly to the steering wheel. All right so far, he thought, now let's try turning the corner . . .

Fortunately, the street was only half a mile from the Royal Hospital and by the time they reached the building Graham was feeling more confident. The ambulance lurched up to the casualty entrance and came to a juddering halt.

'I thought you said you could drive!' Peggy was out of the van at once. The sky was still roaring with the sound of bombers and night-fighters, the anti-aircraft fire was rattling on all sides and as Graham looked up he saw the red flares of parachute mines dropping steadily through the darkness. It looked too near for comfort . . . He ran to the back of the van and shouted urgently.

'Get 'em out, Gladdie. There's something big coming. Get 'em out and into shelter, for God's sake!'

Gladys dragged her thoughts together. She was feeling slightly better now and aware that the people in the ambulance with her had all been injured. I'm not hurt at all, she thought. I'm just making a lot of fuss over nothing. *Tired*!

How can I say I'm tired, when there's people getting killed . . .

'Out, quick,' she said, and together she and Peggy helped the man out. He looked bad. He ought to have been on a stretcher, she thought, and helped him as gently as she could.

'I can't . . .' the man said, and began to crumple. Instantly, Graham was at his side. He swung the man's good arm over his shoulders and gripped him about the waist.

'Come on, mate. It's not healthy out here.'

The two women climbed out by themselves and staggered in through the casualty entrance. Peggy went with them, handed them over to a nurse and then hurried out again. There were other people about too. A doctor, some nurses, porters, another sailor on his way out. One of the porters came out with Peggy and gave Gladys a nod.

'Good girl. There's some char inside if you want it.'

Gladys shook her head. 'There isn't time –'

'There is,' Peggy said. 'You need it. We all do. We've –'

Whatever else she had been about to say was lost for ever as one of the mines struck the roof of the casualty department and blew the building apart. At the same moment, another bomb fell in the main courtyard and destroyed the main entrance. Fire broke out at once and the blaze spread across the whole of the front of the building. To the pilots high above, it must have seemed then that all Portsmouth was afire and that no more need be done to bring this ancient city to its knees.

Neither Gladys nor Peggy saw the sight.

Gladys was saved by her battered old ambulance, which had protected her from the main blast. She was knocked unconscious by a piece of flying debris, and when she came round later she found herself in St James's Hospital with a broken arm.

Her mother was in the next bed. She had been thrown over thirty feet across the yard and landed in a flowerbed. She was covered in scratches – 'from one of those dratted rose-bushes', she said – but otherwise, miraculously, she was uninjured. She was kept in for a few hours for observation and then allowed to go home.

Graham Philpotts, along with the doctor and everyone else who had been in the casualty department at that moment, was killed at once.

CHAPTER TWENTY-SEVEN

They had a funeral for little Cyril Nash, though there was little left to put in the coffin. Sometimes, it seemed as if they just buried a coffin, for the sake of it. As if you couldn't feel properly finished without a funeral.

Cyril was buried a few days after the big raid. What he'd been doing down Powerscourt Road, nobody could make out, and they wouldn't even have known he was there if Micky and Jimmy hadn't told them. The boys had lain in the garden, on the edge of the crater, all through the night, drifting in and out of consciousness, and only been found next morning by accident, by some other boys who were climbing about in the wreckage. The boys had dragged Micky out and got him to a First Aid post, where he was given hot tea and wrapped in blankets, but they hadn't been able to do anything for Jimmy. He'd had to wait until a proper rescue team arrived, headed by the young woman doctor, Una Mulvaney, and when he had finally been lifted clear he had lost a leg.

'Poor little bugger,' Granny Kinch said when Micky was brought home in an ambulance van. He'd been kept at the First Aid post for most of the day, until Dr Mulvaney was sure he was fit to be moved. 'That'll put paid to 'is footballing. 'Ave to 'ave a nartificial leg now, 'e will. Thank Gawd it wasn't you, our Mick.'

'Oh, my Micky's got a charmed life,' Nancy remarked. She hadn't even known Micky was missing, for she hadn't been at home when the raid had started and had made the most of it in a dark corner with a sailor. No point in losing good money, after all. 'Knows 'ow to look after 'imself, Micky, does.'

'All the same, 'e didn't oughter bin out in it,' her mother said. 'Worried sick, I was, 'ere all by meself listenin' ter the bombs. It coulda bin you, blowed to bits,' she told Micky severely. 'Then where would you've bin, eh?'

'All over Pompey, I s'pose,' Micky answered, but the cheekiness in his voice was more wavery than usual. His memories of the raid were garbled now, but he could feel with his body the terror of being trapped in the cellar, the panic as the house collapsed about them. He could still taste the dust and smoke, and his eyes were sore from grit and the red flare of the sky. It had seemed an eternity that he had lain there, with bricks digging into his ribs and a sharp spike of wood scratching deeply into his thigh and the cacophony of planes, bombs and guns resounding all about him. He did not know for sure whether it had been real, or a dream. He had a feeling that it had been totally real, but that from now on it would be a recurring nightmare.

'That Micky Baxter ought to be locked up somewhere,' Frank said. 'He's a holy terror. He leads other boys into trouble and gets off scot-free.'

'He had concussion. He nearly died,' Jess said, but in her heart she agreed with Frank. It was terrible to think of little Cyril Nash, killed for the sake of a bit of boyish mischief, and Jimmy Cross with only one leg. It didn't seem right that Micky, who had been the ringleader, should be able to strut about the streets, looking cocky again.

May brought more furious attacks on Portsmouth, Liverpool and London. Dawn scarcely penetrated to the capital city through the smoke that hung like a funeral pall over thousands of stricken buildings, and the firefighters battled through three days and nights to control the flames that threatened to sweep away the rest.

In Portsmouth, nine high explosive bombs fell near the Hilsea Gas Works and on the main railway line to London. Houses were damaged in all the nearby streets and several people killed. One of them was Jess Budd's aunt Nell, who had let Frank and Jess live in two rooms of her house when they had first got married. Jess heard the news with sorrow and went to look at the house where she had started her married life.

'Poor auntie Nell. She had a sharp tongue, but she was good-hearted, she'd never see anyone go in want. We had some good times in that house.'

'Well, she never knew a thing about it, there's that to be thankful for.' Frank held his wife close. 'And she had a good life. As good as anyone can expect, these days.'

'I know.' Jess sighed and straightened her shoulders. She wiped her eyes. There was never time for proper grieving. The blows came thick and fast, as fast as the bombs, and all you could do was take a deep breath and carry on. Carry on, carry on. Keep smiling through. Don't let Hitler win. Are we downhearted? *No* – let 'em all come!

'We're giving as good as we get,' people said, but did that really help? As far as Jess could see, it just meant more and more people killed or homeless. More and more misery.

She went up to Annie's to tell her about Frank's auntie. Her sister was in the kitchen, baking an eggless sponge. She looked tired and there were lines of worry etched on her face.

'Ted's still bad,' she said as she put the kettle on for a cup of tea. 'It's hit him real hard this time. The doctor don't know what to do with him.'

Jess sat down at the kitchen table. Ted had been found on the turret roof, curled up in a corner and sobbing like a child. Annie had had to call Frank to come and help her, and together they'd unwrapped his arms from about his head and led him down the stairs. Bed had seemed the best place and they'd given him some sweet tea and waited for the shock to wear off, but Ted was still there, staring dry-eyed now at the ceiling and refusing to move. It was almost as if he'd had a stroke.

'The doctor says it's nothing like that. Just shock. He says that last raid was too much for him.' Annie glanced at the ceiling and lowered her voice. 'If you ask me, it all comes from Dunkirk. He would go, and you know how scared he was of

425

even going across the harbour at night. Seeing all them poor soldiers being shelled and machine-gunned where they stood – well, he's never got over it, never. He has awful nightmares.' She poured the tea and sat down opposite Jess. 'I don't think he'll ever be the same again.'

'Oh, Annie! He'll get better, I'm sure he will.' Jess reached across and touched her sister's hand. 'It's all been too much for him, but he'll get over it. People always do.'

'Do they?' Annie gave a short laugh. 'What about old Herbie up the road? He was shellshocked in the last war and he's never got over it. I can remember him going off, a fine figure of a man he was, and always laughing. Half the girls in Copnor were in love with him. And a year or so later he was back, a wreck, frightened to crawl along the pavement, jumping half out of his skin if a door slammed. He's hardly been across the doorstep since and they say his poor old mother still has to cut up his food as if he was a baby.'

'Ted won't be like that,' Jess said uncomfortably, but she knew that Annie was right. Some people never did recover.

But it was no use letting it get you down. Like the old song said, there was a silver lining to every dark cloud, and you just had to look for it. *Turn the dark cloud inside out* . . . And there *were* spots of brightness in the gloom, and if you tried you could raise a smile, on even the worst of days.

One of the brightest spots was Maureen. Now fast approaching two years old, she was toddling everywhere, always with a smile on her face. She could talk well and had begun to ask questions. Her favourite word was 'why'.

'Why does the sun shine? Why is it dark? Why is that flower red? Why is the leaf green? Why does Henry scratch his ears? Why – why – why?'

She never asked why a war was being fought, why she must spend every night in an air-raid shelter, why the darkness was filled with the noise of aircraft and bombs. But, standing at her mother's knee one day and hearing the adults talk about 'peace' she furrowed her brow and asked, 'What's *peace*?' And could not understand the expressions this brought to their faces, nor the reason for the sudden tears in her mother's eyes.

Another bright spot was the letter written each week by Tim and Keith. Jess could imagine them, sitting down together to try to think of things to say. She was amused by the large handwriting, straggling over two or three sheets of paper, on both sides, to make the letter look longer. The letters were singularly uninformative – 'We went to church on Sunday. We went to school. We played' – but she treasured them all the same. Usually, they finished up 'How is our Baby?' and she would write back and tell them all the things Maureen had said and done, and what Henry the cat was doing, mostly sleep, in front of the fire if he could get there, and about the garden and allotment. She kept talk of the bombs and the war out of her letters, unaware of the fact that this was what the boys most wanted to hear.

'Children shouldn't have to think about such things,' she said, but Tim and Keith were avid for news. To them, war was still exciting and such protection kept it so. They knew little of the destruction, the misery, the injured and the homeless. They saw the planes fighting overhead and danced in ecstasy, recreating them as they zoomed along country lanes with arms held wide, pretending to be Spitfires and Hurricanes. They watched the glow in the sky as Portsmouth or Southampton burned and never thought that their own families might be in danger. For the next few days they played firemen, dousing the flames. They longed for an enemy aircraft to be shot down somewhere near the village so that they could take its crew prisoner and be awarded medals by the King himself.

All through the bombing, people tried their best to live normal lives. They went to the pictures and saw films like *Spring Parade*, with Deanna Durbin, to bring a little glamour into their lives, or *Spare a Copper*, with George Formby to bring fun. They saw Laurence Olivier and Vivien Leigh in *21 Days*, and Bette Davis and Charles Boyer in *All This and Heaven Too*. They went dancing and watched football matches, they visited each other for Sunday afternoon tea and played cards and Ludo and Snakes and Ladders. They listened to *In Town Tonight* on Saturday evenings and Gert and Daisy handing out household tips in *The Kitchen Front* on weekday mornings. They coped with ever-tightening rations, with milkless days, with baking cakes with no eggs. They dug their gardens and grew vegetables and made clothes for themselves and their children.

In other places too, the war went on. Turning her attention to nation after nation, Germany threatened Yugoslavia with total destruction. Rommel arrived in Libya and launched his African offensive. The Allies were evacuated from Greece and, a few weeks later, from Crete. Rudolf Hess, Hitler's deputy, parachuted into Scotland and was imprisoned in the Tower of London. The Italian army surrendered in North Africa, and Britain rejoiced as the *Bismarck* was sunk, a fitting vengeance for the sinking of the *Hood*.

'It's not over,' Frank said. 'Not by a long chalk. He's just drawing breath.' He tapped the newspaper in front of him. 'Look at this. They're starting on the plans to make tunnel shelters in the hill. They wouldn't be doing that if they didn't think we were going to need them. They reckon they could get five thousand people in them.'

On the first of June, another announcement appeared in the paper and Jess read it with dismay. She showed it to Peggy Shaw when her neighbour came in for a cup of tea.

'Clothes on ration! We can't buy anything now without coupons.'

'But we haven't got ration books for clothes.'

'No, we're to use our margarine coupons instead. See, there's a list here of all the things we can get. An overcoat or mac'll be sixteen coupons, a pair of trousers six, a skirt seven, a pair of boots or shoes five. We've got sixty-six to last us the year.' She frowned thoughtfully. 'I suppose it's not that bad. I mean, we've got stuff already, it's only whatever we need new. Mind, wool's rationed as well, you have to think of that, and material – three coupons a yard. It says you can get clothes for children under four without coupons though, that'll help with the baby.'

'That's if they've got the stuff in the shops,' Peggy

remarked. She was still pale and shaken after the night when the Royal Hospital had been bombed, and had not regained her usual brisk energy. Both she and Gladys had been relieved of their duties with the ambulance for the time being, though they both went to the First Aid post anyway, to help in whatever way they could. Peggy had tried to dissuade Gladys at first, but had soon given up. 'I don't need two hands to pour tea,' the girl had declared. It was as if she couldn't rest, as if she wanted to win the war all by herself, to make up for losing Graham.

Jess looked at her neighbour with sympathy. 'How're you feeling now, Peg?'

'Oh, all right. I mean, I'm all right in meself, I just can't get it out of my mind, that's all. That mine, landing right on the hospital, it seems criminal. I was talking to the doctor only a minute before, ever so nice he was, and you could see he was dead beat but he was still looking after people. That man we took there, and the two women all blown to kingdom come.' She shuddered. 'And Graham Philpotts. That's what I can't get over. Young Ginger. Him and our Bob knocked about together quite a bit when they were little. I remember him tying a string to my door-knocker one day and hiding round the corner.'

'He was a terror,' Jess agreed. 'But there was no harm to him, you know. Our Betty thought a lot of him for a while, till they split up.'

Peggy nodded. The whole street had known that Betty Chapman had been going out with Graham Philpotts. And just because they'd parted brass rags didn't mean she couldn't be sorry he was dead. 'How's she taken it? Our Gladys is proper upset.'

'Well, she's cut up about it, who wouldn't be? But she don't say much these days. She's changed since she went out to the farm.'

'They're all changing,' Peggy said. 'My Gladys and Diane, your Annie's two girls. They're all changing, Jess. Maybe for the better, maybe not. But there ain't a blind thing anyone can do about it. All we can do is hang on – and try to give each other a bit of strength.'

*

Strength.

It was the one thing that Alice Brunner needed most desperately, and the one thing it seemed impossible for her to have.

It was over a year now since Heinrich had been taken away, and would soon be a year since the *Arandora Star* had been sunk. Slowly, she was beginning to face the fact that he must be dead.

And so unnecessarily. Since the sinking of the *Arandora Star*, there had been a change of heart over the treatment of 'aliens'. So many had, like Heinrich, lived in Britain for many years, had made their homes here and adopted it as their own country. Their families were British. Many of them had suffered in Germany and wanted nothing more than to see Hitler beaten and sanity returned to their homeland. And yet, they had been treated as undesirables, and deported as if they had been criminals.

Ordinary people, like Jess Budd and her husband, had respected Heinrich Brunner and men like him. And for once, ordinary people's voices were heard. They reached Parliament itself and caused a bitter debate in which the whole system was denounced as a 'bespattered page in our history'. The interned 'aliens' began to be freed.

They were coming home. Alice had read about it in the newspaper. Over fifteen thousand of the twenty-seven thousand who had been snatched away, were being allowed home. And Heinrich could have been one of them.

He should never have been taken away, she thought bitterly.

She got out of bed, on that first morning of June, and looked out of the window. There had been a raid during the night, but it had been short-lived and she had not bothered to go to the shelter. What was the point, when Heinrich was dead?

In the garden, there was an old apple tree. Heinrich had loved that tree. He would watch it blossom in April, and talk of how it reminded him of an apple tree in the garden where he had spent his boyhood. His mother would sit under it, sewing clothes for her family or shelling peas. He would look for the first pale green leaf to unfurl, and the first tiny apple to form. He would touch the deep creases of its bark, almost as if he were fondling it.

Alice stared at it and realised that it must have blossomed this spring without her noticing. It was in full leaf, the creamy white flowers gone, and she knew that if she looked more closely she would see the small green apples hanging on its boughs.

All this had happened, and she had never noticed.

Alice felt a sharp pang of guilt. It was as if she had betrayed her husband, who had loved the apple tree. She had neglected it, one of the things he loved; because he was not here, she had brushed it aside as if it were of no value, and let its beauty go by unrecognised.

And how much else have I neglected? she thought.

The back door opened and she saw Joy come out into the garden. She carried an old shopping basket, filled with washing – her own and Alice's underclothes and stockings. She must have been up for an hour or more, marking up the newspapers which the paper-boys must by now be delivering, and doing these bits of washing. Alice watched as she hung them out on the line Heinrich had fixed up between the apple tree and the kitchen wall, and felt another stab of guilt.

I've neglected her too, she thought. Our daughter, Heinrich's daughter, I've let her do the work I should have been doing. I've let her shoulder all the responsibility of the shop. And now I'm even letting her wash my knickers. A girl not yet fourteen years old, losing the last days of her childhood because of my selfishness.

She turned away, overwhelmed by the extent of her neglect, neglect her friends, like Jess Budd, had tried to warn her about. and which she had not understood but now saw clearly, as if a veil had been stripped from her eyes. I've been living in a fog, she thought.

She looked into the mirror and was shocked by what she saw. A woman looking older than her years, her face grey and lined, her hair coarse and unkempt. The blue eyes, which Heinrich used to say were the colour of robins' eggs, had faded and there were anxious lines around them. Her mouth looked pinched and her cheeks hollow, as if she had false teeth and had forgotten to wear them. Her neck was gaunt and lined.

If Heinrich came back now, he would not recognise her.

'What have you done to yourself, Alice Brunner?' she asked aloud. 'What have you let happen?'

A surge of feeling flooded through her and she was so unused to it that for a moment she scarcely recognised it for what it was. For almost a year she had struggled with grief and hope, the two blurring into despair. She had turned away from pleasure, thinking it disloyal to Heinrich, and in the same way had brushed aside any emotion other than bitter misery. Now, for a few seconds, she could not identify the emotion that swept through her body like a clean, sharp wind.

Anger. It was anger. Anger with the system that had taken Heinrich from her, anger with the enemy who had sunk his ship and brought about his death – for she was certain now that he must be dead. His own countrymen! But most of all, her anger was directed at herself.

'You're a mess, Alice Brunner. A selfish, self-pitying mess. And it's time you pulled yourself together and started to do what Heinrich wanted you to do, what he *trusted* you to do. Be a proper mother to his daughter.' She thrust her hands through the greying hair, lifting it away from her neck, piling it loosely on top of her head in the style she knew he liked. 'And if you have to be his widow, be a widow he'd be proud of.'

For Gladys, the night of the third blitz brought more than a broken arm and the loss of someone she'd begun to grow fond of. As soon as she was out of hospital, she began collecting leaflets on the women's Services.

'I don't know whether to join the Wrens or the WAAFs,' she said to Olive Harker, who had come down the street to see how she was. 'Or even the ATS.' She smiled, but it was a twisted smile and without merriment. 'One thing I do know, it won't be the Land Army like your Betty.'

'I wouldn't join that either,' Olive said. 'She seems to have spent the whole winter trying to pull up frozen vegetables. You should see her hands – they're as rough as a navvy's and I don't reckon she'll ever get the dirt out. Mind, she says it's not so bad now spring's come. The lambs are sweet.'

'Well, I want to be in an armed Service,' Gladys said. 'I want to feel I'm fighting.'

'But they don't arm women, do they?'

'They don't yet. Who's to say what they'll do if the war carries on?'

The two girls were silent for a few minutes. Then Olive said quietly, 'I was ever so sorry to hear about Graham. I quite liked him when he was coming to our house for Betty. He always had a joke.'

'I know. Mind, I hadn't seen much of him since he moved over to Gosport, and he used to get on my nerves when he came round to play with Bob when they were little. I thought he was a bit of a nuisance. And if it hadn't been for him, our Bob could have been going out with your Betty. But he'd changed, Livvy. Grown up, I suppose. That last night – I could see he'd been working like a slave to get people out of bombed houses. And he drove my ambulance . . .' Her voice shook. 'It should've been *me* in the hospital that night, Livvy. They were *my* casualties – I should've taken them in. Graham shouldn't ever have been there . . .'

Olive gazed at her in pity, unable think of anything to say that would comfort her friend. Dimly, she could understand the feelings that were churning through Gladys's breast. Guilt that Graham had been killed 'in her place'. Relief that she was still alive, and further guilt that she felt such relief. They coiled round inside her like a bitter snake chasing its own tail.

'He wouldn't have wanted you to think that way,' she said. 'He liked being in the Navy. He enjoyed it. He thought it was fun – all of it. He knew he might be killed, but he could still find something to laugh at, even in the raids. He wouldn't have wanted you to be miserable over him.'

'I know. But I can't help it. He's dead, and I'm alive. I feel that if I could just do something – something to make up for it . . .' Gladys shook her head and Olive sighed. Perhaps she was right. Perhaps Service life would be the best thing for her. Perhaps the only way she could find true relief was by taking Graham's place, by offering herself to serve in his stead.

'I should think the Wrens would be best for you,' she said, thinking of Graham in his matelot's uniform. 'The Navy, that's what you'd be good at.'

'D'you really think so?' Gladys looked again at the leaflet she had obtained. It showed a girl in dark blue uniform, saluting, and across it were the words '*Join the Wrens . . . and free a man for the Fleet.*'

The girl had blonde hair. It was almost ginger. Almost the same colour as Graham's.

'It seems right to join the Navy,' she said thoughtfully. 'Being in Pompey.'

'Well, it's up to you,' Olive said, feeling slightly alarmed. She was fairly sure that the prospect of Gladys in the Wrens would not be at all welcome to Gladys's parents – especially to her father. He hadn't yet stopped reminding them all that he'd never been in favour of her learning to drive, but nobody'd taken any notice of him and now look what had happened. He wouldn't stop, either, as long as Gladys's arm was in plaster, and probably not even when it was out.

Gladys looked at her. 'What about you, Livvy? D'you ever think of joining up?'

'I don't think it's going to be a matter of *thinking* about it,' Olive said. 'I think we're going to have to. We've already had to sign on for war work. It can't be long before we're conscripted, if we're not already in a job.'

'We've both got jobs,' Gladys said, 'but I suppose they don't count those as war work.' She looked at the leaflet again. 'I'm going to join the Wrens,' she said decisively. 'I'll apply now and I'll go in as soon as my arm's better. "*Free a man for the Fleet.*" Well, maybe I'll be able to give 'em one back for the one I took.'

'Gladys, you didn't *take* him,' Olive said. 'He was working in the raids. All the sailors were. He could've been killed anywhere that night.'

'But he wasn't. He was killed doing my job. Anyway, it's done now, nothing can bring him back.' Her eyes filled with tears as she thought of the merry-eyed sailor who had knocked her mother's door and run away when he was a small boy, who had grown into a flippant, irresponsible lad, who had become a man during the blitz and come to her aid when she needed it. 'All I can do is try to make up for it.'

Olive was silent. Then she said, 'I'll talk to my Derek. I think you're right, Glad, we ought to join up. But I can't do something like that without talking it over with him first.'

'Don't you think he'll want you to?'

'I think he'll say if I want to do it, I should. But I still can't do it without talking to him. It's different when you're married.'

'I suppose it is.' Gladys looked at the leaflet again. Then she moved her shoulders as if a heavy burden had just slipped away from them. She raised her head and gave Olive a grin. 'D'you know what? I feel better already! I know what I want to do and nobody's going to stop me.' She lifted her right arm in a copy of the salute being given by the girl on the leaflet. 'I'm going to join the Navy. I'm going to be a Wren. I'm going to fight for my country and I'm going to *enjoy* it – just like Graham did!'

For Betty, Graham's death had come as yet another blow.

Safety in the countryside seemed to have a bitter twist when almost everyone you knew was in danger. Since coming out here she had known three young airmen, all shot down; her great-auntie Nell, bombed in her own home; her sister, suffering the loss of her first baby; Kathy Simmons, killed with her little one in her arms; her friend Gladys, injured; and now Graham – who had said he loved her, who had wanted to marry her, who had begged her to let him make love to her – wiped out in the space of a second.

How could she expect Dennis to survive? She folded the telegram that her mother had sent to tell her of Graham's death, and stuffed it into the pocket of her dungarees. It was happening to everyone, everywhere.

How long before she received another yellow envelope, another telegram telling her that someone she loved was dead?

Erica came out of the cowshed and saw her leaning over the orchard gate. It was a fine morning, the June sunshine turning the dew to a pearly film over the gossamer grass. A few late lambs were under the trees with their mothers, clustered together in a corner as they plotted a new game.

'Come on, Betty. It's no good standing there mooning over the lambs.'

'I know. It just seems so strange, us out here, safe, and everyone we know in danger. I'm just wondering whether I did the right thing, joining the Land Army.'

'Of course you did. You like it. You're good at it.'

'That's not the most important thing,' Betty said. 'The most important thing is helping the country. Liking things and being good at them are things for peacetime.'

'And war too,' Erica said staunchly. 'Look, Betty, I've learnt a lot since I came out here. Remember what I was like to start with, insisting on my own room, saying I wouldn't stay where there was a CO?'

Betty smiled and nodded. 'Yvonne and me thought you were a proper toffee-nosed little squirt.'

'Well, so I was,' Erica said. 'And I was worse after Geoff was killed. But since then, well, I've thought about things a lot.' She bit her lip and looked down at a small, newborn lamb which had come up to the gate to stare at them inquisitively. 'Geoff used to tell me off, you know. About the way I treated Dennis. He said everyone had a right to their opinions and Dennis wasn't a coward. I wouldn't listen to him, I didn't *want* to listen to him, but now I know it's true. There's not many men would go and do what Dennis is doing.'

'I wish he wouldn't,' Betty said. 'He's not a coward, but I am. I'm imagining him getting blown up all the time. I just don't see how he'll get through alive. I just can't believe he will.'

Her voice broke and Erica moved to lay a small, roughened hand on her sleeve. Her own voice was ragged as she answered.

'I know how you feel, Betty. I really do. Every day, I thought of Geoff going up in his plane and never coming back. And one day, that's just what happened.' She paused, gathering strength to continue. 'Maybe it will be the same with Dennis. But there's nothing we can do about it, Betty. We just have to take whatever we can, and make the best of it. We just have to love them while they're here.'

The newborn lamb called to its mates and they came over in a small, bleating throng. They pressed against the gate, gazing up at the two girls. Betty reached down a hand to scratch the top of a hard woolly head and the lamb jumped, startled.

'I suppose you're right,' she said. 'I *know* you're right. But – it's so hard, Erica. The waiting – being brave – just getting through the days. It's so hard.'

'I know,' the blonde girl said, and she moved a little closer and put her arm round Betty's shoulders. 'I know . . . But we can do it, Betty. We're all stronger than we thought. And Dennis is still alive, and let's hope he'll stay that way.' She paused, then added, 'At least you do have hope.'

Yes, Betty thought, I do have hope. I can hope that Dennis will survive. I can hope that the war will soon be over. I can hope that Olive and Derek will be able to be together and have a family, and that Colin will come home one day. And I can hope that Erica will find someone else to love, even though she'll never forget Geoff.

She turned from the gate and felt the telegram crinkle in her pocket. She had parted from Graham before he had died, recognising that their love had never been more than a brief infatuation, that in other times would have fizzled out with no hurt feelings on either side. But he would always have a special place, deep in the corner of her heart, for he had been the first boy to kiss her, to tell her that he loved her, and the first for whom she had felt a tremor of emotion. Despite their arguments, there had been a sweetness about it that she could not forget.

And had no reason to forget. For her love for Dennis was of a different kind, an enduring kind. And as Erica said, she could have hope. She could love him while he was here.

That was all that any of them could do – the girls who were left behind.

All Orion/Phoenix titles are available at your local bookshop or from the following address:

Mail Order Department
Littlehampton Book Services
FREEPOST BR535
Worthing, West Sussex, BN13 3BR
telephone 01903 828503, *facsimile* 01903 828802
e-mail MailOrders@lbsltd.co.uk
(Please ensure that you include full postal address details)

Payment can be made either by credit/debit card (Visa, Mastercard, Access and Switch accepted) or by sending a £ Sterling cheque or postal order made payable to *Littlehampton Book Services*.
DO NOT SEND CASH OR CURRENCY.

Please add the following to cover postage and packing

UK and BFPO:
£1.50 for the first book, and 50p for each additional book to a maximum of £3.50

Overseas and Eire:
£2.50 for the first book plus £1.00 for the second book and 50p for each additional book ordered

---

BLOCK CAPITALS PLEASE

name of cardholder ....

address of cardholder ....

postcode ....

delivery address
(if different from cardholder)
....
....
....

postcode ....

☐ I enclose my remittance for £.................................

☐ please debit my Mastercard/Visa/Access/Switch (delete as appropriate)

card number ☐☐☐☐☐☐☐☐☐☐☐☐☐☐☐☐☐☐☐

expiry date ☐☐☐☐   Switch issue no. ☐☐

signature ....

prices and availability are subject to change without notice